DESERT SKIRMISH

"We're taking incoming," Bradford said. "We're coming over the side and into the hole."

Just then an explosion rocked the fallen-in roof of the factory twenty feet behind . . .

"Come on in," Murdock said on the Motorola.

"Yeah, getting a line on the shooters," Gardner said. "Look to be about a hundred yards north of us. Putting twenties on them now."

Murdock stood in the opening. One more rocket came in. It went high overhead and hit in the middle of the fallen-in roof. Murdock figured it was a shoulder-fired rocket. He heard the twenties go off.

"Oh yeah," Gardner said. "We got them pinned with the twenties. Now Fernandez is picking them off using the thermal imager. We figure there were about ten of them. Not more than two or three left who can move. Get on with your work down there."

"That's a roger, Gardner. Protect our backs here. Good work. See you soon."

D0971946

SEAL TEAM SEVEN
HOSTILE FIRE

KEITH DOUGLASS

BERKLEY BOOKS, NEW YORK

*Special thanks to Chet Cunningham
for his contributions to this book.*

www.chetcunningham.com

This is a work of fiction. Names, characters, places, and incidents either are the product of the author's imagination or are used fictitiously, and any resemblance to actual persons, living or dead, business establishments, events, or locales is entirely coincidental.

SEAL TEAM SEVEN: HOSTILE FIRE

A Berkley Book / published by arrangement with
the author

PRINTING HISTORY
Berkley edition / May 2004

ISBN: 0-425-19649-6

BERKLEY®
Berkley Books are published by The Berkley Publishing Group,
a division of Penguin Group (USA) Inc.,
375 Hudson Street, New York, New York 10014.
BERKLEY and the "B" design
are trademarks belonging to Penguin Group (USA) Inc.

PRINTED IN THE UNITED STATES OF AMERICA
10 9 8 7 6 5 4 3 2 1

Dedicated
To those Special Forces
Who have carried
The brunt of the fighting
Against the worldwide
Terrorist threat

SEAL TEAM SEVEN

THIRD PLATOON*
CORONADO, CALIFORNIA

Rear Admiral (L) Richard Kenner. Commander of All SEALs. Based in Little Creek, Virginia.

Captain Harry L. Arjarack. Commanding Officer of NAVSPECWARGRUP-ONE, in Coronado, California. 51.

Commander Dean Masciareli. Commanding officer of Navy Special Warfare Group One's SEAL Team Seven in Coronado, California. 47, 5' 11", 220 pounds. Annapolis graduate.

Master Chief Petty Officer Gordon MacKenzie. Administrator and head enlisted man of all of SEAL Teams in Coronado. 47, 5' 10", 180 pounds.

Lieutenant Commander Blake Murdock. Platoon Leader, Third Platoon. 32, 6' 2", 210 pounds. Annapolis graduate. Six years in SEALs. Father an important Congressman from Virginia. Murdock has a condo in La Jolla. Owns a car and a motorcycle. Loves to fish. Weapon: Alliant Bull Pup duo 5.56mm & 20mm. Speaks Arabic.

ALPHA SQUAD

Elmer Neal. Senior Chief Petty Officer. Top EM in platoon and third in command. 34, 6' 1", 200 pounds. Divorced. Fifteen years in Navy, four in SEALs. Expert chess player and good bowler. A buzz cut on his hair. Weapon: Alliant Bull Pup duo 5.56 and 20mm with air-burst round. Speaks German and French.

David "Jaybird" Sterling. Machinist Mate First Class. Lead petty officer. 24, 5' 10", 170 pounds. Quick mind, fine tactician.

*Third Platoon assigned exclusively to the Central Intelligence Agency to perform any needed tasks on a covert basis anywhere in the world. All are top-secret assignments. Goes around Navy chain of command. Direct orders from the CIA and the CNO.

Single. Drinks too much sometimes. Crack shot with all arms. Grew up in Oregon. Helps plan attack operations. Weapon: H & K MP-5SD submachine gun.

Luke "Mountain" Howard. Gunner's Mate Second Class. 28, 6' 4", 250 pounds. Black man. Football at Oregon State. Try-out with Oakland Raiders six years ago. In Navy six years, SEAL for four. Single. Rides a motorcycle. A skiing and wind surfing nut. Squad sniper. Weapon H & K PSG1 7.62 NATO sniper rifle.

Bill Bradford. Quartermaster First Class. 24, 6' 2", 215 pounds. An artist in spare time. Paints oils. He sells his marine paintings. Single. Quiet. Reads a lot. Has two years of college. Platoon radio operator. Carries a SATCOM on most missions. Weapon: Alliant Bull Pup duo 5.56mm & 20mm explosive round. Speaks Italian and some Arabic.

Joe "Ricochet" Lampedusa. Operations Specialist First Class. 21, 5' 11", 175 pounds. Good tracker, quick thinker. Had a year of college. Loves motorcycles. Wants a Hog. Pot smoker on the sly. Picks up plain girls. Platoon scout. Weapon: Colt M-4A1 with grenade launcher, alternate Bull Pup duo 5.56mm & 20mm explosive round.

Kenneth Ching. Quartermaster First Class. 25, 6' even, 180 pounds. Full blooded Chinese. Platoon translator. Speaks Mandarin Chinese, Japanese, Russian, and Spanish. Bicycling nut. Paid $1,200 for off-road bike. Is trying for Officer Candidate School. Weapon: H & K MP-5SD submachine gun.

Vincent "Vinnie" Van Dyke. Electrician's Mate Second Class. 24, 6' 2", 220 pounds. Enlisted out of high school. Played varsity basketball. Wants to be a commercial fisherman after his current hitch. Good with his hands. Squad machine gunner. Weapon: H & K 21-E 7.62 NATO round machine gun. Speaks Dutch, German, and some Arabic.

BRAVO SQUAD

Lieutenant (J.G.) Christopher "Chris" Gardner. Squad Leader Bravo Squad. Second in Command of the platoon. 28,

6' 4", 240 pounds. From Seattle. Four years in SEALs. Hang glider nut. Married to Wanda, a clothing designer. No kids. Annapolis graduate. Father is a Navy rear admiral. Grew up in ten different states. Weapon: Alliant Bull Pup duo 5.56mm & 20mm explosive round. Alternate: H & K G-11 submachine gun.

George "Petard" Canzoneri. Torpedoman's Mate First Class, 27, 5' 11", 190 pounds. Married to Navy wife Phyllis. No kids. Nine years in Navy. Expert on explosives. Nicknamed "Petard" for almost hoisting himself one time. Top pick in platoon for explosives work. Weapon: Alliant Bull Pup duo 5.56mm & 20mm explosive round.

Miguel Fernandez. Gunner's Mate First Class. 26, 6' 1", 180 pounds. Wife, Maria; daughter, Linda, 7, in Coronado. Spends his off time with them. Highly family oriented. He has family in San Diego. Speaks Spanish and Portuguese. Squad sniper. Weapon: H & K PSG1 7.62 NATO sniper rifle.

Omar "Ollie" Rafii. Yeoman Second Class. 24, 6' even, 180 pounds. Saudi Arabian. In U.S. since he was four. Loves horses, has two. Married, two children. Speaks perfect Farsi and Arabic. Expert with all knives. Throws killing knives with deadly accuracy. Weapon: H & K MP-5SD submachine gun.

Derek Prescott. Radioman Second Class. 23, 6' 3". Comes from a small town in Idaho. Expert marksman. On the Navy rifle team before SEALs. Played college football at University of Idaho as a tight end. Is an expert kayak man who does ocean runs when he has a chance. Unmarried. Speaks good Japanese. Weapon: H & K G-11, which fires caseless rounds.

Jack Mahanani. Hospital Corpsman First Class. 25, 6' 4", 240 pounds. Platoon medic. Tahitian/Hawaiian. Expert swimmer. Bench-presses four hundred pounds. Divorced. Top surfer. Weapon: Alliant Bull Pup duo 5.56mm & 20mm explosive round. Alternate: Colt M-4A1 with grenade launcher.

Wade Claymore. Radioman Second Class. 24, 6' 3", 230 pounds. Unmarried. Played two years of Junior College football. A computer whiz. Can program, repair, and build computers. Shoots pistol competitively. Lives in Coronado. Weapon: Alliant Bull Pup duo with 5.56 & 20mm explosive round.

Dexter M. Tate. Second Class Electrician's Mate. 23, 5' 11", 190 pounds. An African-American. Computer literate, loves to dive on old shipwrecks. Rides a motorcycle. Weapon: Alliant Bull Pup duo 5.56mm and 20mm lasered air-burst round.

1

Haifa, Israel

Asrar Fouad eased back from the table at La Scalla, the best restaurant in town, and touched a linen napkin to his mouth. Steak and shrimp, one of his favorites, and excellently prepared as always. Too bad it would be one of the last servings for some time here at the Twenty-First Century Hotel. He had paid his bill with a Bank America credit card and added a ten-dollar tip. Whoever owned the card would be surprised at the price of the meal as well as the tip. He smiled, his light brown complexion now shaved smooth, his brown eyes pleased. His features were understated and refined, all polish and poise. His suit had cost four hundred dollars at the best men's store in Haifa. He would return it that afternoon as unsuitable. He smiled at the pun. Fouad took one last drink of his coffee, kept brim full and hot by an attentive waiter, then stood and walked out of the hotel's famous dining room and into the street.

He turned left and strolled up Shalom Street. He had plenty of time, almost a half hour. The stores were busy, and the usual Arabs and Israelis were hard at work keeping the mundane activities of their lives in motion. All that would change soon. He walked four blocks, admiring the stores and their goods. One day every Arab nation in the world would have such luxurious merchandise. He turned and retraced his steps, going into the alley a half block down from the Twenty-First Century Hotel. Here even the alley was kept remarkably clean.

Sadoun Kamnil, eighteen years old, waited where he was supposed to, near the rear entrance to a small leather goods store. Sadoun was small for his age, the result of a restricted diet of poor food in his tiny village on the West Bank, when

1

there was any food at all. He came from Fouad's village near
the Jordan River. Sadoun was five feet nine inches tall and
had a Western-style haircut, wore glasses, and had a round
face that smiled easily and laughed at the slightest hint of
humor. Now his face was stiff and his wary eyes looked at
Fouad, then to the front of the alley.

"Did you see any police, any army patrols?"

"No, neither. It is as we planned it, as we talked half the
night. You are a student looking for work. There always is
a shortage of busboys at this restaurant. The two guards at
the entrance will be pleased to show you where to go inside."

"This padded jacket looks all right?"

"We have used them before. Yes, they will not suspect.
It is starting to get chilly here in the evenings. You will walk
in with confidence, but not bravado. You are a student hunting a job. Your English is almost good enough."

Fouad watched his charge. He was wavering; Fouad had
seen it before. "Sadoun, my friend. You are a hero of your
people. You are on a mission of great importance. You remember the pledge that you made last night?"

"Yes, that I will gladly carry out this mission. That I will
go to it with joy in my heart knowing that I am serving my
people."

"Right, Sadoun, right. You are a hero to your village, to
your family, to every Palestinian."

"And my name will be in the Holy Book in the mosque?"

"I will enter it there myself for all to see. You are striking
a blow for Palestine. You are bringing the day closer when
we shall have a homeland of our own, and we can spit on
the Jews and send them running back to their small country.
This is our destiny, to fight the criminal Israelis who stole
our land and our homes and our towns. This is the way that
we fight against their tanks and their helicopter gunships and
their soldiers who murder countless of our finest young men
with no equal response." Fouad looked at his watch. "It is
almost the peak time for the dinner crowd. We should be
going."

Tears sprang into the young man's eyes. "Yes, yes, I
know. It is just that I will be leaving so much. I understand

it is my duty, my privilege and my honor, a role that must be played."

"Not every man is given the chance to be a hero, Sadoun. You know this. Your family knows it. All of them will be well taken care of. Hezbollah will give them thirty-five thousand dollars reward for your heroism. And your name will be written in the Holy Book as a martyr for Allah."

"I know." He blotted the sweat from his face and set his jaw, then wiped his face with his hands and dried them on his trousers. He reached in his right-hand pocket and took out the three-inch-long, inch-square plastic box. "The red button. First I push the black one, then the red one, correct?"

"Yes, but only when you are ready."

Sadoun Kamnil took a deep breath, pushed the box back into his loose pocket, and nodded. "I am ready. You will not be far behind?"

"I'll be there in case anyone tries to stop you. The army is usually not around at this time of day."

They walked down the alley to the sidewalk. Kamnil went out first and strode resolutely toward the hotel. Fouad came thirty feet behind him. The youth walked with barely concealed impatience, as if he had made up his mind and wanted to complete his mission before he could back out. Fouad trailed him, watched him go to the door of the hotel and smile at the armed guard standing there. Fouad came close enough to hear the conversation.

"Work? You're looking for work?"

"Busboy."

"Always need more." The guard frowned. "Isn't it warm for such a heavy jacket?"

"I left early this morning; it was cold then. Do I go inside here to apply?"

The guard nodded. "Yes. Past the desk clerks and around the restaurant to the door marked 'Personnel' down that hall. You can't miss it. Good luck."

Kamnil said something in thanks and walked into the grand Twenty-First Century Hotel. He went past the desk, noticed two more guards there, and continued on toward the restaurant. It was a classy one; most of the people wore suits and fancy clothes. He had just stepped inside when the head waiter in a tuxedo frowned at him.

"You can't come in here dressed that way," the waiter said.

"I'm meeting some friends," Kamnil said.

"You'll have to have a jacket and tie."

"Not this time," Kamnil said. He ran down two steps into the center of the large restaurant and pulled out the small box. The head waiter charged down the steps after him. Kamnil lifted the detonator and pushed the black button, then the red one.

The explosion of ten quarter-pound blocks of C-5 plastique hidden inside the padded jacket Kamnil wore disintegrated his torso, blew the far windows out, sent tables, silverware, and bodies flying into the air, and buckled the ceiling, bringing half of it crashing down on the screaming diners. A huge cloud of dust, smoke, and burning flesh gushed out the windows and into the main part of the hotel and the street.

Two fires sprang up and licked at the torn-apart timbers and furnishings in the restaurant. More than a dozen victims had been blasted through the windows into the street, most of them dead or dying. Screams of the wounded came before the smoke had blown out of the huge room. Fire sirens went off. Hotel security men rushed into the restaurant with guns out, but could only stand and gape at the destruction and death. Slowly they started to help the closest injured.

Across the street, Asrar Fouad stared at the smoke pall, as did others on the street. Some began running forward, perhaps to help the injured. Police sirens wailed and police and rifle-carrying army men rushed up. Fouad watched for a few moments, then smiled grimly and walked the other way up the street and away from the destruction.

The Fist of Allah had struck again.

Coronado, California

Gunner's Mate First Class Miguel Fernandez stood a domino precisely at the end of the long line and looked at his daughter, Linda, seven.

"Go ahead, honey, start them. Push the first domino."

Linda, dark-haired, and often with a serious expression, grinned now. "It's your turn, Daddy. I did the last one."

"Go ahead, then we'll make a really big circle. Did you know we can make a circle out of the dominoes? Now push this line down."

She did and squealed in delight as the dominoes fell, one striking the next and then the next, making a small turn and then hitting a tower of dominoes a foot tall and knocking it down with a crash.

"I did it, I did it. I smashed the tall fort," Linda squealed.

From the sofa, Miguel's wife, Maria, watched her two favorite people. She put down the newspaper and studied the pair. Linda looked up at her father.

"Daddy, what do you do?"

"What do you mean, honey?"

"This morning in school, all the kids told us what their fathers do. One is a carpenter and he builds houses. Another one works at a bank, and one drives a taxi. What do you do? I didn't know what to tell them."

"Well, Pumpkin, next time they do this, you tell them that your daddy is defending their country. I'm in the navy and I help keep everyone safe."

"Oh, okay." She sat on the floor and began setting up the dominoes on the coffee table. "You said we could make a circle?"

It hit him like an out-of-control Mack truck. Yeah, he's in the U.S. Navy, he's a SEAL, and his real job is killing people. Miguel frowned and looked over at Maria. She concentrated on their daughter. He was right. His main job was killing people. Sure, bad people who deserved to die, or people who were on the wrong side of this undeclared war on terror. But the fact remained that his job was killing people.

His hand jigged the wrong way and the partial circle of dominoes fell down before it was done.

"Daddy, be careful," Linda said.

"Sorry. I'll put it back better than ever." He worked on the circle but his mind raced. Pictures swam in front of his eyes about the dozens, maybe hundreds of times he had "made certain" that a wounded enemy was dead. How many times had he "taken out" an enemy soldier or terrorist with his sniper rifle? Dozens? Hundreds? He was a killer. He killed people for a living. He pushed back and sat on the floor. His knees were weak, his head spun out of control, and his whole body began to shake. A class-four headache pounded into his frontal lobe and wouldn't stop.

Maria looked at him with a curious frown. "You okay, Miguel?"

He looked up, surprised to see her there, surprised he was still in his living room and not in some jungle or desert getting ready to "eliminate" an enemy roadblock. "Huh? Oh, yeah, fine. Just a wandering thought. I'm fine."

But he wasn't fine and he knew it. His work had never bothered him before. How long had he been a SEAL? Six years? How many times had he used his weapons? Why was he asking all these damned questions now?

"Daddy, can you help me with the circle?"

"Oh, yeah, Linda. Here, let me put the final few in. Maybe I can do it this time without dumping the whole thing." He concentrated on getting the last four dominoes in standing tall and closing the circle. "Okay, sweetheart. See if it works."

"No, Daddy, I'm supposed to share. So it's your turn."

He looked at Maria, who lifted one hand in her own defense. He worked up a small grin and touched one of the dominoes. It fell forward and in the best "domino" fashion smashed into the next one, and the string ended in a slightly oblong circle of fallen plastic oblongs.

"We did it, we did it," Linda cried in delight.

That night Miguel sat on the edge of the bed staring at his pajamas. He had one foot in the leg hole and could only stare at the other half of the garment on the floor. Maria sat down beside him and rubbed his forehead.

"The headache still there?" she asked. "I can get you three ibuprofen."

He reached over and touched her shoulder, then kissed her forehead. "No, honey, the headache is gone. It's another problem."

Maria watched him. All evening he had been withdrawn, moody, not his usual happy self since the big domino challenge with Linda. She knew something was bothering him, and she hoped that she could get him to talk about it.

"Can you tell me?"

"Nothing like that. Nothing classified or secret." He sighed and looked at her. He knew better than most of the SEALs in his platoon that it wasn't just the men who were SEALs. The wives and families of the men were involved and affected in an extremely complicated way as well. "Nothing . . . no, it is something. I'm wondering maybe we should talk about my getting out of the SEALs."

Surprise flooded Maria's soft brown features. "Now you must be joking. You not a SEAL? You back in the black shoe navy? It would kill you in six months. What happened out there this time?"

He looked away. He tried never to worry Maria about his job. Yeah, his job of killing people. He jerked on his other pajama leg and stood up. "Lots of things happened out there, Maria. Some I can't talk about."

"Did you lose any men KIA?"

He looked up, surprise on his face. Usually she tried to stay detached so she wouldn't worry. They both understood this. "No, we didn't lose anyone. We did have four men shot up. Senior Chief Sadler was hit pretty bad. He's over at Balboa Naval Hospital. He'll make it, but I doubt that he'll ever be in one of the platoons again. He almost died."

"Who were the others who were wounded? I know most of the men except maybe the latest replacement."

"Ching got tagged in the thigh but nothing serious. He'll be back to active duty in another week. Jefferson is in Balboa, too, and will be there for two or three months, but should come out as one fighting machine. Howard took two rounds in his legs but nothing serious, and he'll be back in another week. So we're in fair shape for the shape we're in."

"Then why are you so depressed? You've been grunging around here all evening."

"Linda got me to thinking when she asked me what I do. Actually I'm a U.S. Navy SEAL and my job is to protect our country. To do that, sometimes I have to . . . to shoot at people. I've never told you . . ." He stopped. "Oh, damn. Why in hell did I have to start thinking about this? We were rolling along just great . . ."

"Sweetheart, anytime you want to step down from the SEALs and go back to the black shoe navy, I'll be right there in your corner rooting for you. Whatever you decide to do, you will have my wholehearted support."

He kissed her and gave a long sigh. "Fourteen," he said. "There have been fourteen since I started with the platoon six years ago."

Maria frowned. She shook her head. "I don't understand. There have been fourteen what?"

Miguel stood, paced the width of the bedroom, and came back, then paced it again. He stopped in front of Maria. "We've lost fourteen men killed in action since I started working with Third Platoon."

Maria's eyes went wide; she sucked in a quick breath. "Really? Fourteen men in the platoon have been killed? And you knew all of them?"

"I knew some better than others. Fourteen, that's almost a whole platoon." He sat down on the edge of the bed and grabbed her hands. "In all of those operations we've been on, I've only been wounded once. You remember that. My stay in Balboa. I took a round in my shoulder and one in my upper chest. I survived. It suddenly came to me that maybe I'm pushing the odds here. Maybe on the next mission there's going to be a bullet with my name on it, and there won't be one goddamned thing I can do about it."

"Miguel, you stop talking that way. Stop thinking that way. You are a survivor. You're smart and you're good, and you don't do stupid things and expose yourself to those bullets. Now just stop it. Come to bed and stop thinking about all of that."

Miguel tried a grin that didn't work. "Is that an order, ma'am?"

"Damn right that's an order. You might as well kick out of those pajama pants right now. It'll save a lot of time later on."

Miguel laughed softly. The crisis was over at least for now. But he knew he was going to be doing a lot of thinking the next few weeks. Did he owe his wife and child more than he was giving them? Did his tempting fate and singing shrapnel and hot bullets put his family at risk as well? If it came just right, he'd have a talk with Murdock. Now, there was an officer who could help a man get through a problem. At least most problems. Maybe not one like he had right now. Still, it was worth a shot with Murdock.

2

Coronado, California

In the small office of Third Platoon, SEAL Team Seven, Lieutenant Commander Blake Murdock stared across the micro-sized desk at his second in command, Lieutenant (j.g.) Christopher "Chris" Gardner. Murdock, six-feet, two-inches tall and 210 pounds, was in the best shape of his six years in the SEALs. His brown hair was almost businessman length. He hadn't cut it since before they went on the last mission. On the off chance they needed to infiltrate into civilian territory, three or half a dozen young men with buzz cuts would stand out like a beacon.

Chris Gardner tossed a pair of papers in front of Murdock and nodded. "Yeah, I talked to the master chief and he cut orders for the senior chief at First Platoon of Team Three to come up for a look-see. This man had requested a transfer to Third whenever the chance came."

"What do we know about him?"

"His name is Elmer Neal, he's a senior chief, and came up fast. Something of a hotshot, but from what I saw before, extremely good with the men. Top quality leadership all the way. He's been a SEAL for three years, has been blooded, and looks good for the job. He's divorced, has two kids who are with their mother in the LA area. Is said to be a whiz at chess and is in a bowling league where he averages a hundred and seventy-three. He's winding up his desk up there and will report here at fifteen hundred."

"Sounds good. Now, what about the replacement for your squad? How is he doing?"

"Been on board for about a week. We've done a little training with him but not much. His name is Dexter Tate.

He's a second-class electrician's mate and is our squad petard man. He's not blooded, and I want to see how he reacts in our live firing exercises. We're going to the desert for an overnight, right?"

"Bright and foggy tomorrow morning. We pull out on the bus at oh-four-thirty."

"Might as well stay up all night. No, I'm kidding. That means I'll hit the sack about eight-thirty tonight."

Gunner's Mate First Class Miguel Fernandez popped his head in the door. "Oh, you're busy. Cap, I'd like to talk with you sometime today, if you can do it."

"Lots of time, Fernandez. How about right after our afternoon walk in the park?"

"Sounds good." He waved and left.

"Fernandez, hasn't he been around here a long time?" Chris asked.

"As long as I have, six years. Only four men still in the platoon who were here when I came on board. Fernandez, Lampedusa, Jaybird, and Kenneth Ching. They are the best. I depend on them lots of times because I know they'll come through. Fernandez didn't look like a happy camper. Wonder what's bugging him."

"Maybe too much SEAL. I've seen it happen before."

"It does happen, but I'd hate to lose a good one like Miguel."

Murdock tossed the training sched at Chris. "So, this morning a soft sand run down to the kill house range and we do some live fire on the inside rooms. Then we swim back with full gear. Your men ready?"

"Will be. We taking the recuperating guys?"

"Ching should be up to it, but I'll give Howard another few days. He needs to check with the medics anyway."

Chris looked at his watch. "So, we'll see you in about fifteen." The Bravo squad leader eased out of the chair and out the door. Murdock stared at the stack of papers he had to get through. What he needed was a good paper pusher, only the roster didn't call for one. Part of the job, Sailor, he told himself and dug into the stack. With any luck he'd be done before the morning workout.

He wasn't. The platoon fell out at 0830 in full field gear.

In the SEALs the officers went on the same training activities that the men did, from the OC (obstacle course) to the twenty-mile hikes in the desert. The officers had to be in just as good shape as the men when it came to functioning in combat. And combat was their job. Not the full division charge, but the more refined and sophisticated special forces operations that called for stealth, ability, and on-the-site ingenuity, skills, and firepower.

The training that morning had them running in the soft sand along the Pacific Ocean strand that stretched from Coronado down to Imperial Beach and the navy radio towers. About a six-mile jaunt. No, it isn't Coronado Island, as some like to say. Coronado is a bulge of land on the end of the six-mile strip of land, an isthmus, between the huge San Diego Bay and the ocean, from Imperial Beach to Coronado. No island about it. The fancy pants of Coronado liked to call it an island, and Murdock had long ago decided there wasn't anything he could do about it.

Jaybird led the run down through the soft sand. He was officially Machinist Mate First Class David "Jaybird" Sterling, a six-year veteran of the platoon and small at five-ten and a hundred and seventy pounds. But he made up for his size with a fast mouth and the ability to jazz up the platoon.

"Come on, you ladies, you think this is some fucking quilting party? Keep up, you laggards, or you'll drop and do a hundred. Right, Cap?"

Murdock grinned. "You've got the con, sailor. Steer your own course."

Three miles down the picturesque beach in the bright morning sunshine, Jaybird led them onto the hard sand, then ankle deep into the foaming waves as they broke and rolled up on the shore. The footing was better and the SEALs could cool off their feet. Water and being wet was nothing new to SEALs. Most of them felt more at home in the water than they did on land. However they were trained to fight from the air, on land, and on, or coming out of, the water.

They arrived at the Close Quarters Battle house dug into the sand near the navy radio towers. The CQB was a three-room house built eight feet deep into the sand and soil of the isthmus. It was built of concrete-block outer walls, bullet-absorbing inner walls, and a bulletproof ceiling so no stray live rounds could leave the building. The SEALs worked through the CQB house, or kill house, as it was also called, at least twice a week.

Just inside the first room the shooters' feet hit pads that triggered computer-generated terrorist dummies that popped up from hiding with weapons firing at the good guys. The drill was to get through the three rooms taking out as many of the terrorists as possible and not kill any of the hostages, who were identified by bags over their heads.

"Bravo leads off," Murdock barked. "Get in there and let's have some good scores on the other end. Go."

Two men from Bravo Squad ran to the door, stepped inside, and began firing with live rounds at the terrorists who popped up. The men never saw the same combination of terrorists or positions twice. There were over fifty thousand combinations of positions in the computer.

Murdock watched the men flaked out in the sand. Most were talking, some just resting. Not a man in the platoon smoked that Murdock knew about. They needed all the lung power they could get. The old World War II call of "Smoke 'em if you got 'em" was nowhere to be heard.

He looked at Fernandez. He sat alone to one side, his arms around his knees, staring off into the Pacific Ocean. He had asked to talk. Murdock wondered if it was some family problem, or financial. Those were the two top winners in the counseling sessions he sometimes had with the men. He'd find out after their training day.

Murdock went to the far side of the kill house and took the printed-out results of the men going through. He read them, then passed them on to the team members.

J.G. Chris Gardner and Canzoneri were the first men through. They came up with a combined score of seventy-six.

"Is that all?" Canzoneri wailed. "I was sure we were in the eighties."

"Would have been if you hadn't chopped that one hostage down in room three," Chris said and they both laughed.

Murdock monitored the rest of Bravo Squad, then went

out front to take Jaybird through as the first of Alpha Squad.

"I've got the right," Murdock said as they stood at the front of the kill house.

"Leaves me the left," Jaybird cracked; then they were inside. Two terrorists with a woman hostage between them popped up on Murdock's side and he blasted the first with three rounds from his Bull Pup on 5.56, shifted, and cut down the second one before he could fire. Jaybird had blown away one terr right on top of him, then almost didn't see a late-comer at the far corner he hit with three rounds before they moved on to the second room.

Jaybird and Murdock came out with an eighty-one score.

When all sixteen men were through the course, Murdock named the new man, Dexter Tate, to lead the swim back to the grinder.

"We'll go three miles on the surface, then drop down to fifteen feet with your buddy cords and go the last three miles. Everyone clear?" Murdock asked. The men wore their cammies and floppy hats, no wet suits today. They had on their Drager rebreathers so they wouldn't leave any telltale bubble trail. Each man had his assigned weapon over his back and his combat vest and what was left of its normal load of ammunition.

Murdock moved Bravo Squad out front and brought up the rear with Jaybird. They were tethered with the usual six-foot buddy line. Murdock watched as the platoon plowed through the Pacific Ocean just beyond the breaker line. It was a straight shot up the six-mile route back to the SEAL home.

When they arrived at the grinder, they moved around the current class of tadpoles and assembled near their headquarters.

"Scores are down at the kill house," Murdock said. "Concentrate. Get with the program. We have to keep sharp because we never know how much lead time we'll have until the next trouble spot blows up and we're on a fast plane to combat. Let's break for chow and we'll work the O course this afternoon. There will be recorded times there as well. Get into some dry clothes and we'll see you later."

Murdock and J.G. Gardner showered and changed into

dry cammies. When they came back to the office, they found a man waiting for them.

"Sirs, Senior Chief Elmer Neal reporting."

Murdock checked him out. About six-one, maybe two hundred pounds. He didn't look his thirty-four years. He had a buzz cut and a slight sunburn from not enough outdoor work. His cammies were fresh and looked pressed. His floppy hat had a certain angle to it that Murdock liked.

"I thought you said fifteen hundred," Gardner said.

"Yes, sir, but I finished up early and figured a couple of hours could be better spent here. If it's okay, sirs?"

Murdock held out his hand. "That's fine. Good to have you on board, Senior Chief. You can show us your muscle on the O course right after chow. You find a locker that suits you?"

"Yes, sir. Everything stowed and ready. I'll need to pick up the gear they didn't let me bring: rebreather, vest, my new weapon, the rest of the goodies from the armory."

"We'll get it as soon as we're back. I hear you like to play chess. We lost our best player when Lieutenant DeWitt got his own platoon. Is it true you have a bowling average of a hundred and seventy-two?"

"No, sir, my average has slipped down to one seventy. I've lost my line, somehow. I need more practice. Do you bowl?"

"Just for the fun of it now and then," Murdock said. "I'm always glad when I can get to a hundred. Hey, see you after chow."

By 1550 that afternoon the members of Third Platoon were all down and panting. The O course is probably the toughest one in the world. It has killer obstacles that make even the most efficient on the course bellow in rage and fury. Murdock dropped to the sand after he had heard his recorded time: six minutes and forty seconds. He had done better. Jaybird came through with a five-minute-and-twenty-eight-second time. Then the men watched as Senior Chief Neal took the last barrier and sprinted for the finish line.

"Five twenty-two," J.G. Gardner called out. "Best time of the day. Congratulations, Senior Chief. Jaybird is going to buy you a six-pack." The rest of the SEALs cheered.

"Hey, I buy it, I drink it," Jaybird called out. The senior chief grinned. He was panting too hard to respond.

The SEALs were released for the day at 1600, and a short time later, Murdock looked up from his desk to see Fernandez standing in the door.

"You have time now, Cap?" The commander of any navy ship is called the captain, and sometimes the SEALs called Murdock Captain or Cap since he was in charge of their platoon, their ship.

"Lots of time, Fernandez. Come in and sit down." Murdock noticed a line of sweat on the SEAL's brow. He had a strange expression and sat quickly, then kept moving his hands around as if he didn't know what to do with them.

"Relax, Fernandez. We've been together now for six years. Hey, anything I can do for you, I sure as hell will. Now, what's been bothering you?"

"That obvious? Yeah, I guess it is. I dragged down Rafii's and my score on the kill house to forty-eight. Then on the O course I came in at almost eight minutes. I'm all messed up, Cap."

"Family trouble?"

Fernandez shook his head.

"Then it must be money problems. You short on cash?"

"Not that either, Cap. Either one would be easy. What I'm fighting with right now is something that must have been coming on for a while, only I wouldn't recognize it. It's basic and goes deep. Cap, I'm just not sure that I can be a SEAL anymore."

3

Baghdad, Iraq

Asrar Fouad had been in Baghdad for two weeks setting up
a meeting with the new president of Iraq, Omar Kamil. He
had wondered when some of Saddam Hussein's men had
killed Hussein two years ago, if that would make any difference in Iraq's posture in the Middle East. Would this newly
elected president be as vicious and dictatorial as the man he
deposed? He would, he did, and he carried to the extreme
many of the plans that Hussein had made. Now he was ac-
tively searching for outside help in his war against America.

The chance had come through an intermediary who had
been in contact with some of the al-Qaida cells in Palestine.
Fouad had been to Afghanistan three years ago and taken all
the specialized training in guerrilla tactics that he could get.
He had led an al-Qaida cell in Palestine for the past two
years. They had been active years, as he worked his way up
the organization until he was one of the top planners for
suicide bombers going into Israel. Now he had been invited
to Iraq to talk with the president. Even with the invitation he
had to wait two weeks to get an audience. He heard that
most outsiders had to wait a month or two for a meeting with
the great man.

He sat in a small anteroom on the ground floor of a three-
story building in Baghdad that could be described only as
functional. It was made of rock and concrete blocks, unpainted and rearing over a section of the city of over five
million people that was part industrial and part residential.
Not the worst part of the city, but near to it. Two colonels
of the Iraqi Army sat across from him. They did not look at
him or in any way recognize that he was in the same room.
They had stepped out of an elevator moments before. One

of them held a radio to his ear, grunted, and stood. The other came to his feet and they marched across the room.

"Mr. Fouad, stand up so we can search you," the shorter man with the radio said.

"I have no weapons, not even a pen or pencil. I have only my brain and it's not easy to search."

"No smart talk. Arms out wide, spread your legs." They patted him down, making certain he had no knife, no weapon of any kind.

"Now come with us." They went to the elevator, which now stood open. The two colonels went in first, then Fouad. There were only coded buttons on the control panel. One of the men closed the door and hit one button. The elevator began to go down. Fouad had no idea where the leader of Iraq might be today. It was said that he moved twice a day and never slept in the same bed two nights in a row. This to make it harder for an assassin to find him.

The elevator came to a slow stop and the door opened automatically.

"Out," the taller colonel said and nudged Fouad, who stepped off the car into a short corridor decorated with garish murals of the glorious history of Iraq. Twenty feet down the corridor they came to a huge, blast-proof, foot-thick steel door that resembled a large bank vault door. It swung open as they approached. Fouad hesitated.

"Inside," the colonel barked.

Fouad stepped past the huge door, but the two colonels stayed outside. Inside he found himself in another corridor, this one brightly lighted with pictures of Iraqi soccer stars painted on the walls. A pair of military guards with submachine guns slung on their shoulders nodded to him and waved him forward down the corridor to another huge blast-proof door. Beyond it two new armed soldiers greeted him. They ran metal detector wands over him until they were satisfied he had no metal objects, and then they led him down the long hall to a normal-sized door. One of the men knocked. A moment later the door opened and a civilian in a black suit nodded.

"Asrar Fouad?" the man asked.

"Yes. I have an appointment to see President Kamil."

"Your passport and identity papers."

Fouad handed them to him. The man did not look at them. They had been checked twice before in the ground-level building. He must have passed or he wouldn't be down here. He wondered how deep in the ground they were.

"Please follow me," the black-suited man said. They went through the normal door into the next room, which was set up as a luxurious Iraqi hotel suite. It had a large living room, with four doors opening off it. The furnishings were a mixture of Iraqi and Western, with upholstered chairs and couches in three conversation sets. Oil paintings dotted the walls, and soft music came from hidden speakers. A woman without a veil brought in a tray filled with fruits and nuts and small cakes and put them on a low table.

To the left was a modern office with computers, several large screens, two desks, leather swivel chairs, file cabinets, and a TV set. One of the chairs turned and a small man with a heavy mustache but otherwise clean shaven, with lots of dark hair and heavy brows, looked at Fouad. He didn't stand.

"Ah, yes, my friend from the West Bank. I'm pleased that you could come. We have much to talk about. Come, come, and sit near the table and the fruit. May I bring you something cool to drink? A cola or a lemonade? Let's relax. I want to hear how things are going in Palestine. We're never sure how true the news reports are. Come, come."

Fouad walked to the office and sat in the upholstered chair that President Kamil pointed to. Kamil was smaller than his pictures suggested. He must stand on a lot of boxes for photos. His black hair was shaggy and almost framed his face. His eyes came at Fouad in an intense stare, and he knew the president was evaluating him.

"Try the figs and the dates," the president said. "They are the new crop, just coming in. Delicious. Dates must be the perfect food. So sweet and good and they'll keep for years."

Fouad tried one of the dates and smiled.

"Now, Asrar Fouad, I can tell you are an anxious man. A man who has so much to do and so little time. I understand that we have some mutual friends. They have told me that you have a plan to help me bring America to her knees."

"Yes, President Kamil. I do have a plan that has been in

the works for half a year. We have teams in place. We have the logistics worked out. Only the last minute, in-fact preparations are waiting to be made. We will strike at the ultimate target that every soldier of Allah dreams about."

"But you need my assistance. This is what my friends in al-Qaida tell me. I was distressed when the news finally came out that our great friend Osama bin Laden was killed by the terrorist Americans in their criminal bombings in Afghanistan."

"Yes, a tragedy, but it perhaps has brought us closer together, cemented our many al-Qaida cells throughout the world into a more workable organization."

"The plan that you sent to me is practical? You can make it work despite the increased security in criminal America?"

"Yes. The security there is laughable. We have penetrated it dozens of times with materials and goods about the same size and weight that we will need to slip our ultimate cargo into the United States. We do it from Mexico where the border is as porous as a sponge. It is there that we have the most secret operatives in place in their Border Patrol, and the inspectors who evaluate the truck shipments going through the San Ysidro border checkpoint."

President Kamil took a slow drink from a tall sweating glass that had been sitting on a coaster on his desk. He returned the glass, then peaked his fingers in front of his face and stared through them at Fouad. Neither spoke for a few moments. Then Kamil swiveled around and picked up a sheaf of letter-sized pages from his desk.

"This is the only copy?"

"It is. Our people have everything memorized. Usually we put nothing like this on paper, but you asked for it, so we provided it."

"I can assure you this document has not been duplicated here in Iraq." He pushed the pages into a shredder near his desk, and the machine turned the paper into a dozen different shapes and slices. "Now, you can breathe easier. There is no evidence."

"Yes, now that it is gone, I am feeling less vulnerable."

"I have a question," President Kamil said. "You realize that our package is not as sophisticated as those of the West.

It is larger than we thought it would be and heavier, but it works. We have tested them underground three times with perfect results. Will you use a ship or aircraft to transport the package?"

"Our plans now call for an air shipment. It will be crated and camouflaged as medical MRI equipment to sustain the fiction of its size and weight. We have checked the limit on some of the cargo aircraft, and it will fit through the doors and meet all of their requirements."

"Is this the best plan? You said you couldn't guarantee us New York or Washington, DC, or even Chicago."

"Mr. President, this is not a war-winning blow. It is a strike at the heart and soul of America. It is a psychological killer that will have the Americans running around like rats inside their borders looking for a safe haven. This one blow will set back the American economy five years. It will be so devastating psychologically that Americans won't trust anyone again in the whole world. We expect that they will withdraw more than a half million troops that are now in place around the world. They will say they need them home to protect their borders from an invasion. They won't even trust their elected officials who are supposed to be helping them."

"We are giving up one of our most treasured assets."

"We are well aware of that, Mr. President. We thank you, and the whole Muslim world thanks you. But you have told us that you don't have the capacity to deliver the package where you want to. The only possibility would be a suicide aircraft, and you're not sure that you could even get that over a suitable target. This is the best way to do the job. This is cooperation at the highest level between Islamic nations and groups. It is the way with which Allah will be pleased."

President Kamil took another drink from the glass. Fouad wondered if there was something more potent in the glass than just the lemon drink. He had been in the West long enough to know of the pull, the addiction, of strong drink. For a man who had everything, anything he wanted, the temptation of some form of alcohol would be overpowering. Fouad was partial to gin in his drinks. Partly because it could not be seen, and partly because of the sting, the bite, and the flavor of the redistilled alcoholic liquor.

"I'm not worried about Allah. I'm more concerned how Omar Kamil will feel. How will I be affected? Will the West track the bomb back to me? I will be the prime suspect. The West, the savage Americans, do not yet know that I have a nuclear capability. What will they do once they learn of it? Invasion is a strong possibility. They could sweep in here overnight without the sanctions of the United Nations and wipe out our forces before we could get our aircraft into the sky. Would the Americans be that furious for losing one of their cities?"

"They will be angry, yes, but cooler heads will prevail. The Americans tend to anger quickly, and to cool down fast. They will suspect you, but there is no way to prove where a nuclear weapon comes from. There is no residue, no telltale parts, and no fingerprint of any kind they could possibly use. Without hard evidence they would have to rely on their suspicions. Al-Qaida will at once take credit for the act and let the Americans speculate where we obtained the bomb. They will discuss and debate the question for days, and then weeks and then months and the sting will wither and the hot blood will cool, and they will take no action against anyone. They won't be able to be sure where the bomb came from. There are thirteen nations in the world now with nuclear weapons. The bomb could have originated from any of them."

President Kamil's eyes drifted shut then came open. He sipped the drink and his voice took on the hint of a tremor. "Just how quickly can this all be done?"

"It took us two years to plan and carry out the strike on the Twin Towers and the Pentagon. This is much simpler, and more direct. Only a handful of people will be required. From the time you turn over the device to us until we detonate it over an American city, we have timed it out to be thirty days."

"So quickly." He frowned. "That doesn't give us much time to strengthen our defenses, to get in better radar, to post ships at sea as an early warning network."

"Believe me, Mr. President. You will have no need for defenses other than your normal routines. America will not attack. Did they attack anyone after the Twin Towers? Yes, they did go into Afghanistan, but that was a slowly developing campaign. There they had many leads pointing to bin Laden."

"Thirty days." The president shook his head. "This seems like a dream, that we can deliver one of our weapons on the hated Americans, and have it accomplished in only thirty days." He took a long pull at the drink and waved his hand. The same woman as before, in long robes, came in at once, replaced the drink with a new one that was already sweating on the glass, took the empty one away, and hurried out of the room.

"Mr. Fouad. I've been battling with this decision for the past two weeks. I've talked to about half of our generals, our defense minister, all of the top people in my government. The consensus is that we go ahead with the plan. The generals, to a man, recommended that we do not give you a bomb. They counseled that we keep them for use to forward our own goals. Just the threat of the use of a nuclear bomb can have a great effect on a small country nearby. That was their suggestion."

"The military leaders make a good point, Mr. President. But you said your other advisors, the civilians, were in favor of the plan?"

"Yes. The final decision is mine. No one else's. No one to blame but me if it goes wrong." He stood and walked with slow steps to one wall where there hung a bright painting, carefully lighted, that showed a luxurious green garden brimming with a rainbow of blooming flowers, and trees, and a small waterfall in a shallow stream. He studied the painting for what seemed to Fouad for five minutes. When he turned he smiled.

"Yes, you shall have your bomb. Our facility is in the desert, out where a mistake would not be so tragic. I'll have it crated and concealed as best as we can. Where will you fly it from?"

"Assuming the bomb is in the desert west of here, we will transport it by truck to Jordan. We should have no trouble crossing the border. We will proceed to the northern city of Irbid. From there we will charter an airfreight craft and fly it away toward the Atlantic Ocean. That's all I should tell you right now. You'll have no trouble pleading that you don't know how this happened, because you really won't know. The plan I sent you is a practical one, but not the exact one that we'll use. Our final plan is much better, slicker and with more chances to succeed. Mr. President. It's an honor and a pleasure doing business with you."

The ex-general smiled and held out his hand. "I hope it will bring pleasure to all of Islam. Now, I realize that your group is usually short on cash. Would you accept a gift from Iraq of fifty thousand U.S. dollars, to help along the project?"

"Mr. President, I'm overwhelmed. Yes, the U.S. dollars will come in handy as we move across the globe. Now, the timetable. We'll need a tractor and an enclosed trailer, to get the package into Jordan and then north. We have contacts there that will cooperate with us with no questions asked. We already have made tentative arrangements with the air-freight company in Irbid."

"I've given orders to provide you with a truck and trailer sufficient to make the trip and to conceal the bomb with bales of raw cotton. It should work well all the way into Jordan. Good luck."

The two men stood, shook hands again.

"Mr. President, just to satisfy my curiosity, how far underground are we?"

"It's a common question. We are a hundred and fifty feet deep into the bedrock of Iraq. No bomb of any type can come anywhere near touching this room."

Fouad smiled. "I'm glad I'm not claustrophobic." He turned and a guard appeared to lead him out of the room and back to the surface. An eager smile showed on his face. Now that it had been decided, he couldn't wait to get the plan into motion. Watch out, America. Al-Qaida is coming for a quick visit.

4

Lieutenant Commander Blake Murdock looked at one of his longtime SEALs who sat across from him in his office. He'd just heard Fernandez say he didn't know if he could remain in SEALs.

"Fernandez, I know something of how you're feeling right now. I think nine out of ten men in the military who are in the front lines and have to pull the triggers on rifles, or bomb release buttons or machine guns, have had the same feelings you're having. I had a bout with doubts in my second year. You didn't know anything about it. The only one I told was the master chief and Masciareli. Boy, that was a mistake going to the commander. I had been on something like fifteen missions by then and the body count was starting to get to me. What the hell was I doing going around the world gunning down these other human beings? So my government said they were bad guys and deserved to die. Why was I their executioner? I pounded it around in my brain for almost two months. Worked through two missions in the process, and came out with one main conclusion for me. My take on it wouldn't mean a thing to you. It's something that every SEAL has to work out for himself. Now, with that as an introduction—tell me how you feel."

Fernandez looked up, the frown still staining his long face.

"It's like you said. I kill people for a living. My little girl this morning asked me what I did. The kids at school told what their dads did for a living, and Linda didn't know. I told her I was in the navy and I went around the world protecting the United States. Then it hit me. What do I do? I shoot people dead."

"Where did that line of thought take you?"

"Down a deep, dark trail. I remembered the dozens, maybe fifty times I've 'made certain' on some of the bodies. Then the hundreds of men I've dispatched with my rifle and sub gun. Just who the hell said I was qualified to decide who lives and who dies in this big fat world?"

Murdock watched Fernandez. It had taken six years to hit him this hard. He was in it right up to his mouth and it was rising. He had to do something or Fernandez would drown in his own self-applied misery.

"You don't decide who lives or dies, sailor. That's my job. I tell you what to do and you goddamn well better do it. That's why you're a SEAL. That's why I'm a SEAL. Somebody upstairs tells me what to do, and I tell you and the whole fucking platoon and we do it or we die trying. You know how many men have died in this platoon on my watch?"

"Yes, sir. Fourteen."

"Right, fourteen. Almost a whole damn platoon planted in the deep dark earth or buried at sea. Fourteen good men."

"I knew every one of them."

"You did. You and I are not among the departed."

Fernandez took a deep breath. "I guess that's something to be thankful for. But still . . ." He stopped and looked away. Tears brimmed his eyes, then ran down his cheeks. He slashed at them with his hand. "There ain't no fucking crying in SEALs, Commander." He shouted the line and they both laughed.

"Every SEAL I've ever known has cried at one time or another. Maybe crying can help. Have you talked to your priest?"

"I'm Catholic, but not a good one. I seldom go to mass. Almost never go to confession. What do I say? Forgive me, Father, for I have sinned: last week I put my submachine gun to the heads of twelve men and blew their brains out?"

"Easy, Fernandez. Just try to relax. Nobody is judging you. You're one of the best SEALs in the platoon. Not just the shooting, but the other things. You've held your squad together when it could have shattered and come up with six dead. You've had some ideas and plans that dug the whole platoon out of deep shit more than once. You're a team player, you cover the man's back in front of you, and you expect the man behind you to take care of your ass. You're a SEAL, which is a fucking lot more than just taking out a few terrs now and then.

"Yes, we shoot a lot. We also rescue people. What is it, three or four embassies we've gone in and pulled over a hundred people out of the fire. Remember that senator in China where he shouldn't have been and we went up the river in a rubber duck and brought him and his wife and daughter out to safety? Remember all those times, sailor?"

"Yes sir. Some high points. But how many Chinese men did we kill on that mission? Two at the front door, one at the back door, and two inside as I remember. Were that senator and his family worth the lives of five human beings?"

"What about the EAR, Fernandez? You've used it several times to put down the enemy without a casualty. We almost never harm civilians. If somebody's army is shooting at us, we have a right to shoot back. If we shoot better than they do, we win."

"Right. In a fair firefight, I have no big problem. If we have better weapons and take them out, that I can live with. But to go up to a wounded enemy and kill him . . . that's what's bugging me the most. I know, I know. These are situations where we simply can't leave a wounded enemy behind or it would compromise the whole mission and could mean that half or more of our platoon would wind up in graves registration. I know that. And still it bugs me that we have to make certain on the wounded."

"I can solve that one in the future."

"Not always. There could come a time when I'm the logical one to do it."

"So I take the second most logical person to make sure and we keep moving. Okay, you're off the list for making sure. That should help. You're one of the best men I have, Fernandez. You'll be taking care of the new man in your squad the way you always do. Teaching him what he didn't learn in the six-month training cycle. Who is your new man?"

"He's Second Class Electrician's Mate Dexter M. Tate. Looks to be about twenty-two or -three, an inch under six feet and maybe a hundred and eighty-five pounds. He's a nut about free diving on old ships in the ocean and he rides a motorcycle to work. Oh, yeah, he's a computer nut and loves his Bull Pup."

"That's it?"

"Well, we've only talked a few times. Seems like a nice guy. Oh, he isn't married."

"Fernandez, see what I mean? Is there another man in Bravo who knows as much about Tate as you do? Not a chance. You're his sponsor; you'll be there if he needs you. You do one hell of a lot more in Bravo than just pull a trigger."

"Oh." He frowned. "Well, maybe so. I never thought much about the other things. Kind of routine."

"Routine, like saving somebody's life. Where was that when you dragged one of your squad out of the line of fire? You took a bullet, but your buddy didn't get killed, and you lived to fight another day, as we say."

"Well, yeah. Somebody had to do it."

"Somebody? There were three others closer to that man than you were. None of them jumped out there to save his ass. You did. Fernandez saw a job that needed doing and he risked his hide to do the job and took an enemy bullet in the process. That's one hell of a lot more than just routine." He paused. "You talked with your wife yet about how you're feeling?"

"Not much. I just barely touched on it last night."

"That is a job you have to do."

"I know. She's never said a word about my quitting, but I know she curls up and almost dies every time we go on a mission. It's tough on her. She'd be ecstatic if I quit the SEALs."

"But would you?"

"I don't know. That's what I'm trying to figure out."

"Your wife and your priest, in any order—that's your assignment. You want to take tomorrow off and do it?"

"We're going to the desert tomorrow for some live firing."

"Right."

"I should be there to take a hand with Tate if he needs it. He hasn't done much live firing lately. You know, give him some pointers, some shortcuts."

"You playing papa bear, right?"

Fernandez grinned. "Hell, I guess so. Just kind of built in. Like the old fire horses would get all revved up when they heard the fire bell."

"Okay. I guarantee you won't have to make sure on anybody tomorrow. It's a one-day trip. Get back late tomorrow night. Be sure to tell Maria that."

"Maybe the wives could have a night out. I'll see what Maria can set up. There's three of them—Ardith, Maria, and Wanda Gardner. I'll talk to Maria about it. A movie, maybe."

"Fernandez, this will clear up, this will pass. When it does, then you'll have decided if you want to remain a SEAL or go back to the black shoe."

"I'd die of boredom back there. Which might be a good thing for a family man. Damn few of us married guys in the SEALs. We'll see. Right now I don't know what in hell I'm going to do."

"We need to get this cleared up before we have another mission. You know that could come at any time."

"Tell me about it. Usually it's on Maria's birthday or one of the big holidays." He snorted. "Damnedest thing. I still love it. The rush of getting a mission nobody else knows about but the president and two or three other big shots, and then we go jetting halfway around the world to do something that nobody else on this old earth can do. Now, that is one hell of a rush."

"Stay hard, SEAL. Now get out of here and talk it out with Maria. Let her have her say."

Fernandez came to attention, snapped a salute, did an about face perfectly, and marched out the door. "Hey, maybe I'm getting in some practice in for the black shoe navy."

Murdock waved and looked back at his desk. The damn paperwork. It was nearly 1700. He'd look at it in two days. Up early for tomorrow.

Ten minutes later he headed for the new condo in the edge of La Jolla. The traffic wasn't all that bad. He came off the

San Diego Bay Bridge on Interstate 5 and headed north. Then through San Diego and out the same interstate to the Grand Street off-ramp, and soon he was in the south end, the lower income part, of La Jolla, just blocks from Pacific Beach. He parked on the street, leaving the assigned underground parking slot for Ardith's car. She usually pulled in about twenty minutes of six.

Upstairs in their condo he checked the phone answering machine. Two messages: "Honey, I'm sorry." It was Ardith's voice. "I'll be a little late getting home tonight. Small emergency I have to fix. I'd think I'll be in about seven. Love you."

The second one was a mortgage company looking for business. He deleted both and checked in the freezer. The Hungry Man super dinner looked about right. He could thaw with the best cooks around. He set it for the seven minutes in the microwave and settled in with the newspaper. He scanned the front page to see if he could see any hint of where they might be heading next. More action in Afghanistan, where they'd routed some more holdouts in caves. A combined Special Forces team found four Stinger anti-aircraft shoulder-fired missiles, over a hundred thousand rounds of rifle ammunition, and hundreds of mortar rounds. The whole ammo dump made a tremendous explosion and sealed the cave. Not much chance of Third Platoon going there.

Iran was heating up again. An American diplomat had been gunned down in usually stable Yemen. Two men on a motorcycle raced up beside the diplomat's car. One man used a submachine gun and riddled the rear seat window and the man inside the car. The attackers sped away, were soon lost in the heavy traffic, and escaped. No one had taken responsibility for the crime at the last report. No, they wouldn't go to Yemen.

He gave up, fished the roast beef dinner out of the microwave, and ate it right out of the plastic tray. Surprisingly, it tasted good and there was plenty of it. He went back to the paper.

Ardith charged in at seven-thirty. She was tall, slender, with a mass of long blond hair that cascaded over her shoulders. She was the daughter of the senior senator from Oregon and had worked for him in Washington for six years as an assistant counsel. She came west when she had a job offer she couldn't refuse. Today there were worry lines around her eyes and she slumped against the wall.

"Tough day at the office?" Murdock asked.

Ardith laughed, ran to him, and hugged him soundly, then kissed him and kicked off her shoes. "Yes, Master. A furious day at the office. The client changed his mind, then when we did what he wanted he changed it back to the way we had it in the first place. My boss is taking him out to dinner, but I begged off. So what's new at your zoo?"

"Mostly routine. Oh, Marie Fernandez might be calling you. We'll be in the desert tomorrow and home about midnight. Miguel thought maybe you three could take in a movie or something."

"Sounds good."

"Miguel is having some worries about being a SEAL. He's re-evaluating his job, his career, the whole thing. I think he'll come out of it okay, but you never can tell. I've lost three good men who decided to go back to the black shoe navy. One of them went to officer candidate school, so he doesn't count."

"Miguel, he's been with you a long time."

"Six years. Now what can I thaw out for you for dinner?"

"Anything in there that will get hot. I could eat a horse. Let me get out of these work clothes and dress down a little. Desert tomorrow? You get a new senior chief today?" Murdock nodded. "How do you like him?"

"I think he'll do fine. Doesn't look like Sadler will make it back. He got shot up a little too much. We'll have to wait about four months to see."

He stuffed the chicken breast with broccoli and cherry pie desert into the microwave and set it for five minutes. He turned it on and looked at the paper again. Nothing in the international news that sounded critical. He was about to tune the TV set to CNN when his cell phone chimed. He'd forgotten to turn it off. He flipped the phone open.

"Murdock here."

"Good, I caught you." Murdock recognized the master chief's voice at once. "Sir, we're getting our tails twisted again. I got a direct call from the CNO. He said he had a phone call from the President and the Chairman of the National Security Council and they want your platoon in DC tomorrow afternoon for a briefing at Langley. Something hot is cooking but he wouldn't tell me what. You don't argue with the chief of naval operations. You had an early morning trip to the desert planned for tomorrow. We have you booked on a biz jet for oh-eight-thirty. You're to come in full combat-ready gear, double loads of ammo, and all weapons. No Dragers or wet suits. This sounds like a dry land operation."

"Yes, Master Chief. North Island Air at oh-eight-thirty. Gives us lots of time. Have you talked with Miguel Fernandez lately?"

"No, why, is he in trouble?"

"Not a bit, just wondered. We'll be ready and on board. We have two new men, but they'll have to earn their pay as they learn. We'll let the men check in over the quarter deck at the sched time of oh-four-thirty and take it from there. Any hint where we're going?

"Not a glimmer, lad. Not a Chinaman's clue."

"Right. You sleep in in the morning. We've got the bus on call at oh-five-hundred. See you when we get back. Oh, does Masciareli know yet?"

"I'm about to call him. He's gonna piss his pants again."

"Yeah, be good for him. Take care, Master Chief." He took a deep breath. Now he had to tell Ardith they were on call again. She would not be pleased.

5

Murdock drove into the parking lot outside the Quarter Deck at oh-four-thirty. There were already six SEALs there jawing at each other around their cars. They waved and trooped together across the Quarter Deck and to SEAL Team Seven Third Platoon's quarters.

"Break out your new desert cammies," Murdock told the men. "We won't be going to the desert today; we have a mission, only nobody but the president knows what it is."

"How's the time?" Jaybird asked.

"Lots of it. We don't take off from North Island NAS until oh-eight-thirty."

"Time for chow," somebody chirped.

"Yes," Murdock said. "The bus leaves here at oh-eight-hundred. We go ready to fight. Weapons, double ammo, no Drager or wet suits, so we're on a land mission. Fill in the rest of the men when they arrive. Gardner, on me."

Lieutenant (J.G.) Gardner walked with Murdock to the small office and couldn't keep the curiosity out of his voice.

"So where are we really going, Cap?"

"DC, then Langley, Virginia, and a briefing I'd guess by the spooks at the farm."

"Couldn't they do it with encrypted radio messages?"

"Evidently not. They may have more in mind than a briefing. The last time they invited us to Langley we came out looking like a ragtag bunch of Arabs."

"We're going to infiltrate some Arab country?"

"Possible. We've done it before. Check out your squad and be sure that every man has his assigned weapon and double ammo. That's going to mean ammo bags for the Bull Pups."

"Will do, Commander," Gardner said and hurried out the door.

It was a little after oh-seven-hundred when Murdock called home. Ardith should be about ready to drive to work. She picked up on the second ring.

"Yes, good morning."

"Hi, Ardith. A small change in plans. I won't be home for a while, maybe a couple of weeks. We just got a new mission. We fly out this morning at oh-eight-thirty. Wanted to say good-bye."

"I guess that new furniture we talked about looking for will have to wait. It hasn't been long since your last trip."

"True. You know the routine. When they call, we go. You take care of things there. I've got to go. See you soon."

"Soon. Murdock, I love you."

"Love you, too. See you."

He hung up and made a final check on Alpha Squad. Everyone had made it on time at oh-four-thirty. Some of them had breakfast. He found Fernandez checking over his gear. Murdock knelt down beside the SEAL and spoke so no one else could hear.

"You sure you want to go on this one?"

"I'm sure, Cap. I decided when I first heard we had a mission. The old fire horse. No way you can keep me out of it."

"You talk with Maria?"

"For about two hours. She understands how I feel, and that I'm not sure which way I'm going to go. She said it's fine with her either way, but I know she'd rather I drop out and go black shoe."

"I can order you to stay on base."

"I know. But I don't think you'll do that. You don't want another washout."

"Not that. I have to decide if you might endanger another man or your squad." He looked at Fernandez. The SEAL stared straight and even at him, eye to eye. There was no wavering, no indecision on Fernandez's part. "Okay, sailor, you on for this walk in the park." Murdock stood. He nodded curtly and went back to the office.

The navy driver had pulled in the navy bus they were going to go to the desert in at 0840, sweating because he was late. He heard the news of the changed plans and promptly sacked out on the front seat.

The bus dropped off the sixteen SEALs in full battle gear at 0815 on the short runway next to a sleek Gulfstream II that the navy called the VC-11. It is the same as the civilian model with the exception of the added military communications gear and some interior layout changes. The craft is usually used for flying military top brass and VIPs around when they needed to move in a rush. It carries a crew of two and has seats for nineteen passengers.

The VC-11 has a broad, tall vertical tail with a full-height rudder, swept horizontal stabilizers on top of the vertical "T." It uses insert elevators. Flight controls, flaps, spoilers, landing gear, and brakes are all operated by two independent hydraulic systems. Two Rolls-Royce turbofan engines power the craft.

It's seventy-nine feet long, twenty-four feet high, and has a long-range maximum cruising speed of 581 miles an hour. At cruising it can jump over 3,712 miles without refueling and has a ceiling of 43,000 feet.

The SEALs settled into the deluxe first-class, passenger-style seats, stowing their ammo sacks, combat vests, and weapons wherever they found enough room.

A male second-class petty officer came in from the front cabin and talked to Murdock. Then the CO of the platoon bellowed out an order. "Listen up," he said. The chatter stopped and the second class waved.

"Morning. I'm Tanner. You have any questions, ask me. We'll be taking off promptly at oh-eight-thirty. Commander Johnson is our pilot. She is one of the best. Our flight time to the Washington National Airport will be four point seven two hours, depending on the jet stream. The jet goes from west to east, so it could boost our speed by a hundred miles an hour. We've taken meals on board. As soon as we take off and gain altitude, I'll be bring you box breakfasts. Just after twelve hundred, you'll get a lunch prepared by the North Island NAS Officers' Mess. Any questions?"

"Yeah, who has the beer concession?" Jaybird cracked.

"That would be Commander Janice Johnson. However, she's a little busy right now getting ready for take off. Any other questions?"

"Yeah, why are we landing at Washington National instead of Andrews Air Force Base?" Canzoneri asked.

"I don't know. I have no need to know, and that matter may be classified. Let's have a good trip." The crew chief vanished back into the forward cabin.

Murdock looked at J.G. Gardner. "So why are we landing in downtown Washington?"

"Got me. I know that airport is a lot closer to Langley than Andrews, which is maybe fifteen miles east of DC in Maryland."

The box breakfasts were routine, but the noon meal was great, served on china with silverware.

They landed early, barely four hours into the flight. The plane taxied to the end of the runway and took a narrow concrete strip to a building painted dull green, with two closed vans and three airport police cars in front of it. A light colonel came out of the closest van and marched over to where the crew had just let down the steps on the VC-11. Murdock met him at the steps.

"Commander Murdock?"

"Yes, sir," Murdock said, saluting.

"Anderson here, I'll be your official guide. Have your men bring all of their equipment, weapons, vests, everything. We're a little early, which will make the chief happy. Remember to set your watches. It's three hours later here than on the coast."

They loaded into the vans and drove. The closed vans were the twelve-passenger type but had no windows other than the windshield and those in the front doors.

"This feels like a goddamned tomb," Hospital Corpsman First Class Jack Mahanani said.

"You've done this before?" Gardner asked. The squads were each in a separate van.

"Once or twice I can remember," Fernandez said. "This must be a high-level operation to pull us in here rather than jet us right to the hot spot."

"We gonna be here long?" Dexter Tate asked.

"Who knows?" Fernandez said. "When they tell us to go, we'll go."

Fernandez tried to watch out the windshield, but he couldn't see much. They had lost three hours so it was just past 1600. Fernandez grinned. He had seen the same roadside fruit stand twice now. The drivers were taking them on a confusing joy ride before settling down at the Farm, the famous training ground for United States CIA spies and operatives.

It was another half hour before the van came to a stop. The guard in the front seat opened the rolling door from the outside.

"End of the line. Everyone out."

They came out and automatically formed into a column of ducks and awaited the next command. The army colonel waved at Gardner and he brought his men up near Murdock's squad.

"Gentlemen, this is the CIA Farm. You've heard of it. Most of you have been here before. We have some business to take care of before you head out on your mission. These guides will lead you to your quarters. In twenty minutes there'll be a chow call, and then at oh-nineteen-hundred we have a meeting. Leave all of your weapons, even your hideouts, and your ammo and gear in your quarters. A guide will be on hand to lead you to the meeting. That's all. You're dismissed."

The guides waved and the SEALs marched over to a pair of low-lying buildings that looked more like college campus dorms than barracks. Inside, though, they were barracks, with double bunks and room for sixty men. The two officers stayed with their men. They went through the same chow line and were ready when the guides came to take them to the meeting.

They entered a three-story brick building with ivy blanketing half the near wall, and went up to the third floor. The conference room looked like one from a major corporation. The oval walnut table was twenty feet long, with chairs all around the outside. Already in the room were four men, one in an army general's uniform and three civilians.

The SEALs stood in two ranks along one side of the table

and the four other men sat down. Deputy Director of the CIA Glenden Swarthout nodded at the SEALs.

"Gentlemen, it's good to have you here again. We're facing a problem that has been growing for sometime but was confused with false information, rumors, and downright lies. Now we have the facts and we're prepared to act on them.

"Our top agent in Iraq has told us that the government there now has four operational atomic weapons. They are crude but functioning. We have no information on what they plan to do with them, but we can't afford to wait and find out. Those weapons must be destroyed as quickly as possible. We know they have staged at least three underground explosions, and from all reports the weapons worked as planned.

"Right now, we're not even sure where the bombs are. We know they are in the desert, probably at least two hundred miles west of Baghdad. That could be anywhere in a large arc of locations. Your job is to go to Iraq, infiltrate the country, learn where the bombs are, and destroy them. Next you will take out the production facility where they have been manufactured. A big task? You bet. A deadly important one? One of the highest on our agenda. Most of you have been here before and taken our quick Arabic and Iraqi indoctrination program.

"By this time you've probably figured out that we can't infiltrate sixteen men into Iraq. We can put in three, and we hope all will be fluent in Arabic. We have few resources in Iraq. Our best man there is continuing to send us vital information on this problem. I realize you men are not experts on nuclear weapons and how to destroy them without blowing up the whole countryside. We will be sending an expert along with you. Some of you know this person. She's Katherine 'Kat' Garnet. You've worked with her before. She comes on station here tomorrow morning. She will be dressed as a man to avoid female restrictions in any Islamic country we are in.

"We will know tomorrow if we can use Saudi Arabia as our staging area. Our relations with that nation have been good, and when we tell them that Iraq has these weapons and may use them on its neighbors in a drive for new territory, we believe they will give us total cooperation. Saudi

Arabia has a border with the far western section of Iraq, in the edges of the Syrian Desert. If the bomb location is in the desert, we will be much closer to it from Saudi Arabia than from Kuwait, but if we can't use Saudi Arabia for staging, it will be Kuwait. Are there any questions so far?"

Murdock stepped forward. "Sir. You said we don't have an exact location of the weapons yet. So we'll have to go to Baghdad, meet your man there, and ferret out that location. For this we would take in only three men. Then when we know the location, the rest of the platoon can move in from Saudi Arabia?"

"That was our best plan so far. Rather than work up from Kuwait with our three men, we are considering an airdrop from the northern edges of the Iraq Southern No-Fly Zone, which we patrol regularly, so aircraft there would not arouse suspicion."

"How close can you get our men to Baghdad with that airdrop?" Jaybird asked.

"About forty miles, which is a lot better than the three hundred and seventy-five miles from Kuwait to Baghdad."

"Then Kat would remain with the bulk of the platoon in Saudi Arabia while our three men dig out the location?" Murdock asked.

"That is our suggestion." The deputy director looked at the SEALs, then at the others at the desk. "Are there any more questions?"

Murdock spoke up. "I'm assuming that we'll use all non-U.S.-made weapons and that we'll have all non-U.S. uniforms and gear for the fighting part of our platoon, so we leave no fingerprint of our presence."

"Right. You've been there before. The three men who go into Baghdad must be as Arabic as possible. Who will you send, Commander?"

"Our key man is Omar Rafii, a native of Saudi Arabia and totally fluent in Arabic. I'll be the second one. My Arabic is passable. The third man I want along is Kenneth Ching. He speaks four languages and picked up well on Arabic on our last outing when we needed it."

"Good. You three will start your training at eight o'clock tomorrow morning. The rest of the platoon will report to our

uniforms and wardrobe department. We'll probably go with
Kuwait army cammies for you. Miss Garnet will be outfitted
with the rest of the platoon."

He pulled down a large scale map that showed Iraq and
portions of the nations around it. "So you can orient yourselves. If we don't get confirmation from Saudi Arabia before
you fly out, we land in Kuwait, then we'll work from there.
Our timetable looks like this. Training tomorrow and the next
day. We want you three to be as invisible as possible while
in Baghdad. That way you can stay alive. We want your
Arabic to be as colloquial as possible. Three days from today
you'll fly out in another VC-11, heading for the Middle
East." He nodded to the men. "Thank you all, and have a
good night's sleep. Tomorrow we get to work."

The general and the three civilians stood.

"Ten-hut!" one of the SEALs bellowed. The SEALs
snapped to attention as the general and the civilians walked
out of the room.

6

Baghdad, Iraq

Salah Rahmani watched his two sons and his wife at the breakfast table. She had captured his heart four years ago and he had married her at once. Now he was a family man and had to start thinking about his responsibilities. The food and living conditions were adequate, but not nearly as good as they could be in the United States. But first he had his commitment to the CIA to be as useful here in Iraq as possible. He prayed that he could get out soon. There had been some hints about his loyalty in the past, but nothing came of it. He had not been aware of any innuendo that the president's secret police suspected him. He knew the dangerous track he walked. There was absolutely no margin for error. One miniscule misstep and he would be shot down at his desk or wherever one of the elite hit squads found him.

He had been back in Iraq for four years. He was born here, and before he left he had graduated from the top military academy in Baghdad. He placed first in his class and was recruited to go to college in America and take ROTC training to learn as much about the American military system as possible. He wouldn't exactly be a spy, but he was to soak up as much U.S. military information as he could. While in the States he fell in love with America, with the people, the government, the relaxed, marvelous way of life. It took a CIA man only two months to turn him and convince him to become a spy for America in Baghdad.

He quit college and took a four-month course at the Farm at Langley and went back to Iraq with his college degree and his commission as a second lieutenant in the U.S. Army reserve. Both were fabricated by the CIA. Since then he had been increasingly important as a source to the Company

41

about Iraq and what the government really was doing. In Iraq he had been assigned by the War Ministry to the American Forecast Desk and had told them just enough about the U.S. Army's operation to keep them happy. In his position as a captain in the Iraqi Army he was privy to some but not all of the Iraqi military plans. He did have an up-to-date plan for the placement of antiaircraft guns in and around Baghdad.

The most dangerous part of his life was transmitting his reports to the CIA via the SATCOM. The small CIA version of the satellite radio had come into his hands in various pieces and he assembled it and made contact. The radio was so advanced that it spurted out the transmissions in a tenth of a second, far too quickly for any triangulation to pin down its location. He had the foot-high, four-inch-square radio hidden in an unused chimney in the flat that he rented from the government.

Two days ago he discovered that Iraq's push to develop a nuclear weapon had been a success. He had kept the U.S. up-to-date on the progress over the past three years. He learned that the military now had four nuclear bombs. They were crude by Western standards, but operational. Iraq had already exploded three in deep-well tests far underground. There had been no international recognition of the tests. The Iraq Ministry of Science had reported a minor earthquake at the same time. Seismographs around the world had recorded the disturbance and scientists agreed that it was an extremely small earthquake located in the Syrian Desert. Now he had to find out where the bombs were kept and, more important, what Iraq's new president intended to do with them. A tough assignment for a lowly captain in the army. It would be the most dangerous intelligence-gathering work he had attempted so far. He had some contacts who might help. He knew that Iraq had no aircraft capable of delivering the nukes over a long distance. They had short-range missiles, but he didn't think they were large enough to take nuclear bombs in their payloads. So what was President Kamil going to do with the weapons? He could bluff his neighbors, threaten to vaporize them unless they allowed Iraq to take over their country without a fight. But would the rest of the Arab world stand for that? No, he must have other plans.

President Kamil was an absolute dictator of Iraq despite the handpicked parliament and the religious courts. He was a master politician as well and was winning over the loyalty of the people. Lately he had granted immediate release to more than ten thousand mostly political prisoners. He had expanded a program to give free pieces of land to all civil servants and military personnel. He had relaxed restrictions on private businesses, allowing people to open stores and small enterprises and to import goods directly from abroad.

In Baghdad he had liberalized some aspects of life. Internet cafes opened that drew hundreds of Iraqis desperate for outside news and eager to conduct business deals by e-mail. E-mail was still restricted to one government-controlled server. But just months ago people were allowed to access e-mail form their homes.

President Kamil was trying to buy the contentment of the people, and so far it was working. Salah knew from his own observation that things were much better for the middle-class people in Baghdad than they were four years ago. The roads were much improved; the telephone system, in total disarray after the Gulf War bombings, was now back in operation and worked well enough so anyone could dial direct anywhere in the world.

Even a year ago the Saddam International Airport had been dark. Today the brightly lit terminal was buzzing with flights and passengers from Jordan, Syria, and Russia. The roads in town were jammed with cars and trucks, among them Mercedes-Benz and Peugeot models. Many of these were imported by the Iraqi Trade Ministry and sold to residents at cut-rate prices.

Salah had been to one middle-class neighborhood recently where a jazz trio serenaded diners in an Italian restaurant with Beatles and Frank Sinatra tunes. Shoppers bought computers from Dubai and grabbed bootleg videodiscs for their new DVD players.

Still, with all the improvements, Iraq remained a dictator-run country with harsh laws and customs.

Salah rode his bicycle to work at the War Ministry. It was only four miles, but traffic was heavy. At his office he carried his bike up two flights and parked it inside so it wouldn't be stolen. Even locked bicycles left on the street were disassembled, and every part not locked down was taken. The parts were put together with parts from other bikes.

Captain Rahmani sat at his desk and worked over a plan for integrating the senior cadets at the military academy into the army at once in case of an attack. He had most of the details worked out and had devised a plan to mobilize them into a self-contained infantry company. There were a few over four hundred seniors at the academy. They would be organized into four platoons, with a regular army company commander, four academy lieutenants, and six sergeants in each platoon.

He printed out the plan and took it to his superior, Major Nabil.

"It's a little rough, sir, but the basic plan is there. All we'd need to do would be grab an infantry captain from the army to be the company commander and draw the cadre from the top students from the academy."

Nabil briefed the plan and nodded. "You have it set up well, Captain. Finish it and we'll submit it with the rest of our emergency contingency plans in case of an invasion." He moved his chair closer to Salah and his voice dropped to a near whisper.

"Did you hear about the four babies we have in the nursery? Looks like they are operational. Half the general staff is sweating bullets trying to figure out how best to utilize them. Do you threaten with them? Drop one in the desert as a demonstration and then say, 'Okay, Syria, we're moving in with occupation troops tomorrow at oh-eight-hundred. Any opposition and Damascus and two and a half million people get vaporized." Major Nabil chuckled. "What a weapon that is! So damned destructive. No defense. Defy us and you die. Quick, simple."

"But then would the West threaten us with a nuclear drop if we invaded another country using nuclear blackmail?" the captain asked.

"Probably." He shook his head. "It's all political now. Not just military thinking. It has to be a political cause and a political stance that is backed up with the military. We could be in a hot spot here for years, and that should mean promotions."

"Yes, Colonel, I'd like your oak leaves." They both laughed. "I hope the top brass doesn't keep those bombs here in Baghdad. Just one little mistake by somebody and boom, we're all atomic dust."

"Oh, no, no problem with that," the major said. "I sit in on one of the planning groups. The whole thing has been done far, far out in the desert. I'd say the four sweethearts are probably closer to the Syrian capital than they are to us here in Baghdad."

"That's a relief. Well, I better get back to work on this contingency plan. Any deadline on it?"

"Sooner the better."

Salah hurried back to his small office and put down the papers. The only thing he could think about was what the major had said. Closer to Damascus, Syria, than to Baghdad. That could put it way out in the Syrian Desert. But there were hundreds of square miles of sand and grass and wadis out there. He had to get a more precise location. But how?

Falda. He had met her several times at military functions. She usually was there as an entertainer, a dancer, sometimes a singer. She was something of a mystery to him. He had heard hints that she might be an undercover spy for the British, but no one knew for sure. She was beautiful, slender with big breasts that she didn't mind showing off.

At noon he went to a phone booth in the lobby of a hotel and made a call. A sensuous female voice answered.

"Yes, good afternoon."

"Falda?"

"Perhaps. Who is calling?"

"Captain Rahmani. You probably don't remember me."

"Of course I do. I remember all the handsome men I meet. You were at the general's thirtieth anniversary party, just last week at the Welcome Hotel."

"Amazing. I wonder if you have time so we could take a walk and talk?"

"That sounds interesting. Nothing we can do over the phone?"

"No, it's more personal than that."

"Now I am intrigued. You know the Grotsky Park?"

"Yes."

"Be there within a half hour. By the Saddam statue."

"I can do that."

They hung up. Salah smiled. She just might be a British spy after all. If she was, he'd find out, and maybe then they could combine their efforts. He hurried out of the hotel and flagged down a cab. This was an emergency. He had to make the meeting on time.

When he arrived in the park, he found her sitting on a bench near the statue. She saw him coming and stood, walking toward him with a dancer's movement, smooth, flowing. She was much prettier than he remembered, and without her stage makeup, she was more approachable.

"You came," she said.

"Of course. We need to talk."

"What about?"

"I understand you spent some time in England?"

"Only a brief vacation."

"Did you talk with any important people?"

"Not a one. Why?"

"Just wondered. I hear many interesting things about you. You move in high official government circles. As a woman, you are given extensive privileges other women don't get. It makes me wonder."

She laughed. "You think I'm a British spy? How interesting. Yes, I am friends with many people. I dance for many functions and I know the men and some of their wives. I am not a British spy."

"Then I won't have to report you to my superiors."

"They wouldn't believe you, anyway. I hear some strange things about you, Salah. Do you know that you are being watched? Everywhere you go someone is following you."

"Why would they do that? Can't they afford a bike of their own?"

"They can and it kills them. They would rather follow you in a car. They take turns bicycling behind you to and from work. They curse and swear at you, but they follow. You spent three years in America."

"It was four years, for my university study. I was sent by the government to learn all I could about the American army and how it works. I was commissioned a second lieutenant in the U.S. Army."

"And now you ask questions about our nuclear project."

"Yes, I'd just as soon it isn't in Baghdad. One mistake by one scientist and we're all atomic dust."

"You know where we keep them?"

"In the desert I would guess, far away from Baghdad."

"Good guess. Oh, we found your fancy radio."

"What radio?"

"The one called SATCOM. The one you sent your spy messages on to the CIA."

"I what? You must have the wrong captain."

"Oh, no, you're the right one. The radio proved that. We're sure that your wife is innocent and knows nothing of your spy work." She signaled and two men in long black coats came and walked beside them.

"We were delighted with the find of the SATCOM, anxious to learn its secrets so we could listen in on U.S. classified messages. You know what happened. When our men opened it without the proper code on the panel, it exploded, killing our three men and totally destroying the powerful radio."

"I still don't know what you're talking about."

"You will, soon. These two men have many questions to ask you. I'll have to leave you now. The big black car just ahead is for you. Have a pleasant afternoon."

Salah Rahmani knew then that they must have been watching him for months. How else would they know about the SATCOM? He hadn't checked on it for two weeks. He jolted away from the woman's side and sprinted into the grassy park, pulled the small H&K P7 semiautomatic pistol from his pocket and turned just as the two special investigators fired their weapons. He felt one round hit his leg and he went down. He fired four times, putting one of the black coats down before he rolled to get out of the line of fire. But three of the heavy rounds from the second investigator's pistol hit Rahmani in the back. One ripped through his spinal cord and another plowed through his lung and lodged in his heart. He died before he could fire again, and with him died his big dream of returning to the United States with his family.

7

The Farm
Langley, Virginia

At oh-ten-hundred that first morning at The Farm, Murdock, Rafii, and Ching came out of the wardrobe building wearing typical Iraqi clothing. All had on cotton pants, belts, white shirts on the outside, and a variety of hats: a New York Yankees baseball cap, one straw hat, and the other a felt floppy. Ching and Murdock had their faces, hands, and arms colored a light brown to more closely match Rafii. He grinned as he saw the transformation.

"Hey, you two can be my homeboys. We'll do fine in Baghdad. I'll be the front man and you guys are my muscle. We'll sweep down one of those streets and take care of anybody who looks cross-eyed at us."

A man they had met early that morning studied them. Slowly he nodded. He was Rolph Sedgewick, a Brit who came to the U.S. before the Second World War and had settled into the CIA as one of its European specialists.

"Yes, you'll pass. I want you to live the parts you'll play for the next two days. You'll eat Iraqi food, hear Iraqi music, ride in an old Renault with Iraqi license plates, and speak Arabic whenever possible. He shifted into Arabic then and Rafii knew exactly what he said. Murdock caught the main idea, but Ching only frowned. The three moved toward the classroom building that Sedgewick had told them about in Arabic. Ching hesitated then hurried with them.

"Will somebody tell me what he said?" he yelped.

"He told us it's class time," Rafii said. "We start to get some basic instruction in things Iraqi so we can stay alive."

"I'm in favor of that," Ching said.

The classroom was set up to train half a dozen students,

with chalkboard, wipe board, desks, projectors, and video. Their instructor met them and introduced himself.

"I'm Taliva, George Taliva for convenience. I'll be your language instructor and hope to make you able to speak enough Arabic to complete your mission. First we have a general introduction to Iraqi society courtesy of some travel agency."

They watched a video of the current street scenes in Baghdad, some of the tourist attractions, and a display of a holiday festival. When it was over, the instructor, an Iraqi who'd spent twenty years in Iraq, let them ask questions.

"I thought Muslim women had to have their faces covered in public," Murdock said.

"That's a general misconception about Iraq," the instructor said. "For decades now Iraqi women have enjoyed greater equality and opportunity than have the women of neighboring Arab countries such as Iran and Syria. Iraqi women have struggled for equal rights for nearly a hundred years. Women in Iraq began taking positions in the mainstream job market as early as the 1920s.

"Under Saddam Hussein's regime, these rights continued. Men and women receive the same salary when doing the same job, and many pursue professions usually thought to be for men. Iraqi women are not required to cover themselves from head to toe the way women are in Iran and Saudi Arabia. Women also receive five years' maternity leave from their employers.

"At the same time, United Nations sanctions against Iraq have created enormous suffering among women and children. Traditionally women had only one job, but now many must hold down two or even three to feed their families. Women-headed families are not uncommon in Iraq, which lost many soldiers in the Iran-Iraq war in the 1980s and again in the Gulf War in 1991. A schoolteacher who once could live relatively well on her salary must now take in sewing and bake goods to sell for extra money. The government makes rations available for the needy, but these last only about ten days a month.

"In Iraq women may hold down jobs outside the home, may drive cars, girls go to school, and they can move about outside the home without a male relative. All of these rights are not granted to women in fundamentalist Muslim countries such as Iran and Saudi Arabia.

"So, when you go into Baghdad, expect to see many women on the streets, and in jobs and doing ordinary things that they couldn't do in other Arab nations.

"However, this is not Hillsboro, Michigan. Iraq is still a military dictatorship. Voting is done for one party and one candidate. The men run the military and the military runs the country. Many laws are strict and the punishment harsh and not fair by Western standards. Soldiers from the army and from the elite Republican Guard are frequently seen on the streets enforcing laws, arresting people, and maintaining the rule of the military.

"After lunch, we'll start our language units, and we will speak nothing but Arabic. Next this morning we have two more films on Iraq. One is from the Iraqi Ministry of Information, so take it all with a large dose of disbelief. It does show Baghdad today in some of its best sides. So watch it closely. The signs won't mean much to you, but relate them to what is going on in the named store or shop. Pay close attention to the restaurant where a jazz combo is playing Frank Sinatra and Louis Armstrong songs. That may sound weird, but it is happening in Baghdad. Listen up."

The two films turned out to be videos and not the slickest production, but good enough to get across the points the makers wanted to show, and to give the three SEALs a lot more information about Iraq.

At noon they went to the visiting chow line and found the rest of the platoon.

"Hey look, ladies," Jaybird shouted. "We've got visitors from outer space."

Murdock bellowed a sharp command at him in Arabic and Jaybird jolted back a step, then the platoon laughed at him. Murdock saw one new member of the platoon. The person was smaller than the rest, dressed the same in desert cammies, but he could see short brown hair sticking out below her floppy hat.

"Hey, Garnet," Murdock called.

Katherine, "Kat" Garnet turned and grinned. "About time

you showed up, Commander. We've been holding the chow line until you got here. My, you've developed quite a tan since I saw you last." He said hello to her in Arabic and held out his hand. She smiled and gave him a hug instead.

She was the same Kat. About five-eight with brown eyes, a tempered athlete's body under the cammies. She did iron woman triathlons just for the fun of it. She had won the classic Hawaiian women's race twice.

"I hear you're going to be going on the picnic with us," Murdock said.

"I'll go, but I get to play with the toys only if you guys can find them. Any idea where they could be?"

"Our only hint so far is that they are in the desert. But that involves hundreds of square miles. We have a man in Baghdad who is supposed to give us the coordinates."

"You and Ching and this man I don't know will be going into Baghdad to help him. Be careful."

Murdock pulled up Rafii. "Kat, this is Omar Rafii, one of our SEALs. Rafii, this is the little lady who makes the atomic weapons go poof instead of bang. At least she did before, twice, and we all survived. We hope she can do it again." The two shook hands. "Kat, are you just as good with a sub gun as you used to be?"

They moved up in the cafeteria line, picked out what they wanted, and soon were seated at tables with real chairs.

"A sub gun. You had to remind me. I'm afraid I'm out of practice. But then I haven't had to kill anybody in the office where I work. You would have to remind me of that."

"Hey, you saved my skin out there in the boonies. I'm not about to let you forget that. I still owe you big time."

She grinned. "You still all tied up with that tall blonde from Washington, DC?"

"No. Ardith lives in San Diego now. We just bought a condo."

Kat scowled for a moment then lifted her brows. "You really know how to spoil a girl's day. Well, I guess it's just business then."

"Right, just business."

After lunch, the three SEALs reported back to the class-room. Sedgewick, their trainer for the day, nodded as they came in. "Before we get started on our language unit, I have some news. Our man in Baghdad who had been feeding us most of our information is no longer communicating with us. He was supposed to give us a general area where the Iraqi bombs were being stored. On his last report he said he had a contact who should be able to get the general area for us. He had a scaled-down version of the SATCOM to use to contact us. It had a built-in safety device. The operator had to punch in a special code to deactivate the self-destruct charges. If it is turned on, or opened in any way without that code, there is a ten-second delay. During that delay the set automatically broadcasts a distress call on all frequencies notifying us that it is in the delay mode and will soon self-destruct. We received the distress call just after twelve-twenty P.M. in Washington and here. If the set is dead, we can be sure that our agent there is either dead, compromised, or being interrogated."

"So we have no help in Baghdad?"

"There's one chance. Twelve years ago we had a top man in Baghdad. He married an Iraqi woman, has a family. When it was time for him to come out, he declined. Said he was retiring and we should send his check to an address in Baghdad. We did. We found out later that he's been on the bottle religiously, that he's never been compromised as an agent, and that he's evidently happy enough living in Baghdad. He does some writing for a Baghdad newspaper as an expatriate who knows America and can tell the Iraqi readers a slant on life they don't know about."

"We still go into the capital and try to find out where the bombs are located?" Rafii asked.

"That's your job. It just got about ten times harder. You can contact this man. His name is John Jones. We have his address. He won't be easy. Lately he's been on the wagon. His wife is helping him. The last time we heard he had a hundred and thirty-eight days clean and sober. The probability is he'll flat out refuse to help you, not wanting to jeopardize his setup there."

"Great, a burned out ex-spy who's now a drunk," Ching said. "Will he be any help at all?"

"We're not sure. For all I know he's a sleeper, still an

agent, but posing as a real-life drunk and waiting until we need him. I've talked with the deputy director, but can't get any confirmation. Even if he is a sleeper, the only one who would know is the director and he wouldn't tell us. You'll have to contact Jones and see if he'll help. If he won't, you'll have to rely on three other sources who might be able to assist you, and might not. You'll memorize their names and contact points before you leave The Farm.

"All this time we're supposed to stay undercover in a land where every man, woman, and child have been indoctrinated to hate Americans?" Rafii asked. "Isn't that a huge problem for us?"

"It's larger than huge. This is also a volunteer mission. Any of you SEALs can opt out at any time right up to boarding the VC-11 day after tomorrow morning."

"We've had tougher operations," Murdock said. "We'll want a complete description of Mr. Jones, and any identifying marks so we can be sure it's him before we spill our guts to him. We don't want to find out he's been replaced by an Iraqi superspy just waiting for somebody to contact him."

"No worry there, Commander. Jones is talking to us through e-mail out of one of the popular Internet cafes that have opened. It's all in the clear and in a kind of doubletalk we used twenty years ago, but damned effective."

"Then can you contact him by e-mail?"

"No chance. We don't want to alert watchers he's getting anything in return from his e-mail talk."

He let that soak in a moment, then went back to business talking in Arabic. He made sure all of them, especially Ching, knew the words he used and what they meant. It would be a long, slow process.

Two hours later, Ching grinned. "Hey, I'm getting some of this chatter. It's a lot like Spanish. Not the same, but there are similar sounds."

"Now say that in Arabic," the leader told him in Arabic. Ching snorted and tried, but he didn't have all the right words. The lessons continued.

In another building the rest of the platoon, under the watchful eyes of the J.G., worked over the weapons choices.

They would keep a number of H&K MP-5D4s. A man in blue coveralls and wearing a blue hat that had "CIA Weapons" embroidered on it shook his head when J.G. Gardner said they would be taking seven Bull Pups with them.

"That weapon has ties to the U.S.," the CIA man said. "I can't approve your taking it."

"H and K makes the body of the weapon, and three other firms are involved in all the components," Gardner said. "The gun isn't even in production yet, so there can be no tie-in with any country. It's got to be with us. It turns any infantryman into an artillery piece."

Gardner handed his Bull Pup to the man. "Take a look at it. The CIA doesn't have them yet. These are prototypes made especially for our platoon. Nobody else in the world has this weapon. Besides that, almost nobody else knows that it is operational by us. We're taking them in."

That decided, Gardner selected other weapons that they would take. Each man picked out a hideout weapon for his ankle. They at last agreed on the German Sauer M1914. It held a six-round magazine of .32 ACP and weighed in at 570 grams, or a pound and four ounces. They would all have the same weapon so they could share ammo if they needed to. They would keep the H&K PSG1 sniper rifle, and the EAR, the Enhanced Acoustic Rifle, that shot out a blast of compressed air for over four hundred yards and put any troops down and unconscious for four hours but left no aftereffects on the victims.

The CIA weapons man was fascinated with the EAR, but Gardner didn't let him look at it too closely. "Hey, we get to have a few secrets, too," he told the gunman. The J.G. asked the man about shotguns.

"Figure we should have one scattergun for close work," Gardner said. The man showed him one made in Spain. It was semiautomatic and the magazine held five rounds. Pump and shoot, pump and shoot.

The SEALs checked their weapons and ammo supply and ordered what they needed. They had brought their own double ammo on the Bull Pups and the sniper rifle. They would need the .32 ammo and magazines, and ammo and weapons and magazines for five of the sub guns. When he was satisfied with the weapons and supply of ammo, J.G. took the platoon out for a ten-mile hike. He talked to one of the guards who gave him a route all on the Farm property.

"Come on, ladies, it's time to sweat," Gardner told them. "We go out at an eight-minute-to-the-mile jog, and after we get warmed up, we get serious. We'll go with full combat vests and weapons. Let's get cracking. We need to be back before lunch."

Kat talked her way out of the march. "I need some re-training on the firing range," she told Gardner. "I want to fire the sub gun, and my Sauer pistol and the Bull Pup. Gardner agreed and had an arms instructor from The Farm take her to the range with the weapons and five rounds for the 20mm and fifty for the other weapons. The CIA weapons instructor was as anxious as Kat to test fire the 20mm.

"Only thing I thought fired the twenty was a fighter jet aircraft," the instructor said. His name was Monroe and he came from Michigan.

At the range Kat went prone, propped the short Bull Pup barrel on a sandbag, and fired off her first shot.

"Not nearly the recoil I expected," she said. "How do they do that?" She fired the next round with the laser sight on an old snag of a tree just off the rifle range. The airburst was spectacular. She let the instructor fire the last three rounds. One was a WP that he used as an airburst on the snag with a brilliant flash of white phosphorous and then a pall of smoke.

"You're right," Monroe said. "This Bull Pup makes every infantryman his own artilleryman. That thing can fire in back of buildings and over the reverse slope of a hill. All you need is a friendly tree."

Kat fired the MP-5 then. The sound and the rise of the muzzle soon came back to her and she could keep the weapon on the target. The Sauer was easy after that.

"This is not a long-range weapon," the instructor said. "It's for defense only and good for ten to twelve feet at the most. If you need it in a sudden confrontation to save your life, just keep pulling the trigger."

Kat went back to the main compound with a slightly sore shoulder and a big grin.

That evening after chow the troops were shown a war film in the recreation center. But Murdock, Ching, and Rafii weren't there. They had night classes in Arabic, Iraqi customs and dress, and the Muslim religion.

8

Riyadh, Saudi Arabia

The sleek Gulfstream II VC-11 landed at Riyadh slightly before dark. They had been halfway across the Atlantic before the pilot received word that he could land here. King Fahd ibn Abdul Aziz had made a special call to the American President to talk about the situation. It was an encrypted call from the American Embassy there. The President had confirmed that Iraq had four atomic weapons and they very well could use them on, or use them to threaten, their neighbors. Saudi Arabia would be a good first choice for Iraq. After a few tense words through interpreters, the President assured the king that this would be a one-time, lightning strike with no tie to Saudi Arabia or to the U.S. That American Navy SEALs would do the work and there would be no atomic detonations to worry about.

He had approved the landing at Riyadh, for the SEALs and an air transport to bring in additional support and vehicles to move the SEALs and a small group of soldiers toward the northern Saudi border.

Their usual CIA contact, Don Stroh, met them at the airport and led the way to an army complex where they would stay until the exact location of the bombs was known. Murdock, Ching, and Rafii would fly out on the VC-11 the next day, for Kuwait, which would be their jumping off point for Baghdad a day later.

Murdock whacked Stroh on the back when he saw him. "You old billy goat, I didn't think you were in on this one."

"What's not to be in on? I set up the whole thing. Actually I bring you goodies. Wait until it gets dark. Have I got a new toy for you guys."

"Is she pretty and is she willing?" Jaybird called.

"So Jaybird made the cut?" Stroh asked. "I thought he was on the trading block, going back to Second Platoon."

"They wouldn't take him," Gardner cracked.

"A new toy, like what?" Murdock asked.

"Get settled in your quarters and I'll show you. Probably right after chow. Hope you like this Saudi food."

"Dog stew?" Lam asked.

"Cat curry from what I hear, but it's tasty," Stroh said. "I'd stay and chat, but I'd miss the first seating at the officers' mess."

The quarters they were trucked to were about the same as what they were used to. A barracks is a barracks. Only single-story bunks here. They had chow at the enlisted mess and found they were eating a stew of some kind.

"Hell, eat up, you guys. This is pure beef stew," Luke Howard said and they all relaxed.

After chow and back in the barracks, Don Stroh came in with two small boxes.

"Jaybird, go down there to the far end of the room and wait. Just stand there, don't get wise."

When Jaybird was in place, Stroh took a device out of one of the boxes. It was about half the size of a football, had a handhold on it and a strange lens out the front. In back there was a viewing screen.

"Okay, Murdock, kill the lights." Stroh held up the device and aimed it at where Jaybird should be. Nothing showed on the screen. He moved the device back and forth then stopped. A weird white glowing figure showed on the black screen. "Jaybird, you're crouched down beside a box up there but I can see you. Bang bang, you're dead. Stand up, Jaybird, and walk across the back of the room there."

"What the hell is that?" Fernandez asked.

"It's called a thermal imager. Aim it at a spot and it picks up the thermal signals from a body, or a large animal. They've been around for years, but now they made this small handheld one especially for firemen to use in burning buildings. I talked them out of four of them for you misfits. They have a special adapter so they can be mounted on most of your weapons. They'll fit easily on the Bull Pup. I want each of you to come up here and work this thing."

He handed it off, and one by one the SEALs and Kat checked Jaybird moving around. They told him exactly where he was and what he was doing.

"Ain't it about my time to see through that thing?" Jaybird called.

"Omar, go up and be the target," Murdock said. He had his turn with a second imager and followed the Saudi on the screen up the aisle between the bunks and then lost him. They found him crawling around a bunk.

When they turned the lights back on, the men were convinced.

"Oh, yeah, I like it," Vincent Van Dyke said. "Much better than night vision goggles."

"Twenty times better," J.G. Gardner said. "We can nail guys creeping up on us. Blow them out of their socks. This is the best new weapon we've had since the Bull Pup. It could get us out of a terribly murderous situation."

"That thing sure bugged me when you were spotting me in the dark," Jaybird said. "I figured I was completely hidden then an arm or a foot would be enough to give me away."

"Bravo Squad gets two of them," Murdock said. "Alpha takes one and we'll take the other one to Baghdad. We'll keep it handheld so it will be easier to conceal. Then, too, we won't have any long guns with us."

"Murdock without a Bull Pup?" Jaybird asked. "Now, there is a first."

"Had to happen sometime," Murdock said. "We three leave first thing in the morning. Tomorrow night we should be in Baghdad. Any questions so far?"

"This is the weird place," Kat said. "Nobody here knows that I'm not one of the guys. Can we keep it that way?"

"Aw, Kat, you just want to watch us undress when we hit the sack," Bradford said.

"I grew up with three older brothers. Unless you guys are not all that normal . . ." She stopped and the SEALs laughed. "Don't worry, I'll try not to embarrass you. I will be in the far end of the barracks, however."

"Good idea," Murdock said. "In this country women must be covered head to toe at all times, they can't drive a car or work outside the home, and they can't be in public without a male member of their household. Fundamentalists rule here. Yes, keep your hat on and no makeup."

"Hell, she don't need none," a voice shouted. The SEALs cheered.

"For you new men, I don't know what you think. These old-timers are just mad because I can outrun and outswim all of them. They'll settle down after a while."

"You really win a full iron woman triathlon?" somebody asked.

"Three of them to be exact. But we won't be doing much biking or swimming on this one. Now, if any of you want to disable the bombs we're finding, I'll trade places with you."

"Hey, no way," Derek Prescott said.

"Teen hut!" somebody bellowed. The SEALs snapped to attention. Three U.S. Air Force officers walked into the barracks.

"At ease, men. Just a little visit. I'm Colonel Livingston. I'm your official host for your stay here. My staff of two and myself will do everything we can to take care of you. Whatever you need, talk to Major Wilbur or Master Sergeant Phillips. We'll work with the Saudis to let you do your conditioning. No live firing, so keep all ammo out of your weapons. When we know where you need to go along the Iraqi border, we'll get you up there, probably by truck, but maybe by Saudi choppers. Is Commander Murdock here?"

"Here, sir," Murdock said, snapping a salute. "Reporting for duty."

The colonel returned the salute, then shook hands. "Good to meet you, Murdock. You've got a tough one coming up. I almost wish I was going with you. I'm not exactly sure why you're going in there. They tell me I have no need to know. Good luck up there. You won't be here long. Your VC-11 is being serviced. You'll take off at oh-seven-hundred for a short hop to Kuwait, only two hundred seventy-five miles almost due north. Don't mess up the place—that's my current post."

"We'll be gentle," Ching said.

"Good. Now, about your jaunt to Baghdad. You'll be going in from Kuwait in a chopper. We'll use a version of the

Black Hawk. The Navy has flown one in from a carrier. It's the Seahawk, the SH-60 you call it. You fly on the Iraqi deck all the way to the thirty-third parallel, which is the top of the Southern No-Fly Zone. We've had choppers in the area before so it shouldn't cause that much of a flap. We'll keep you covered all the way with a beefed-up group of fighters. If any Iraqi planes make any moves toward you, they will be taken out. We owe them a couple anyway.

"After we drop you, the chopper will take a southwestern course that will put it into Saudi Arabia along the border somewhere, and we will go in and find it. The bird can do six hundred ninety-one miles so the distance is not a factor. Speed might be. It can make only a hundred and seventy-eight miles an hour. So flying time into your drop point is roughly two hours. The planning team considered all factors and decided this was the best way to get you near the target. We have no practical fixed wing aircraft for you to bail out of near the thirty-third parallel. This particular bird is fitted with external gun and rocket pods and can give you some quick ground support if you need it. Any questions?"

"Two hours to get there?" Murdock asked. "Won't they have a lot of people there to greet us? How can we stay all the way under their radar?"

"We've done it before, Commander. It works. We went in almost to the same spot a year ago to pick up a downed pilot. Everyone returned safely to Kuwait."

The colonel looked at the other two SEALs. He continued. "Your take-along weapons must be highly concealable. You're not soldiers; you're just three men on their way to Baghdad in the dark. We will leave Kuwait at darkness minus ten. Which puts us into your drop zone at about twenty-one hundred. Then you'll have eight hours to get in or near Baghdad and the chance to contact the man you're going to see before daylight. We have his current address. Rafii will be your main man on this trip. He knows the territory."

"We haven't picked out weapons yet, Colonel," Murdock said.

Don Stroh spoke up. "I've talked with the colonel, Murdock. We suggest you go with handguns only. Even if you all had Ingrams and you were detected, you wouldn't be able to shoot your way out. Iraq is an armed camp. Almost every household has one or two weapons, mostly army rifles. Men and boys spend their vacations taking weapons training and learning house-to-house fighting techniques. This must be a stealth campaign. As silent as possible. But no silencers on your pistols. Much too heavy and too hard to conceal. We suggest two pistols. A hideout on your ankle and a larger weapon in your belt or the middle of your back."

Murdock looked at his two men. Both nodded. "We agree with you on the weapons. Don, anything more on the location of the devices?"

"Our communications link with our main man is down. Our only hope is that you can activate Mr. Jones."

"I'm not at all happy with our intel on this. It seems like we are learning less and less about our mission as we move along. What if Jones has been compromised or turns us in when we get there? You going to bring in a Marine battalion and blast us out of town?"

Don Stroh shook his head. "Actually, sir, we don't have the slightest idea who you are. You're certainly not U.S. citizens and no chance are you American military. Just three soldiers of fortune who happen to speak English. Could be South African, or English, or even Australian or Canadian."

"I guess I deserved that, Stroh. Thanks for the new toy. It could be a game breaker."

"Gentlemen, if that's all?" the colonel asked.

"We're up to speed, Colonel, thanks," Murdock said. "See you in the morning?"

"Oh, yes. I'll be riding along with you to help move things along in Kuwait. Lots of rank over there, but I'll have Don Stroh along with me to take care of any objections."

"Don gets all the cushy assignments, Colonel Livingston. But I've got to warn you if he tries to talk you into going fishing, have a whole bunch of reasons not to go. He can really louse up a fishing trip."

"Oh, yeah, Murdock. Who caught the most edible fish on our last trip out of Seaforth in San Diego?"

"Three sand bass as I remember, about a pound and a half each. Who caught the most legal log barracuda?"

"Who eats barracuda?"

"Last trip out I went overnight and woke up to a hot albacore bite. We boated ninety-three albies, about forty yellowtail, and twenty skipjack. I caught one of each."

"Fish stories," Stroh said. "You have pictures, of course."

"Sorry, no camera."

Colonel Livingston frowned. "You two have known each other for some time?"

"Over five long years, Colonel," Stroh said. "He's trying to outlast me on the job."

"Murdock, you better be careful on this one or it could be your last mission," Colonel Livingston said. "The Iraqis are furious about something right now. Last reports there were anti-American demonstrations all over Baghdad."

The colonel and his staff turned toward the door.

"Teen hut!" Senior Chief Elmer Neal barked. The SEALs snapped to attention until the door closed.

"He had to tell us that," Ching said.

"Hell, won't bother Rafii none," Jaybird said. "Things get too hot he just drops his pistols, melts into an alley, and finds him a hot woman to shack up with."

Rafii snorted. "Commander, can we take Jaybird with us? We need a sacrificial goat to appease the Iraqis."

Murdock grinned. "Maybe later. Right now I'm getting into my bunk. I have an early call. Then it's off to Baghdad."

9

Kuwait City, Kuwait

Murdock looked out the front window of the closed van as it drove across the tarmac from one side of the big airport to the other. Security was tight around the field. Snipers had been shooting into the area, and Murdock had heard that the locals were busting their balls trying to nail them down. The van pulled to a stop thirty feet from an SH-60 that sat there without its rotors turning.

Master Sergeant Phillips drove the van. He motioned to the chopper. "Thought you would want to meet the crew. Be ten hours or so before you take off."

"Good," Murdock said, and the three SEALs dressed as Arabs left the van and hurried over to the bird. The side door was open. An armed man jumped out of the chopper and challenged them.

"At ease," Murdock bellowed. "Commander Murdock and team. Want to get a look at your bird before we fly out tonight."

The man in suntan cammies relaxed and grinned. "Right, Commander, knew you were coming. Your costume threw me. You look damn good."

"Hope we can fool the other guys," Ching said. They checked out the chopper. They had seen lots of SH-60s before. This one had mounts for door machine guns but none in place. A lieutenant came out of the cabin and stared at Murdock.

"Commander, you the same Murdock who used to throw beer around in San Diego?"

Murdock looked up. "Streib. I'll be damned. You finally got your wings. You used to bitch enough about getting to go to flight training. Looks like you're doing okay."

"I'm getting by. I'm on a six-month blue water, then it's back home to Seattle. Hey, let me tell you about rain."

"Been there," Murdock said. "Can this crate get us up to the thirtieth parallel without clipping any trees or mountains?"

"I hope to hell we can. Went up that way once before. No real problems. Just so the damn civilians will keep their rifles quiet."

"Pick up some ground fire?"

"Oh, yeah. They know that the Iraqi flyboys won't be down this far, so they whale away."

The van horn beeped.

"I think that's Mother calling," Murdock said. "We're due somewhere. See you about sunset."

Back in the van, Don Stroh frowned. "We hear about more demonstrations against the U.S. in all the big towns in Iraq. In that country that means women out there marching and firing off their rifles right alongside the men. Seems weird. Well, not much we can do about it. You get in, find Jones, and convince him to help you, then radio us where the cache is and we'll start converging on it."

"If you get to the bombs before we do, go right ahead and do the honors," Murdock said. "We could have some trouble moving in that direction."

"Trouble is your middle name, Murdock," Stroh said. "You're lucky there isn't any good fishing around here."

"Right now I have all the angling I can take care of. I'm feeling naked already without my combat vest and my Bull Pup."

"Get used to it." Stroh grinned at Murdock's discomfort. Then he sobered. "Oh, did anyone tell you that you have three days to find out where the devices are?"

"Three days? Why?"

"They didn't tell me. They want this all cleared up in five days. Three for you and two for Kat and her buddies on the boom-boom."

"Not even Kat can blow them up if she doesn't know where they are. If it takes us four or five, you'll have to live with that. We set with this little radio, this poor man's SAT-COM?"

"Right. We talk only if we have news. Time it at twelve noon and midnight. Don't call us, just transmit. We'll be receiving all the time in case you have a problem. After your message we'll give you a ten-four to let you know we got the call."

"When do we eat?" Ching asked. "I want a damn full belly before I get into all that Iraqi chow."

"Mess call is at noon today and again at four," Stroh said. The master sergeant will be your guide. Then by seven o'clock you're at the chopper pad."

"What do we do until the food?" Rafii asked.

"We sleep," Murdock said. "We won't get much where we're going. Stroh, you have some bunks we can claim?"

At 1850 they stepped on board the S-76 and closed the side doors. The three SEALs sat on the floor and looked for something to hold on to.

"Two hours," Ching said. They had been sweating in their Arab costumes, but once they were in the air, the inside of the bird cooled off. The pilot had waved at them as they boarded. Now he had his job to do, and he had to do it well or all of them would splash down on some barren Iraqi hill in one huge fuel-induced fireball.

An hour into the flight Murdock heard some pinging on the side of the ship. "Ground fire," he shouted, and the others nodded. The noise of the engine and the rotor made normal conversation impossible.

A half hour later the crew chief came back and signaled to Murdock to come forward. In the cabin he watched Streib fly the chopper. He turned and shouted.

"Early by ten. Three minutes to the LZ. Get ready."

Murdock nodded and went back to his men. He motioned them up. "Two minutes to the LZ," he shouted. The men adjusted their clothes, then made sure the belt pistols were in place and stood beside the door waiting for Murdock to open it.

The wheels hit with a soft thump. Murdock rammed the door open and the SEALs jumped out and sprinted straight north away from the sound of the machine that could bring any nearby natives to the scene with their AK-47s up and firing on full automatic. They surged away fifty yards, then dove to the ground and listened. The chopper could barely be heard. It had jolted into the air ten seconds after the wheels hit, and rocketed south at full throttle.

The three SEALs in their Arab costumes lay on a small rise. Nowhere ahead or to the sides could they see any lights. Murdock had taken the handle off the thermal imager to save two inches of bulk. He brought it out now and scanned the low land in front of them.

"Hold it. I'm getting something." He laughed softly. "About twenty goats up there a hundred yards. Most of them down and sleeping. If there's goats, there's a goat herder close by. Let's go around then to the left."

The ground here was rocky and barren, with an occasional planted field. "We're supposed to be about fifteen miles from the major highway north to our left," Murdock said. "The Tigris River is about fifteen miles to our right. Our best move is to get to the highway and see if we can con a ride into Baghdad."

"It's how far north?" Rafii asked.

"About thirty miles, but we'll run into houses and villages long before then."

"I remember one place—Kahn Azad," Rafii said. "Our family had relatives there. I think I had three cousins there. I wouldn't know them from Jaybird now."

"No help there," Ching said.

They stood and hiked soundlessly fifty yards to the left, then turned north at a steady trot. A half mile up a gentle valley they could see lights ahead.

"We could use a car," Murdock said.

"You find a car and I can jump the wires to get it started," Ching said.

They worked ahead slower now. Soon they passed a pair of houses with no lights. There were no vehicles by either building. Another quarter mile farther along, Murdock went to ground and the two men followed. He had out the imager and scanned two houses that still had lights.

"A big dog at the right-hand place," Murdock said. "He hasn't spotted us yet or smelled us. We've got the wind in our faces so he can't smell us. We go around these places."

They found a dirt road that led to the left. They needed
fifteen miles in that direction so they headed down the road
at a trot. Now there were more houses. Rafii spotted a car
near a small home. Murdock scanned the area.

"No dogs, no guards. Ching, let's see what you can do.
We all go in and push that old sedan a quarter of a mile
down the road. It's slightly downhill so that will help. Then
you do your wire work."

Ten minutes later the car was a half mile from any building. Ching went to work with his knife and in two minutes
had the engine purring.

"Don't know what the hell make it is," Ching said, "but
it has half a tank of gas, so let's roll."

Twelve miles to the left they found the main north-south
highway. It was bigger than they had figured.

"There will be road checks on this one," Rafii said. "Not
real blocks, but a slowdown and look over. Probably a pair
of Home Guards there who will pull anyone to the side who
looks suspicious."

"We can't shoot our way through," Murdock said. "We
have to stay silent. Rafii, you drive and talk up a storm. If
we hit a checkpoint, Ching and I will be sleeping."

"Football," Rafii said. "If they wonder where three men
are going at night, I'll say we're part of a football team
playing in Baghdad tomorrow. There's always some kind of
tournament going. Yes, football, they call it. It's soccer to
you guys."

"Not the Dallas Cowboys, I figured," Ching said.

They drove. There was little traffic. Murdock didn't know
if nighttime driving was restricted or not. He didn't think it
was. Rafii said they had passed three small towns he remembered. "Not more than five miles to the city," he said. Then
he swore in Arabic.

"Checkpoint just ahead. Not a big one. One army truck
to the side. These may be Home Guard guys. If so, they are
tough and well trained. Get to sleep, you guys. Just no snor-
ing."

The old car pulled up to the block. There was one car
ahead of them. The driver in the other car talked to the soldier, who waved the rig on through. Rafii pulled up and

stopped. He had out his papers. They had been made and weathered and worried and were as authentic as any in the land. He held them out to the guard.

"Quiet night?" Rafii asked in Arabic.

"The way I like it. Where you headed?

"Football stadium. We'll sleep in the car tonight. We play at ten o'clock tomorrow."

"Just three of you?"

"The others are ahead of us. We had to work all day. The other bastards got off early."

"Who you playing?"

"Don't know. The draw is tomorrow."

Another car pulled up behind them. The guard gave him back his papers. "So get moving. And boot in a couple of goals for me."

They were through and past the check.

"Nice going, Rafii," Murdock said.

"We could have taken him out easy," Ching said.

"Sure, but he had a relief man in the truck," Rafii said. "I saw the radio in his pocket. All of these checkpoints have radios now or telephones. Good thing we got through clean."

Murdock rode in the front seat. He looked at Rafii. "What's Jones's address in Baghdad?"

"Twenty-two-oh-three Bahar Lane. It's in a section where poets, writers, starving artists, and musicians used to live. I don't know what's there now. You know this is a big city, almost five million bodies now."

"Been here before," Murdock said. "That's why we have a local native as our guide. Can you find the place?"

"Know about where it is. Then we follow my nose to get the right street. Not like we had a map."

As they neared the city, they saw streetlights and stores and shops along the way. More and more houses and some industrial areas cropped up. Then they were in the middle of the five million people who made up Baghdad. The highway vanished, and they rolled into a maze of narrow one-way streets, thousands of lights, and in places, swarms of people. They had to stop for a surge of people who crossed the street. About half of them were women. Strange in a Muslim country. Then Murdock remembered their training. This was not a fundamentalist Muslim nation. On the corner a garish sign glowed.

"The sign says coffee and jazz," Rafii said. The music gushing out from the open door was pure Frank Sinatra singing "My Way" in English. Three blocks later Rafii turned into a side street and nodded.

"Oh yeah. I lived about two blocks from here. Came back several times. Almost didn't get permission to leave the last time. Now I know for damn sure where we are. Another ten minutes unless we get run over by the gangs."

A short time later, Rafii eased the old sedan to the side of the street and pointed. A house made of wood and plaster set back from the curb. A Citroën sedan was parked in front of it just off the street. A steel fence shut off the front of the yard, and a gate in it was closed. Rafii pulled out and drove two blocks away.

"Everybody out. We don't want this rig tied to us in any way if the farmer reports it stolen. We walk back. I'll make the contact. Both of you stay in the shadows of the houses at each side."

"Go," Murdock said.

Lights glowed from two windows that showed to the street. It was a two-story house and in better condition than most of the others around it. Rafii moved up the sidewalk, past the parked Citroën and up to the gate. He looked it over for a few seconds, then opened it and went to the side of the place and evidently to a back door. Murdock frowned and waited. He wished he had talked them into bringing the Motorolas. The small personal radios would have been damn handy right then. They waited.

It was almost ten minutes before Rafii appeared at the side of the house and waved them forward. They went up like black ghosts and around the side of the house.

"Yeah, he's here. He isn't happy that we dropped in on him, but he expected this would happen. He knows that the CIA man here was cut down. Right now he's angry, about half-drunk and had been about ready to mount one of two partly clad women when I knocked on the back door. That he'll never forgive me for. The rest of our mission is open to persuasion."

"You tell him why we're here?"

"Nope, just that we're working with his old outfit and it needs some of his help."

They slipped in a black rear entrance, went through a dark room and then into a lighted one. A man sat on a well-worn couch. He had a full beard that needed trimming. His mustache covered his mouth. Small nearly black eyes stared out from below heavy brows. His hair was black streaked with gray and Murdock couldn't guess how old he was. From forty to sixty-five. His face was puffed and fat, showing splotches of red and brown. Even before he stood, Murdock guessed he was eighty pounds overweight. When he came to his feet, it was with an effort. He had to push down on the couch with both hands. He wore an Iraqi white shirt and white pants, now stained with what Murdock figured was tobacco juice. As if to confirm it, Jones turned and spit at a bucket that sat at the end of the couch. Half of the stream of dark brown juice went into the improvised spittoon.

"What son of a bitch gave you my address?" he asked.

Murdock stepped forward. "I'm not sure, Mr. Jones. Do you know a man by the name of Don Stroh?"

Jones roared with laughter, his eyes teared, and he slapped his heavy leg with a meaty hand. "That old bastard is still alive? Stroh the Stickler we used to call him. What a fuckoff. He must be a big shot in the Company now if he's still kicking."

"He's alive and in Kuwait," Murdock said. "You know about the CIA man here who they lost."

"Didn't lose him. I know exactly where his body is. But he's not much good to the Company now." He scowled at them. If there had been women in the room, they had left. He didn't offer to let the men sit down. "What the hell can I do to help you? I have no fucking contacts anymore. The police used to watch me like a cat on a rat. Now they leave me alone. I like it that way. I get enough booze, enough to eat, and enough women to keep my whanger happy. What more could I want?"

"Iraqi President Kamil now has four functioning nuclear bombs," Murdock said.

"Oh, God. Just what we were afraid of." Jones sat down

and nearly broke the couch. He waved the SEALs to sit.

"What the hell can I do about it?"

"We don't know where they are. We want you to help us tie down the location."

Jones laughed. He wiped tears from his eyes and shook his head. "Find them? You must be nuts. I ask two questions about those weapons and I'm skinned and my head is paraded through the streets on the end of a pike pole. Not a chance."

Murdock sat on a wooden chair and watched Jones. He didn't say a word. Jones shifted his bulk on the couch. He wiped one hand across his face.

"Christ, what's he planning on doing with them?"

"We think he'll set off one in the desert somewhere as a warning to his neighbors. Then he'll threaten Syria or Saudi Arabia. If they don't lay down their arms and join him in the greater Arab Union, he'll bomb them out of existence. He'll keep it up until he owns every Arab nation in the Middle East."

Jones nodded slowly. His eyes took on a hard glint. "The bastard could do it. Or he could sell a weapon to some terrorists, al-Qaida, for example, who would use it to blow up some American city. That's al-Qaida's dream: nuke an American city."

"We need to know where they are, so we can destroy them," Murdock said.

"The three of you?"

"No, sixteen of us—seventeen, actually. We're Navy SEALs, and the rest of the platoon is waiting in Saudi Arabia."

"SEALs, huh? Heard about you fuckers. You're supposed to be hell on earth. Maybe so—you got in here without getting caught. Oh, damn. I figured I was out of the loop for good. Why the hell they trying to sucker me back into the action?"

"Because you're the only hope we have. Nobody else in Baghdad can do what you can do. We need to find out where the weapons are, and we have only three more days."

"Three days?" Jones snorted, reached for a dark bottle, and took a long pull from it. He wiped his mouth on his white sleeve and shook his head. "Hell, take more like three months. My contacts are all gone, dead, or executed. What the hell can I do in three days?"

He slammed his fist into the couch, picked up a pillow, and threw it across the room. "Huda," he bellowed. "Huda, get your pussy in here. We've got company. Bring in some of that good beer I've been saving. I'm not sure, but I think I'm back in business. Hell of a long vacation. What can a man do when his country gives him a call? Hell yes, I'll help you—that is I'll try to help you—find out where the nukes are. Won't be easy. You got one of them fancy SATCOM radios I hear about? Hey, I've got the Internet. Huda, where the hell are you? You go deaf, woman? Get your little ass in here with the beer."

10

Baghdad, Iraq

Murdock and the other SEALS accepted brown bottles without labels, and Jones waved at the woman dressed in a skirt and blouse who brought them.

"These Iraqi women are not downtrodden like those in the fundamentalist countries. They have rights, can drive, go to school, even teach school and enter all sorts of businesses and professions. Most are frightened that any kind of a regime change here would put the Iraqi fundamentalists in power and push the women back into the dark ages. Huda is bright, speaks English fairly well, and is a great help to me."

"Can she meet with any of your former contacts?" Rafii said.

"Ah, yes, the turncoat. You are an Iraqi; I can tell by the way you speak English. Your Arabic must be perfect. The short answer to that question is yes, no, and maybe. It depends who it is and how well-concealed the meet is made."

"How can we help?" Murdock asked.

"Mostly by staying inside this house so no one will see you, and not making any noise. The telephone system is back in operation after a long time in ruin after the Gulf War. Let me make a call or two. No, we don't have cell phones yet, but the land lines do quite well. Huda will show you up the stairs, where you can get some rest. If I need you tonight, I'll call."

The SEALs stood and followed the Iraqi woman out of the room and up a closed stairway to the second floor. There were three rooms; the largest had two beds and dressers.

"I'm not a damn bit sleepy," Ching said.

Murdock scowled. "Sailor, on a mission like this we sleep whenever we get the chance. We might not get another bed this good for two or three days. So we sack out."

Going into enemy territory this way put a serious nervous energy drain on the men, and Murdock knew it. All three were sleeping within ten minutes.

Sometime later, Murdock felt a hand on his shoulder. He looked up without moving and saw Huda.

"It's time to come downstairs," she said. "Just the commander."

Murdock nodded and swung his legs off the bed. "Did he make a contact?"

"He'll tell you." She led the way down the stairs to the big living room. Jones looked better to Murdock. He had trimmed his beard, combed his hair, and put on a different shirt. He sat at a desk at the side of the room. The telephone was in his hand as they came into the room. He spoke rapidly in Arabic. Murdock caught only a few words. He said something else, then hung up and turned to Murdock.

"How is your Arabic?" he asked in that tongue.

"Not the best, but I can get by," Murdock answered in Arabic.

"The small one, is he fluent?"

"Yes, fluent and colloquial. He was born here."

"Good. We have a meet. All three of you should come. Are you armed?"

Murdock showed him the pistol and the thermal imager.

"Oh, yes," Jones said after turning out the lights and trying the imager. "Now, there is a tool we can really use. You ready? Get your men. We have fifteen minutes to get to the meet."

At the curb they got in the six-year-old Citroën and Jones squeezed into the front seat to drive. He slipped through the first mile without lights. Then he turned them on and went through a brightly lighted section, before turning into an alley a mile away and stopping in a parking lot behind a four-story building. Jones waved at Murdock before they got out.

"I'm not sure this will produce anything. She's a contact I've had for ten years, but I haven't talked to her in five. I used the same coded words as before and she replied in kind and here we are. Her code name is Gypsy, which she isn't and she's a bit of a rebel in her own land. She has wide contacts and keeps her ears open. She's an artist of quite good talent and makes a living selling her pictures. I'd guess she's still on the Company payroll as well. Every few hundred dinars help these days. We should meet no one else but her here, but if we do, let me do the talking."

They went through a door in the back of the building. Darkness engulfed them like a black fog. They could see no lights at all. Murdock aimed the thermal imager around and found no live bodies.

"I remember this place," Jones whispered. He grabbed Murdock's shirtsleeve and they moved forward slowly, step by step. After twenty steps Jones paused. He whispered.

"Yes. I was right. A door just ahead. We'll all get to the side wall when I open it. He moved Murdock to one side and Murdock pushed Ching and Rafii to the wall. They all flattened against it. Jones opened the door. Murdock saw a thin shaft of pale light cut into the darkness, and Jones let out a held-in breath.

"Yes, good. Now a little light. We move ahead. Stay close behind me."

Again the four men made a slow movement forward. Murdock couldn't make out any details in the room. It could be a warehouse, an office, even a garage. He had no idea. Ahead he saw a half-open door. They angled toward it, and again stopped near it. Jones looked into the room from the side of the door. More lights were on now. Murdock saw that it was living quarters: chairs, a table, some rugs on the wooden floor. In the dim light he had trouble making out anything else. A voice in Arabic probed out of the semi-lighted room.

"About time you got here, Jones. I've been waiting. I thought you were out of the business."

"Gypsy, you always were the innovative one. When did you set up this man trap?"

"Long ago. How do you like it?"

"Feels like your style. I have some friends with me."

"So I gathered from your coded words. Come in and close the door and we'll find some more lights. My guess is that they are not with the Company."

"True. But men whom you can trust with your life. They are trusting their lives to you."

"Way I like it. Should we switch to English?"

"Yes," Jones said in English.

The lights came up, and Murdock saw the woman sitting in an upholstered chair on the far side of the room in what looked like a small office area. It had a desk, two file cabinets, bookshelves, and on the end of the desk a small TV. That all went into Murdock's mental computer in a fraction of a second. Then his eyes concentrated on the woman. She was seated, but he could tell she was small, thin almost to anorexia. Her hair was obviously a dark wig that framed her face. Her cheeks were slightly sunken, her eyes deep set and dark, her skin lighter than most Iraqis. She wore a silk blouse and a skirt. She had folded her hands in her lap.

"These are the Americans? Good job with the clothes and makeup. Yes, excellent job. Except for the small one. He is a real Iraqi. You wonder if I'm still with the Company? Only on the extreme fringes. I have no control. I have no responsibilities. I have stayed alive. I have my work. I paint."

"We hear that you have sensitive ears and many contacts," Murdock said. "Excuse my abruptness. My apologies. I am Commander Murdock; these are two of my men. We are U.S. Navy SEALs, and right now we are on a terribly short time schedule. Do you know why we are here?"

"There is only one reason I can imagine. You are worried about Iraq having nuclear bombs."

"That we are," Jones said. "Our sources tell us that Iraq has four operational nuclear devices, probably crude bombs."

"Your sources are correct," Gypsy said. "Few people in or out of the government know about this program. Oh, we have known that there was a push to get the bombs before our neighbors did. But I had no idea that the development was complete. Not until three weeks ago. Knowing it isn't of much value. What are you Americans going to do about it?"

"We're concerned that President Nabil could use the weapons on Israel," Murdock said. "If he does, there will be an immediate retaliation and perhaps half a million Iraqis would die instantly, with another half million dying slowly of radiation poisoning."

"Yes, I and a select group have discussed this both ways in the past few days," Gypsy said. "The bomb is a multi-edged sword that cuts so many ways. The threat of using it was enough to stop the Cold War by the two most powerful nations on earth. Now with the proliferation, the threat again becomes real on a smaller scale, but real enough."

"We need only two simple facts, Gypsy, that we hope you can help us with," Murdock said. "We need to know where the bombs are being made and where the four completed ones are being held."

Gypsy laughed. It was a dry, mirthless sound that had a chilling effect of Murdock.

"What you ask for, Commander, is impossible. How would I know such information? I don't. How could I find out these 'simple facts' for you? Not without a dozen times endangering my life and that of anyone associated with me. If they knew I was even talking with you gentlemen, they would kick my doors down and machine gun me into Allah's bosom in a second. There is nothing you could offer me that would even start me on such a search."

"How about half a million U.S. dollars?" Murdock asked.

Gypsy sucked in a breath. Her black eyes glowed for a moment. "That is a tremendous lot of money, a hundred and fifty thousand dinars. Enough for me to live on the rest of my life." She laughed again. "Plenty for that, since my life's future would be no more than two weeks long. How could I explain such wealth? No, not money."

"Think of the million faces of your countrymen, women, children, soldiers, all of whom would be vaporized in an instant if President Kamil dropped one of his nuclear bombs on Haifa," Jones said. "Think of those souls, and know that right now you might have the ability to prevent such a disaster."

She frowned and reached for a long black cigar that lay smoking in a metal ashtray on her desk. It was crooked and about the diameter of a cigarette. She took a long drag on the cigar and inhaled it, then blew it out slowly. A ragged cough racked her. She closed her eyes and rode it out, then smiled.

"One of my small vices. You are unfair. I am a simple painter who mixes the oils well and has a certain talent that I can use to paint what will sell in this feeble market for artwork. I am not a world-class spy. I do not know or have the skills that Mr. Jones here has, or at least had several years ago." She took another drag on the cigar but this time did not inhale.

"Gypsy, you have helped me in the past. We have worked well together."

"And the Secret Police almost killed me because of it. But now, after these five years, even the Home Guard has tired of watching me. The Secret Police no longer monitor my phone or shadow me when I go out. My friends are not questioned and I am at peace to live my life and paint my little pictures and try to make a living."

"Baghdad would be the Israelis' first target," Murdock said. "You could very well be one of those vaporized."

"Glorious. Then I would not have to worry about the Secret Police or about John Jones or Commander Murdock." Her laugh came again, only not so cold this time. She sighed and put the cigar back in the ashtray, but left it burning.

Gypsy stood and walked the length of the room, then back. Murdock figured she was no more than five feet tall and might weigh ninety pounds dripping wet. She marched now more than walked. "Did you know that I was a major in the Women's Guard during the Iranian war? I commanded four hundred women, all armed with rifles." She smiled and did another tour of the room. "Luckily we were not called into battle. We would have been a disaster."

She went back to the desk and sat in her chair and doodled on a pad on her desk. When she looked up, Murdock saw that she had made her decision.

"Yes, it very well might be the death of me, but I will help you. I know an army colonel who is overly fond of illegal Scotch whiskey. He has been known to brag sometimes about his accomplishments when he's drunk."

"Is he a part of the team that worked on the nuclear program?" Murdock asked.

"If all of his bragging is true, he headed the program. With Khaled it is hard to tell when he is bragging or telling the truth. He is a typical colonel who has been given too much power and far too many privileges."

"When can you see him?" Jones asked.

"Tonight. He likes late-night get-togethers."

"Here?" Murdock asked.

"Oh no. He likes his comforts, which I can't offer him here. He lives in a big house with servants."

"Would he have anything in writing about the program?"

"Not a word. He says it's all verbal. He's most proud of the fact that nothing ever has been written down."

"What else can we do?" Murdock asked. "There must be others we could talk to. What about men who have worked on the program? There should be many back in town."

"Yes, but they have been warned not to talk. I met two of them, and they said they had been away fishing for eight months. We have no seacoast, no fishing fleet. They were on the project. The pay was double the usual and they were sworn to secrecy."

"What type of workers were they?" Rafii asked.

"The silent ones. Yes, the ones I talked to were construction workers. Built the barracks, houses, laboratories, and warehouses. Finding one of them might be possible. One was picked up by the Secret Police a month ago and we haven't seen him since. The other one is still around. He drinks a lot. Yes, you might find him at his favorite illegal booze house."

"Booze house?" Ching asked.

"A house where ordinary people smuggle in whiskey and beer and other illegal drinks and sell them to friends and neighbors." Jones said. "Usually extremely hush, hush."

Gypsy reached for a phone. "Let me call this lover man and see if he is hungry tonight. He almost always is. If he is, I'll go see what I can find out without getting myself shot. I'll give you the address of the booze house. Only two of you can go there."

Twenty minutes later, Murdock and Rafii parked down the block from a house with a light on in the window. It was rundown, with litter in the front yard, and pushed up against buildings on both sides. It was the start of an abandoned business district that had deteriorated badly.

They walked back to the house and Rafii took the lead. He knocked on the front door as he had been told. A door opened a crack and Rafii whispered his name. Then the door closed, and they went around the side of the house to the rear door and found a man sitting on the steps smoking.

"Rafii?" he asked.

"Yes, a friend told us about your place. First time here. Do you have any tonight?"

"Every night," the smoker said. "You are new. Twenty dinars to get inside."

"So much?"

"Going rate."

The men both took out twenty-dinar notes from worn purses. Each had been given three hundred dinars before they left Kuwait. Murdock also had five thousand dinars in a money belt inside his undershirt. The man checked the notes carefully in the pale light from the open rear door, then waved them inside.

The house had all the windows blacked out. Inside the first room they found the bar, a table with a dozen bottles of whiskey, gin, other liquors, and more bottles of beer. Each bought a beer for five dinars, then sipped at the strange brew while they circulated. More than twenty people filled the room. Less than half were women, but all those were in Western dress and with no veils. A record player punched out a soft jazz tune in the background. They looked for a man Gypsy said was called Sharif. She had described him as a taller-than-normal Iraqi man with a trimmed beard, eyeglasses, and a hearing aid. He was about forty and had lost two fingers on his right hand.

They found him in the second room, talking to a striking young woman with perfect dark features, a slender body, and big breasts. Rafii moved up, pushed the woman aside, and spoke quietly to the man. His eyes flared for a moment then he nodded slowly.

Murdock moved up to cut off anyone standing nearby, and he heard the offer.

"Yes, we just want to talk," Rafii said in his soft voice

with a hint of persuasion. "A hundred dinars if you come outside with us and talk. We're not the Secret Police."

"Talk about what? I'm just a poor construction man. I know nothing important."

"Good, then you won't mind making a hundred dinars. That would buy a lot of booze for you, Sharif, my friend."

"You know my name. That is upsetting. Nobody here knows my name."

"We won't hurt you in any way. We're friends, trying to help Iraq. Let's go outside. Okay?"

Murdock grinned at the use of the "okay" word. It was nearly a universal word these days. He quickly surveyed the area. He never liked to walk into a room or a building that had no immediate outlet. Here the paper-covered windows would have to do.

Before Sharif could answer, a whistle blew and two shots thundered in the other room.

"It's a raid by the police," Sharif bleated.

"The windows," Murdock said, slipping into English. He grabbed Sharif and pushed him toward the black paper-covered window six feet away. "Jump through," Murdock said, remembering that much Arabic. Sharif's eyes flared. He looked at the door, where men and women were charging into the room to get away from the police. Murdock ran three steps forward, put his crossed arms in front of his face, and dove into the black paper window. The four-foot-square window smashed outward. Murdock did a quick curl, hit on his shoulder, and rolled through the dirt and weeds.

Sharif came out right behind him, and then Rafii. The three jumped up and ran just as a submachine gun chattered off a dozen rounds from the shattered window, searching for them.

11

Murdock followed Sharif, who should know the territory. The tall Iraqi dodged behind a pile of wooden boxes next to a building. A moment later Rafii surged in beside them. The chatter of the sub gun continued for a moment, then stopped.

"They are arresting those inside," Sharif said. "Hurry this way before they send out men to hunt us." They ran again, to the street, down a full block, then up an alley and into a small house behind a larger one.

Sharif turned on a light and stared at the two SEALs.

"Something about you seems different," the Iraqi said. "I don't know what it is. If you are Secret Police, then I'm dead. You did save me from them back there. For that I and Allah thank you. This is my home. You wanted to talk. I owe you that much."

Rafii had been listening carefully. He touched Murdock's shoulder and nodded at the tall man.

"I understand your worry," Rafii said. "We are trying to help Iraq, help her despite what your president wants to do. We will not hurt you in any way, do you understand that?"

"Yes. If the Secret Police had caught me back there, I would have been in prison for years. It would have been the third time at a booze house. I have had no work since I came back from my fishing trip."

Rafii smiled. "Fishing in the desert is hard work. We need to know where you were fishing."

Sharif looked away. He shook his head. "I promised that I would never tell. It is a state secret."

"You built the facility, Sharif. Do you know what they manufactured out there in that desert?"

"They told us not to even guess at it. Not our business. We built the place; they used it."

"They put together Iraq's first nuclear bomb out there in the desert," Rafii said.

Sharif jumped to his feet, disbelief swarming over his face. "No. You must be joking. We can't do that. We don't have enough scientists, enough material. Who taught us how?"

"We don't know, but Iraq now has four nuclear bombs, and if they drop one on Israel, there will be an immediate response. Two or three nuclear bombs will fall on Baghdad, killing a million people. We are trying to prevent that from happening."

"A million . . . dead?" Sharif shook his head and turned away. "And I helped build the place they were made."

"You can still help save Baghdad from destruction."

"How?"

"Tell us where in the desert this secret complex is and how we can get there."

Sharif shuddered. His thin hands came up and rubbed his face, then he looked at Rafii. "If I told you, they would kill me."

"The Secret Police or the Home Guard will never know. We won't tell them. You will have enough money to live for years, if you don't start spending too much. You will be saving your country."

Sharif sat on the worn couch and held his head in his hands. Rafii and Murdock sat down nearby and waited.

"No one would know?"

"We will tell no one. No one knows that we have come to see you."

"I would have some money, so I wouldn't have to beg from my relatives?"

"Absolutely. Enough to live on for years."

Sharif stared at the floor. "It is in the desert."

"Is it underground?"

"Yes, but just two feet of dirt and rocks are on the roofs of the buildings, making them invisible from the air or the ground."

"Where are they, Sharif?"

"Far into the Syrian Desert. Beyond Muhammadiyah."

"That isn't even in the desert," Rafii said.

"Far, far beyond there, on the highway leading into Jordan.

"How far from Jordan?"

"I don't know. We were blindfolded for the whole trip both ways in the trucks."

"Was it more than two hundred kilometers?"

"Oh, yes, much more. I heard some drivers talking at a rest stop. They said they figured it was more than—"

Gunfire splattered through the thin outer door and into the room. The door crashed inward and two men ran into the room firing submachine guns. Murdock and Rafii dove to the floor pulling their pistols. Murdock had a clean shot on the first submachine-gun wielder. He put two shots into his chest and the man crumpled. Rafii took a round in the left arm in the first barrage, then rolled to the floor, drew his pistol, and fired four times, cutting down the second gunman near the door.

Murdock lifted off the floor and jerked the sub gun from the man's dead fingers. Then he kicked the second gunman, who groaned once before he died. Murdock went to Rafii, who held his left arm.

"Caught one, Skip. Not too bad. How is our pigeon?"

Murdock looked at Sharif. The construction worker had taken the brunt of the attack. He had one minor head wound and three rounds in his chest. They had missed his heart. Blood bubbled from Sharif's mouth.

Rafii held him where he lay on the blood-splattered couch.

"Sharif, you're hurt bad. Now you've got to help us. How far was it to the construction site?"

Sharif shook his head. "Long ways," he said. Blood came out of his mouth.

"Over three hundred kilometers?" Rafii asked.

The Iraqi's head nodded.

"Over four hundred?"

Instead of nodding this time, the construction worker's head rolled gently to the side and one last breath gushed out of his lungs.

"Out of here," Murdock growled. They each picked up a submachine gun and took two magazines from the civilian's pockets, then peered out the back door. Nothing moved in the alley. They darted out the door into black shadows. Nothing happened. They ran back the way they had come. At the street they hesitated again. No one was on the sidewalk. No cars moved along the pavement.

They walked now, heading back where they had left the stolen car two blocks from the booze house.

"We have a start," Rafii said. "Over three hundred kilometers and on the highway to Jordan. There are few roads in the desert. This one goes through Muhammadiyah. I know the place. We have a start."

"Over three hundred kilometers. That divided by 1.6K to a mile would be about a hundred and eighty-five miles or so. How far is it from Baghdad to the Jordan border?"

"You're testing my geography. It's roughly three hundred and seventy miles by air from Baghdad to the Jordanian border. By road it's more than that but not a lot. Almost no one lives beyond Muhammadiyah, which is only about twenty miles from the Euphrates River."

"And this Muhammy town is how far from the Jordanian border?"

"Not sure. Maybe two hundred miles."

"Are there any settlements out there in the desert at all?"

"Damn few. Maybe one or two."

"Would they build a setup like this near a village?"

"Hard telling what President Kamil might do. He's a dictator just like Saddam Hussein was. He can put it wherever he wants to."

"Maybe in a valley or a large wadi where it would have some protection."

As they approached the car they had come in, they blended into the shadows and watched it. No one stood guard over the car. They could see no one watching it. Two blocks ahead they saw many lights and car engines racing and a lot of shouting. The arrests must still be going on. After five minutes, Murdock stirred.

"I'll do a walk-by," Murdock whispered and eased onto the sidewalk and moved up past the stolen car. He saw nothing to worry him. He went back, stepped inside, and started the engine. Murdock drove down to where Rafii waited.

"How did they find us there with Sharif?" Rafii asked.

"They must have had scouts out watching for any runners," Murdock said. "When they saw the three of us, they tailed us, then brought in the guns."

"At least Sharif's worries are over," Rafii said.

Murdock pulled over and stopped the car. "You better drive, Rafii. I'm lost already."

Gypsy drove her own car, an ancient British sedan, the ten miles to the general's luxurious house. It was provided by the regime, as were the two maids, a driver, a handyman, two cooks, and his own dresser and butler. Colonel Kahled Ibrahim had just finished watching a sexy Western film when the call came from Gypsy. The film motivated him. It was late, and he had the meeting tomorrow with the president, but he invited her over. She would come in the side entrance and no one would know she had been there. It was safest that way. He could do as he pleased, but he was well aware of the president's narrow view on women. He was often too fundamentalistic for Ibrahim's tastes. Every man to his own.

As a door closed softly Ibrahim looked up and smiled. She would come in with her top garment loose and showing her small breasts. Breasts were not her best feature, but he humored her. A moment later she came through the door into his den. It contained a large couch, a giant TV screen, radios, and a desk in one corner with a telephone. He spent most of his time there. To his surprise, Gypsy danced into the room without anything on above her waist.

"Yes, yes, I like the new entrance, little one. What pleasures and surprises do you have for me tonight?"

"Many surprises, but first a drink. I crave some of the vodka that you like so much."

Ibrahim beamed. "A woman who knows good drink," he said and produced a bottle and two glasses from his desk. They both drank and he fondled her small breasts.

"I'm told a woman's breasts enlarge with milk when she has a baby. Have yours done that?"

"Once, so long ago I don't want to think about it."

"A boy?"

"Yes."

"Where is he now?"

"With Allah."

"The war? Was he killed in the war with Iran?"

"No, with the Americans. His captain killed him."

"His captain? How?"

"Sent him on a suicide mission to determine how quickly the American motorized infantry was advancing. Put him on a motorcycle and told him to ride until he saw them, then turn and race back and report."

"Did he get back?"

"No. He saw them, then they were all around him and he was cut down by machine guns."

"In every war . . ."

"But not for officers. How many wars have you been in, Kahled?"

"Only two. Wounded but not killed." He finished his drink and poured another. He smiled at her, pushed his hand up her leg, and rubbed her crotch. "You remember what you promised me the last time you were here?"

"Yes. Do you still have the box?"

"I have guarded it better than the state secrets I know." He went to a closet and returned with a cardboard box a foot square. "So?"

Gypsy laughed and opened the box. She took out a folded plastic sheet and spread it on the carpet on the floor. It was thin and covered a space ten feet square. In the middle of that she put down a folded piece of canvas that was four feet square. She pushed out the folds until it lay flat. Gypsy took tubes of paint and jars of color from the box and smeared them on her arms, hands, shoulders, stomach, and breasts. Then she lay down on the canvas and began writhing and sliding and rubbing the paint from her body onto the flat surface. She stood twice and nodded at her work. Then she slipped out of the skirt and put paint on her legs and waist and dropped on the canvas for more splashes with her paint-smeared legs. For the final touch, she pushed her crotch flat and hard against a paint buildup in the center of the canvas, then eased up and stepped away.

"Bravo, yes, amazing," the colonel said. He lifted his third glass of straight vodka and drank. "I want you to sign it for me. When it dries, I'll be able to sell it for three hundred dinars."

"At least," she said and dropped on the couch. He moved to her, already opening his pants and sliding down on her paint-etched body.

An hour later she held his head in her naked lap and stroked his face, now streaked with paint from her body. He had kept drinking and now was so near passing out she had to stop the drinks.

"So how did you stay busy today, Kahled?"

"Busy, always busy. Had to send men to the desert. Defending what doesn't need defending."

She lifted her brows. "I thought all of Iraq needed defending. The enemy is always waiting for us to leave an opening."

"Not defending against an enemy, protecting what we have."

"What could we have in the desert that would be worth a hundred armed men?"

"Not a hundred, two hundred and heavy weapons."

"You're joking. Our men are needed on the borders in case Israel sends in planeloads of paratroopers, and tanks and infantry."

"The borders are well protected." He belched. His eyes flickered shut, then she kissed them and they opened. "We had to drive within a hundred and fifty kilometers of the Jordan border. Bastards made me go with them. Then the long drive back home. At least my sedan was air-conditioned."

"Nothing in the desert is that important to take you away from Baghdad, and your good food and drink."

"True—no, not true. This is important. The future of our country. So important that the president himself told me to take the troops out there and be sure they had the best positions around the complex."

"Was two hundred enough?"

He blinked. His eyes closed and opened slowly. "Need one more drink."

She poured vodka in his glass, just a sip. "There, that's the last of the bottle."

He drank it and threw the glass on the floor. "Important? Oh, yes, so fucking important you would be surprised out of your wits. You could do a painting about them. About the first one. A huge picture, massive explosion, enormous cloud rising . . ." His brows went up and he laughed. "Talking too much. You always bait me. Talking too damn much." His eyes drooped closed and she knew this time they wouldn't open. But they did, and he sat up quickly and stared at her, not looking drunk now at all.

"You are a spy. I told everyone. They wouldn't believe me. Five years ago we had enough to shoot you, but they wouldn't let me. I proved to them that you were working with the Americans, but they said impossible. You had painted a mural on one of Saddam's castles, and he loved it. He ordered us to leave you alone. But now you are asking questions no one can ask. The desert is off the scale; it is so secret that not even all of the general staff know about it. I know. I supervised the work.

"And now I'm calling in my guards and they will shoot you as you try to escape. It's been interesting. And I have the last body art painting the famous Gypsy ever did." He stood to move to his desk. Gypsy darted there before he did. The drink had slowed him. She caught up a wooden pencil with a sharp point and whirled as he lunged toward her. She had put the eraser into the palm of her hand and let the six inches of pencil stick out between the middle fingers of her fist. As he lunged toward her, she held out the pencil, her wrist straight with her arm. Colonel Kahled Ibrahim saw the pencil and ignored it, until it drove into his chest, piercing his skin, slanting between ribs, and sinking six inches into his left lung.

He let out a sharp cry and staggered to the left. It tore the pencil out of her hand, but it remained in place. The colonel fell to one knee, then dropped on his face on the rug just short of the desk. The pencil hit the floor and drove the rest of the way into his lung. He tried to roll over. His arms flopped helplessly. Gypsy stared down at him, then turned him over. If he lived, she died.

As simple as that.

She caught up a metal letter opener from his desk. It was eight inches long, tapered steel and sharp on one side, coming to a point. She knelt beside the large man and watched his face distorted in fear and agony. Then she held the letter opener in both hands and stabbed it downward, directly at his heart. The point hit a rib and stopped. She moved the point over half an inch and drove the opener downward. It sank into flesh and into his heart.

She lifted away from him. His breathing was labored for a moment; then he died and his bladder emptied, staining his pants dark brown. Gypsy watched him a moment. He was dead. Could they tie her to him? She didn't think so. She hurried to where she'd left her clothes and put them on. She cleaned off her face with a towel from the adjacent bathroom, washed off her arms, and then found her purse in the hallway. She went out the same familiar way she had come in. The guards were at the far side of the compound and wouldn't see her go out the side gate, which had a lock on it that could only be opened from the inside, or left unlocked as it was tonight when she came. She walked six blocks to where she had left her car. Only then did her heart stop racing. She had killed him. There would be no way to tie her to his death. Even the body art painting could have been done by any amateur. She had killed him.

He said she had been suspected five years ago. Were they still watching her, only doing such a good job that she couldn't tell? Had she led the three SEALs into a trap that would cost them their lives and that of John Jones? She found her car where she'd left it and drove quickly back to her quarters in the old warehouse. She parked down the street and walked up to where she could see the area in back of her place. She watched for ten minutes, but saw no one smoking, heard nothing, saw no shadows move. Nothing. She walked slowly, then darted into the entrance and waited, her heart thudding against her thin chest. Again, nothing happened. She went on inside and closed the doors and locked them. What if the SEALs were not back from the booze house? A moment later she saw the four men in her living room and she collapsed on the couch. None of them asked about the paint splotches still on her face, in her hair, and on her arms.

Nobody said a word. She let some of the panic drain from her then looked at the Commander.

"So, Navy SEAL. What did you learn at the booze house?"

Murdock told her. "Sharif is dead. Must have been the Secret Police. They had submachine guns. These submachine guns."

Gypsy stared at the pair of sub guns like many she had seen before. "So the Secret Police are dead, too. Lovely. Now the animals will all be out looking for revenge."

"Did you learn anything from the colonel?" Rafii asked.

"Only that he took out two hundred armed men to defend the factory, and that it's within a hundred miles of the Jordan border. We've got it bracketed. Now all we have to do is find it."

12

Kamil Gardens, Iraq

Asrar Fouad settled into the lean-back upholstered chair in the guest house at Kamil Gardens and smiled grimly. Yes, everything was on schedule and going as planned. The big trailer was loaded; the tractor was full of diesel fuel and ready to drive. They would leave the first thing in the morning. He had spent most of the day hiding the nuclear bomb in the forty-foot trailer. It was shielded with lead blankets that would prevent even the minutest quantity of radiation from escaping. The bomb itself was in a wooden crate nearly six feet wide and ten feet long.

The West would call it a crude, overly large bomb. But it was a nuke that worked, which was all that Fouad cared about. The crate was tucked into the trailer, which had been loaded with dozens of bales of raw cotton. The cotton could be the key in the success of the mission. The fiber was grown in great quantities in northern Iraq, and was one of Iraq's few export products. This truckload was heading straight for Jordan, continuing down the road toward the border. Once into Jordan, the road continued southwest through the heart of the Syrian Desert to As Safawi, where the highway turned northwest to Al Mafraq and then on into Irbid in northern Jordan and only a few kilometers from Israel.

Then the critical phase of the mission would come. They had to unload the crate at the airport and get it into the transport plane without arousing any suspicion or an in-depth inspection by the Jordanians. They had no export license for the crate so it could be touchy. He hoped the men he had bribed would be in place. Fouad sipped on the cold drink he had been provided, something carbonated with lemon. The guest house was one of the few air-conditioned in the whole complex, and the temperature remained at a steady sixty-eight degrees year round despite the summer temperature of over a hundred and twenty degrees out in the desert. He looked at the selection of movie videotapes and decided not to indulge himself with a Hollywood epic. Instead he would get to bed early and be ready for their five A.M. start.

Fouad was impressed again by the huge highway tractor that he had talked President Kamil out of for the trip into Jordan. It was the latest model from Germany, huge, a diesel, and carried enough fuel in its saddle tanks below the cab to drive the rig for six hundred kilometers. He figured this run would be about five hundred and twenty kilometers, so they wouldn't even have to stop for fuel. The big tractor had hitched up with the sleek trailer and pulled out on the highway from the concealed, underground manufacturing area slightly after five A.M. Fouad was pleased to be leaving Kamil Gardens, the name given to the production facility where the bombs had been created. He was used to hours of delay in getting most of his projects underway in Iraq. Time here was not as important as it was in the West. But this project was moving along on schedule. He smiled then, thinking about his surprise for the Americans. Things would slow down considerably all over a paralyzed America once he exploded his bomb over a big U.S. city. He had not decided yet which metropolis it would be. Once he was across the U.S.-Mexican border at the Otay Mesa inspection station near San Diego, California, in his disguised truck with the bomb, he could chose from San Diego, Los Angeles, or San Francisco. It would be a marvelous time for him, deciding which city to turn into a nightmare of death and vaporization.

Fouad watched out the truck's windows. The cab was air-conditioned and even had a small freezer. He watched the barren, burned brown Syrian Desert roll past the window. They weren't making the kind of time he'd hoped they would, but the plan was moving along. This was the start of the end. He sighed. Waiting had always been a trial for him. At least he had brought along enough food and drink from the dining room at the Kamil Gardens to last for three days. Even at eighty kilometers an hour on the poor roads, they

should be able to make the trip in half a day, one full day at
the most. He didn't worry about the border with Jordan. They
were on good terms with that nation and the cotton import
would be welcomed by the industries in Jordan. Actually the
cotton would be sold there in Jordan to help cover their
tracks. He had all the papers he needed, including an import
license and the required documents to get the load of cotton
across the border. Now all he had to do was have a pleasant
nap in the big seat, or have another sandwich and a cold
drink. Yes, for the moment, life was good. He was a bit on
edge, and would be until the package was into the Jordan
airport and loaded on the chartered air transport plane. There
would be no trouble there. Already two Irbid airport officials
in the international freight section had been properly com-
pensated for the help they would give the shipment. All was
ready and awaiting the package. Fouad laughed softly, bringing a look from the driver. The driver was not one of his
men, and had no idea that there was anything in the trailer
besides the cotton. He had no need to know, another part of
the plan to keep the secret. Fouad talked with the driver for
a few minutes, then waved and closed his eyes. It was time
for a nap. There would be plenty of action soon.

Baghdad, Iraq

The same morning the big German highway tractor left Kamil Gardens with its load of cotton and one nuclear bomb,
Murdock and his men, and ex–CIA agent John Jones, sat at
the breakfast table in Gypsy's quarters in the converted warehouse. They had just eaten fried goat meat and a hash of
eggs and potatoes. The coffeepot kept perking.

"So, we fall back on plan B," Ching said.

"What the hell is plan B?" Rafii asked.

"First it means we take a look at that scratch you got last
night. Roll up your sleeve." The wound was an in and out
that had nipped an inch of flesh. It hadn't bled much. Rafii
had tied a kerchief over it to stop the blood flow last night.
Murdock took it off gingerly.

"Gypsy, you have any alcohol and some bandages?"

She did and brought them. Murdock cleaned the wound
on both sides, then wrapped it tightly with a white roller

bandage and fastened it with tape. It wouldn't show under the shirtsleeve.

"So plan B?" Rafii asked.

"We make it up as we go along," Murdock said. "Gypsy, do you have any other contacts that might have some idea where the bomb factory could be?"

"Absolutely none if I want to stay alive. Yes, women here in Iraq have it better than any females in the Muslim world, but we also have a dictator who executes his enemies and any who protest his policies. This bomb must be top secret. I'm surprised that he let as many of the construction men who built the project live as he did. A lot of them must be mixed in with the concrete in the foundations out there in the desert."

"Any contacts that wouldn't get you in trouble?" Murdock asked.

Gypsy wrinkled her brow. She had pulled her dark hair back into a ponytail and had not put on any makeup. "I paint pictures, not my face," she had told them the first thing that morning.

She shook her head, then stopped. "Oh, there could be one but it's an outside chance. When things get slow, I teach master classes in beginning oil painting. It's easy and brings in a few extra dinars." She took a long drink of her coffee, frowning and shaking her head. "No, probably not."

"Hey, if there's a chance, and it won't hurt you, we have to give it a try," Murdock said.

She took another sip of the coffee and put down the cup. "It is a long shot. One of my students has a big family, and he said one of his brothers had been on what he called a fishing trip into the desert. He's an engineer, specializes in putting up buildings for the government. His brother had laughed and said his kin went on four fishing trips and didn't bring back a single fish."

"Fishing trip, the same term the construction worker used," Murdock said. "Let's get in contact with the engineer."

"Do you have a list of those students?" Rafii asked.

"Should be here somewhere."

Five minutes later she found the list and ticked off the brother of the engineer.

"How do we get him to tell us how to get in touch with his brother, without getting suspicious?" Ching asked.

"More coffee, please," Murdock said. The five sat at the table, working on the third cup.

John Jones stood and walked around the kitchen. When he sat down, he grinned. "Got it," he said. "Gypsy, you contact this guy and tell him you're giving another master class, and you're short one person. Ask him if his brother would like to take the class. A lot of engineers think they're artists. It could work. Get his phone number or address so you can invite him to the class."

Gypsy laughed softly. "My friend, Mr. Jones, you are a sneaky bastard, but I like you. I think it might work. I have something of a reputation around town. He might be pleased to be invited to study under the great Gypsy."

Rafii let out a long-held-in breath. "That's good, but what can I do? I keep thinking about all those construction workers. A lot of them must be out of work now. Where do they hang out? They don't have a union hall, but there must be a spot where they get together and swap lies."

Gypsy grinned and pointed a spoon at him. "Rafii, how did you know that? You haven't lived here since you were four, you said."

"My father was a carpenter here. I remember what he used to tell us about working."

"There is a spot, two of them actually," Gypsy said. "The men do talk and tell tales about their work. It could be a good place to go if you can listen a lot, talk little, and blend in."

"I'm a top-notch blender," Rafii said.

"I'll give you the two addresses. Take my car. Both these places are across town. Right now I want to call my ex-student and see if we can talk to his brother."

A half hour later, Rafii pulled Gypsy's sedan of uncertain vintage to the curb and watched the coffee house across the street. It was not one that offered jazz as a sideline. No boisterous crowd. In the outside chairs and tables he saw men, only men, bending over cups of coffee. One or two had tall drinks of some kind. He slid out of the car and walked up a block, then crossed the street and came back on the other side. He went into the shop, bought a cup of coffee, and eased back out to a table with no one else at it. He listened. The men talked in low voices and he could make out nothing.

A few minutes later the place filled with men, most in working clothes, some with beards, most without. Two came up to his table and motioned. He waved them to chairs and they gave their names. Ali was the tall, thin one. Sami was shorter, heavy with a beard. He told them his name and they nodded. They talked to one another, not trying to include him. This time he could hear.

"No work again today?" Ali said.

"True, not for two weeks now," Sami said.

"Maybe we're in the wrong business. My wife's brother is a baker and he's making a good living."

"But he works all night," Sami protested. "I like to sleep at night."

Ali looked at Rafii. "No work for you either?"

"Not much of anything since the desert. The fishing trip was fine but now, nothing."

Both men frowned. "We are not supposed to even remember the desert," Sami said. "We could be shot."

"Who is listening?" Rafii asked in a soft voice. "Besides that was a year ago."

"By now you must be hungry," Sami said with a chuckle.

"I mean I haven't had a job that lasted more than a week," Rafii said, figuring he had overplayed his hand.

"The fishing was good, but that damn long ride each way was what killed me," Sami said.

"Still, I'd do it again," Ali said.

"Carpenter?" Rafii asked.

"No. Concrete, forms, slabs, even some liftup concrete walls."

"Good work," Rafii said. "I'm just a carpenter."

"The damn trip was what killed me," Sami said. "Eight hours in that damn covered truck."

"We did it in seven," Rafii said. "You must have stopped somewhere."

"Oh, yeah, forgot. We had to stop for fuel in Ar Rutbah. Then that damn dirt road due south."

"Dust got into everything," Rafii said. "Why didn't they pave it or put the blacktop down?"

"That would make it an arrow straight at the secret place," Ali said. "They aren't that stupid. They camouflaged the dirt road after every truck went down it. Fake bushes and brush. It was a lot of work."

"Is the government hiring again?" Rafii asked. "Heard something about work out at the airport."

"Just talk," Ali said. "We've been hearing that for a month now. They might never get to extending that runway."

Rafii finished his coffee. He stood. "Maybe there'll be something tomorrow," he said. He waved and walked down the street a block, crossed over, and strolled back to the car. For a moment he wasn't sure which car he had come in. Then he remembered the dent in the left front fender and climbed in. Yes, the key fit and engine started. So they were south of Ar Rutbah. Now all they had to figure out was how far south.

13

By the time Rafii had driven back to the old warehouse where Gypsy lived and painted, she was pacing the floor waiting for him. He told them what he had discovered, and Ching got the SATCOM out and set it up to broadcast.

Gypsy grabbed the car keys and headed for the street. "I told my student's brother that I'd meet the engineer at a cafe, and I'm going to be late. So he'll have to wait. Not sure what I can find out, but we'll see what he says about painting, and about the desert. Maybe I can talk him into painting some desert scenes. This shouldn't take more than two hours at the most."

She had changed clothes and now wore a colorful skirt, a blouse that barely hid her breasts, a red scarf around her neck, and a light linen jacket. She also wore makeup, but just a little.

Ching had the SATCOM set up at an open window in the back of the second floor of the building where the dish antenna could look into the sky. The improved SATCOM had a dish that was barely four inches in diameter, much smaller than the one Ching was used to. It also was twice as easy to zero in on the satellite. He made the adjustments and handed the mike to Murdock.

"Underground One reporting. We have a location. In the desert south of Ar Rutbah, a small village on the highway to Jordan. Don't know how far south. On a dirt road. We'll get there as soon as we can. Running down one more lead. Underground out."

The message went out in a burst that lasted only a tenth of a second and would be almost impossible to triangulate, even if the Iraqis were listening for any broadcasts. They put the SATCOM away and Murdock began pacing.

"How long do we wait for Gypsy?" he asked Jones. The former CIA agent shook his head.

"She'll be back when she thinks she has what we need. No telling when that will be."

"We need transportation," Murdock said. He looked at Jones. "Can you get us a car with a full tank of gas that will run until we get to that little town out in the desert?"

Jones frowned. "You want a throwaway car? Why not just steal one?" He shrugged. "Yeah, I know. Even the Iraqi police can find a stolen car now and then. So let me make a call. I have at least one favor coming in this town. You want an older car that runs well. Let me use Gypsy's phone."

He left the room and Murdock had his two men check what equipment they had. They would be ready to move as soon as Gypsy came back.

Jones was back in five minutes.

"Done," he said. "It's a four-year-old Chevrolet, of all things. Runs good and has good tires. What you do is use it as long as you can. In two days the owner is going to report it stolen. That way he should get it back without any problem. The cops here are good on returning stolen cars when they find them."

"When do we get the car?" Murdock asked. "We know enough to get moving right now."

"You're not ready yet. You'll need food and water. Lots of water. It's going to be a hundred and twenty in the desert for the next week. Sap the juices right out of you. You'll need at least a gallon of water a day. It's almost two o'clock. Best to travel at night. So get some rest now, and I'll get food for you to eat before you go and for the trip. Meat now, cheese sandwiches for later. We don't want any spoiled meat in the desert heat. Go, go get some sleep. It won't be dark for six hours yet, and the car won't be here for two. Go."

Murdock grinned and waved his men up the stairs, where they saw some mattresses on the floor. John Jones watched them go. He chuckled. He hadn't had this much fun in years. Maybe it was time he reactivated himself and got back in the spy business. He could send out a message in his old manner. Or he could have Murdock tell the brass to reinstate him. He'd be back in business. Yeah, he had to admit that he kind of missed the rush he used to get in this business. The last day and a half had been good. Now to get some food and water and the car.

Gypsy walked into the Lily of the Nile Cafe slowly, trying to watch everything around her without seeming to. She didn't want this to be a trap she couldn't get out of. She saw the young man sitting alone at a table near the window, where he was supposed to be. He looked up and nodded. He must have known what she looked like.

She could spot no Secret Police at tables or loitering around the area. Gypsy walked over to the table.

"Hassan?"

He stood quickly, not a trait found in many Muslim men.

"Yes, and you're Gypsy. My brother has been raving about you ever since he failed one of your oil classes."

"Aren't you nice. Thank you." He made no move to help her sit down. They dropped into the chairs.

"I'm having something carbonated," he said, his voice lower now than she had expected. He looked to be about thirty, clean shaven, with darting dark eyes and full brows. He wore a business suit, white shirt and tie, and she knew he must be with some large engineering firm in town.

"I'm not quite sure what it is I'm drinking, but it's cold and it's legal. May I order you one?"

She nodded. "Please. I usually don't venture out in the heat of the day this way. So, are you interested in my next oil class, or was your brother just fooling me?"

He sipped at his drink, then nodded. "Oh, no, I've dabbled in painting from time to time. I like acrylic the most, but I should have a better foundation in oils. When do your classes start?"

"Next month. I'm lining up students now. The class costs five dinars a session."

"That's not a problem, but something else is. Did my brother say anything about what I do?"

"He says you're one of the best engineers in the city for getting large buildings put up. He's proud of you."

"That's all he said?"

"He didn't give me a résumé of your work, nothing like that."

"Good. Now that you've seen that I'm not a monster, may I take your class?"

"Yes, you just passed the test. Oh, your brother did say something that surprised me. He said you had been fishing in the desert. What in the world did he mean by that?"

She saw a sudden change in his expression, from open and pleased to a serious, nearly frightened look.

"He shouldn't have said that, even as a joke. I can't explain it and you should forget you ever heard him say that. People could get in trouble talking about that. Even you, and especially me. Let's just forget all about it. I don't think I should take your class. Excuse me, I have to leave."

He stood abruptly and hurried away without a backward glance. The moment he left the chair, a short man with a beard and hard eyes sat down in his place. He had a sharply defined face with a small nose and heavy brows. He stared at Gypsy.

"Gypsy, we have been watching you more closely lately," the small man said. "Yes, yes, I know about your mural in the palace and that you have been a favorite of the president. But even he will turn away from you over this problem. Why did you talk to Hassan?"

"I invited him to join my next oil painting class."

"That's why he suspected you. Because of his past work, he is especially careful about who he talks to. He wondered why a famous artist like you would have to ask people to be in your classes. That's when he contacted us. We have a heavy file on you, Miss Gypsy. You have done some questionable acts in the past and we have long memories. Even now you have some strange men staying at your quarters."

"They are art students from the country. I provide them a place to stay while they study with me."

"We are finding that hard to believe, Gypsy. We think that it's time you come to headquarters for a talk with the captain. He is an expert on your history. Now would be a good time to go."

Gypsy had a pencil in her small purse, but she didn't see how she could use it here. She had to do something. The

SEALs were in danger but how could she warn them?

"Do you mind if I finish my drink first? It's a hot day outside."

The Secret Policeman nodded. "It may be the last one you get for a while. The captain is not at all pleased with you. Knowing that you mentioned fishing in the desert will make him angrier."

Her mind whirled. How many of them were there? Where were the others? Would she have a better chance here or in the car? If only she had ordered hot coffee, she could have thrown it in his face. She made the drink last, but could work out no plan. There would be at least two of them. They didn't trust their own people enough to send out one man to do a job. Where was the other one? In the car, or watching from the side. It had to be now. She took the pencil out of her purse and wrote on a piece of paper, then she stood, and before the policeman could stand, she threw the rest of her drink in his face, lunged forward with the pencil stiff between her fingers as before, and drove it into his chest. He cried out and pushed backwards. Already the sharp-pointed pencil had plunged three inches into his chest. He grabbed at it, tripped over the chair as he was standing, and fell on his chest. His body weight drove the pencil six inches into his chest.

There were few patrons in the cafe. Two looked the other way. She stepped away from the table and walked toward the kitchen, expecting a man to grab her at any moment.

Just before she reached the door, a shot thundered and she felt the bullet slam past her head and hit the door. A man with a pistol out ran toward her shouting. She ducked behind a waiter just coming from the kitchen with a tray of dinners. She pushed him from behind, driving him toward the gunman. The man fired again, the round pounding into the waiter's chest. He screamed, and Gypsy pushed him forward into the gunman, knocking them both down. She grabbed the pistol, which had skittered out of the policeman's hand. She bent and slammed the heavy pistol twice against the Secret Policeman's head, just the way she had been trained by the army to do. The policeman stopped shouting and his head rolled to one side. He was dead or unconscious.

Gypsy dropped the pistol, ran through the kitchen's swinging doors, and looked for the back way out. She saw a door and went through it, then out another, and she was in the alley. Once outside, she ran the long way down the alley to the street. Then she walked. She had on a light jacket over her dark blouse. She pulled the jacket off and dropped it into a trash can hoping it would make her harder to identify. Then she walked quickly away from the main street. She found a telephone and called her own number. Someone picked it up on the third ring.

"Yes?"

"Jones?"

"Yes, Gypsy?"

"Right. Trouble. They tried to arrest me. I got away. They know there are strange men at my place. Get all of you out of there now. Right this instant. Set up things in the street somewhere many blocks away. Get them moving toward the target with what they have now. Do you understand?"

"Yes. We're moving now. Go to my place. You know the address. Nobody has been watching me lately. Go there now. Walk, don't take a cab. No hurry. Better yet wait somewhere for an hour, then call my home and I'll come pick you up. We're all gone from here."

The three SEALs left the warehouse one at a time and walked in different directions. They would meet two blocks over to the north. Murdock was the last SEAL out. Jones had planned to wait a few minutes more and then drive away in his car. Murdock tried to act naturally as he left the alley and walked down the street. He had to stop himself from checking out every hiding spot. He saw a man come out from between buildings, but too late to avoid him. The man wore a sports shirt and dress pants and he held an automatic in his left hand.

"Stop," the man said in Arabic.

Murdock waved at his ears as if he couldn't hear and kept walking toward the man. The Secret Policeman frowned, said something else, then Murdock was against him, grabbed the gun, pushed it aside, and drove the smaller man backwards between the buildings. Murdock's right hand had the weapon, and his left came up hard, grabbing the man's throat and pushing his head upward. His grip cut off the man's air and pressed hard on both carotid arteries. In twenty seconds the policeman collapsed from lack of blood to his brain. He wasn't dead, just unconscious. Murdock took the weapon, used riot cuffs around the cop's hands and feet, and put a cloth gag around his head and across his mouth so he couldn't scream.

At the front of the buildings, he looked both ways along the street. He saw no one. After walking a block, Murdock jogged toward the assembly point. He found both his men, and Jones and the car, waiting for him.

"What took you so long?" Ching asked.

Inside the car, Jones told them they were advancing the schedule because Gypsy had nearly been arrested.

"She might have killed the Secret Policeman," Jones said. "At least they now will try to hunt her down and execute her. Can she go with you? She's dead if she tries to hide here in Baghdad."

"We can at least get her out of town," Murdock said. "Maybe drop her off at some town along the way. We're going into an intense combat situation."

"She was a major, I believe, in some kind of women's army unit in the Iran war," Jones said. "She might be another shooter for you."

"Doubtful," Murdock said. "We'll get her out of town and then see what happens."

"That car I got for you should be parked outside of my place. If it is, all you need is some more food and water and you can be on your way."

"What about rifles?" Ching asked. "Are any available? I hear every house has at least one for use by the Home Guard."

Jones nodded. "Yes, true. I can get you two. AKs—the older ones but still damn good weapons. Two rifles and about fifty rounds for each. Will that help?"

When they came near Jones's place, he drove right past. All the men checked out the area on both sides of the street. They saw nothing that looked threatening. An old Chevrolet of uncertain year sat in front of the house. Jones turned around at the end of the block and drove back.

"This is the car. So far, so good. Let's get out and inside. I'll load the car with the rifles, food, and water. Then hope that Gypsy calls. When she does, you'll have a place to pick her up. She'll have to go with whatever she has with her. The Secret Police will be all over her place within hours."

Murdock made one more transmission on the send-only SATCOM and told them he had no more information. He repeated the area where they should continue to hunt and said they were on their way. He hoped the rest of the platoon of SEALs had been moving long before now.

The call came ten minutes after they were packed and ready to roll.

"John?"

"Yes, Gypsy. Where are you?"

"I'm in the Green Spa restaurant on Saddam Street. I'm in the women's room. There is one man following me. He has to be Secret Police. I don't know how they found me. Send two of the SEALs to the restaurant. I'll wait until I see them standing just outside the women's room door. I'll peek out."

"They are on their way. Take them about twenty minutes. You have to leave with them for the desert. If you stay in Baghdad, you're a dead artist."

"I know that. Tell the SEALs to hurry. I can stay in here only so long, then that man is coming in after me."

14

Syrian Desert, Iraq

The monotony of the drive soon told on Asrar Fouad. He
had slept for two hours, then the rough road awakened him
and he swore for ten minutes, using every foul word in the
four languages that he knew.

"Why can't they build a road that will last more than two
years?" he bellowed at the driver. The man behind the wheel
was of mixed parentage and stood more than six feet, four
inches tall. He turned to Fouad and snorted.

"Be quiet or I'll throw you out into the desert. Would you
like that, city man?"

Fouad bristled and doubled up his fist. "Do you know who
you are threatening? Haven't you seen your papers with the
signature of the president himself on them?"

"Yes, but he isn't here to help you. You want me to stop
driving and let us bake in the oven here? Or can you drive
this big machine?"

Fouad quieted, shrugged, and stared back out the window.
Once they got to their destination, he would shoot this addled
driver to further cover up the transport. He checked the
odometer on the new dashboard. They had moved over
eighty kilometers, about half of what he thought they would
do in the three hours they had been on the road. It was another one hundred and sixty to the border. There might be a
building there they could cool off in for a time. No, there
wouldn't be. Only an outpost on each side of the border. The
guards might not even have guns. Relations with Jordan had
always been good. There would be no facilities there for
travelers.

He had been surprised at how little traffic there was on
the road. Occasionally a car would pass them. He could re-

member seeing only ten cars and trucks coming from Jordan on the trip. No wonder the road had not been taken care of. Desert sand had drifted over it in some places, making the going even slower.

They passed the border checkpoint two hours later. There was no action by the Iraqi guards. The Jordanian soldiers flagged them down, checked their papers, and opened the back doors of the big trailer for a quick inspection of the jammed-tight bales of cotton. In three minutes they were on their way again.

"How much fuel do we have left?" Fouad asked.

"More than three-quarters of our supply, plenty to get us all the way to the big town," the driver said. "Go to sleep. We have a long run to As Safawi. We've come a hundred and fifty kilometers. The next stop is over two hundred and twenty." The driver reached down into the cooler, took out a bottled drink, and unscrewed the top. He took a long pull from the pale green liquid and grinned. "Fuel for me," he said.

Two hours later they met a roadblock somewhere outside of the little town they were heading for. A Jordanian tank blocked the roadway, with an army truck on each side. Six armed men stood behind the tank. An officer came out to the stopped truck. Fouad climbed down from the high cab to meet the captain.

"Our border guards told us you were coming. They want me to check your documents. Is it really the Iraqi president's signature on your export license?"

"It is, sir. He's concerned that we are not exporting enough cotton, so he personally moved this truckload into the system. I think you'll find our papers in order."

The Jordanian captain leafed through them and nodded. "You are right. It does look authentic, the signature. Fine with me. You may proceed." He gave a signal and the tank wheeled its big gun around as it turned and aimed the cannon directly at the truck; then it rolled to the side, leaving the center of the road open. They drove through.

They soon came to the small town of As Safawi, which consisted of only ten buildings. Fouad wondered why it was there, what sustained it. A mine, perhaps, nearby. Ten kilometers beyond the town the desert road turned northwest and Fouad started to feel better. This endless desert should soon be behind them.

"About seventy kilometers to Ar Mafraq," the driver said. "It's the main town in this governorate. It's a real town. We'll stop there and take a break. Buy something to eat. You'll pay. It always works this way."

Fouad seethed for a moment, then relaxed. Let him have his fun. It wouldn't last.

An hour later Fouad jumped and looked out the window. He rolled it down and let the hot air pour in as he stretched out the window looking at the trailer.

"We've got a bad tire—can't you feel it? A heat blister. We've got to stop. Pull over just off the road."

"Tires are all fine. The readouts on the control panel show all are up to pressure on air."

"That readout doesn't show blisters on the melting rubber. Pull over, damn it, right now."

The driver shrugged. "Yeah, okay. You're the boss. I still say . . ." He looked up at the anger on the smaller man's face and shrugged again. He pulled the rig to a stop at the side of the road and they both got out.

"It's on my side," Fouad said. The driver came around the front of the rig and bellowed in rage.

Fouad had out his pistol and fired six shots into the big man's chest so fast he didn't crumple until the last 9mm round penetrated his left lung and he went down, sprawling into the dirt and sand of the Syrian Desert, dead before he hit.

Fouad waited two minutes to be sure the man was dead. No cars or trucks came by. He grabbed the driver's hand and pulled him ten meters into the rocky landscape, well away from the side of the road, and left him behind a scrub growth that looked starved for a drink of moisture.

Fouad climbed back into the cab, shifted the rig into drive, and moved it back on the road. He'd had two days of instruction in driving the big new highway tractor in Baghdad before they hooked up the trailer. It was much simpler than flying a jet plane. He eased the unit up to speed and hummed a little tune as the kilometers melted away.

When he reached the larger town of Al Mafraq, he was hungry. He found a place he could park the big truck, went into a cafe, and sat where he could see the truck out the window. He had a mutton stew meal with desert and hurried back to the truck. If he kept moving at this pace, he could get to the airport at Irbid before dark. The plane and the bribed customs inspectors would be waiting. He had memorized the route and knew that from here there were only a little over forty kilometers to the big town and the airport. He speeded up. The road was better now, and he made good time. Before dark he hoped to have the package safely on board the jet cargo plane. As soon as it was securely tied down, they would take off, with him on board, as well. He touched the money belt inside his shirt. The flight had been prepaid, but he had enough money to pay for it again if he needed to. He had twenty thousand Jordanian dinars as well as twenty thousand U.S. dollars. He could buy his way out of any problems or trouble. He yawned. An old habit when he began to get nervous. Now it was only a matter of a few hours before he would take the next big step in his grand plan to humiliate the Great Evil, to blast one big American city into vaporized ruins.

Baghdad, Iraq

In the restaurant where she had hidden, Gypsy peered out the inch-wide slit where she had opened the door a crack. She stared at the wall across from the women's rest room. No one stood there. She checked her watch. It had been twenty minutes since she called Jones. Where were they? She went back into the rest room and into a closed stall and locked the door behind her. She stood, shifting her weight from one foot to the other. She heard women come in, chatter, run water, use the stalls. Then a rough man's voice sounded as if it came from the open door.

"Gypsy, I know you're in there. In five minutes if you don't come out, I'm coming in and breaking your arm and dragging you out."

She heard the door close and excited talk by three or four

women who must have been in the room. She opened the stall door and stepped out. She went to the door and pulled it back an inch and looked out.

Yes. The two Americans stood against the wall, looking out of place and nervous. She pushed the door farther, waved at them, and they both walked toward her. She hurried out and they flanked her as they moved toward the outside door.

"Stop!" a commanding voice bellowed in Arabic. The three kept walking. A shot thundered into the room, echoing like a thunderclap in the closed area. The round went into the ceiling. Murdock turned, a pistol already in his hand. He fired three times at the Secret Policeman who still pointed his gun at them. The man jolted a step backwards, then turned and fell on his side to the floor.

Murdock, Rafii, and Gypsy hurried out the door, ran down the street to the alley, and surged into it. Murdock stopped them. He watched behind them but saw no pursuit. They ran through the alley to where they had left the car and got in.

"Gypsy, in the back, lie down on the seat, and cover up with the blanket."

Ching sat in the rear seat and helped hide her.

"There will be an alert out as soon as they find their man. Rafii, guide us out of this downtown area and to the west. We need to find that highway that darts across the desert toward Jordan."

They had gone only a dozen blocks before they saw a police car with flashing lights rocketing toward them. It flashed past them.

"Heading for the restaurant and their dead buddy," Rafii said. "Won't be long now before we have cops all over the place. Gypsy, what's the best way out of town east?"

"Find the Hussein Parkway and head east," Gypsy said. "Then watch for the turnoff to Al Kazimiyah. That will be the highway to Jordan. I don't remember its number. It will be close to a small river."

Ten minutes later they found the parkway, and soon the turnoff to the highway leading west.

"This is the main highway?" Murdock asked. "It's only two lanes."

"We're lucky it's blacktopped," Gypsy said. "Our glorious president would rather spend money on missiles and bombs than on roads and bread. We're holding on by our teeth here." She sat up and frowned. "I guess I should say the Iraqis are holding on, since I won't be with them much longer." She looked out the window. "I really didn't expect to be alive by this time," she said. "Once the Secret Police get a kill order on you, there's no way to last more than a day or two."

"That's when there aren't three U.S. Navy SEALs watching your back," Ching said. "I hear you can fire an AK-47?"

Gypsy turned to him and smiled. "Yes, that I can do. I was second in marksmanship in my women's army battalion of four hundred. Oh, I forgot to tell you. The colonel said that he took two hundred troops to the desert to protect the bomb plant. He said they had heavy weapons. Would that be fifty-caliber machine guns and maybe some shoulder-fired rockets?"

"Probably, which is not good news for our side," Murdock said.

A half hour later they were through the little towns near Baghdad and racing down the road almost due east. The Chevy's odometer was calibrated in miles not meters, so it must have been an import.

"How long until it gets dark?" Murdock asked.

"Probably about seven o'clock," Gypsy said.

"How big a gas tank on this bucket?" Ching asked. "Maybe fourteen gallons? If this crate can get twenty miles to the gallon, we'll be lucky. That's two hundred and eighty miles. How far is the target?"

"We figured about two hundred and forty to that little town, then whatever south we need," Rafii said. "We might have enough petrol."

"If we don't?" Gypsy asked.

"Easy," Rafii said. "We dump this one, steal a car in that town, Ar Rutbah, and drive south until we hit those two hundred troops."

"Just how the hell do we link up with the rest of the platoon?" Ching asked.

"All we can do is use the SATCOM and tell them where

we are," Murdock said. "They'll have to come find us. Or if
we hear a firefight somewhere, we circle around and try to
get behind the good guys."

"Lights ahead," Ching said.

Murdock saw them about the same time. Looked like a
pair of army trucks parked across the road. They were at a
hundred yards now and no way they could fade into the
desert. Murdock slowed and Rafii slid under him as Murdock
went high and they changed places, with the Iraq native now
driving. He rolled up to the barrier. Near the two trucks stood
four soldiers, each holding a submachine gun at the ready.

"What's our story?" Rafii whispered. Before anyone could
answer, one guard tapped on the window that was halfway
down.

"We don't get much traffic this late at night," the guard
said. "Where are you from and where are you going?"

15

Rafii held out his papers. "We're from Baghdad and we're heading for a little town called Ubaylah. Hope we haven't missed it. They didn't tell us it was this far out here. My uncle's funeral. Tomorrow morning. We should have started earlier. What time is it, anyway?"

The guard shrugged. "You didn't miss it. Not far now. You'll come to Ar Rutbah. A few kilometers past that place you turn right. A funeral? It's a bad time to die."

"Anytime is bad for dying. Did you see a fairly new Citroën coming this way? I thought our relatives would be ahead of us."

"Haven't seen them tonight. Maybe you beat them." The soldier guard looked at Rafii's papers in the beam of his flashlight, then handed them back. "Time? I don't have a watch. Get out of here so I can take a nap."

Rafii waved at the guard, the trucks pulled apart, and the old Chevy eased through, then sped up and drove away from the soldiers.

"Good thinking, Rafii," Gypsy said. "Funerals are highly important in this country. Almost everyone comes to a good funeral."

"We should be fairly close," Murdock said. "We need to decide when to ditch the car and hike."

"We drive until we get stopped or see lights around the place," Rafii said. "If there are any lights."

"We've got the two sub guns and our pistols if we get stopped at a checkpoint," Ching said. "They'll have at least one, maybe two or three, on that dirt road. My guess is we get stopped not far down the dirt road from that little town."

"If we don't want to advertise that we're here, we better

ditch the truck before we get stopped," Murdock said. "Gypsy, you have good shoes on?"

"I can hike in what I have. No heels. I could use a shirt if one of you has an extra one. It gets cold out here in the desert at night."

"Rafii," Murdock said.

Rafii grinned and took off the shirt he wore as he drove. Murdock held the wheel as he got it off his shoulders. They all had put on two shirts before they left Gypsy's place. Rafii was the smallest of the three; even so, his shirt hung on Gypsy like a blanket. She pinched it in and then tucked it into the top of the long skirt she wore that came almost to her ankles.

"Ready for duty," she said.

"You get one of the AKs," Murdock said. "Let's load up and get ready to travel."

Ten minutes later they saw lights ahead.

"Has to be the town," Rafii said. "Now all we need to do is find that dirt road leading south. I'll turn left off the main highway and work the back streets until we find something that looks like it could take a lot of heavy trucks, which must have had to run down this way just to build a complex out here. Everyone keep your eyes open. Even in the dark we might be able to spot something."

"Just after midnight," Murdock said. "Most of these houses are dark. Let's hope there isn't much military in town, and that the cops are all taking a break."

Three blocks down on a back street, Rafii pulled the Chevy to a stop. Fifty yards ahead a string of headlights cut into the night.

"Army trucks," Rafii said. "Like our six-by-sixes. Covered, haul men or equipment or supplies. Could be a nightly supply train to prevent it from being spotted by the satellites."

"Let them get a couple of miles ahead of us," Murdock said. "Then we'll follow them as far as we can. Move when you're ready, Rafii."

They waited five minutes after the last truck had gone past.

"I counted eighteen," Ching said. "Haul a heap of stuff in all those trucks."

"Let's hope they aren't two hundred more defensive troops," Murdock said.

Rafii pulled the Chevy onto the dirt road. The dust had settled, and they saw the camouflage fake trees and shrubs that evidently would be pulled back into the dirt trail before daylight.

"Not a straight road," Rafii said. "Taking some gentle curves one way and then the other. Make it harder to pick up by the satellite."

"We're two miles down the dirt," Ching said as he watched the odometer. "I'd say we're overdue for a checkpoint."

Rafii stopped and cut the lights, then he crept forward, trying to get his night vision established. "I want to see them before they see us," he said.

"Lock and load," Murdock said. The other three pushed magazines into weapons and checked chambers.

Two miles later, Rafii slowed and stopped. "I've got some lights about half a mile down the road. Could be a checkpoint or another truck coming this way. Up to you, Cap."

"Drive off the road to get the Chevy out of the wash of any truck lights," Murdock said. "We're on our shank's mares from here on in. Let's get the SATCOM up and running."

When the Chevy ground to a stop in the deep sand thirty yards off the dirt road, the four got out and Ching set up the SATCOM on the hood and positioned the antenna. Murdock took the handset.

"This is Underground One. We are in the area near the bomb factory. We are north of it. Figure you're coming up from the south. We'll try to circle the complex, when we find it. We're about five miles south of the town of Ar Rutbah on a dirt road. Our information is that there are two hundred troops defending the factory and they have heavy weapons. Be careful. Hope to find you soon."

The transmission went out in a quick burst when Murdock pushed the button. They looked at each other in the darkness.

"Okay, troops, we move. Rafii and I out front with the

sub guns, Gypsy with her AK follows us by ten yards and Ching brings up the rear with the other AK. If ten yards is too far to see each other, close it up. We'll stay at least fifty off the dirt track. Rafii, you keep the road in sight; I'll be on your left. Remember, this is a silent move. No firing unless you need to, to save your skin. Let's move."

There was almost no moon out and Murdock was both pleased and worried about that. A little moonlight would help them stay together and keep the road in sight. Too much and they'd be easy targets. He brought out the thermal imager and watched the area ahead as they walked. Nothing hot showed on the black screen. Then for a moment he saw something white skitter across the view screen and disappear. A desert hare, maybe a coyote. Did they have coyotes in the Syrian Desert? Murdock didn't know. He watched where he walked now and scanned ahead every two or three minutes.

They had moved out less than five hundred yards when Rafii dropped to the ground. Murdock saw him and went down. Behind him he saw the other two drop to the rocky desert sand. A moment later two sets of headlights bored through the darkness and they heard the growl of truck engines. Rafii skittered back beside Murdock.

"Sounds like they are loaded," Rafii said. "Hope they aren't hauling the bombs out to some strategic airstrip. Does Iraq have any planes big enough to haul a heavy, crudely made bomb aloft?"

"Not sure," Murdock said. Then they stopped talking as the two trucks rolled through the dirt on the road, setting up a good cloud of dust that settled back almost in place, with no wind to whip it around.

The two trucks moved slowly, and when they were past, Rafii jumped up, moved to his position, and waved the small party forward. Murdock was glad it was trucks and not a checkpoint. They could have a dozen men strung out at outposts on both sides at a roadblock. He certainly would. He hoped the Iraqis figured they were more secure than that.

They hiked for a half hour and in the distance could see a soft glow against some low clouds. Murdock brought them together still fifty yards off the dirt track.

"Gypsy, how are you doing?"

"Great. I'm a walker at home. This is no problem. We used to do twenty-mile marches in the battalion. I'd forgotten how heavy these damn AKs really are."

"You have some spare mags?"

"Three of them, in my shirt pockets."

"Let's pick up the pace. We're going to jog for two miles and see where that gets us." Murdock took the lead and set the pace. He didn't want to lose Gypsy. He put her right behind him and told her to sound off if she wanted to stop. She nodded.

After the first half mile they could see the lights in the distance. Not a lot, but in total darkness just a few stood out. Then, they all snapped off in a nanosecond.

Murdock stopped the crew.

"My guess is that they know a satellite is coming over and they don't want the lights to show. Damn smart of them. We've got the direction. We must be another three miles away. Let's keep moving. The satellite will be gone in ten or fifteen minutes. My guess is that the lights will come back on then."

They hiked forward again, Murdock using a bright star in the lightless night for his direction. Twenty minutes after the lights snapped off, they came back. Murdock put the people down on the ground and stared at the complex. They were closer than he had expected.

They were less than half a mile from the first building. It was one story and a line of trucks was parked near it as if waiting to unload.

"Damn," Ching said. "No fences, no barbed wire, no guard towers, just that one building and about twenty lights around it. Where is the factory?"

"Underground like the man told us," Murdock said. "That building must be an elevator housing to get goods down to the people working and living below."

"So where are the two hundred troops?" Gypsy asked. "They can't defend much underground."

"We might be right on top of them," Murdock said. "If I were defending this place, I'd take twenty squads of ten men each and position them in a ring around the factory. Put them out five hundred yards, which means we could be stumbling on them if they are there."

"Wait and listen" Rafii said. "These troops are well known for lack of discipline—jingling equipment, laughter, even smoking."

The other three looked at Murdock. "So we move and we listen," Murdock said in a soft whisper. "For starters we head due east away from the factory. We get out another half mile, then go south again to circle this place. Quiet, and listen for any enemy sounds. Rafii, lead out east."

Murdock dropped back beside Gypsy. He reached out for the rifle and she shook her head; then when he caught the barrel, she nodded and let go of the ten pounds of rifle and rounds. Murdock shouldered it with the muzzle up on the strap and moved forward.

They had gone what Murdock figured was almost a mile when Rafii dropped to the ground. The rest did the same. Murdock crawled up through the rocks and sand, and now and again cactus of some kind, to where Rafii lay at the edge of a wadi. The gully was twenty feet deep here and seemed to Murdock like it gradually became shallower as he looked south.

Murdock used the thermal imager. "Nothing," he said.

"Listen," Rafii whispered.

They did. Murdock heard it then, faintly but it was there—muted laughter, some conversation, the jingle of what could be mess gear, then a low soulful tune on a flute.

"Around, or through?" Rafii asked. "If they have a fire, we could wipe them out in our first volley."

"Too much noise. The next squad would surely hear and send out scouts. We stay silent and go around them. Find a place we can cross this wadi without breaking our legs."

The spot came south two hundred yards. Everyone knew about the Iraqi troops and moved silently. The flow of sudden downpour rainwater had formed a new small wadi that came in from the right, carving down the side of the larger gully. They went down there and up the far side, which wasn't as steep. They swept east again another half mile, then turned south.

Two more miles and Murdock turned them back west

again. They could just make out the faint lights of the elevator house at the factory. Murdock figured they were two miles south of the complex now and moved another five hundred yards to hunt a wadi they could vanish into if daylight came before he expected it to.

Rafii found another wadi five minutes later, and the four of them dropped down the eight-foot slopes and rested on the smooth, dry watercourse bottom.

"We're here," Ching said. "Now what the hell are we supposed to do?"

"First, we tell the rest of the platoon where we are," Murdock said. "Ching, do the honors again."

Ching set up the SATCOM and zeroed in the antenna at the orbiting relay satellite in the sky.

"This is Underground One," Murdock said. "We're in position about two miles south of the factory. Nothing shows aboveground except one camouflaged elevator house. I've an idea it may lower into the ground when not in use. We're waiting. I figure the factory is about eight or nine miles south of Ar Rutbah, which may put it in the Southern No-Fly Zone. How do we connect up with you guys? Out."

Ching lifted his brows, put away the radio, and slumped against the side of the wash. Murdock moved upward so he could see over the top of the wadi, and aimed the thermal imager into a small downslope. He passed it over the area several times but came up with no hot-blooded man or animal. They hadn't had time to work out any kind of a hookup plan before they left Kuwait. It was his job to get his platoon back together again before they attacked the factory. He shook his head. He had absolutely no idea how to contact the rest of the platoon. All he could do now was wait and see what developed the rest of the night, and hope that tomorrow in the daylight they could hide from any roving Iraqi patrols.

16

Saudi Arabia
Near the Iraq Border

Lieutenant (j.g.) Chris Gardner called his platoon together in the dust and dirt of the Syrian Desert fifty yards from the Iraq border. It had been a rugged day for the man now in charge of the Third Platoon of SEAL Team Seven. Twenty-four hours ago they had permission from Saudi Arabia to launch an attack on the bomb factory in Iraq from Saudi soil. They had flown into the small village of Ar Ruthiyah in two helicopters. The settlement was little more than a checkpoint for entry into Iraq on a dirt road. The Saudi army presence there was twelve men and one officer. Since almost no one ever came through the Syrian Desert into Saudi Arabia over this route, the men had little to do.

They were excited about the presence of U.S. helicopters and military men. A Saudi captain made the trip to assure his countrymen that all actions were under orders. The checkpoint was less than five miles from the border.

"First, we turn on the SATCOM and keep it on at all times from now on," J.G. Gardner said. "It's our only link with the commander and his men in Iraq. We know that the bomb factory is somewhere south of the little Iraq town they pinpointed. Our maps show that we are about eighty miles south of that town. Our last transmission from Murdock put the bad guys maybe ten miles south of the town. So we can chopper into the area and hit an LZ five miles away from the bomb factory at night and stay unnoticed.

"From there we work north until we find the bomb site or we find Murdock and his people. Then we recon the place and figure out how to take it down and get the nukes."

"Didn't Murdock say there could be two hundred troops

up there?" Jaybird asked. "Where will they be while we're doing this?"

"Fighting mad, I'd figure," Gardner said. "That's our job. Eliminate the troops, if they are there, then take on the factory."

"Didn't that transmission say the whole place was underground?" Fernandez asked.

"It did. Make it tougher, but not impossible. There must be air vents, exhaust shafts, and probably a good-sized elevator. We'll know more once we get to check it out in the daylight."

"How long has Murdock been in there?" Canzoneri asked.

Gardner wiped his face with his left hand, a small habit he had taken to lately. "That could be a problem. He was on his second night when he called us. That was last night. I hope we didn't miss a transmission while we were in the air since our SATCOMs couldn't hold on the satellite while we were flying. He's somewhere near the bombs now and has been most of today. We'll get in there as fast as we can with first dark, and hope he's still ready to show us the bombs."

"The captain says it gets dark here about eighteen hundred," Senior Chief Neal said. "So we take off in about thirty. Everyone had his gear checked? Double ammo. Miss Garnet, do you have everything in your special kit that you'll need?"

"Yes, sir, Senior Chief. I'm ready to go."

"Good. Senior Chief, you'll take Alpha Squad in one chopper and I'll have the rest of Bravo with me," Gardner said. "Miss Garnet with Bravo. Any questions?"

"We gonna have to walk out eighty miles?" Bradford asked.

"Not a chance. This is in the Iraq Southern No-Fly Zone. We own the air in there. We can call on air strikes if it comes to that. We have along a laser that we can use to pinpoint a target for the air jockeys. When the place is reduced and the bombs destroyed, we'll get our same two choppers in to pull us out. They have a SATCOM on the ground here and can communicate with the radios in the choppers."

"We've got a transmission, Lieutenant," Bradford said.

"Underground One here," the SATCOM speaker said. "Where the hell are you guys? Figured you'd be here last night. We've been playing tag and catch me if you can all damn day. We're still about five miles south of the plant. My guess is fifteen miles below that little Arab town. The natives seem to go to sleep at night here. That is the Iraq army, which is made up of the elite Home Guard. They headed back toward the factory about an hour ago. Looks like damn maneuvers out here. Squads of ten charging all over the place. They had a good workout, but never spotted us. My guess is they don't know we're here. You should be able to chopper in within fifteen miles of that town up there and not be heard by the Iraqis. If we hear you, we'll spot a red flare in a wadi where you can see it and the Arabs can't. Better go. Get in here, you guys, we got work to do."

"That's it, Lieutenant," Bradford said.

"Okay, we have our LZ, fifteen south of Ar Rutbah," Gardner said. "Let's load up. We're leaving fifteen early. Move it."

Five minutes later they lifted off the ground. The pilots had plotted their route to the small city, and the distance. They would come down in an LZ at what they figured was fifteen miles due south of the town. Flying time: twenty-six minutes at 147 mph.

J.G. Gardner still worried it. He wasn't sure he liked having a woman along on a combat mission like this one. He'd talked to her three or four times. She assured him she could use a sub gun or a rifle and that, yes, she had killed men in combat. She might have killed more than he had. He sat beside her in the chopper. She gave him a thumbs-up and he grinned. Anybody who could win a triathlon must have a lot of guts. From now on she was just another SEAL in a combat situation.

He went to the front to watch out the windows. They were about a hundred feet off the desert. As they passed fifteen minutes on the flight clock, the pilot lifted up to five hundred feet so they could spot a flare if one lit off below them. At twenty minutes they had seen nothing. At twenty-four, Gardner yelped.

"Flare, one o'clock, one red. That's our guys. Nobody else could see their signal." The pilot talked to the other chopper flyer and they had seen it, too. The birds came down fifty feet apart on the desert floor fifty yards from the flare. The second the wheels touched the ground, the SEALs jumped out and ran toward the wadi. They got out of the chopper's wash and dropped to the ground spread out in a defensive arc.

Gardner saw the men coming from the other chopper and waved them to his position.

"Lam," Gardner whispered. "Get up there and make contact. I figured somebody would be up here by now."

"Roger that, Lieutenant," Lam said. He lifted up and moved silently forward. He soon vanished in the night air that was starting to cool. The men were all sweating. They lay in the sand and rocks waiting for the contact.

Less than two minutes later, Lam materialized silently out of the darkness and waved. "We found them. Murdock says come on in."

The rest of Third Platoon hiked the fifty yards to the edge of the wadi and looked down. A small fire burned against the far bank. Four figures waved at them as they slid down the six-foot incline to the flat floor of the dry watercourse.

"Good to see you guys," Murdock said as he stood and held out a hand. Gardner shook it and frowned.

"What is this, chow time?"

Murdock took another bite of one of the cheese sandwiches they had brought with them and grinned. "It is now. I hope you guys brought food and water. We could take another look at the place tonight, but so far I don't see one fantasy way in hell that we can even get inside this monster, let alone destroy it with the bombs we brought."

He watched the men greeting each other then got their attention. "Men, I want you to meet the person who found out where this place was for us, and in the process compromised herself and became a kill target. Let me introduce Gypsy, our benefactor."

Gypsy had hung in the background; now she moved up and waved. "My English she isn't so good but best I can do. Better I am here than dead in Baghdad. Where is this woman scientist, this Kat Garnet?"

Kat come up and hugged Gypsy and they moved to the side and began talking.

Murdock sat down with the men. "This sucker is underground all right. We don't know how far. I'd guess it has at least four feet of concrete on top and then two feet of sand and rocks on top of that to make it impossible to spot. You brought that laser the brass talked about?"

"We did, and we have Prescott, who took a day of training on it and can make it work," Gardner said.

"We sure as hell might need it," Murdock said. "Those troops we saw were working the area in a circle around the factory. We heard there were two hundred. Could be more than that. They live out here. We almost ran into two kitchens. No bedrolls—they sleep on the ground. All day is given over to patrols, interlocking patrols with ten-man units. They range from a mile to three miles from the complex, so we never could be sure where they might show up. We had to back off and wait them out."

"So how do we get close enough during the day to get Prescott in there to use the laser?" Jaybird asked.

Murdock scowled. "My guess right now is that we don't. We go in at night and have the bombers primed and ready to go. They are going to need the bunker busters, those babies that can penetrate ten feet of concrete before they explode. Once we laser it and they get their first sightings in on it, they can plaster it with a dozen of the busters and that should do the job."

"So how can we be sure that we've destroyed the four bombs?" Wade Claymore asked.

Everyone looked at Murdock. "We can't. After the bombing, we'll have to send in a small team, three or four with Kat, and see what we can find. Once the place is wrecked, they may pull all the troops out and bring in the scientists and construction men to start seeing what they can salvage. If they do that quickly, we'll have a good chance to get in and get out."

"Sounds like a suicide mission," Senior Chief Neal said. "Doesn't sound like SEAL work."

"We don't do suicide operations," Vinnie Van Dyke said.

Everyone was quiet for a while. The two women had moved back to the group.

"I don't know about you guys, but my job out here is to

get those four bombs destroyed," Kat said. "I'm going in there if I have to go alone."

"We won't let you do that," Murdock said. "If it comes to a three- or four-man unit going in, we'll be with you. First we have to find out how to get the damn bunker busters in the neighborhood. Bradford, you have our regular SATCOM that sends and receives?"

"Yes, sir. I can have it set up in about thirty seconds."

"Do it."

A minute later Murdock keyed the mike after setting the transmission to the one Don Stroh usually used.

"Murdock to Stroh. Come in, big buddy, we've got a problem."

He waited. Nothing happened. He made the call twice more. There was no response. "Turn it to the CIA channel," Murdock said. Bradford did. "This is Underground One in Iraq. I need to talk to Don Stroh. Can you raise him for me?"

The response was immediate.

"Underground One. Stroh is in Kuwait. He's probably turned off his set. I'll contact him by land line. Call again in thirty minutes. Out."

It took them almost an hour to raise the CIA man in Kuwait.

"Murdock, this better be good. Pulled me away from the best steak I've had in years. These Kuwaitis really know how to cook."

"Bunker busters," Murdock said. "We need a dozen of them out here in the boonies tomorrow night."

"Tomorrow? It's that hard a site? Must be. You know the navy doesn't carry them around. We'll need the air force to fly them in. They can land here in Kuwait, I'd guess. You have the laser?"

"We do, and a man who can work it and a target to set up for you but only at night."

"Night is no problem. Getting the hardware in place might be. I'll call my boss and have him ring some tails. What time is it in DC? Damn. I'll call anyway. What time tomorrow night?"

"Anytime after dark. We'll set up a time when you get the bombs in Kuwait."

"You know how much just one of those busters costs?"

"You know how much one nuke on San Francisco would cost?"

There was a moment of dead air. Then Stroh let out a long sigh. "Yeah, you're right. I'll get the gears grinding. Might have to fly them in from Germany. I don't know. I've got to make some calls."

"Underground out."

He sat down against the side of the wadi. He had put out two guards, one on each end of the gully. They all had to get some sleep now since tomorrow they would be moving around to stay out of the way of the roving patrols.

Kat came up and sat next to him. "Hey, Gypsy tells me you had some action in Baghdad. Got shot at and everything."

"Yeah, true, but we won." He scowled. "Oh, damn. Mahanani, you got your goody kit?"

"Never without it. My CO's orders."

"Find Rafii. He took a round in the arm and I forgot to check it. He could be hurting."

"Rafii got shot and you forgot about it?" Kat asked. "You must have been busy. How could he forget about it?"

"Happens. Heard about this Marine in 'Nam who was in a vicious firefight with rockets and grenades. He was throwing grenades with his right hand and it wasn't until the short firefight was over that he realized that his left hand had been blown off. It can happen. There's such a surge of adrenaline during combat that it wipes out everything else. Rafii wasn't hit that bad, an in and out I think he said. But, yeah, we've been busy."

"Can I help him?"

"Mahanani can do it."

"Good seeing you again, Murdock."

"Good seeing you, too. You married yet?"

"Nope. You?"

"Almost. We have a new condo we bought."

"Sounds serious."

"It is."

"Murdock, we've got to get those four bombs. The President is afraid that Iraq will sell them to the highest bidder, probably some terrorists like al-Qaida."

"You hobnobbing with the President again?"

"When he calls, I drop everything and run right over to the Oval Office. Be surprised how intimidating that place is."

"I've been there."

She nodded. "Right, you told me about that. Anyway we have to destroy those bombs before they get spread around. That's why I've got to go in there and try. Even if I don't come out."

"You'll come out, Kat, or none of us will. Now, get some sleep. I don't want to have to carry you on my back tomorrow."

"Hey, sailor, that will be the day. Remember I can outrun you any day of the moon."

"The moon has days?"

"Absolutely. Good night, sailor."

One of the guards woke up Murdock at midnight. He had the graveyard shift. He always took his turn. Besides, he wanted to see the sun come up over the desert. For the first two hours he played with the thermal imager. Twice he saw small animals. He'd have to find out what they were. Once he thought he saw the flash of headlights far to the north. Then he decided it must be a flash of dry lightning. Too far away anyhow to worry about rain. He remembered once they were almost trapped in a gully when rain in the mountains poured down and the ravine suddenly filled with water twenty feet deep. Not this time.

The sun came over the eastern horizon. At the lip of the wadi he figured he could see twenty miles to the east. The red glow of the sun was muted somewhat by a ground haze that sent slivers of gold and red throughout the desert. Then the huge red orb broke free and the heat warmed him from the night desert chill. All too soon it would be too warm and then hot and then miserably hot.

At first he didn't believe it. Then the spot on the far sky raced closer and he could see that it was an aircraft. A jet? Or an old piston plane? He couldn't tell. He ran back to their camp, roused everyone, and told them to blend in with the sides of the gully in case the plane came directly over them.

Murdock stared at the craft over the lip of the wadi. He couldn't be sure if it was coming right at them. Then it turned, and from what he figured was less than half a mile away, it swept down to a hundred feet and powered straight down the wadi where they hid.

17

Murdock looked at his men, who had flattened against the walls of the wadi. All had pulled floppy hats down over their faces and their brown and tan desert cammies helped them blend in with the sand and dirt. The four of them in gray and brown shades of Iraqi clothing melted into the background as well.

He moved his head an inch so he could see where the low-flying plane would come from. It was a small, high-wing craft that could seat no more than four and must be used for scouting and recon around the facility. He had seen no airstrip, but here it would take a bulldozer only an hour to level out a dirt landing field.

He could hear the sound of the plane now. It might be over one more wadi, maybe fifty yards away; he couldn't be sure. Then he saw it, amazingly close, no more than a hundred yards to the left and a hundred feet in the air. It dipped its right wing and made a gentle turn away from them, coming close to the ground, then continued the turn and climbed as it headed back the way it had come. Murdock held the team in place for another two minutes, then called out.

"Relax, I think he missed us. If he spotted us, we should be hearing from a mounted patrol within half an hour. Let's talk."

The men and women gathered around. Kat and Gypsy sat close together whispering and grinning, laughing now and then. It seemed to Murdock that they had bonded like long-lost sisters.

"Bradford, crank it up and let's see what our chubby buddy from the Company has to say." When the SATCOM was aligned with the closest satellite, Murdock took the handset.

"Big Daddy Kuwait, this is Underground One."

The response was immediate.

"Yes, skinny little buddy, I'm here. You cause me more trouble. I had to get people out of bed. Well, turns out we do have some of the GBU-28s on station here in Kuwait. That's air force talk. They are delivered by the B-52 Stealth bombers. I can't say where they are or where they might come from, but some are now on station in Kuwait awaiting your orders. How's that for hot copy?"

"Not bad, Company Man. At first dark we'll move into position about five miles from our OP. We should have the GPS coordinates for you on the target around twenty hundred. Then we'll light up the target with the laser designator and hope we can coordinate the attack."

"Sounds like a winner. Oh, while we're on the air, some details. The GBU-28 is a weapon developed and tested and put into operation in twenty-eight days back in February of 1991. This is unheard of speed in munitions creation. The critter is four thousand six hundred and thirty-seven pounds and has six hundred and thirty pounds of tritonal high explosives. It has a four-thousand-four-hundred-pound penetrating warhead. The bombs are made from modified army artillery tubes because of their great strength. Only two of these weapons were used in Desert Storm, but many have been dropped in Afghanistan.

"The bomb is fitted with a GBU-27 LGV kit and is only fourteen and a half inches in diameter and nineteen feet long. Tests show that it can penetrate twenty feet of concrete and up to a hundred feet of soil without heavy rock formations. You were right; they don't cost much, only a hundred and forty-five thousand dollars each. Any questions?"

"We light up the target with our laser designator and keep it on until the bombs fall, right?" Murdock asked.

"Right, we trained your man on that."

"Will there be more than one bomb run by the B-52?"

"We don't know. I'm not sure how many of the bombs the B-52 can carry at one time. We'll get back to you on that. If we don't, or our commo goes out, just keep the target lit up until the planes go away."

"That's a roger, Company Man."

"Be careful out there. After the hit, those Iraqis left alive are going to swarm like enraged hornets."

"That's for sure. We're out."

"Why doesn't all of that HE go off when it first hits the concrete?" Jaybird asked.

"I've seen pictures of them," Gardner said. "It has a charge right on the nose that helps dig through the concrete, then blasts on through and explodes when it's underground."

"How much destruction will they do under that concrete roof?" Kat asked.

"We don't know," Gardner said. "But any explosion inside a concrete box like that will be magnified by ten times in the concussion, the blast, the shrapnel effect of blowing things apart. Will it take out a completed nuclear bomb? I have no idea. Let's hope we get to go inside and see for ourselves."

"Worst scenario," Murdock said. "We hit it with two of the bunker busters. That building could be a hundred yards long, size of a football field. Would two bombs totally destroy it? Probably not. So what do the Iraqis do?"

"If the nuclear bombs are intact, they get them to the surface somehow and truck them out of there to another site," Fernandez said. "They know this plant is compromised, so they want to cut their losses and get the bombs to a new safe place."

"Good, good," Murdock said. "So we need to plan for that. We need a team with twenties somewhere north of the factory and within half a mile of the dirt road to take out the trucks if they try to bug out with the nukes."

"Why not hit them as soon as they come out of the building?" Senior Chief Neal asked.

"Easy," Kat said. "We need to know how many of them survived. If they truck out only two, that probably would be it. If we hit the first one at the elevator or the crane that brings it up, they might not try to move any others."

"Hey, Kat. Your momma didn't waste her money on your schooling," Jaybird cracked.

"The lady is right," Murdock said. "What else do we need to talk over?"

"How to stay alive until dark," Gardner said.

"You're the experienced one there, Lieutenant," Murdock said. "The con is yours."

For the next four hours the platoon stayed in the wadi. Gardner had lookouts a quarter of a mile ahead and spread a quarter mile to each side to watch for roving patrols. None came near until after noon. The scouts scurried back and the platoon did a quick retreat down the wadi and then over a quarter of a mile to avoid the two ten-man patrols that were converging on their old position. Gardner had the rest area policed, searched, and combed and brushed before they left, to give no indication anyone had ever been in that gully.

By dusk they had moved twice more and Murdock readied the men for the hike to the factory.

"We all get as close as we can," he said. "Gardner tells me he believes the farthest out the patrols are on their night watch is about a mile from the elevator. We're still on the right end of the factory to find the lift. At first dark we'll move forward and get into position. Then I want Gardner to take three men and two Bull Pups and hike a mile north along the dirt road. Stay a quarter mile off it and sit down and wait. If you see any trucks coming north on the road after the bombers hit, blast them. We have our Motorolas. We'll tell you if we think they are hauling out any of the nukes. Any questions?"

"Yeah," Howard said. "Can you check with the SATCOM to be sure that our choppers are in position just across the border in Saudi Arabia waiting for our call for a ride?"

"Good idea. Bradford, set up and contact them at the base. Do we have their call sign?"

"No, but Don Stroh should. I'll get it."

Ten minutes later the sun dropped below the western horizon and they headed toward the bomb-making facility. Lam took the point and led them down gullies and over small ridges and into a slight rise that he figured was a mile from the edge of the factory. He was surprised when the lights came on and they watched as the elevator shaft lifted straight up out of seemingly virgin desert.

"About a mile and a quarter," Lam said. "Those lights sure seem bright out here in nowhere."

It was totally dark by then and Murdock used the global positioning system box to pinpoint where they were. He wrote down the figures on a pad and then watched as Prescott picked out his spot of dirt, unstrapped the high-powered laser designator from his back, and set it up. He sighted in on the easy-to-see elevator building and told Murdock he was ready. Any people in the target area being electronically illuminated by the laser would not know it was happening.

"Light them up," Murdock said. Prescott turned on two switches, adjusted his aim a moment, and nodded.

"We're set. We're on target waiting for the big bird."

Bradford handed Murdock the ready-to-go SATCOM mike.

"Company Man, your ears on?"

"Ready and waiting, Underground."

"Your target is lighted up with the laser designator. Do we leave it on now or turn it off and wait for the planes to take off?"

"We have two birds, each with a pair of eggs. They just got a five-minute alert and will be taking off at that time. Flight time to your position at six hundred and fifty-two miles per hour is barely a warm-up. It's four hundred and ninety miles, the pilot tells me, and estimated flight time is forty-five minutes. They'll be on an Iraq overflight all the way but expect no trouble."

"If they take off in three minutes, their ETA will be . . ." Murdock looked at his watch in the beam of his pencil flash. "That would make it twenty-fifty-three. Right. We'll turn off the designator now and save on the battery. We don't want it to go dead before they get here."

"Right, Underground. I'll let you know if they are late in their takeoff. Otherwise, good hunting."

The platoon had gathered around the radio and heard the low-volume speaker. Now they drifted away.

"Gardner, take your men with two Bull Pups. About a mile. When you get to your spot, check in on the Motorola. A shallow wadi would give you great cover."

"What I was thinking. We're out of here. If no trucks come, bring us back so we can get in on the assault, or whatever."

"Will do."

Prescott turned off the laser. The only difference they could hear was the cessation of a slight hum. Then they waited.

Kat sat down beside Murdock. "Is this going to work? I mean, can the bombs kill those four nukes in there?"

"We don't know. The first one or two blasts might bring the whole roof down on the bombs and smash them into junk. Four or five or six feet of concrete is a load. I remember that double-deck freeway in Oakland when the top one collapsed on the lower one during the earthquake. Only one guy survived under that mass of concrete, and that was a miracle."

"Won't this be reinforced with rebar?"

"Probably. But six hundred pounds of high explosives going off in a contained area creates a tremendous effect."

"So we'll hope." She frowned, silent for a moment. "How will we know if all four of the bombs are in there? I mean, if the place is a total wreck, we still have to go in and count heads, or bombs in this case."

"True. We just have to wait and see, but not wait much longer. How are you and Gypsy getting along?"

"She's so wonderful. I love her like a sister. She's an artist, did you know that? Made a living painting. Now that takes talent, and in Iraq it must have been horrendous. She's going out with us and I'm going to set her up in Arlington with a nice little studio. She'll be making a living within six months."

"Planning ahead is good. Now how much more time?" He used the shielded pencil light and checked his wristwatch. He had banned glowing dials or numerals on watches in his platoon after one of his men was shot in a close encounter when the other guy aimed at the SEAL's glowing watch face. "Looks like we have another twenty minutes. Prescott. Turn on the laser in ten minutes."

"Aye, aye, Commander."

Gypsy moved up and sat beside Kat. Gypsy now wore a pair of cammie pants one of the men had given her.

"Is this going to work?" she asked.

"We hope so," Kat said.

"How will we know?"

"That's a problem," Murdock said. "No matter how much or how little damage the bombers do, we still have to go in there and verify the bombs are ruined, or destroy them ourselves. That is, Kat has to destroy them."

"If you go in and Kat goes in, then I go, too," Gypsy said. She held up her hand as Murdock started to protest. "This is my country, Commander. Building those bombs is partly my fault. I sat by and let it happen along with about twenty million other Iraqis. I'm going. Remember I can use this AK-47."

Murdock watched her face in the thin moonlight for a moment then nodded. He looked into the darkness. "Bradford, you've kept the box on receive?"

"Yes, sir. No transmissions for us since that last one from Stroh."

The Motorolas came to life.

"Murdock. This is Gardner. We're in position about a mile north of the lights and a quarter off the dirt road. Found a nice little three-foot-deep wadi we can use as a firing platform if we need to. I'm not betting one way or the other. We can take out four or five six-bys if they come this way. Let us know what's happening."

"Right, Gardner," Murdock said. "We're about fifteen out from the drop. Stay loose and watch for any night activity by those damn ten-man patrols."

"Will do. Out."

They waited. To one side Kat and Gypsy talked in low tones. Murdock looked at his watch three more times. After the last one he used the Motorola. "Okay, men and women. My watch shows the flyboys should be here within two or three minutes. Everybody lock and load and keep your eyes open. The minute that first bomb hits, these wadis may come alive with two hundred troops. We don't know what they will do. Steady as it goes."

"How high will they be on the bomb runs?" Jaybird asked on the radio.

"No data on that," Murdock said.

"Doesn't matter much," Gardner said on the net. "Once the bomb's guidance system locks on the illuminated target, it zaps down a straight line at the target. This isn't a missile, so it doesn't have lightning speed, just gravity, but directed gravity."

"We might not hear the birds, then?" Canzoneri asked.

No one answered.

A minute later Lam used the radio. "Cap, we've got company. Back side of the wadi, maybe fifty yards out. One of those damn ten-man patrols is coming our way. I don't see how they can miss us."

18

"How many silenced weapons do we have?" Murdock asked. "Sound off, now on the net."

A moment later he knew: two MP-5s and one sniper rifle. "You three, move up toward Lam where you can spot the patrol. Pick off the men on the end of the line. Do it quickly. Be sure of each shot. Go."

Luke Howard crawled up the side of the three-foot-deep wadi he had found near Lam, and looked into the night. A moment later Kat slid in near him with her MP-5. Jaybird came down on the far side of Kat with the other MP-5. They all stared into the blackness.

"How could Lam spot them?" Kat whispered.

"He has cat eyes and elephant ears," Jaybird whispered back. Then he pointed. "There, to our left just a bit. Ten of them; no, nine. Let's get to work."

Jaybird fired the MP-5 when he figured the line was thirty yards from them. The MP-5 is not a long-range weapon, but he saw one man double up and go down. Kat had waited for Jaybird, then she fired as well on single shot. She knew she had fired true. She saw a man stumble and fall. Had she killed him? She shook her head and sighted in on the next man. Howard had been firing since he first saw the line. He went for the far end and put down three of them before one of the men shouted and the rest of the patrol hit the ground. Kat saw one lift up, and she aimed and fired. The man pivoted backwards and she couldn't see him anymore. For a moment the thrill of the hunt had carried her along. Now she closed her eyes and felt sweat on her forehead. She had just killed another man, maybe two. This was not why she had come on this mission. But it was part of her job if the mission was to be accomplished. She brushed moisture from her fore-

head and concentrated on where the remaining men must be.
She could see no movement, no bodies. She wished that she
had the thermal imager. She had just killed again. How long
would it take her to get over it this time? She closed her eyes
and a heavy weight beat down on her shoulders.

A man at the far end of the line of Iraqi soldiers lifted up
to run back the way they had come. Howard cut him down
with two shots. Then all was silent.

"Cap, we put down six of the nine," Jaybird whispered
into his Motorola. "I think the others are crawling back the
way they came. Should we pursue?"

"Negative," Murdock said. "At least they didn't fire, alert-
ing anyone else. Let them go. Keep watch. We should have
some action from those planes at any minute."

"I've got aircraft, two of them," Lam said. "Might be at
ten or fifteen thousand, coming our way."

"Right, Lam. Alert, everyone. Keep your eyes open. We
don't want any more surprises. Prescott, is that laser on and
working?"

"Up to speed and lighting up that elevator shaft."

"I've got three trucks coming into the factory from the
north," Gardner said. "We let them pass. Might be on hand
for the reception. I can hear the planes now, too."

A minute later they all heard something. It wasn't the
whish, whish, whish of an artillery round going over. It was
more of a whistle of air rushing past a falling object. They
all watched the factory complex and the elevator building.
One truck geared down and stopped in front of the building.

At almost the same time a flash lit up the sky and a roaring blast thundered across the desert. Moments later the
ground shook as the penetrator bomb, the GBU-28, exploded
underground.

Seconds later a second bomb flashed as the first charge
bored a small hole through the concrete and the nineteen-
foot-long bomb blasted into the underground complex and
detonated the main charge. Again the ground shook. The
other two trucks had stopped short of the elevator house. The
third bomb struck the elevator structure itself, and it and its
lights evaporated in the blast; and the third huge explosion
reverberated through the ground to the SEALs over a mile

away. One more flash came, the fourth, followed by the resulting detonation of the six hundred and thirty pounds of tritonal high explosive deep underground.

Smoke poured out of where the elevator shaft used to be. Murdock studied the complex with binoculars Jaybird had brought for him. The near side looked like it had sunk ten feet below the desert level. Farther along he saw another huge ball of smoke gushing out of the underground factory. He used the thermal imager and scanned the front of the area. He saw one man near the truck. He lay on his back, evidently wounded. Another form near him glowed for a moment, then the image faded into the black background.

Nowhere else did he spot any live figures. Where were the workers and the scientists from the nuclear bomb factory? Another exit? An emergency exit? He scanned again, and this time far down the side he saw more than twenty images of men as they ran out of a depression in the desert and hurried away from the complex.

Murdock talked to his Motorola. "Lam, you know where those dead Iraqi soldiers are?"

"Yes, sir."

"Go out there and bring back one of the uniforms. Move fast."

"I'm gone."

"Rafii, find me. I'm near the laser."

Two minutes later, Rafii slid in beside Murdock. He let Rafii look through the thermal imager.

"Quite a bunch of them out there. We need you to go down and find out what they're saying. Talk to them. Get an idea how bad it was underground. Learn if the bombs were destroyed or if they are still inside and if so how many. We have to know this. If you can find somebody in charge, bring him back with you. Tie him up and gag him if you have to. We need a body to question."

Just then the ground shook again and this time there was a rumble of breaking and smashing. Murdock used the binoculars on the factory. "Most of the roof of the place has crashed down. It must have flattened everything inside. Almost all of the factory is now nothing but a ten to twenty-foot hole in the ground. Lam, where is that uniform?"

"Coming. This dead guy didn't want to give it up."

Murdock used the thermal imager to look at the surrounding desert. He spotted three groups of soldiers moving slowly toward the factory. He wondered how many more there were. Had there really been two hundred? They had spotted no more than fifty in their travels.

Lam slid in beside Rafii. "This must be for you. Hope it fits. Oh, it's got three bullet holes in it, but there isn't much blood."

Rafii snorted and pulled off his civvies and put on the uniform including a floppy hat.

"Take an AK with you, Rafii, and go now," Murdock said. "Keep your Motorola out of sight, but give us a radio report as soon as you can. Move it."

"I'm going most of the way with him," Lam said. "Nothing for me to do here."

Murdock frowned, then nodded. "Gardner, put twenties into those two trucks you have out there. When they are reduced, come on back here to the home base."

"That's a roger. Give them something new to think about."

"I want everyone here on a perimeter defense," Murdock said. "You silent weapon guys get back here fast. We don't know who might come calling. We're holding tight here until we get more intel on the factory's insides."

Murdock heard the familiar crack of the 20mm rifles and soon the explosion when the rounds hit the two trucks. One of them burst into a fireball of vaporized fuel and soon both were burning furiously.

"Scratch two trucks," Gardner said. "Returning to home base. Don't shoot us as we come in."

Lam and Rafii jogged toward the dust pall that showed even in the desert night. It hovered over the factory that now was a hole in the ground.

"We get there, you stay in the boonies, and I'll go in and see what I can find out," Rafii said. "My guess is there weren't many soldiers inside. I can fake it coming from one of the protection units."

They jogged down a wadi that would lead almost to the edge of the factory area. There were no fences, no protection.

Fifty yards from the gaggle of men they saw and heard just outside the factory, the two SEALs stopped.

"Stay here," Rafii told Lam. "I'm going to appear out of the dark for a report for my sergeant."

"Luck," Lam said.

Rafii nodded, went over the lip of the wadi, and jogged toward the men standing around talking. As he came closer, he picked up bits and pieces of conversations.

". . . then suddenly the whole side of the wall caved in and I ran like hell. I heard the explosion, but we've had accidents before."

". . . I saw my supervisor blown through a wall and land in a heap near my desk. Didn't know where to run."

As Rafii came up, the civilians paid no attention to him. He looked from one small group to another until, in the shifting moonlight from the partly cloudy sky, he saw a man who could be a boss of some kind. He wore a white shirt and a tie. His jacket had one sleeve partly burned away. Rafii hurried up to him and gave a salute.

"Sir, I'm here from my unit to ask for orders and to evaluate what happened. Was it an accident?"

The man in the shirt and tie snorted. "No accident. We were bombed. You were outside; did you hear the aircraft?"

"We heard nothing until the explosions."

"Four years of work gone in an instant," the man said.

"The bombs, they are safe?" Rafii asked.

"No. One of them was smashed when the first part of the roof fell in. The other two are in a position where we might be able to lift them out and save them. We have a crane and a backhoe. The work has begun already. Your army units can't help. We were worried about land invaders, probably from Saudi Arabia. We didn't think about penetrating bombs."

"Then we should maintain our positions?"

"Do whatever you wish. You will be relieved when the general is ready. There is nothing you can do here. We must get these men out of the desert and into that small town as quickly as possible. All of our food and water has been smashed into dust. I have one radio that still works. Baghdad knows about this attack. I'm sure they will send out rescue units and food and supplies. Now get back to your unit. The military is not in good favor with our men."

"My lieutenant asks that you come back with me to explain what he is to do with his men."

"Impossible. I have duties here. Half of our staff was killed. Dozens of workers are injured. I have to stay here to direct—"

Rafii moved quickly beside the man. His pistol pressed hard into the man's side.

"You will come with me now, or die on this spot. Your choice. I really don't care one way or the other."

"You must be joking . . ." The man's face clouded and he squinted at Rafii. "You have an accent that I don't recognize . . ."

Rafii pushed the pistol muzzle harder into the man's side.

"We will walk directly away from the men here. You will not look or speak to any of them. Otherwise you are dead. Do you understand me completely?"

"Yes. When we find your lieutenant, I will order him to cut out your eyes, then to chop off your balls and shoot you in both knees before he kills you. Enjoy life while you can, you traitor."

"Keep walking, and no more talking. Hurry."

Fifty yards from the factory, Lam saw them coming and met them with a gag and plastic strips to tie the man's hands behind his back.

Lam grinned. "You did good, little buddy. I might put you in for a silver star."

"Is that good? I'd rather have a two-week leave in Maui."

"Who wouldn't?"

They worked ahead quickly but with Lam out front watching and listening. He spotted a ten-man patrol to the left, but they were heading for the factory complex and didn't see the three men crouched in the darkness.

Fifteen minutes later they came near the wadi where the SEALs lay.

Lam went in first. He took his time. Soon he spotted where two of the SEALs lay facing outward with guns at the ready. He moved slowly, without a sound, and, working between them, passed both without their knowing it. He came up behind one and dropped on the sand beside him.

"Watch closely out there. Lam and Rafii are coming," Lam said.

Mahanani jolted to one side. "Lam, you son of a bitch. How did you do that? I've been watching for you."

"Trade secret. Rafii, bring in our guest."

Ten minutes later Murdock sat beside the supervisor from the bomb plant. Rafii had convinced him it would be better for him if he talked.

"What do you have to lose now? The bombs are destroyed, and your plant is a total loss. You said one of the bombs was smashed and was leaking radiation."

"Yes, the six-feet-thick concrete roof fell directly on it. It killed four men and two more were doused with radiation. They died almost at once."

"The other two bombs you said are intact?" Rafii prompted.

"Yes, they are in a section at the extreme far end. They were ready for shipment. The slab roof held on one side, so they were spared being smashed flat."

"You're starting tonight to get them out?" Murdock asked.

"Yes, a backhoe and a crane."

"But you have no trucks," Murdock said.

"Before I came out here, I told Baghdad of the disaster and they are sending rescue units and trucks to take the bombs away."

"When?" Rafii asked.

"They will leave Baghdad at daylight."

"When will you have the bombs to the surface?" Rafii asked.

"My men are experts at this. It should take them no more than six hours, unless the rest of the roof caves in."

Murdock motioned to Rafii and the two walked away. Lam stood over the Iraqi.

"Why don't we save them the trouble of lifting out the bombs?" Murdock said. "How much military did you see around the area?"

"None at all. One squad had started to hike into the place, but they hadn't made it there yet."

"If they can lift the bombs out of there, we can lower Kat

into the hole and she can do her thing on them with timers."

"Should work. We take the whole platoon in as backup."

"Now, what about the fourth bomb? We know they had four. He's talking only about three."

They went back to the supervisor where he sat in the sand, and Rafii knelt down in front of him.

"You're doing fine. You may live to see your children. Now, tell us about the other two nuclear bombs that were built at this facility."

The man held up both hands. "Three bombs, we only built three, that's all we were ordered to build."

Rafii's fist slashed out and drove into the man's jaw, slamming him to the side, where he sprawled in the sand and rocks of the desert. Rafii jumped up and pushed his boot down on the supervisor's neck, pressing his face into the sand.

"For a man about to die, you seem unusually stupid. You will tell me about those other two bombs in ten seconds, or you will die in extreme pain where you lie."

19

Rafii kept his boot on the supervisor's head, pressing the side of his face into the sand.

"Yes, I am with the Americans here to blow you apart, but I am also a Saudi Arabian. I know how pain feels, and I know how to inflict it in ways the Americans would never do. Do not think you can fool me. Now, I ask you once more. How many bombs did you build and where are they?"

Rafii took his foot off the prisoner's head and he sat up warily. He looked closer at Rafii and nodded. "Yes, I can see you are one of us. So I will tell you. We built three bombs and one left the complex yesterday. I don't know where they took it. The other two are still inside the wreck of our building."

"Only three bombs?" Rafii asked.

"Yes, only three."

Rafii shot the man in the right knee, shattering the bones, bringing wails of pain and fury from the supervisor. He sprawled on the dirt again, wailing and screaming. Rafii slapped him hard twice and the man stopped screaming. Tears streamed down his face. He held his knee with both hands, trying to stop the gush of blood that spurted out of arteries and pooled on the sandy soil.

Rafii knelt in front of him, the pistol aimed at the supervisor's heart. "Now, big important man, how many bombs did you build and where are they?"

"Yes, yes, we built four, complete. Two more in early stages. Four are done. They took one away in a big tractor trailer truck yesterday morning."

"Four bombs?"

"Yes, on the grave of my father, only four completed bombs."

"One was smashed flat by the roof?"

"Yes, destroyed and leaking radiation."

"Is it away from the other two bombs you're trying to get out?"

"Yes, other end of the plant. No radiation around the two undamaged bombs."

"Good, you did good. How many soldiers guarding the area?"

"Only thirty. Two truckloads left two days ago."

"Good." Rafii and the man had been speaking in Arabic. Murdock got most of it, but Rafii filled him in on the basics.

"So, the quicker we go in, the better," Murdock said. "Lam, out two hundred yards and take a look at the place. We'll be leaving shortly."

Gypsy came up to Murdock. She held out her hand. "Give me your pistol. This evil one is of no more use to us. Right? You take no prisoners, right?"

Murdock nodded. He gave her his automatic. "Wait until we're gone fifty yards, then catch up with us."

He called the others around. "We're going into the complex and Kat will destroy the two bombs left. Then we have to try to track that fourth one that is out there in the desert somewhere on a highway tractor truck. Let's move. Squad order. Bravo first. Five yards separation. Go now."

Gypsy waited behind as the others left; then she stood in front of the supervisor who had tied part of his shirt around his shot knee. He looked up, surprised to see her.

"Who are you?" he asked.

"I am a real Iraqi patriot. And a close family member of two young men your Secret Police killed because they were suspected of being spies. Only suspected, and they were innocent. You and your kind killed them. Now I will kill you in partial payment."

"No, I had nothing—"

The sharp report of the weapon echoed down the wadi. The round entered the supervisor's forehead, fragmented into a dozen hot chunks of lead, and blasted through the man's brain, killing him instantly.

Gypsy looked down at the dead man in the faint light, and then kicked him in the head twice, once for each of her nephews who had been shot by the Secret Police. She shook her head as she hurried to catch up with the rest of the SEALs. When she tagged on to the end of the Alpha Squad, no one asked what had happened or where she had been or what the shot was. They didn't have to ask.

Five hundred yards from the sunken nuclear bomb factory, the squads stopped. Lam had been out ahead by a hundred. He came back. He reported to Murdock.

"They're working out there. Somehow they rigged up lights—off emergency generators, I'd guess. Must be fifteen men there with that backhoe and a crane. So far I didn't see anything that looked like a bomb. They have men and cables in a hole they have dug near the back wall of the factory."

"Military?"

"I saw part of one squad standing around. Not in any kind of a defensive mode."

Murdock turned to Kat. "Are you ready with your gear?"

"Ready and waiting. I can rappel down if I need to."

"Good." Murdock pulled the men in around him. "We'll move up to a hundred yards and go into a line of skirmishers. We saturate the area with twenties, and then move ahead fifty yards and recon the place. We might have some return fire by that time. Let's move."

They kept ten yards apart now, usual combat procedure. When they were only a hundred yards from the lights, they spread out in a line facing the bomb factory.

Murdock used the Motorola. "Okay, twenties. I want each man to put three rounds in and around those lights. You snipers take any forms you see moving. Fire when ready."

At once three twenties fired and Murdock brought his Bull Pup up and sighted in. The first two rounds were airbursts immediately over the crane and backhoe. Murdock saw through his scope some men scattering as he fired. He saw one round hit the crane and blow the engine apart. Three rounds later, all the lights in the area went out.

When the twenty-one rounds of the 20mm high-explosive shells had been fired, Murdock ordered the men ahead to fifty yards. There had been no return fire from anyone near the end of the bomb factory.

At fifty yards it was still too dark to see much. Murdock

waited. Something didn't seem right. He used the radio. "Anybody have any bad vibes about this place right now?"

Lam came on first. "Skipper, I don't like it. No return fire. Where are those thirty rifles?"

"Something wrong," Jaybird said. "Maybe a squad in reserve out in the dark waiting for us to move in."

"It smells," Gardner said. "They have some resources they haven't used yet. We just don't know what they are."

"Lam, do a half circle from here around to the left. Stay out a hundred and see what you can find. Take a Bull Pup and the thermal imager with you in case you get into a firefight."

"Done, Cap. I'm gone."

They waited.

Kat lay in the sand beside Gypsy. "When we get back to the States, I'm going to set you up in your own little gallery. You will live with me in my apartment. My roommate got married and left, so I've plenty of room. I figure you can paint for six months, and then we'll have enough pieces to open a gallery somewhere. Oh, not one on the best street in town, but somewhere you can get some exposure, some notice."

"It's a dream. The Company said they would take me out if I got into real danger of being exposed and shot. I didn't think the Secret Police would ever catch me, but evidently they had doubts about me for a year or more. I was lucky. I just hope it can happen."

"It will happen, Gypsy. We have connections. I work directly for the President. He can do anything. The Company owes you a retirement check every month." Kat nodded in the darkness and put her hand on the Iraqi woman's shoulder. "It will happen."

The radios spoke softly then.

"Oh, yeah," Lam said. "I have about a dozen ghostly white forms up here about halfway around. Their weapons all lined up on the spot where the backhoe sits. They have a machine gun and two rocket launchers. I'm putting an airburst over the group, then a quick HE on the machine gun, and another one on the rocket launchers. Any left I'll pick off with the 5.56. Any questions?"

"Go," Murdock said.

They waited. A moment later an airburst lit up the desert for a lightning-fast second, then the booming sound of the detonating round came over the half-mile distance. It was followed quickly by two more 20mm rounds going off. A third and then a fourth sounded before the radio spoke.

"Okay, I'd say the threat is over. The rocket launchers are down and the MG is a bunch of scrap metal. I got all but two of them who were running scared. They lost their rifles and are heading deeper into the desert. I'd say the next move is yours, Cap."

"Roger that. Good shooting. Get back here fast. We won't leave until you hook up. Besides, I want that imager."

"Moving," Lam said.

Five minutes later, when Lam jogged into the platoon, Murdock had given out the assignments. Alpha Squad would go in with assault fire by all weapons. Bravo Squad would move a hundred yards across the face of the target to stay in reserve for any more surprises. They would be in a perimeter defense and keep alert for any troops in any direction.

"Kat and Gypsy, on me. Line of skirmishers. When you are on line, sound off."

Two minutes later Bravo Squad had double-timed to the left to get into position and the last Alpha Squad man checked in.

"Let's do it, walking assault fire. One round every five seconds. No automatic. Let's do it, now."

The first shots sounded in the quiet desert darkness. Then the shots came one after another as the men and two women marched forward. Kat set her mouth in a firm line and triggered her MP-5 every five seconds. Beside her Gypsy fired her AK-47 from the hip, aiming at the dark bulk of the crane and backhoe ahead of them. For a moment there was no return fire. Then a few shots came from the two vehicles.

"Automatic fire, let's run forward," Murdock barked into the radio. At once the firing increased as the weapons went fully automatic in five-round bursts. It staggered as they changed magazines; then it picked up again.

Murdock came to the crane first. The long arm had slumped into the depression that had been the bomb factory.

He took cover behind the smashed cab and could hear no more return fire. He pulled out the large, two-cell flashlight Jaybird had brought for him and, holding it at arm's length, shined it around. A shot came from the right and he turned and fired six rounds from the 5.56 Bull Pup into the area.

There were no more shots from anyone in or near the bomb factory. More flashlights came on and shined into the hole. Murdock stood at the very edge and looked down fifteen feet. A man lay there holding up one arm. The other arm was a bloody mass.

"Okay, okay, okay," the Arab shouted.

"Rafii, on me," Murdock shouted. "Just behind the crane."

Rafii ran up beside his CO.

"Man down there. Talk to him."

Rafii leaned down and shouted in Arabic at the man below.

"You in the hole. Anyone else alive down there?"

"No, two with me but they are dead. All dead. Artillery shells. All dead."

The side of the dug-out hole next to the slanting roof of concrete had a sloping side.

"I'm going down," Rafii said.

"Go," Murdock said.

Rafii slid down the side with his flashlight beam playing on the wounded man. He checked the Iraqi quickly, took a pistol he had, and looked around. He aimed his light around the open space between the slanted roof slab and the concrete wall it rested on. Then Rafii vanished under the slab. He came back to the side a moment later.

"Skipper, looks like the real thing down here. Better send Kat down with her gear. Two big mothers, fifteen, sixteen feet long. Lots of metal and wires. Fat little jobs, maybe four feet across."

"Any more Iraqis down there?"

"Don't see any, Skipper."

"I'm coming down with three men to clear the area before we risk Kat."

Kat had knelt down beside Murdock.

"I'll wait here," Kat said. She snapped on her flashlight to check below. At once a rifle fired from down near the end of the fallen roof. Another rifle answered it on automatic fire. Murdock recognized the heavy sound of the AK-47. The rounds came from the top of the ground. It had to be Gypsy firing. When the shooting stopped after twelve to fifteen shots, they heard a scream from across the way, then silence.

Murdock took the closest three men and went over the side and down to the bottom. They worked into the vacant area under the slanted slab. The spot they had to clear was only thirty feet deep and ten feet high at the wall. The fallen roof tapered down rapidly and hit the concrete floor of the structure fifteen feet from the side.

"I've got two KIAs," Jaybird said on the radio.

"I've got another down and dead," Luke Howard reported.

"Any live ones?" Murdock asked.

"None here. Clear in this section the farthest back," Jaybird said. "I'd say were clear."

"Clear," Murdock repeated. "Kat, come on down but be careful. How many flashlights you want down here to light your work?"

"Four should be enough. I'm sliding down."

Murdock met her at the edge of the cut and lit her way back to the first large device. Kat checked it from one end to the other.

"It's the real thing. I need to take off two panels and put in the explosives. I don't have the C-4. I want two pounds for each one."

Murdock used the radio. "Who has the C-4? We need eight of the quarter pounders. Gather it up and get it down here."

As he spoke, he heard gunfire on the surface. Then the radio came on.

"We're taking incoming," Bradford said. "We're coming over the side and into the hole."

Just then an explosion rocked the fallen-in roof of the factory twenty feet behind where the backhoe stood.

"Come on in," Murdock said on the Motorola.

"Yeah, getting a line on the shooters," Gardner said. "Look to be about a hundred yards north of us. Putting twenties on them now."

Murdock stood in the opening. One more rocket came in.

It went high overhead and hit in the middle of the fallen-in roof. Murdock figured it was a shoulder-fired rocket. He heard the twenties going off.

"Oh yeah," Gardner said. "We got them pinned with the twenties. Now Fernandez is picking them off using the thermal imager. We figure there were about ten of them. Not more than two or three left who can move. Get on with your work down there."

"That's a roger, Gardner. Protect our backs here. Good work. See you soon." He looked around and saw most of his men, who had slid into the hole when the shooting came.

"Where's Gypsy?" he asked Jaybird.

"Haven't seen her."

"Gypsy, you have your radio on?" Murdock called. There was no response. "Gypsy, are you down, hurt? Where are you?"

Nothing.

"I want all but four of you back up to the top and find Gypsy. She must be hit or she'd respond. Move it."

The men crawled up the slope and over the top. Murdock went inside to where two men each held two flashlights. Kat had used impact wrenches and screwdrivers and had removed a two-foot-square panel near the nose of the first bomb.

She took one of the lights and looked inside.

"Oh, yeah, they got it right, but it's easy enough to blow apart. We'll blow up the trigger and fusing end and leave nothing that can set off the chain reaction."

"Any radiation?"

"Sure, but not a lot. We won't use that much C-4. I might cut back on the amount. Now let me get to work."

"How long on each one?" Murdock asked.

"About an hour. This has to be done right."

Murdock left and crawled up the dirt slope to the surface of the desert. He used the radio.

"Anybody found Gypsy?"

Ching came on. "Yeah, Skipper, just found her. That first sniper in the box must have hit her. Then she nailed the bastard. Not sure how bad she's hit. Shoulder, maybe her chest. Better get Mahanani over here."

"I'm running," Mahanani said on the radio. "Stop any

bleeding if you can. She doesn't have much blood she can afford to lose. Be there in about five minutes. Where are you from the crane?"

"About fifty feet south of it, twenty feet from the edge of the cave-in. Can't miss us. I'll have a red carnation in my lapel."

Murdock ran to the south looking for Gypsy and Ching. As he ran, the radio came on again.

"Skipper, I've got two trucks coming down the road from the north," Gardner said. "Could be reserves coming in from that little town. That supervisor said he talked to Baghdad after the bombing. What the hell you want me to do about these two trucks?"

20

Murdock kept running toward where he could see Mahanani bending over someone. "Two trucks," he said on the Motorola. Let them get within half a mile of you, and then hit them with your twenties. You have enough rounds?"

"We have three twenties and fifteen rounds per gun."

"Stop the trucks and then airburst the troops if there are any inside, which there must be. Reinforcements, Iraq style. No air, thank God. Keep me posted."

He came to the two on the ground and knelt beside Gypsy. Mahanani had his shirt spread over her and was working on her upper chest.

"She's in and out of consciousness," the medic said. "Shock mostly, I'd guess. You have an extra shirt? We could use some. Hey, guys, bring us some shirts, south of the crane."

"Breathing?"

"Ragged and shallow. Probably some damage to her right lung. We need an airlift out of here pronto. Can you use the SATCOM and get a bird?"

"Bradford," Murdock said on the radio. "Move to me south of the crane. Get the set aligned, we need to talk."

Murdock watched the medic. He had cleaned and bandaged the wound. The rifle bullet probably went right on through.

"She must have fired at that sniper after she was hit. That's one gutsy lady. Save her for us, Doc. I'll get a chopper here as soon as we're finished with the damn bombs. They have to be first priority. I know, I know. But it's got to be this way."

He lifted up, ran back to the crane, and called down into the pit. "Kat, how you doing?"

"A half hour more here, then about forty minutes on the other one. Senior Chief Neal is taking the plate off on the other bomb. That will help. So about an hour and a half, more or less."

"Don't waste any time. You heard about the trucks coming in. We'll have a fight. Then we need to get Gypsy out of here as soon as we can. She took a round into her lung."

"Shit," Kat said.

Murdock pulled back, caught Bradford, and had him set up the SATCOM and align the small dish antenna. Before he was done, they heard the twenties go off just north of them.

"They came and we're shooting," Gardner said. "We've stopped both trucks and I can see maybe twenty men scattering out of each truck. We're on airbursts now. Some of them will get away, so we'll have to watch for them."

"Nail all you can. Follow them with the thermal imager and harass them with the twenties. Save a few rounds. We might need them before we get out of here."

"How bad is Gypsy?"

"Not good. We need an air evac as soon as possible. Kat says about an hour and a half more. I'm going to talk to Stroh now."

"That's a roger."

Bradford handed Murdock the handset. "She's ready. We're on the frequency we usually use for Stroh."

"Underground looking for Big Daddy."

The response was immediate.

"Yes, Underground. Progress?"

"The sky guys came and dropped about two-thirds of the six-foot-thick roof into the complex. One of the bombs was crushed and is worthless. Two more are getting Kat's treatment now. Our report by an insider supervisor is that they made four and one left yesterday morning by highway truck heading north. We don't know where it might be. That's your problem now."

"We're on it. They could have gone to Baghdad for a flyout on a sale, or maybe to Jordan. We're out of assets in Baghdad, but we do have good people in Jordan. We'll check the airports for any private charters out of there today. Money in Jordan can get any information. Any casualties?"

"Yes, one of your Company people from Baghdad. She's with us and took a round through her lung. We need air evac as fast as possible. Where will they be coming from?"

"My home port from where you took off."

"That's two hours away," Murdock said. "I thought they might be closer, where Gardner came in from."

"We could do that. You need two. When will you be ready for a pickup?"

"Get them here on our red flares an hour and a half from now. It might be starting to get light by then. We've got ten or fifteen men from the home country contesting our right to go on living. We're working on them. How long from Saudia Arabia to us?"

"Twenty minutes to the border, but we don't have the medical there she'll need. Two hours from Kuwait to you and two back. Best we can do for top medical help."

Murdock sucked in a long breath. Even if they got out of Iraq to Saudi Arabia, that wouldn't save Gypsy. "Okay, get those birds warmed up and moving from Kuwait. We'll see you here in two hours. The pilots have the coordinates. Two hours, get their asses in motion."

"It's done; the air chief here is listening. They'll be in the air in five minutes. Stay safe. Let me know when the bang-bang comes eliminating those other two nukes."

"Will do. Underground out. Gardner, come in."

"Go, Skipper."

"You heard my talk with Stroh. We've got two hours to wrap this up. How is your seek and destroy doing?"

"Two trucks burning. We figure we nailed about half of the Arabs. That leaves fifteen out here somewhere. You better put out some security down there. We won't come in unless they get behind us. They probably will circle, so watch your hind side."

"Right. Thanks, Gardner."

Murdock looked around. It wasn't getting light yet, but it could in another two hours. "Mahanani, you hear Gardner?"

"Yeah, Skipper."

"See if you can gently move Gypsy into some cover—a wadi or a ditch or something. We could be taking fire soon."

"Done, Skip. Jaybird and I moved her about ten minutes ago. Little wadi about three feet deep. She's stable now, or as stable as I can get her. I pumped in two morphine and all the liquid antibiotics I have. She's still in and out of reality. We're talking four hours to medical help?"

"Afraid so."

"That will be touch-and-go."

"Right, Doc. Kat, can you talk?"

"Since I was two."

"Who do you have helping down there?"

"The senior chief and Vinnie Van Dyke. I sent Jaybird and Howard up a few minutes ago. You'll need them. I'm almost done with the first one. Second one won't be so hard. Another thirty, maybe fifty minutes."

"Take your time. We have two hours. Let's make certain. I don't want to crawl in there on a hangfire."

"Oh yeah, I'm with you, Skipper. Out."

"The rest of Alpha on me at the crane," Murdock said.

Soon the five men were there. "You know the situation. Best bet is that other squad of Iraqis out there will come at us from the south. So we want a picket line. Space yourselves thirty yards apart along the end of the complex to the right. Lam, take the thermal. Use your twenties on them if possible. We've got plenty of rounds and the kill ratio is higher. Doc, you stay with your patient but keep a lookout to the south. Don't gun down any of our guys, though. Questions?"

"Will it be light by the time the choppers get here?" Ching asked.

Murdock looked at Rafii.

"In this area, this time of year, should be daylight by oh-six-hundred. It's now about oh-four-hundred. So it will be just getting light when the birds come."

"Let's hope this squad doesn't have any RPGs with them," Jaybird said.

Murdock looked up. "Gardner. On those truck hits, did you hear any secondary explosions, like maybe rockets or RPG ammo?"

"Yeah, we did hear some, three or four, then the fuel tanks blew and that was all we heard."

"So, the troops in the field might have some heavier firepower. Let's keep alert. Get out there, stay in touch, and keep quiet. Lam, lead them out." He watched the men. Besides Lam there were Jaybird, Howard, Ching, Bradford, and Rafii. Bradford had left the set aligned on the satellite and all Murdock had to do to talk was hit the talk button on the handset.

He called the north squad. "Gardner, any ghosts on your thermal imager?"

"Nothing except some small animals I think must be rabbits. We haven't seen or heard of any of them since the big blast. Maybe they headed back north?"

"Probably not. At least not if one officer or one noncom survived. Just keep on the alert. We should be wrapped up here in less than an hour.

Twenty minutes later they had heard nothing more from the Iraqi army squad. Kat called to tell Murdock her status.

"I've just finished one, made all the internal changes I wanted to, and I have placed the C-4 inside but it has no timer or detonator. That comes last after the next one. Moving there now. Yes, the senior chief has the panel off so I can get right to work. I need him and Vinnie to hold the lights. Now that I've done one, the next one should wrap in about thirty minutes. Later."

Murdock kept watch to the south, but could see nothing. He tried to make the time go by faster, but it wouldn't. He checked twice with Kat, who said she was almost done.

"Taking longer than I figured. I'm going to be on this one most of an hour."

Later in the picket line of defenders across the south flank, Jaybird shielded his penlight under his shirt and checked his watch.

"All you locals out there in radio land, the time this morning is oh-five-oh-two. Which means we could see the start of the dawn in a half hour. Maybe we should find some wadi protection rather than up here in the good target area."

"Good idea, Jaybird," Murdock said. "I'm settling in on the side of the cut here like in a big foxhole. Those ten or fifteen riflemen aren't going to sit out there and wait for us to move."

Ten minutes later Murdock heard rifle fire from the south.

"Oh, yeah," Lam said. "We got company. Still dark

enough they can't see much, but they figured out we're out here waiting for them. They popped up out of a wadi about two hundred from us, I figure, and jolted off a few shots and then vanished."

"Anybody hit?" Murdock asked.

"No rounds came even close," Ching said. "I think they were looking for some muzzle flashes from us."

"The thermal gadget helping any?" Murdock asked.

"Oh, yeah, now it is," Lam said. "I've got two of them crawling out of a branch wadi maybe fifty yards out." The radio went dead, and a moment later Murdock heard three three-round bursts from an MP-5.

"Oh, yeah, two down and dirty," Lam said. "They won't try coming around that end again."

"I've got a pair of uglies moving in up here," Gardner said. "I'll wait until they come in close and nail them. We're spread out the way Lam and his bunch are. I've got this pair of Iraqis on the thermal and they are dead meat in about two minutes."

The sound of an explosion came over the radio earpieces.

"What was that?" Murdock asked.

"Must be an RPG," Lam said. "Hit down the wadi about thirty yards. Missed us. No muzzle flash so it must have come from a gully somewhere south of us."

"Probably RPG-Sevens," Jaybird said. "The antipersonnel grenade they throw is good for over twelve hundred yards. No telling where they fired them from. Bad news is they can bring down a chopper. Remember we lost three or four Blackhawks in Mogadishu, Somalia, back in 1994. RPG-Sevens shot them down."

"Don't they have antitank rounds, too?" Lam asked.

"Sure do. The launcher is forty millimeter and it can throw an antitank round out a thousand yards," Jaybird said. "Now, what do we do about the damn things?"

"We find them and take them out with our twenties before they can use their forties," Murdock said. "The Russians used to assign one RPG man to each squad. That could be the ratio here. So maybe they only have one RPG with them. Gardner, you see anything more up there?"

"Nope. We took out the two men we spotted. Haven't seen or heard anything else."

"Okay, we assume then they have one RPG and it's to the south. Lam, work down some of those tributary wadis and see if you can sniff out where the bastards are. Don't get yourself shot and don't get on the surface. They must be watching the top just like you guys are. Going to be dawn in about thirty. Move fast while you can. Bradford, this SAT-COM ready to go?"

"Ready, sir."

Murdock picked up the handset where the SATCOM sat on the lip of the drop-off and pushed the send button. "Big Daddy, talk to me."

The response was slow, but it came. "Yes, Underground. Our birds are in the air. Their ETA your place is less than thirty minutes."

"May have some bad news. We've got a squad of Iraqi infantry and they evidently have one or more RPGs. The old seven type probably, but mean enough to knock down a chopper. We're hunting them now, but not sure we'll find them before your birds get here. Did you give the chopper pilots one of our Motorolas?"

"I did, little buddy. I remembered getting broadsided before because the birds couldn't talk to you. Five miles is about all the range they have, or maybe six or seven when they are in the air."

"As soon as we hear them coming, we'll talk to them and throw out a red flare. Right now, we're on a search and destroy. Out."

Murdock put the SATCOM back in place. "Kat, how are you doing?"

"Another ten minutes and I'll be done. This bomb is different from the first one. Don't know why. I can do both of them. Give me ten and then time to set the fuses and we'll all choggie out of this neck of Iraq."

"We pull back how far?" Murdock asked.

"Two hundred. I'm having Senior Chief Neal rig the wall that's holding up the roof slab so it will blow out the wall and let the whole thing drop down and crush the bombs.

He'll set that timer for two minutes after the charges on the bombs go off."

"Good, I like it. Get finished. It's almost light out here." Murdock watched the darkness slip away and the first traces of dawn creep over the desert.

"Senior Chief, you read me?"

"Right, Skipper."

"Okay, you've got the con here. Get the three of you out of there when the charges are set. Give yourself at least five minutes to make the move. Then find a wadi up here on the surface to drop into. I'm heading out to where Lam is hunting for the RPGs."

It took Murdock five minutes to get out to where the rest of the squad had the picket line. They were in a gully that ran parallel with the bomb factory.

"Lam went down that one," Jaybird said, pointing to a branch of the wadi. "He's been gone fifteen and we haven't heard a word. He traded me for my Bull Pup."

"Lam, you on the scent out there?" Murdock radioed.

"Fucking close. I can hear some chatter, but can't see anybody yet. Oh damn. Just around a bend in this ten-foot-deep gully, I can see them. Six, maybe eight of them, and they have three RPGs."

"Let me get up there," Murdock said. "You have a twenty?"

"Yes and four rounds."

"I'm coming. Lead me in. I go to the first branch to the left—is that the direction?"

"Second branch, and go right. I'm about fifty yards from the turnoff."

"Be there in five. Hold your fire." Murdock took off at a sprint, got to the first-branch wadi, went past it to the second. That's when he heard the sound of the two choppers coming in. He ran ahead again. If he didn't get there in time, the RPGs could knock down their ticket out of there.

"I hear it, too," Lam said. "About two miles out. You better get here quick. Otherwise I'm going to have to do it myself."

"I'm no more than a minute away. Two rounds are better than one. I'm running, Lam. If I don't get there in time, you take them out with the twenties. We can't afford to let them get off a single round."

"I'm sighting in and waiting, Skipper. Shake a leg. Those birds are getting closer."

Murdock frowned as he ran. "Jaybird, don't throw out that red flare until we get these RPGs taken care of."

"You best hurry, Skipper," Jaybird said. "The birds are zeroing in on the smoke still coming up from parts of the factory."

Murdock scowled into the growing light and surged down the flat bottom of the wadi toward where Lam must have been waiting.

21

Murdock panted as he rounded the small turn in the five-foot-deep wadi. No Lam ahead. He could hear the sound of the choppers now coming in from the southeast.

"Skipper, Gypsy isn't sounding good. She's wheezing now and her pulse is so low I can hardly find it," the medic said. "Where are those damn flyboys?"

"Coming. First the fucking RPGs. Lam, where are you?"

"I can hear you, Skipper. Next curve on the wadi and you have it."

"Underground, this is Bird One. We don't see a flare."

"Hold it, Bird One, circle or something. We've got some RPGs down here we need to shoot up."

"That's a roger, Underground."

Murdock came around the next small turn and saw Lam belly down in the dirt next to a sharper curve. He ran up and dropped beside him.

"I'll do a contact round, Skipper. You do an airburst. They're up there about fifty yards."

Murdock leaned around the lip of rocks and sand and saw the uniforms. "That's a go, swabbie. On three. One, two, three." Both men fired. The twin reports of the twenties startled the Iraqi soldiers, but they had no time to react as the 20mm rounds exploded almost at the same time. Lam's contact round blew two men into the air and riddled one RPG launcher with dozens of penetrating shards of shrapnel. Murdock's airburst sent hundreds of razor-sharp metal fragments blasting down on the eight men who crouched in the gully.

Both men at once fired second rounds, and the next time they looked around the bend in the wadi, they saw only one man standing. He stared down the gully at them and lifted his RPG. Murdock's contact 20mm exploded in front of him before he could fire. The explosion set off the round in the RPG launcher and tore the soldier apart who held it. He jolted backwards, one of his arms missing and his torso riddled with shrapnel.

The SEALs looked again, saw no one alive, and Murdock hit his radio.

"Jaybird, throw out that red flare. Kat, how are you coming?"

"Flare is on the way," Jaybird said on the net.

"You eliminated the RPGs?" the new voice on the Motorola said.

"Yes, Bird One, you should have one red soon to land. Kat, what's your status?"

"We're all three out of the crater. Senior Chief Neal set the charges on the wall, and we punched up the boom-booms for five minutes. That was a minute and twelve seconds ago. Right now we're hoofing it fifty yards away and finding ourselves a hole."

"Blast set for about three minutes from now, everyone. Bird One, wait about five before you land. We want to see what happens at the bomb hole."

"That's a roger, Underground. We're holding."

Murdock could hear the choppers then. The sound came and then diminished, then came again. They were circling.

Murdock and Lam ran back down the wadi to where they could get out easily, and then jogged toward the line of pickets they had set out. Just as they got there, Murdock felt the ground shake.

"Fire one," Lam said.

A gush of smoke and dust blasted out of the opening behind the crane. Then a second explosion came, followed at once by a third. More smoke and dirt gushed out of the hole; then they heard a rumbling and saw the slanted roof on this end of the factory shake and then slide into the hole that had been the bombs' home.

Murdock, Lam, and the rest of Alpha Squad hiked back toward the crane. They met Kat and Neal, who were both grinning.

"Looks like you did it," Murdock said.

Kat nodded, her smile bright. "Oh yes, we did. The slab

dropping down seals those two bombs in there so no radiation can come out. They should be safe there for about a thousand years."

"Flare now, Skipper?" Jaybird called on the radio.

"Flare now, affirmative."

Murdock hurried forward and found the gully where Gypsy lay on a bed of cammie shirts. He knelt down beside her. She opened her eyes.

"Kat got the bombs?" she asked, her voice husky, so low Murdock had to strain to understand.

"Yes, all three are destroyed. Now our job is to get you safely out of here and to a good doctor."

"I like this one," she said and smiled. Then her face tightened and her eyes closed. She gasped as pain drilled through her body. She shuddered, then nodded and opened her eyes.

"Hurts some," she said.

Fifty yards behind Murdock, the choppers both landed on an open space.

"Load up," Murdock said to his mike, and he saw men moving toward the two birds. "Howard and Canzoneri, come over to where Gypsy is. I'm standing and waving."

The four men held each other's wrists under Gypsy and moved her as gently as possible to the chopper door. Eager hands helped take her inside and put her on a cargo pad on the floor.

"Everyone on board?" Murdock asked. "How many bodies in the first chopper?"

Gardner responded. "We've got eight here. Kat's with us."

Murdock counted. "We have ten including Doc and Gypsy. Eighteen is our number. Cleared for takeoff."

Just then an explosion shook the first chopper.

"RPG incoming," the pilot shouted into his Motorola. "It didn't miss us by much. We're out of here."

The second chopper pilot lifted off at the same moment, and when the bird was twenty feet into the air, another RPG round went off where the craft had been sitting. They felt some pings and the sound of whining shrapnel, but nothing that came through the skin of the chopper.

Both helicopters slanted south at top speed and a minute

later Murdock relaxed. They must be out of range of the RPGs by now. They were dangerous and deadly but better at short range than long. He touched his radio mike. "Bird One, what's your flight time to Kuwait?"

"I have it an hour and forty-eight."

"Good. Can you advise them we have wounded and we'll need an emergency team at the landing site ready for one critical."

"Will do that, Underground. Congratulations on your mission. Talk about hairy. You SEALs do good work."

"We had help from one brilliant and gutsy lady, and a second lady who is leaving her country to help us. Get us to medical help as soon as possible."

Murdock went over to Gypsy and held her hand. She was unconscious. He gripped her hand and she stirred, then opened her eyes.

"Dream. I just had a dream. Wild. Abstract. Nothing fit anything else. Almost a nightmare."

Mahanani hovered nearby. "Gypsy, do you need some more morphine? Is the pain too much for you?"

"What pain? I'm with friends." Her scratchy voice was hard to hear over the roar of the chopper. Mahanani took her pulse and scowled. He went up to the pilot.

"Tell the medics at the airport to have a portable defibrillator on their gurney and everything else. Her heart rate is so slow I'm afraid it'll stop before we get there."

The pilot nodded and made the call to his home base.

In the chopper the SEALs sat and watched the struggle for life. For a time Mahanani hovered over Gypsy, watching, testing her pulse and listening to her breathing. At last he leaned back, his face near a smile as he nodded.

"She's stronger. I don't know where she finds the strength, but she's doing better than I hoped. At this rate, she might make it."

Twenty minutes from touchdown, Gypsy cried out in pain and tried to sit up. Murdock and the medic held her down. Mahanani took her pulse and frowned.

"So damn low it almost isn't there. Make this damn machine go faster," he shouted into the chatter of the rotors.

When they landed, Murdock had the door open and saw
the team of white-coated medics running forward with two
gurneys. One was empty, the other loaded with machines and
material. Two men jumped into the chopper and checked her
with their stethoscopes. One frowned and shook his head.
The other called for the paddles. They came into the chopper
on their long cords.

"Three hundred," the medic shouted, then, "Clear." The
paddles contacted Gypsy's chest and shoulder and made her
slender body jolt upward. The stethoscope came again, held
by the doctor. He shook his head. "Four hundred," the doctor
called and the paddles hit her again, jolting her upward off
the pad then down.

The doctor with the stethoscope nodded. "She's back," he
said. "Let's get her out of here and into emergency."

Two hours later Murdock and Kat paced the waiting room
near the operating suite. An hour before, a nurse had come
out and told them that Gypsy was still in critical condition
but they had stabilized her. The bullet had gone through her
chest, lung, and out her back, and most of the damage had
been repaired. Her right lung had collapsed, but they had it
working again it and it was functioning well.

"There's a little more repair work we need to do, and she
isn't out of danger yet, but her chances look extremely good.
She's a tough little lady. We'll let you know how we're
progressing."

At last they both sat down and stared at each other.

"She's with the Company, right?" Kat asked.

"Yes, a part-time player, but they owe her."

"If they don't give her a retirement or put her to work,
I'm going to go to the President about it. He owes me at
least one favor. She could be invaluable in their Middle East
Section."

"Without her we wouldn't have found the bombs," Murdock said. "You're right. Our country owes her."

It was still morning in Kuwait. They had landed in one
of the military airfields close to Kuwait City where the U.S.
had set up a large contingent of Americans and dozens of
aircraft, all air force. Murdock had seen that his men were

sent to a barracks for some rest, showers, and chow. He told Don Stroh where he would be but hadn't heard from the CIA man since.

Stroh walked into the room, saw them, and sat down beside Kat.

"If this cowboy gives you any trouble, let me know, Kat, and I'll have him shipped to Adak up in the Aleutian Islands to count polar bears on the icecap."

"Hey, good fishing up there," Murdock said.

Kat grinned at the two jawing at each other. "Since you asked, your agent is stable and should make it," Kat said. "Is the CIA going to give her a job stateside, or give her a medical retirement?"

"She isn't staying here?" Stroh asked.

"No, she's coming back to the States with me and living in my apartment."

Stroh lifted his brows. "Well, that was a fast bonding."

"She took a bullet for me, Stroh, and then gunned down the sniper before she collapsed. We owe her."

"I'll talk to Washington. Right now we've got more problems."

"Where is the other bomb?" Murdock asked.

"We're not sure. The Israelis have been tracking a man they call Asrar Fouad for over three years. He's chaperoned more than a dozen suicide bombers into Israel. Now they think he's moved up in his chosen profession. We've had intel about somebody shopping for a functioning nuclear bomb. This person worked the Russians, went to Ukraine and tried the Odessa caves, but found the price too high. The word is that he then contacted those who had produced nuclear bombs to buy or co-own one. One trace showed him in Baghdad recently.

"Yesterday he was spotted by one of our people in Jordan, not in the capital but in a northern city called Irbid. Okay, we're making some assumptions here. Baghdad airliners are not welcome in many nations. On the other hand, Jordan Air, a freight hauler, can literally fly the world.

"A few more background facts. The Israelis captured one of Fouad's right-hand men. I won't say the Israelis used torture, but they extracted quite a bit of general information about Fouad. One of his dreams is to set off a nuclear weapon on a U.S. city. We now know that he was in Baghdad. Iraq has nuclear bombs. One of them got away. We think Fouad sold Iraqi President Kamir on the partner plan. Kamir furnishes the bomb; Fouad transports it to America and detonates it."

"That's a bucket full of assumptions," Murdock said. "What do we know in hard, cold facts?"

"Fouad wants to nuke America. Fouad has been in Baghdad. Baghdad has one nuclear bomb left. Fouad was spotted yesterday in Jordan. It's a closer drive to Jordan from the bomb site than it is to Baghdad. Those are our facts."

"Can your man in Jordan check the airfreight companies?"

"Unfortunately no. He was killed this morning in an apparent auto accident."

"So, when do we leave?" Murdock asked.

"I've been authorized to send three men to Jordan to try to check out the sightings. You and your two best Arabic speakers leave in two hours. You'll go as Saudi nationals on a Saudi Airlines flight from the civilian airport here. No weapons, not even a knife. Tight security on these planes. You'll stop in Amman and continue on to Irbid. There are two airfreight lines up there. Jordan Airfreight and Middle East Air Freight. Both solid, legitimate carriers. They say money can buy anything in Jordan. That might be the case here. You'll each have five thousand dinars. It takes three dollars to equal one Jordanian dinar. We better move. We have new Saudi Arabian–type civilian clothes, Saudi papers for each of you. Rafii and Ching are ready to go. You better get a shower and hit the officers' mess. I'll keep you informed about Gypsy. Best way to contact me will be by regular telephone. Let's go."

Murdock looked at Kat. He touched her shoulder. "Thanks for all of your good work, and take care of Gypsy. We owe her. Stomp all over Stroh here if he gives you any trouble. Stay with Gypsy until the Company gets her a passport and lands her with you in New York."

"Count on it," Kat said, staring hard at Stroh.

• • •

Two hours later the three SEALs took off from Kuwait City Airport on the Saudi Airlines jetliner. They did a lot of nodding and used simple Arabic words and probably looked like foreigners, but that was no big problem here.

Rafii sat next to Murdock on the two-seat side of the aircraft.

"Maybe eight hundred miles to Amman," he whispered. "That's about two hours, depending on the route. We'll go south some so we don't overfly Iraq."

"Be early afternoon when we get on up to Irbid. Let's hope the airfreight outfits are at the airport. We'll use a taxi. My big worry is that we're at least a day behind Fouad, if this is where he went. Stroh and his brain trust could be all wrong on this. President Kamil of Iraq might be going to use that bomb himself."

"Let's hope not," Rafii said. "If he drops it on Israel, they for sure will retaliate with a nuke and the big nuclear war could be started."

"So this time Stroh and the Company better be right, or the whole damn world could be in big trouble," Murdock said.

22

Irbid, Jordan

Rafii took the lead as they left the plane with their carry-on bags and walked outside the airport terminal. He hurried directly to a waiting taxi at the head of the line and talked briefly with the driver. He nodded and the three SEALs climbed into the cab. It turned out to be a short drive around the outside of the airport to a rear gate where the transit aircraft and the two airfreight companies were located.

Rafii told the taxi driver to wait, and the three went straight to the closest firm, Jordan Airfreight. The building was old, needed painting, and crouched beside a large hangar where they could see three twin-engine jet planes and two smaller propjets. Inside they found a counter with a man sitting behind it playing cards. He looked up, then made one more play. He was darkly Jordanian, with a full mustache, no beard, slightly slanted eyes, and a forehead that bulged slightly like he was a cranial genius. He heaved to his feet and Murdock saw that he was at least three hundred pounds. He scowled at them, then asked what they wanted.

"I'm looking for a large, heavy shipment that went out of here last night or this morning. Must have weighed at least a ton. Large wooden crate. Anything like that on one of your planes?"

"Customers' business is their business," the clerk said. "We don't talk about it." He took a ponderous step to the right and looked over a sheaf of papers on a clipboard.

Rafii took out a wad of bills and began laying Jordanian twenty-dinar notes on the counter. The clerk watched him from dark eyes now hooded with heavy brows. Rafii stopped and the man looked up. Rafii shrugged and put the rest of the bills in his pocket. The large man moved ponderously toward the money, but Rafii covered it with his hand.

"The information first. If it's worthwhile, you get the money."

Heavy shoulders shrugged, and then his hand darted out and caught one of the dinar notes. He stepped back and chuckled.

"No heavy cargo here in two weeks. Boss is angry about it. Saw lots of lights over next door last night. Ask them." He held the bill up. "Go with Allah."

Rafii turned with the rest of the bills in his hand, and the three left the office. The outfit next door was a half a block away. They walked as Rafii pushed the bills back in his pocket. The taxi trailed along behind them.

"Money can buy most anything in Jordan," he said. "Maybe we get lucky on this last stop. If not, we phone Stroh. Maybe they have a new lead."

On the way to the office of Fast Air Freight, they passed the open hangar door. It was a large building, with two twin jet transport planes inside being serviced. The FAF logo stood out on both planes in a bright red against the white body color.

Inside they found a counter behind which was a young man sitting at a desk with a phone bank. He looked up and smiled.

"How may I help you gentlemen?"

Rafii bristled. "You sent out an illegal shipment last night on one of your charter planes. We need to know who sent it and where it went."

The young man stood and frowned. He fussed with his hands, and a thin line of sweat popped out on his forehead. "I'm afraid I can't help you. I didn't work last night."

"Get your supervisor or your boss. Get him here right now!" Rafii's voice had risen to a thundering level. No one else was in the office. The young man wiped his forehead, nodded, and hurried through a back door.

"Might never see him again," Murdock whispered.

"He'll be back," Rafii said. "Twenty to one."

"You're on for a tenner," Ching said.

A moment later the rear door opened and an older man, with a full beard, a vigorous walk, and hands that showed he had done his share of hard work, came in. He wore a New York Yankees baseball cap and a large smile.

"Now, what seems to be the trouble?" the man asked.

"None, if you tell us what we need to know. Who sent the large, heavy crate last night and where did it go?"

"Well now, that is company business. We're not allowed to give out the names of shippers or where—"

Rafii reached across the counter and grabbed the man by the throat. He pressured both carotid arteries and the supervisor's eyes went wide and his arms flailed for a moment, then his voice squeaked out.

"Okay, okay."

Rafii let go of his throat but kept his hand wrapped around the man's shirt front just under his chin. The man swallowed twice, rubbed his eyes with one hand, then nodded.

"Yes, yes, a heavy shipment. It was listed as farm machinery. Very heavy. Too heavy to be regular farm equipment. But the man paid. He paid extra to get the crate loaded last night and the plane cleared for takeoff."

"A charter?"

"Yes, the only freight on board. It took an hour to get it placed exactly right in the body of the aircraft so it wouldn't interfere with the flight characteristics."

"The manifest," Rafii demanded, holding out his hand that had come off the shirt front.

"I really shouldn't." The supervisor's eyes went wide and he took a step back as Rafii moved his hand toward the Arab's chin. "Why not? I didn't like the man. He was a Saudi, slick and sleek and had to have his way with everything."

Out of his pocket Murdock pulled a picture that Stroh had supplied.

Rafii handed the picture to the Jordanian. "Is this the man?" Rafii asked.

"Yes, the mustache is the same, but now he has the start of a full beard, maybe two weeks' growth."

"Where is the plane going?" Rafii asked.

"The flight plan calls for it to go to Portugal to stop for fuel. The man said he would file a new flight plan there."

"What kind of plane is it?" Rafii asked.

"It's a BAC One-Eleven. A Romanian-made plane."

"Payload and range," Rafii snapped.

"Range is up to twenty-three hundred miles. Payload is a hundred and eighteen passengers or in the cargo version over twenty-one thousand pounds."

"Plenty," Rafii said. "Show me the manifest."

The man frowned and Rafii reached for him, but he stepped back again and took a file from a nearby desk. He leafed through it a moment and came up with four sheets of paper. Rafii looked at them and nodded. He took out three twenty-dinar notes and pushed them at the man.

"You don't need to tell anyone that we were here, agreed?"

The man stared at the money a moment, and then nodded. As Rafii and the others left, he grabbed the money and pushed it into his pocket.

Outside, Murdock took over. "We need to find a phone," he said. Rafii signaled the taxi and it pulled up beside them and stopped.

The driver took them to a pair of phones well away from the roar of jets taking off, and Murdock tried to direct dial the number that Stroh had given him in Kuwait. It didn't work. Rafii got on the phone and with an operator got through.

"Stroh, Murdock."

"About time you called. What's happening?"

Murdock laid out the action for him. "Maybe your people in Lisbon can nail the plane before it takes off?"

"Not likely. But it sounds like we guessed right and we have a tail on the right guy, with the bomb. He has almost twenty-four hours head start. You say the FAF logo is bright red on a white body. That will help. Not a lot of BAC One-Elevens out there. We'll put out a worldwide watch for it on the Internet and offer a reward. It's worked in the past."

"So we go to Lisbon," Murdock said.

"Yes, but you won't get a nonstop. We can put one agent on it in Lisbon. Maybe we can find out something. Fouad will have to file a flight plan there. Whether he tells his true next destination could be a problem. Get there as fast as you can. Rafii can do it for you. Probably have to go back to

Amman, then to Athens if you're lucky and on to Rome or
Madrid. You might not make it for twenty-four hours, depending on layovers between flights. You can get out of your
Arab clothes anytime you want to. Now, get moving. I've
got some radio calls to make."

They had to wait an hour for a flight to Amman, and then
Rafii went to work with the ticket people and managed to
get flights to Greece and Rome.

"We'll have to rebook when we get to Rome, but the first
plane to Athens leaves in an hour and will take half the night.
If we can book out of Athens, we should be in Lisbon by
noon tomorrow."

"Too damn slow," Murdock brayed. "He could be halfway across the Atlantic by then, or into London. We don't
know where the hell he's heading."

"Isn't Lisbon a jumping off spot for crossing the Atlantic?" Ching asked. "From Lisbon to Nova Scotia. Halifax, I
think, is the town."

"How far is that?" Rafii asked.

Murdock frowned. "As I remember, the Azores islands
are about a thousand miles due west of Lisbon. Stop there
for fuel if needed and then head on out to Halifax another
sixteen hundred."

"A big jet like the BAC could make it in one hop," Ching
said.

"Enough talk," Murdock said. "When does the damn
plane leave out of here for Athens?"

Lisbon, Portugal

Remedios parked her Volkswagen in front of the Lisbon Air
Freight office and hurried inside. She knew one of the men
there—that would be a help. Her phone call had come
through less than twenty minutes ago with an ultra-urgent
note on it. When the Company called, she swung into motion
as fast as possible.

Inside the small office she saw Carlos, the man she knew,
and waved him over.

"Need a special favor, my friend," she said. She was
wearing a tight white blouse and smiled at the thirty-year-
old clerk.

"My pleasure, Remedios," Carlos said with a grin.

"Not that, at least not now. I'm looking for a flashy air-freight plane. It's a BAC One-Eleven with large red logos on the side saying 'FAF.' Any ideas?"

"Don't see many BAC planes around here. It's Romanian. I can ask around. When did it come in?"

"My source said sometime early this morning, maybe before daylight."

"Only three other airfreight outfits here that it could stop at. It would need fuel and a new flight plan probably. You check with the tower for a flight plan, and I'll make some calls."

Remedios called the tower and, after being transferred to three different people, had her answer. No FAF freighter had filed a flight plan within the past twenty-four hours. She went back to Carlos. He shook his head.

"Sorry, nobody has seen a BAC around here today. Of course, if it came in before daylight, it would be hard to spot and the men who worked then have gone home. Wish I could help you. When are we going out to dinner?"

"Soon, Carlos. Soon. Right now I'm in a short-time situation. I'm going to check with the other three freight guys and see what they know. Thanks for your help." She put on her best smile, then turned and hurried out to her car.

A half hour later she looked for a phone. None of the men at the other three big airfreight outfits had seen a BAC plane, or any other with the red FAF logo. She called her contact and told him. He would pass the word on to Don Stroh.

Asrar Fouad heard about the woman in the Volkswagen asking questions at the airfreight firms. He even saw her once when she went into Lisbon Air a hundred yards from where he watched. She had come out, looked around, and then driven away. Fouad relaxed. It had been a tough day. His contact man had not been in place when the plane arrived at 3:40 A.M. He told the pilot where to taxi the big transport, but when they arrived in front of the hangar barely wide enough for them to enter, the big doors were closed and all the lights were off. It had taken him two hours to get his man out of bed and into action. They at last rolled the big plane into the hangar just before daylight. They closed the doors and went to work.

That's when the trouble with the flight crew started.

"We can't fly out of Europe," the pilot said. "Our company is not licensed to go any farther than Lisbon."

"Tough, we're going to the Azores, then to Halifax, Nova Scotia," Fouad said.

"We can't fly there," the copilot said. "We'll lose our jobs and get thrown into jail."

"You'll fly where I tell you to," Fouad rasped.

The copilot roared in rage and charged at Fouad. He pulled his automatic from his belt holster, and when the copilot didn't stop, Fouad fired twice. Both rounds hit the furious man in the chest and he fell at Fouad's feet. The pilot rushed up and knelt beside him. He put his fingers to the man's throat and looked up.

"He's dead. You killed him."

"He attacked me," Fouad said. "No problem, you can fly the plane alone. You *will* fly it alone." He waved the pistol at the flight engineer and the pilot. "In back, all the way back to those cargo blankets. You men get to take a nap until time for us to fly out of here. Move, I have lost my patience. Oh, carry your dead friend with you. We can't have this blood all over the plane."

Fouad put them on the cargo blankets, tied their hands and feet, and told them that if they made a sound, he would kill them.

"You'll get food before we take off. Right now I have other work to get done. Be quiet, or you die. I can get a pilot anywhere to fly this old tin airplane."

Outside the plane, Fouad checked with the two men in the hangar. They were supposed to do some repainting. The small firm's spray guns had failed to work, and they had to repair them. An hour later the work was underway, spray painting out every sign of FAF on the plane's sides and tall rudder.

After that they stenciled on new logos, not nearly as large, and in a gentle blue color. The letters were DAF, for Domestic Air Freight. There was a real DAF freight company in Morocco, but it seldom came this far north. The pilot wore no uniform so that was not a problem. He had the fake credentials and certificates he needed for the plane and its destination. Now all he needed was several thousand pounds of fuel, and a flight plan. He would file the flight plan thirty minutes before his takeoff and list London as his destination. If anyone were following him, the new logo and the flight plan should send them on a false scent that would give him the free time he needed.

He had slept most of the flight to Lisbon. The galley had been stocked with enough prepared dinners for a dozen men and he'd had his choice of several different meals.

Now on to the Azores and then to Halifax. He was making progress. He had two men in Halifax who would smooth the way for him there. He planned on a quick turnaround on servicing and fueling before he headed south. North America. He was almost there. The Fist of Allah would pound the Americans into the dust within a week. That was his timetable. The rest of his men were in place and ready. All he had to do was get the bomb to its final destination and then fly away a safe distance. It would be the ultimate thrill, the rush of a lifetime. When he saw that beautiful mushroom-shaped cloud rising over an American city, he would have fulfilled his grandest dream.

Once more he checked the paint job. These modern paints dried almost instantly. Five minutes after applying them, they were dry and rock hard. He looked at his watch. The pilot and flight engineer had eaten dinners from the plane's galley. Time to move the plane to get fuel, then his radioed flight plan and the takeoff. It was only then that he realized he hadn't eaten since they landed. He could go to a restaurant in the terminal, but that would be one more spot where he could be recognized. His beard had not grown out as much as he had hoped it would. He went into the plane and to the refrigerated area of the galley and took out a pair of dinners. He would heat them up in the microwave and have a feast. He selected from two of the bottles of wine and settled down to his meal. When he finished, he would untie the flight crew and get the craft moving. Then in a matter of an hour they would be on the runway waiting their turn to take off.

The Fist of Allah was about to strike again, and this time the whole world would know about it and perhaps about him, depending how well he had concealed his identity. Either way it would be the crowning achievement of his life.

23

Remedios sat at her small desk in the jewelry store she owned in the best shopping area of Lisbon. She had three trusted employees who ran the store, which left her time to take care of any Company work that needed doing. She frowned thinking about that airplane that must have landed at the airport but then promptly become lost. Where had it gone? There was no new flight plan. She didn't know what it carried, but it had ignited a firestorm of activity by the Company like none she had seen in years.

Her contact at the U.S. embassy had been insistent. She had tried pulling in all of her credits and favors, but nothing had worked. The phone rang, and as usual she let the manager answer it. The woman looked in her door and nodded.

Remedios picked up the phone. "Yes, this is Starlight Jewelry. How may I help you?"

"Remedios, it's Carlos. I think I've found your BAC One-Eleven. There's an old hangar I thought was still closed, a quarter of a mile over. Ten minutes ago I saw a plane pull out of there and then start the engines and taxi away. It was white but didn't have the large red FAF on it. There were some other initials I couldn't quite make out. It was a BAC One-Eleven I'm sure."

"Damn, sounds like a quick paint job. Did they file a flight plan?"

"I checked with the tower just before I called. A BAC did file and listed its destination as London."

"Thanks, Carlos. I owe you. Dinner tomorrow night at eight. Pick me up. Bye."

She hung up and called the embassy.

The receptionist answered.

"Good afternoon, this is the United States Embassy in Lisbon. How may I help you?"

"Harvey, please."

"Just a moment."

"Yes?"

"Remedios. A friend saw the plane. The FAF was painted out and it had a new logo in its place but he couldn't read the letters. The tower reports a BAC took off five minutes ago with a flight plan listing London as its next stop."

"I doubt that," the voice at the embassy said. "It could be going anywhere. With Fouad's hatred of us, it's probably heading for the Azores and then the U.S. He could do a flyover of New York City without refueling again after the Azores. He could trigger the bomb at a thousand feet and kill two million people."

"Is he the suicide type?"

"Washington has been talking about him all morning. Their profile shows him not to be. But get him hyped on something and he could psych himself up to do it. So we've got to play both sides. Have you checked with air traffic control to see if there's a BAC One-Eleven heading for the Azores?"

"We can do that?"

"Not your problem. I'll do it. First I've got to contact Washington yesterday. Thanks. Out."

Remedios hung up the phone and frowned. There was absolutely nothing else she could do.

Murdock and his team hit Lisbon twelve hours after the BAC jetliner had taken off. Murdock used a land line and called Stroh. He was back in Washington, D.C. Stroh filled the SEAL in on what they knew about the BAC.

"We have no assets in the Azores, never thought we'd need them. No chance to backstop him there. We have run out of time. If he's twelve hours ahead of you, he's already landed at the Azores, refueled, and could be over New York or Washington right now. If we'd known in time we could have had the Halifax authorities stop the plane for a customs inspection, or a health inspection, but it must be too late now. Always a chance the plane broke down in Halifax. We'll give

them a call and see. We doubt he's going to London. If it is
the Azores, we can call and check. Wish us luck. As for you
and your team, exchange some of your dinars and get your
asses back to the States. This guy has the potential of sui-
ciding out with a nuke blast over New York City. His plane
has the range. But we don't think he'll do that. He must have
landed in Halifax. If he's in a rush, he would refuel and get
the hell out of there fast. We have cooperation up there in
Canada, but we're not sure of the plane. We can't flag down
every BAC that comes in there. Even if he's still there, which
I doubt, he could slip through the cracks.

"He'll need fuel. If he plans on landing in the U.S., he'll
be met at any airport in the country big enough to set the
BAC down. We can do that. A top alert went out six hours
ago, and every cop at every airport has a description on the
plane and color. The air traffic types will watch for any BAC
planes coming in. But we are probably too damn late."

"He won't stop in the U.S.," Murdock said.

"Why not?"

"Al-Qaida has shown a preference for Mexico to get into
the U.S. Now Canada is on higher alert since the nine-eleven
disaster, where their borders were violated. He'll go to Mexico, then pick his U.S. target, and fly to a border city nearby."

"We've got it all in the think tank here. Get your tootsie
out of there and on a plane. See you in my office in D.C. as
soon as you get here."

Over the Atlantic Ocean

Asrar Fouad settled into the fourth seat in the cockpit of the
BAC aircraft and smiled. They were flying at thirty-four
thousand feet to avoid as much as possible of the jet stream
coming at them. He had held a long talk with the pilot and
the flight engineer in the Azores. He had kept them inside
the plane and had his gun in his hand most of the time. They
said they were not authorized to fly outside of Europe. He
told them they would fly the plane where he said, or they
would die. He told them they all would be rich men when
the flight ended. He would present each of them with fifty
thousand dinars, more than a hundred and fifty thousand dollars. They could go back home and quit work and live in

luxury for the rest of their lives. To show his good faith, he gave each of then five thousand dinars.

It had helped quiet their concern. He told then he had paid the operators of the aircraft a huge sum for the trip, and he would not let them stop him or change his flight plans. He told them they would land in Halifax, Nova Scotia. None of them had ever been there before.

"It's a modern airport with all the facilities," he told them. "The Halifax air traffic controllers will find us about sixty miles at sea and bring us in."

The pilot nodded. "That I know. Our aircraft's transponder will pick up the incoming radar signals from Halifax and broadcast an amplified, encoded radio signal in the direction of the detected radar. Our transponder signal tells the Halifax controller the aircraft's flight number, altitude, airspeed, and destination. We'll show up on the radar screen as a blip with this information beside it."

"So, we're just another cargo plane coming into Halifax," the engineer said as he watched the autopilot flying the plane.

"Just another one," Fouad said. "We'll file a flight plan for the Azores thirty minutes before we take off. I told you we can't waste time now. We check in with the Halifax tower, get refueled, and get in line to take off. Only we don't go back to the Azores, we head south for Nassau in the Bahama Islands.

"You said somebody might be looking for us?" the pilot asked.

"Looking, but not finding. Canada won't be worried about us as long as we follow the procedures, and we'll do that until we get out of their airspace."

"But won't the flight controllers in the U.S. pick us up?" the pilot asked.

"We'll stay far enough off the coast so the locals won't even see us," Fouad said. "Say, Boston is interested in us, but can't find us on its screens. Their ASR, Airport Surveillance Radar, can reach out sixty miles. So we'll stay well beyond that range. They won't worry about us because they won't know we're there. They are required to handle only those planes that are in their airspace.

"We have a bigger problem. Boston is the air traffic oceanantic center for the Atlantic Ocean. It maintains radio contact with planes flying across the ocean. They are supposed to report every so often with their position, their speed, and the identification. Then Boston tracks them across the ocean. But they can do that only if the plane radios in its position."

"But we won't do that?" the engineer asked.

"For sure we won't do that. Air traffic doesn't care who flies up and down the coast as long as the plane doesn't come west into U.S. airspace. If a plane comes into that space, the Air Defense Command takes over and asks by radio who the plane is and why it's coming in. If there is no response from the plane on the ADC radar, a pair of jet fighters scrambles and they meet the plane and find out what it is and why it didn't respond. So we stay well out of that area.

"Once we leave Halifax, Boston Oceanic won't know we are there. Now it's clear sailing. No way that the Oceanic people can track us without our radio positions."

"We stopping in Miami?" the third man in the cockpit, the flight engineer, asked.

"Not a chance. Remember that route I blocked out for you? You can put it into the machine now. We go down the coast about seventeen hundred miles and land in Nassau, the Bahamas. We pick up fuel there, then take off and turn to the right, miss the tip of Florida by at least sixty miles, and the Miami air controllers, and head through the Gulf of Mexico for Mexico City."

"Your first plot showed that we could make it without refueling after Nassau. Do you still say that?"

"Depends how much head wind we hit. But we should be able to get there with plenty of our fuel to spare."

"Good," Fouad said. "You guys fly the plane. I'm going to have a nap. Let me know when we hit Halifax airspace." He scowled at them. And remember, I can fly this plane. Any deviation from my orders and you both get killed and I fly the plane into Mexico City. Let me know when we're approaching Halifax."

The Azores

Murdock went to the airport manager in the Azores and found a confused and irritable man. He spoke enough English that they could communicate.

"I know nothing of this plane. Yes, yes, it landed here, a BAC One-Eleven. But at that time we had no reason to question it. It landed, refueled, filed a flight plan for Lisbon, and took off. Nothing unusual. Now your government tells me it could be carrying terrorists. How was I to know?"

"What was the logo on the side?" Murdock asked. "What airline did it claim to be?"

"He listed it as DAF, Domestic Air Freight of Morocco."

"Is there such a company?"

"Yes, but we rarely see it out here."

Murdock frowned. "At least we have a logo and color. When did the plane take off?"

"A little over nine hours ago. You'll never catch up on a commercial flight."

"Did your flight control radar show them heading for Lisbon?"

"Yes, but it reaches out only sixty miles."

"And they could have reversed their course and you'd never know it." Murdock slammed his palm down on the desk and left without another word. Nine hours. That meant the craft they hunted could already be in Halifax, or maybe refueled and gone on the next leg of its flight. He called Stroh on a pay phone, was surprised to get through so easily, and reported what he knew.

"So, we missed him in Halifax. I've had a report by one of our men there. He's found a record of the plane landing, fueling, and taking off. The flight plan said the plane was heading back to the Azores. We'll try Halifax again. They might know something more now. Their air traffic control should have something on him."

"If the plane has a transponder."

"They have to now to get off the ground."

"You still think he's heading for Mexico?"

"Yes."

"We'll work on it. In the meantime, get yourself into town. We may need you south of the border."

"Where is the rest of the platoon?"

"On their way. Kat raised all sorts of hell and got Gypsy a free pass home. She's been yelling at my boss and threatening to go straight to the President. Which she could do. I think the Company got her satisfied. She's staying in Kuwait until Gypsy is well enough to fly; then they both will come back. Gypsy will go on the payroll when she's well. Kat is pleased and all is well on that score."

"When will the platoon hit the States?"

"Who knows? They're hitchhiking back on military planes when there's room and when they're coming this way. Give them three or four days."

"My flight was just called. We're out of here. See you tomorrow."

In Washington, D.C., Don Stroh put the phone down and rubbed his face with both hands. In fifteen minutes he, six other Company men, and the FBI contingent had a meeting with the Director of the Department of Homeland Security. Twelve men were going to figure out what to do? Better they asked the man on the street. Mexico still looked good. He wasn't sure of the range of a BAC One-Eleven. If it took on extra fuel, it might be able to fly from Halifax down the coast. It could refuel in Bermuda or the Bahamas and then have enough juice to get below Florida and slant over into Mexico. Where in Mexico? Mexico City would be an idea. Lots of air traffic. Easy to get lost in the jumble. It was a big, busy airport.

What about air traffic control over the ocean, off the coast? He knew some of the radar that picked up incoming planes could reach out for sixty miles. There were no checks or tracking of planes over the ocean, except by radio. Planes could fly up and down the coast as long as they didn't punch into U.S. airspace. If they did, they would answer to the Air Defense Command.

Stroh sipped at a cup of hot coffee and nodded. He could call the Air Traffic Control System Command Center and ask if with the new security they were monitoring flights farther off the coast now. He could, but he wasn't going to. He was sure of the sixty mile limit. Mexico, it had to be Mex-

ico. But where in Mexico? He was thinking in circles. He
and Murdock had gone over this before. A nap. He needed
a nap. A research outfit said that workers who took a half-
hour nap during the day awoke refreshed and worked at a
much higher efficiency level than those same type workers
who plowed straight through the day. Yeah.

His office door opened and Milly pushed inside. She was
forty, thirty pounds overweight and didn't care, and had yo-
gurt every day for lunch. She grinned at him.

"Hey, Mr. S. Time for your meeting. The main conference
room. Looks like quite a bunch coming in. You want me to
run interference for you?"

He groaned, stood, picked up his notes from his talk with
Murdock, and angled for the door.

"This time I've got to do my own downfield blocking,
but thanks, Milly. Next time for sure I'll get you out in front.
If Murdock calls, have him give you a number. I'll need to
talk to him as soon as he hits town."

"Yes, Mr. S. I'll do that." She smiled. "You get in there
and get this thing straightened out."

"Wish I could, Milly. I do so wish that it was that easy."
He walked down the hall and went into the conference room.
Ten or twelve men with notebooks and pads of paper sat
around the big table. The Director of the Department of
Homeland Security rapped his water glass and the men sat
down.

"Gentlemen, thanks for coming. We have facing us what
may be the greatest threat to the United States in our history.
It's up to us to come up with some answers, and some way
to detour, detect, and destroy this nuclear threat that even
now may be hidden in the heart of one of our great cities.
First I'd like to hear from Don Stroh, who has been shep-
herding this situation from the start and has the latest information about the possible location, destination, and maybe
even the target of this nuclear device. Mr. Stroh."

24

Ramstein Air Force Base, Germany

Gunner's Mate First Class Miguel Fernandez sat on his bunk in the transient barracks at the U.S. Air Force base and thought back over his work in Iraq. He shook his head. He didn't even know how many men he had killed. Several. Two, ten, fifteen? He had been on the assault fire and some of the other firefights. Did it bother him? He rubbed one ear that had been itching lately for no apparent reason.

Yes, the killing now did bother him. Was it enough to make him quit the SEALs? He didn't know. Death had suddenly become a factor. After over six years of close and dirty combat with the SEALs, he was starting to feel the strain. Was it the actual killing or the idea that someone's brother or father or son would not be returning home from his military post that bothered him? He simply didn't know. He could go talk to an air force chaplain. No, he couldn't. They were on a fifteen-minute alert schedule. They would have only that much time to get their gear together and rush to the flight line for a ride to the next military base. He hated this hitchhiking. They became just so much cargo for these air transport guys.

So he couldn't risk missing a flight by going to a chaplain. He sure as hell wasn't going to let any of the men in the platoon know how he felt—except Murdock. Death had become more important to him since his grandfather died two months ago. The old guy was almost eighty, but spry and witty and still worked part-time in his small restaurant. He had died with his boots on, or more properly his apron, where he stood at the stove in the kitchen grilling a pair of steaks. He had gone in a flash and there was no chance to revive him when the paramedics came. A heart attack—massive, unstoppable, and deadly.

His grandfather was his first relative who had died in ten years. He didn't think too much about it at the time. The large, extended Mexican family had the usual mass, wake, funeral, and burial. It had all seemed routine at the time. This was simply what a family did when a member died.

Now he realized that the loss of the old man had been more than routine for him. His grandfather had taken him on his first fishing trip and to his first baseball game. Had come to watch him play baseball in high school. His own father had been navy and often out on six-month blue-water trips, so he wasn't home that much. When he was there, he was distant, unresponsive. Not your best hands on Dad. The death of Grandfather Hernando had been a severe blow; he just didn't realize it at the time. Now he was paying for it.

Damn it, he was doing what he had been trained to do. Six long months of training. He was good at this job. It was work that had to be done by someone. They had taken on the country's enemies in dozens of different locales and situations, and had won. He had faced death himself twenty, thirty times in those six years and had survived. Maybe that was what was meant to be? He didn't believe in fate. Man made his own way, and sometimes luck of the draw was a factor, but certainly nothing was preordained. A man lived or died mostly by his own decisions and actions. Sure, a plane might go down and all on board be killed. A chance happening. A man did not have "a time to die." He hated it when people said, "Well, I guess it was Joe's time to go." That was nonsense. No person of even average intelligence could possibly believe that.

So where did that leave him? He didn't know. He'd see how he felt when this mission was over. Maybe it was over. Or maybe they would be chasing that fourth nuke all over the world. He wondered where it was by now. Had the bad guys moved it where they wanted to set it off? That would more than likely be some target city in the United States. He just hoped that it wasn't San Diego.

"On your feet, troops," Senior Chief Neal bellowed. "We have exactly sixteen minutes to get to the flight line. We've got a ticket to fly straight into Washington, D.C., good old Andrews Air Force Base just outside of the District. Move it."

Over the Atlantic Ocean
Along the U.S. Coast

Asrar Fouad grinned as the BAC's radio spoke again.

"Last call, BAF-235. We have no position for you after your takeoff from Halifax on our screens at Boston Oceanatic Control. Do you read me? Do you read me? Please respond."

"Yes. They can't find us," Fouad said. "That's the best news we've had yet. They don't know where the hell we are. That's good."

"I can get in huge trouble for doing this," the pilot said. "Turning off the transponder and not answering the AT control. I'll lose my license at the very least. I could land in jail."

"Don't worry about it," Fouad said. "Who is going to report what happened? Not me, not your engineer. You're safe and going to be a rich man. Hell, you don't even have to go back to Jordan if you don't want to."

The engineer laughed. "Hey, we stay in Mexico City, learn to speak Spanish, and keep the plane to start up our own airfreight business. Or we sell the plane. Must be worth at least two million dinar."

The pilot shook his head. "That would really make us criminals. Jordanian cops would come looking for us."

Later the flight engineer told Fouad they were two hundred miles down the United States coast from Halifax. Boston had been trying to reach them since they cut the switch to the transponder after leaving Halifax. They were a hundred miles off the United States coast.

"So we may officially be dead," Fouad said, smiling broadly. "They had us heading for the Azores, then we vanished. Tough luck, guys, you must be sleeping with the fishes." The Jordanian nationals frowned at his remark.

"Don't worry about it. That's a term from a movie about American mafia criminals. Just keep us heading south and we'll be in good shape. How long until we come to Nassau?"

The flight engineer made some calculations.

"About two and a half hours more," the engineers said.

"Good." Fouad's smile broadened. "Hey, I'm hungry. You guys want another one of those airline dinners?"

They said they did, and Fouad went back to the small galley and heated up meals in the microwave. There were still twenty frozen dinners waiting. It was dark out now. It would stay dark as they came around Florida and headed across the Gulf of Mexico. Fouad's eyes lit up as he realized that the plan was working to perfection. Soon they would be in Mexico City and he would make the final preparations.

Washington, D.C.

Murdock, Ching, and Rafii arrived in Washington's Ronald Reagan National Airport at 0115. Murdock phoned Stroh at his office. A man answered and said Mr. Stroh was in conference.

"Good. Tell him Murdock and team have arrived at National. We'll check into a local motel and wait for his instructions in the morning. I'll call him with our hotel number when we have one."

"I'll tell him that. No, no, wait a minute, the meeting just broke up and Mr. Stroh is coming back in. Hold a moment."

"Murdock?"

"The same. At National, where do you want us?"

"Stay there. I'll send a car for you. We've had a report of a BAC One-Eleven that dropped off radar when it was on a flight plan to return to the Azores. Our team doesn't think it crashed. They could have turned off the transponder, which makes it tougher for the sixty-mile radar to find them. Then they could have turned south. Not that many BAC planes flying in and out of Halifax."

"So, Mexico City?"

"Looks that way. They could be almost there by now. At five hundred miles an hour you eat up the distance. We'll get you into our place, get you new clothes a little less ethnic, and ship you out to Mexico City on a Gulfstream. You'll get into Mexico City fast. Hope you slept on the plane. Yes, we can get you clothes in the middle of the night. This is the Company. Also get you some weapons. The car should be there in about twenty minutes. Meet the driver at the central taxi stand."

"A black Lincoln?"

"The same. Oh, the rest of the platoon left Germany about noon yesterday. Be in here sometime today at Langley."

"Good. See you soon."

An hour later, the three SEALs were checking out their new clothes. They fit. Sport clothes with a change in a modest roll-along suitcase. Each man had a 9mm automatic in his waistband and an Ingram in the suitcase with plenty of filled magazines.

Stroh looked them over.

"Not my idea of the perfect American tourist, but you'll have to do. We've been bombarding Mexico City's airport but can't get much cooperation. They say a BAC One-Eleven has landed without a flight plan, but the crew claimed radio and computer problems on board. They released it and it's somewhere on the big airport, but they had no reason to watch where it parked. Somewhere in the transit or freight sections, they figured."

"I've been at that airport," Murdock said. "There are all sorts of private hangars big enough to hold that plane. We'll have to find it before it takes off again."

Stroh's cell phone rang. He answered it and nodded. "Fifteen minutes. Right. We'll be there."

"A chopper is standing by to get us back to National, where the Gulfstream is waiting. We'll be in Mexico City early this morning. I'm going with you. We have to find that damn plane. It must have the fourth nuke on board."

"We'll give it a try," Murdock said.

Thirty minutes later, the SEALs and Stroh boarded the sleek business jet used mostly to fly VIP visitors around. They had used the plane before. They leaned back the first-class-type seats and relaxed. They knew they would get little sleep once they hit Mexico City.

The pilot told them his flight plan was to Corpus Christi, Texas, then almost due south to Mexico City. The whole run was about twenty-one hundred miles, and they could do that without stopping for fuel.

"Flight time a little under four hours, depending on the winds up there. We'll be at forty-one to forty-three thousand feet, depending on the wind. It's now three-oh-five A.M. Which puts us in the hot tamale town about seven A.M. Snacks in the galley and lots of pillows and blankets. Check in later."

The speaker snapped off and the sleek jet raced down the runway and took off. Each man had twenty thousand U.S. dollars in a money belt around his waist. They were ready to do business in Mexico, where *cohecho,* or bribery, was the way business transactions were done. Murdock had three hundred in ten-dollar greenbacks in his pocket.

"Let's get some sleep," he said. He was sure before their work was done in Mexico they would need it.

25

Mexico City, Mexico
Benito Juarez Airport

Three Mexican CIA agents waited for them at the taxi stand when they walked out of the terminal. Murdock could tell that they were Company men. They didn't wear suits or hats, but each had on a sports coat and a white shirt and tie.

"Mr. Stroh and Murdock?" one of the men asked as they walked up.

"Right, I'm Murdock," he said holding out his hand. The other man shook it.

"I'm Antonio Gutierrez, head of station." He turned to Stroh. "You must be Don Stroh. I've talked with you before but never met you." They shook hands. "There are some messages for you at the embassy. The second car will take you there. They said you should go there first, and then catch up with us."

"Thanks, Antonio. I'll go see what they want, then come back here to the airport." He waved and walked to the second black Buick at the side of the street and stepped inside.

"What do you know about that BAC One-Eleven that landed here sometime last night or early this morning?" Murdock asked.

"Not much. The Company is not exactly on good terms with the powers that be here, and the airport manager bucked us up to the Mexican City Chief of Police, who said he couldn't help us."

"So, where do we start?"

"We have a contact in one of the air-freight companies," Antonio said. "He's going to meet us as soon as I call him."

"Go," Murdock said.

Antonio took out a cell phone and hit the numbers and

chattered in Spanish for a moment. He looked up and waved at a black Buick that pulled up beside them. "That was my contact, Felipe. He said if it's a rogue aircraft, there are more than a dozen old buildings on the north side of the airport where it might be hidden and worked on or just kept out of sight. We'll split up and three of us will work from each end of the old buildings. They were supposed to be torn down, but things move slowly sometimes around here. You and I and one of your men will go one way, my two men and one of yours will be the other team."

They all squeezed into the Buick and drove around the parking lot, through a gate marked, FOR OFFICIAL VEHICLES ONLY, and around a road that hugged the airport's outside fence. Murdock saw the buildings well before they got there. All were old, most unpainted, one had half the roof fallen in. The car stopped at the first one and two of the Mexican CIA men got out. Murdock pointed to Ching, who joined them.

The Buick moved along the access road to the far end of the quarter-mile-long row of old hangars.

"Do these buildings still have electricity?" Murdock asked.

"Some do and some don't. It depends on who the owner knows, and how much he pays to keep the juice on."

They came to the last building, which looked better than the rest. "We might get lucky on our first try," Murdock said. Then he saw a sign with lettering and pictures of three fish.

"This one I know," Antonio said. "A big shipper of fish to outlaying areas in medium-sized transports. We'll go in and look around anyway."

On the south side of the airport, Asrar Fouad stared at his cell phone and swore in three languages. "What's the matter with these people?" he asked the two men who stood near him in a clean, well-lighted hangar that had the large front doors closed. "I asked them for clearance to fly to Monterrey, and they told me I would have to wait for the weather to clear. Weather, where? There's not a cloud in the sky here. Who knows what the weather will be like by the time we fly up there? These people are idiots."

The two Mexican men grinned, understanding little of what he said, which had come out in rapid-fire Arabic. They knew he was angry. So far they had helped him get the plane fueled and even some food restocked in the galley. They had been ready when he landed and routed him to this hangar for transient aircraft. He knew a little Spanish, enough to make them understand what he needed. The strange behavior of the tower made him angry, and he slipped into Arabic out of necessity. He knew no swear words in Spanish.

Now he tried to relax and struggled to find the right word in Spanish. "The weather," he said in Arabic. Then he tried his Spanish. "*Boletin meteorological muy malo,*" he said.

The two men looked up at the ceiling. "*Aqui?*" one asked.

Fouad shook his head. "*En Monterrey.*" The two Mexicans nodded and looked around. There was nothing else for them to do. Fouad seethed. He was ready. He had phoned Tijuana, and it took him an hour to get through. Mexico must have the worst telephone system in the world. He made arrangements on the other end and then filed his flight plan thirty minutes before he asked for take off. That's when they started talking about the bad weather. Nothing he could say in his limited Spanish helped. He would have to wait. He told them he would be at 42,000 feet, but they weren't swayed.

He was in a hurry but did not feel rushed. With any luck the air traffic people would figure his BAC went down in the Atlantic on the way to the Azores. He wondered if they would put out a search party looking for debris. Probably not. He went to the small door in the huge one and looked out. He didn't expect to see a hoard of police cars, wailing sirens, and red lights angling for this hangar to take him into custody. But he checked anyway. He had violated no Mexican laws. Bent a few but hadn't broken any. He knew that the CIA and Interpol had files on him, but first they would have to try to tie him into the cargo he carried, and then get him involved with the BAC. Slim to none, he figured. He had filed his flight plan to end at Monterrey, a big town four hundred miles due north. He groaned. So that was the hold-up. Monterrey must be socked in with fog and he wouldn't be able to land there. Shit! A town he wasn't going to go to was holding up his takeoff. He used his phone again and called the tower to find out about the weather for his flight.

The man on the phone this time said it was starting to clear. The way it looked now, he could take off in another thirty minutes.

"Yes, gracias." Fouad said and hung up. He yelled at his two helpers and had one hook up the tractor to the front wheel and turn the plane around so he could tow it out of the hangar and the pilot could get the engines warmed up and ready for taxiing to the right runway. He hurried inside the plane and told the pilot the good news.

"Great, we'll do our pre-flight check and keep in contact with the tower," the pilot said. He knew enough Spanish to get by with the tower. "Thirty minutes, you said."

"Right, and we head north for fifty miles, and then get on our course directly for Tijuana." He looked at the flight engineer. "You have our course all plotted?"

"Right, fifty north, then northwest to Tijuana. Do we turn off the transponder?"

"Oh, yes," Fouad said.

The flight engineer looked at him with a frown. Fouad wasn't sure he had convinced the man. He'd have to check to be sure that the engineer did turn off the transponder. "We can claim an emergency on the radio and that our transponder is down. They'll have to let us land. Then once there I have thirty men who will swarm the area and get us to a neutral spot where we can transfer the cargo to a specially made truck."

"Then we decide if we want to steal the plane, or radio home and get instructions?" the engineer asked.

"That's it," Fouad said. "Then it's up to you what you do. You'll each have that fifty thousand dinars I promised."

"Good. Now let me concentrate on my pre-flight."

Fouad went to the galley and made coffee. It wasn't the best, but would have to do. He enjoyed playing around in the little galley. He especially liked the variety of frozen dinners that were available.

On the north side of the airport, Murdock, Antonio, and the other Mexican CIA agent had been through six buildings

so far and found nothing but a few vagrants, a lot of rats
and cobwebs, and one small firm still in operation, but no
aircraft.

They paused outside the next building. Murdock figured
there were at least twenty in the row. He saw two cars parked
in front of the one three buildings down the line. They hadn't
been there a half-hour ago. He motioned and the three men
ran to the spot and checked. The man-sized door in a large
hangar door was unlocked. Murdock motioned for Antonio
to jerk the door open and Murdock would go in first with
his weapon drawn.

The door jolted outward, and Murdock surged inside. He
stopped in a blaze of lights. Directly ahead sat a half-finished
sailboat, maybe thirty feet long. He lowered his nine millimeter and waved with the other hand. Two men sat on the
partly finished deck working with narrow strips of wood.

Antonio shouted something to the men on the boat, and
the three attackers went back outside.

It was forty-five minutes later that the two teams met in
the middle and reported no suspects.

"So where the hell is he?" Murdock asked.

"Don't know. Let me try to see if he's filed a flight plan.
The first time I tried, the man said he wasn't authorized to
give it to me over the phone. We didn't have time to go up
to the tower." He phoned and talked for two or three minutes,
but Murdock figured he was striking out again.

Antonio folded his cell phone and scowled. "The tower
master says we're not authorized to receive that kind of information. If I want to go to the tower and show him my
credentials and get them verified, he can tell me."

"Where else on the airport? Any small air freighters?"

"Several. On the south side. Let's go down there and work
them."

They drove around the perimeter fence again and into the
south part of the airport where there were maybe a dozen
hangars with mid-to-large–sized jet transports parked inside
and out. In the third building they tried there was no office,
just two men wiping up oil spills on the otherwise clean
concrete floor. Antonio talked with them.

He became alert at once and signaled to Murdock who went up to him.

"These men say, yes, a plane with DAF on the tail was here. They helped service and refuel it. It took off about fifteen minutes ago. They saw it airborne."

"Damnit, what rotten fucking luck. Now we go to the tower and you show him your papers and get that flight plan destination."

A half hour later, Murdock watched Antonio come out of the airport tower manager's office. Murdock couldn't read his expression. He slumped down beside Murdock and shook his head.

"Not sure if this is good news or bad. Yes, the BAC One-Eleven took off at 0832. It had a flight plan with Monterrey in north eastern Mexico as its destination. Four hundred miles from here. Only when the air traffic men tracked it on their radar, they found it on a different course. It had gone twenty miles north, and then turned northwest. It continued on that course for forty miles until it flew out of the radar's range. The air controllers could not raise them by radio."

"So he filed a false flight plan," Murdock said. "He was really heading northwest. Not many major airports out that way."

Antonio took over. "Where is he headed? Leon is up that way about two hundred miles, but has only a small airport. Then there is Durango on that line, which has a good airport, but why would he go there with a nuclear bomb?"

"He wouldn't. What's on out in the northwest?"

"Hermosillo, about a thousand miles northwest, but it's still two hundred miles south of Tucson, Arizona. Why would he stop there?"

"He wouldn't," Murdock said. "On northwest is Mexicali and Tijuana, both right on the border with easy crossing into the U.S. One of those must be his destination."

"Or he really did go down. Weather was bad and he was delayed on his takeoff. Weather was extremely bad with electrical storms, even funnel-shaped clouds near the Leon area. So he could have gone down."

Murdock stood and paced. Then they went down the steps to the terminal.

"How long would it take him to get to Tijuana or Mexicali?"

"I don't know the BAC that well, but figure five hundred miles an hour. Three and a half to four hours. Depending on headwinds. The jet stream is moving against him, but he could go above or below it."

"Okay, alert our people in those two border towns to monitor the landings of any BAC One-Elevens within the next four hours. If they find one, they should use local law and grab it and arrest everyone on the plane, and check to see if there's a large crate on board that might have lead shielding around it. That's all we can do right now."

"If it doesn't land at one of those two airports?" Antonio asked.

"Then we get on our boots and hire some choppers and run that flight line he took until we find or don't find a wrecked BAC somewhere beyond Mexico City's radar reach."

"We have at least a two hundred mile line to check just for starters from here to Leon," Antonio said. "We better get started."

"Why don't we rent two choppers now and have them ready just in case we need them? Then with any luck we can run that first two hundred mile line before it gets dark."

26

While Antonio made some calls to rent the two search choppers, Murdock called the embassy. Don Stroh came on the line.

"What have you found out about the BAC?"

Murdock brought him up to date.

"I want to go with you on the search. I approve. Sounds like the best bet. How long until they should land at the border cities?"

"Almost three hours. Antonio has your people alerted in both towns who are at the airports keeping watch. Where is the rest of my platoon?"

"They hit Andrews about a half hour ago and checked in with me. I put them on a borrowed Gulfstream, and they should be here by one-thirty, or thirteen-thirty, as you guys say."

"What do we use for quarters down here?"

"No U.S. military facilities. I'm having a man here rent one of the unused hangars in that northern section of the field. Have the choppers flown there, where we can get up and away fast if we need to. There's a fancy hotel right inside the new terminal there, the Hilton Mexico City Airport Hotel. It's on the third level and on the plush side. I don't think they would appreciate our traipsing around in our cammies and toting submachine guns."

"Right. Can we keep the Gulfstream here in case we need to make a run to Tijuana?"

"That's the plan. If the big plane did go down along that route, we'll need all of our troops to dig it out. I've had your men fully equipped with their usual armament, including the twenty-millimeter rounds. We can do that with the private charter. Anything else?"

"Yes, have one of the men at the embassy arrange to bring in catered food to that hangar three times a day until we tell him to stop. I hope you brought your standard CIA-issue credit card."

"I never leave home without it."

"Good. We three knights of the O table are going to find a snack bar somewhere and fill up on fast food before the action gets going again. I figure another two hours and fifty minutes until we should have some confirmation from both towns."

"Your platoon guys may not even have time to stretch their legs after they get here, before jumping right back on that Gulfstream."

"There was bad weather to the north. The BAC was held up for a half hour waiting for it to clear so they could go straight north. They may have run into the back end of it and gone down. That's my hunch right now. We'll see how well it plays out."

"I'm done here. I'll catch you in the airport in about an hour."

"See you then."

Murdock picked up his two men and they headed for the tourist-type food concessions in the huge new terminal. He figured the world's largest city should have the world's best eating spots.

North of Mexico City

Fouad settled back into the fourth seat in the cockpit and worked on his steak portabella with mushroom sauce, peas, carrots, mashed potatoes, and an apple crumb desert.

"We've got weather ahead," the pilot said. Fouad adjusted his headset and mike so he could talk with the crew.

"There always is weather," Fouad said. "Is that good weather or bad?"

"Bad. When we left Mexico City going north, they said the weather had closed in on Monterrey and was building to the west of the city. When we turned northwest, I hoped we could clear it. I can see the storm clouds ahead. They are spiraling up to fifty thousand feet. Lots of electrical activity.

Maybe we should turn around and go back to Benito Juárez Airport."

"Not a chance. Don't even think about it. We're charging straight through. What's the next big town on this route?"

"León, about a hundred miles ahead. I don't think we can make it there, and it doesn't show on my maps as having a runway long enough for us."

"I show a big airport at Guadalajara," the flight engineer said. "Only trouble is it's a hundred and twenty-five miles almost due west of us."

"Forget it," Fouad said. "Why can't we fly through a little bit of lightning and wind?"

"That little bit of lightning could hit us and knock out all of our electrical circuits, putting us down in the jungle," the pilot said. "That wind could rip off the rudder or a wing."

"I don't believe you," Fouad barked. "I've flown in worse weather than this. We're going through, straight through on our heading for Tijuana." He pulled the pistol from his belt and moved forward to the pilot's chair. He pushed the muzzle of the gun against the pilot's head.

"We're going through," he said again. "Either that or I take the controls because you'll have your brains blasted all over the side of the cockpit."

Sweat ran down the side of the pilot's face. He lifted his brows and coughed. "Yeah, okay. We go through. We're at fifteen thousand now. It looks calmer down here. Our forward speed is cut to a little over four hundred due to the heavy head winds and the turbulence. We'll try. May Allah be with us."

"That's for damn sure," Fouad said. "I've come this far and I'm this close. Nothing is going to stop me. Certainly not a little thing like a windstorm and some lightning."

The first rain crashed into the windshield of the BAC like hail. The wipers came on but couldn't keep up. The pilot turned and looked at Fouad.

"This is not good. The rain could turn cold and freeze on the wings. We don't have automatic de-icers."

"Shut up and fly," Fouad said. "Unless you want a nine-millimeter addition to your brains."

A sudden jolt hit the aircraft and Fouad felt himself lifted off the floor, and his hands reached for the top of the cockpit.

"Hang on," the pilot shouted. "An air pocket."

Fouad was on the ceiling of the cabin for what seemed like twenty minutes. He knew it couldn't have been more than ten seconds. He dropped suddenly to the floor and his knees buckled as gravity took over again.

"We dropped straight down over two hundred feet," the flight engineer said. "Hope there are no more of those." The other two men were belted into their seats. Fouad returned to the fourth seat and buckled himself in.

"Keep flying this bucket of bolts straight on our heading," he shouted.

A flash of lightning tore through the clouds, turning the near darkness into brilliant light for a brief moment. Then it was gone and the rain and the rumble of thunder pounded through the plane.

"We're drifting right," the copilot said into his mike.

"Corrected," the pilot said.

The thunder came again, and lightning. The plane jolted and this time Fouad scowled.

"We were just hit by lightning," the engineer said. "Our dampening rods took care of most of it, but we've lost part of our controls to the ailerons."

"Switching to backup controls for the ailerons," the pilot said.

They flew for two more minutes before another bolt of lightning hit the aircraft. The whole plane began to vibrate and swing slowly from side to side.

"We've lost the number-two engine," the pilot said. "We can fly with one, but it cuts our speed to about three hundred and fifty miles an hour."

"Where are we?" Fouad asked the flight engineer.

"About fifty miles from León. No airport there."

"I should send out a mayday and ask for instructions to the closest airport," the pilot said.

"No," Fouad shouted. "We dropped off their radar, remember." He looked at the flight engineer. "You did turn off the transponder, didn't you?"

"I haven't had time yet. I was trying to track the storm."

"Idiot. I should shoot you right here. Pilot, make your

mayday call but don't identify yourself. Clear?"

"That's the first thing they'll ask. Our flight and our location."

"Just ask about weather, stupid. Do it now."

The pilot had just keyed the radio and sent out a mayday call when the third bolt of lightning hit the plane. The whole tail section exploded. The second engine flamed out. The T-tail rudder broke off, and the resulting strain on the heavy engines cracked them loose and the whole tail assembly fell entirely off the plane.

The craft went into a steep dive. The pilot fought the controls, but he had only the flaps and the ailerons to control it and they weren't enough. The big transport spiraled down then flattened out. The three men in the cockpit were screaming at each other. Fouad didn't know what had happened and tried to shoot the pilot. His round missed, and then in a violent spin he lost control of the pistol and it fell to the floor.

From fifteen thousand feet it took only what Fouad thought were seconds for the craft to plunge to the ground. He felt the first ripping and tearing as the cockpit hit first. Huge trees and limbs smashed into the plane; the cockpit's heavy Plexiglas windscreen disintegrated, and chunks of it slashed into the cabin like shrapnel. Before he could even cry out at the pain, Fouad's whole world turned black. The cockpit smashed into the ground at over three hundred miles an hour and crumpled. The wings sheared off; the fuel in the tanks exploded into a huge fireball that engulfed the wings and front of the plane and caught some of the towering trees and brush on fire. The wings and their fuel tanks careened fifty yards forward through the jungle growth, spewing flaming aviation fuel in their wake. The fire burned furiously for twenty minutes. Then when all the fuel was burned up or evaporated, the rain and the eternal dampness of the jungle squelched the blazes into smoking islands, which were soon put out entirely by the heavy downpour. Only a twenty-foot section of the body of the craft remained intact. It had been behind the wings and missed the gush of burning fuel. It lay half-hidden by the large trees and heavy rain forest growth on the slope of a mountain more then eight thousand feet high.

After an hour the rain stopped and the clouds blew away. Soon the birds began to sing again; the animals, frightened by the roaring, burning wreckage that had smashed into their habitat, came out of hiding and went about their daily work of survival.

There was no movement in the smashed and burned cockpit of the BAC One-Eleven that had buried itself ten feet into a small stream that ran down the mountain. All was quiet inside the cabin, deadly quiet.

Mexico City Airport

Murdock, Ching, and Rafii ate at a Chinese specialty cafe in the food mall and had no trouble paying for their meal with U.S. dollars. Murdock figured the dollar was worth about ten pesos. Then they met Antonio at the appointed spot near the tower.

"The time is eleven-fifty-five," Antonio said. "If they got through the storms, they should be landing in either Tijuana or Mexicali in five minutes. I'll call both places to check."

"If they land, your people know what to do?" Murdock asked.

"Oh, yes. If that plane sets down at either spot, there will be a dozen police and agents swarming all over it. They won't have a chance to get away."

"Let's hope," Murdock said. "Then this chase will be over."

Ching shook his head. "They never got through the storm. I've been watching the TV news. Worst storm in two years. Blanketed central and northern Mexico with rain, hail, and lightning, high straight-line winds up to eighty miles an hour. You know what that would do to a mid-range airliner like the BAC One-Eleven?"

"Snap it in half like a balsa wood glider under my foot," Antonio said. "Yes, the weather has been horrendous, and if they flew toward León they were right in the middle of it. When does the rest of your platoon get in?"

"About an hour and a half. Do we have a HQ anywhere around here for the choppers to land?"

"Remember those old hangars we looked at? I rented the one where the BAC had been. The choppers will go there. I told the tower to order the American Gulfstream to taxi over there as well. Let's go to those phones over there. I'm calling Tijuana."

Five minutes later, Antonio shook his head. "Neither airport reported that a BAC has landed, and they have no flight plans for one to come that direction. I called the choppers. They'll be at our hangar in fifteen minutes."

"Let's go meet them," Murdock said.

They paged Don Stroh and he met them at the north entrance. They took a taxi to the north side of the airport. The driver was angry the trip was so short, so Murdock gave him a ten-dollar tip and he was all smiles.

The hangar was about as they had seen it that morning. The two maintenance men were there, glad for the new renters. A catering truck arrived just after Murdock and the others and they stocked up on food.

"Your platoon ate on board the Gulfstream, but it won't hurt to have some extra staples around," Don Stroh said. He unwrapped a sandwich. "Yeah, tuna fish. Can't beat a good tuna fish sandwich."

When the choppers arrived, Murdock, Stroh, and Antonio had worked out a heading from the airport to León.

"If that last fifteen minutes are right on their flight, the plane could have gone down somewhere this side of León," Antonio said. "Only it won't be a straight line from here. The tower said they went out twenty miles north before they headed northwest. Let's recalibrate our heading."

The two helicopters arrived ten minutes late. Murdock checked his watch. It was twelve-hundred-twenty. The two craft were Bell 206 JetRangers. Two pilots and three passengers. They were veterans of the civilian chopper trade and reliable, but not capable of any heavy lifting. They talked to the two pilots. Both spoke only Spanish. Antonio told them what they wanted and what route they wanted to fly. He emphasized that this was a search mission and they needed to be as close to the ground as was safe.

Murdock put Antonio, one of his CIA men, and Ching in one bird. He, Stroh, and the other Spanish-speaking CIA man, who said his name was Hernando, went in the other one. Murdock told Rafii he'd done enough on this mission.

"Take a nap, have a Coke and another sandwich, and meet the rest of the platoon when the guys come. Tell them what we're doing and the odds. If we find anything, we should be back shortly. Depending how far we have to go. At any rate we have to be back before dark."

Murdock stepped into the Bell JetRanger. "*Vamonos*," he called, and the pilot cranked up the rotor and they took off, heading north for twenty miles, then on a northwest track for León.

"What if we don't find it?" Stroh asked.

"If we don't find it, we're in one hell of a lot of trouble. I have no idea where else it could be. Unless they really did disable their transponder and fly somewhere else, like to Houston."

"If they did, we *are* in a lot of trouble," Murdock said. "But Houston is in one hell of a lot *more* trouble. Nuclear bomb vaporization trouble."

27

The Bell JetRanger hit a few pockets of unsettled air that followed the main storm that had passed through central Mexico and was now heading for the Gulf Coast. The pilots had dropped down to a hundred feet over the lush growth of the rain forest below. The two birds flew fifty yards apart on the same course to double the chance of finding the crash site, if there was one. Murdock believed they would find the crash.

"It's got to be here somewhere," he said. "That BAC didn't fly on to Houston. Fouad's best chance was Tijuana. From there he could cross the border in a specially rigged truck, moving across at the busiest time. He could also have bribed three or four border crossing inspectors and paved the way. Once in the U.S. he was home free and could pick San Diego, Los Angeles, or San Francisco as the target. All he had to do was drive into the heart of any city, set a timer on the bomb, jump in a trailing car, and drive fifty miles outside the target zone."

The pilot bellowed something and everyone looked out the windows. The sun broke through scattered clouds as the front moved quickly to the east. Below they could see a scorched spot of the forest. Both choppers circled the area.

Murdock shook his head. "Looks like a small forest fire that somebody put out. Not more than an acre or two. Must be hard for a fire to keep burning down there."

The pilots swung back on their heading for León and dropped lower. They came to a series of hills that pushed them higher and higher, but they kept their distance above the forest at fifty to a hundred feet.

The sun broke out of the last cloud that scudded quickly to the east.

"How far to León?" Murdock asked Hernando, the Mexican CIA man. He relayed the question to the pilot. The answer came back.

"We're about fifty miles to the town," Hernando said. "Looks like they really got a lot of rain through here. Look at the water gushing down these hills."

Below, a torrent of water rushed down a gully, turning it into a river twenty feet wide. It was water that had been dumped onto the foothills above and was just now coming down the slope.

They powered over the hills and up a long valley, but found nothing that looked like a crash.

"Most likely there would be a fire if the plane went down," Murdock said. "It had just taken on a full load of fuel to fly the sixteen or seventeen hundred miles to Tijuana. That much fuel will make a furious fire."

The two pilots saw it about the same time. "Trails of smoke ahead," the pilot told Hernando, who told Murdock. He and Stroh stared out the windows on both sides and tried to see ahead. Hernando went to the front of the little craft and looked out the windscreen.

"Yes," he shouted over the sound of the chopper. "Yes, a gash in the forest. Must be a quarter of a mile long. It's coming up fast, it'll be on the left side."

Murdock and Stroh looked out the left-side windows. It came up quickly; then the pilot slowed the craft and hovered over the middle of the slash through the trees with a large burned area in the center. They could see the middle section of a jet airliner half-buried in the trees and brush.

"No tail," Murdock shouted. "Where's the tail and the DAF logo?" Murdock touched Hernando's shoulder. "Tell the pilot to follow the fire trail. The wings have to be here somewhere."

"They moved slowly above the burned path in the heavy foliage. A line of trees had been chopped down as if with a giant machete. The forest was scorched right down to the ground in two trails. Then they saw what was left of the smoking sections of the two wings.

"Had to have happened today, with that smoke," Stroh said. "How close can we land?"

Murdock asked Hernando. He asked the pilot. Hernando came back shaking his head. "The pilot says he can't see any place clear enough to land on for at least a mile. We wouldn't have a chance to cut our way through that jungle and get to the plane and then back to the chopper before dark. A mile down there is like twenty on a good paved road."

"Have him make another pass and hover over the middle section. Wish I'd thought to bring along some rappel equipment. I could have gone down there."

The bird turned, flew back to the middle of the burned slash, and hovered. Murdock and Stroh stared out the open · door at the wreckage.

"Any survivors?" Stroh asked.

"Don't see any. If they could move, they would have got in the open by now. I'd guess all KIA."

"Can you see any kind of a crate that could hold the bomb?" Stroh asked.

"Could be inside that section, or it could have torn lose on impact and rammed forward into the jungle."

Murdock studied the scene for another two minutes. "Okay," he told Hernando. "Let's get out of here and back to the airport. We've got to rent a bird big enough to have a winch on it so I can go down and make certain that the bomb is on that plane. Then all we have to do is find another chopper big enough to lift the crate out of there. It must weigh at least two tons."

Hernando told the pilot. He radioed the other pilot and they turned back toward Mexico City.

"Be sure the pilots don't radio anyone that we found this plane," Murdock said. "We don't need any competition trying to get the bomb out of there." Hernando went forward and came back with a frown.

"Afraid I was too late. Our pilot had radioed the tower at Benito Juárez Airport that we were hunting a downed jet-liner. He didn't say exactly that we had found it, but the authorities will be asking us questions."

"Not if they can't find us," Murdock said. "Have the pilots fly us back to their home field. They aren't at Benito, right?"

Hernando nodded. "Yes, that should work. This outfit, Helicopters Mexico, has some big birds there. With any luck we can get a chopper today to fly out with a winch to let you down and bring you back up. That way we'll know for sure it's the BAC and the bomb is on board."

"Tell the other pilot where we're heading," Murdock told Hernando. "Be sure he understands that he makes no transmissions to the tower at Benito."

The flight back to Mexico City was quick. But by the time they landed at a small airport just north of the city, and talked to the owners about a larger craft, it was too late to make a safe flight back to the crash site.

Murdock inspected the suggested chopper. It had no winch and was far too small to lift out even a ton. Hernando and Antonio talked with the owners, who shook their heads.

"They say they don't think we'll find any helicopters in the whole area with a winch and that could lift out two tons. Just not much work for them."

Stroh waved him off. "Let's get back to the embassy. He took out a cell phone, called them, and told them to send a car to the small airport to pick them up.

"Let me get to my SATCOM," Stroh said. "We thought there might be some problems down here so we sent a pair of destroyers and a cruiser on an exercise into the Gulf of Mexico. We might have some assets that we can use."

A half hour later at the U.S. Embassy in Mexico City, Stroh used up the airwaves to call his headquarters in Langley, then the chief of naval operations. It took ten minutes and Murdock listened. When the last transmission was done, Stroh grinned.

"You owe me a long-range fishing trip out of Seaforth. We've got a Seahawk that will be visiting us here at Benito Airport. It should arrive about daylight. I'll get clearance from the Mexican air people for the overflight by a U.S. military aircraft. Then it's gravy. The navy will time the flight so it arrives here at Benito Juárez Airport at daylight plus ten and sits down at that north hangar we rented. It's a search-and-rescue type so it has a hoist. They'll pull the torpedoes and armament so we can stuff six SEALs in there if

we have to. It has a range of over seven hundred miles, so
no sweat about refueling until it gets ready to go back."

"How much can one lift and does it have lift hooks on
it?" Murdock asked.

"It does and it can lift over five thousand pounds."

"What's the average vertical lift distance for an S and H?"
Murdock asked. "Can they go down a hundred feet with their
cable?"

Stroh frowned. "I don't know. I'll ask the destroyer captain. I can get him direct on the SATCOM." He keyed up
the set and called the destroyer *Anderson,* DD941. Stroh
asked the question on length of the cable.

"Stroh. I talked to the pilots. They say anything over sixty
feet is risky. They can go up to eighty in an extreme emergency."

Stroh thanked the captain and signed off.

Murdock scowled. "That's in a forest on the side of a
mountain. My guess it's about six to seven thousand feet.
Air is thin up there for the choppers. Those trees looked to
be eighty to ninety feet tall. Lots of them. No place near the
crash site I saw big enough to get down lower. Well have to
find an open place just to lower down, then cut our way
through the jungle to the crash. I'll take two men with me.
We'll need machetes, axes, ropes, and some heavy boots."

"I'll have them for you in the morning. I'll need boot
sizes."

"The rest of the platoon at the hangar?"

"Yes, waiting for you. I'll send you out in a car."

Murdock hesitated. "Think anyone else will be looking
for that plane?"

"Like the Mexican FAA? I don't even know if they have
one."

"I was thinking more like some of Fouad's people. He
must have had someone here setting up things for him. Have
there been any news reports about that BAC plane dropping
off radar in the middle of the big storm?"

"I'll find out. Now get back out to your platoon. Feed
them. I've sent in sleeping bags for them for the night. No
bunks, but better than sleeping on the concrete floor."

"Not much. Let me know about any news report on the

plane. And where do I pick up a SATCOM? Our troops didn't bring one of ours."

Stroh brought him one and sent him and Ching out the door into a black Buick that headed for the airport.

Back at the north hangar, Murdock found the rest of the platoon along with what was left of two cases of beer and the catering truck's supply of food.

"So, is the bomb there?" J.G. Gardner asked.

"Don't know. We'll find out in the morning." He told Gardner and the rest of the men what they had seen at the crash site. "It's a hundred and fifty miles or so northwest of here, in heavy timber and brush and what looks like a junior-sized jungle. Going to be tough just getting to the site, let alone getting the bomb out if it's there."

"Why not call in Kat and have her disable it in place?" Jaybird asked.

"The brass in Washington want to take it apart and evaluate it and see how much Iraq really knows about making these weapons. The experts can learn a lot by dissecting the mechanism."

"You say it might be too dangerous to go down on a hoist out of the chopper," Fernandez said. "Why not just drop down a two-hundred-foot line and rappel down?"

"We're not sure how tall those trees are, or what the wind currents might be in there. We'll pull back a mile, or two or three, if we have to, and keep everyone safe. The fucking bomb isn't going anywhere."

"Anybody else looking for it?" Senior Chief Neal asked.

"That could be a problem. Fouad must have had a cell here in town helping him. Just what they are doing now, or what they know about the crash, is uncertain. If they know the plane went down, it's almost certain they will try to find it."

"So we go in with all of our firepower intact," Lam said.

Murdock nodded. "Okay, we have food, a couple of beers and sleeping bags. Sack out wherever it's best. We have a dawn date with a Seahawk. I'll take five people with me. If we can be lowered down on the winch, three of us will go and inspect the crash. If we have to hike in, all six of us will go. For the drop I want Bradford with his SATCOM, Canzoneri, and Mahanani in case anyone is still alive."

"You think there are survivors?" the medic asked.

"I'd say no, but strange things can happen in an airliner crash. Also suited up for the game will be Lam and Prescott. That's it; let's get some sleep. There will be food here three times a day. Go easy on the beer. We might have a hot firefight before this is over."

Murdock told Bradford to set up the SATCOM and keep it turned on all night. Stroh might want to get in touch.

The next morning at 0515 Murdock came awake to the thumping whine of a chopper rotor. He ran outside in time to see a U.S. Navy SH-60 Seahawk land thirty feet in front of the hangar. The side door popped open and two men jumped out with sub guns at their sides. The motors shut down and the rotors swung slower and slower.

"We're friendly here," Murdock called. The two men trotted over. One had silver railroad bars on his collar.

"Murdock?" the lieutenant commander asked.

"Right, you're early. Glad you could make it. You have juice enough for a three-hundred-mile round trip?"

"Plenty, Commander. We're ready when you are."

Murdock found a pile of boxes outside the large hangar door. Inside were axes, machetes, ropes, and two dozen MREs (meals ready to eat).

Three of the SEALs came out of the small door pulling on their combat vests. Each had his weapon. They looked at the boxes and Murdock told them to put them in the chopper.

Three minutes later all six SEALs were in the Seahawk. The door closed and the bird took off at once. Murdock went to the cabin and showed the pilot where they had found the crash.

"For a hundred and fifty miles, we'll have a flight time of sixty-one minutes," the pilot said. His name was O'Malley, and Murdock liked him immediately. He gave the pilot a Motorola and showed him how to use it.

"That's good for about five miles. Be a way for us to keep in contact. We'll call you back when we're ready to come out or if we get in trouble."

"I'll pull back and find a cleared spot where I can set

down and wait for your call. Just so I keep it within five miles, right?"

"Right."

"Not too sure how close we can get you to the actual crash, but we'll get in as close as we can, and winch you down and up if possible. We want to find out if the package is there just as bad as you do. Take a rest. I'll let you know when we sight the crash."

Murdock went back into the SH-60 and found a spot to sit on the hard metal floor. Maybe now the chase would be over. Maybe. They would know for sure in the next hour and a half.

28

The SH-60 U.S. Navy helicopter flew straight down the heading that the GPS had recorded when Murdock was at the crash site the day before. The SEAL commander remained seated for what he figured was a half hour, then he stood and looked out the window. Trees, mountains, green stuff down below. He saw some towering trees and hoped there weren't a lot of them around the crash site. He knew there were some.

The crash had ended in a gully with a small stream running down it. The slopes on each side slanted up sharply to high ridges that led to higher peaks in the distance. That much he remembered. How close they could come to the site and find a landing spot, he didn't know.

The second pilot, a J.G., tapped Murdock on the shoulder.

"Two-oh minutes to the LZ," the man said and returned to the cockpit. Murdock followed him and looked out the slanted windscreen of the Seahawk. More trees, more ravines and ridges. The craft slanted higher to follow the upthrust of the land.

"Our elevation?" he shouted to the pilot.

"Near six thousand," the pilot shouted back. "Our target is about seventy-two hundred according to my map."

Murdock watched the wet-looking slopes drift under the chopper. It was doing a hundred and forty-five miles an hour, its normal cruising speed. He had no idea what any wind would do to their actual ground speed.

"Is that it?" the pilot shouted.

Murdock looked ahead where the pilot pointed. He saw a thin trail of smoke rising in the still air over a ravine.

"Two miles to target," the copilot called.

"Looks good," Murdock said.

They flew up to the black gash in the forest green and circled it at three hundred feet. The pilot shook his head.

"Commander, no chance in holy hell I can set you down there, even on the sling. Too many tall trees. They're spotted around at just the wrong places. Let's troll for a possible LZ."

The chopper swung downstream on the little gully. Trees and more trees. Some looked shorter here, but there could have been a double canopy sixty feet in the air. Murdock scowled and kept looking.

"There," Murdock shouted, pointing at a blackened section to the left and over the small ridge. "Looks like a fire, lightning strike maybe."

The pilot nodded and swung that way. He dropped down to a hundred feet and circled the area.

"Yeah. I can sit down there. That's a clear LZ. It does look like an old fire. I can stay here. We're not over four miles from the target. Over this ridge, then up the gully."

Murdock tapped him twice on the back and went to the other SEALs.

"Out-a-here in five," he said. He pointed to the door and held up five fingers. The SEALs stood and adjusted their equipment and picked up their weapons.

"LZ?" Lam asked.

Murdock nodded and stood beside the door. He pulled it open and watched the ground coming up to meet them. Thirty seconds later he felt the two front wheels touch the ground and he jumped the two feet to the blackened ground and found it surprisingly solid. He ran out thirty feet and waited for the rest of the men. They came, lugging the boxes with the tools and MREs in them.

When the last man came up, Murdock stopped them. "Let's spread out the tools, ropes, and MREs," he said. "We'll take two axes, all the rope, the MREs, and each one of us gets a machete. Glad they included them. It's going to be tough going through this tangle." When they'd all taken tools, gear, and MREs, they had three axes and a machete left.

"Leave them here," Murdock said. "Move that box into the edge of the jungle and camo it." That done, they headed up the slope toward the crest of the ridge. As soon as they left the blackened area of the fire, they walked into a green wilderness of trees, brush, vines, and dozens of different kinds of plants, even some flowering ones. The ground was damp, and some places seeped moisture out of the hillside.

"This ain't gonna be easy," Bradford said.

"Up to the top and north," Murdock said. "The pilot said not more than four miles, but it could be six."

It was slow, agonizing work. In places they had to hack their way through the growth with the machetes. They took turns leading to spread out the agony.

Almost a half hour had passed before they chopped through the final tangle and reached the summit of the ridgeline. They looked down through the trees and saw a small stream bouncing down the gully, which showed about fifty feet wide at the bottom.

Murdock looked to the north, hoping that he could see the wreck or at least some trails of smoke. Nothing. The ravine took a left-hand turn and vanished behind the shoulder of the mountain. The top of the ridge showed lots of rocks, and rock face in places, which cut down the growth.

"Let's stay on the ridgeline," Murdock said. "A hell of a lot easier going up here than down in the jungle."

"Amen to that, brother," Lam called.

Before they moved ten feet, a rifle round ricocheted off one of the rocks and whined away into the sky. The six SEALs dove to the ground a second later and rolled to their right off the ridgeline and away from the sound of the shot. At once, four more shots slammed over the rocks and into the trees behind them.

Lam edged back up the slope beside a rock and peered over the ridge at the jungle below.

"Nothing but fucking trees," he said. "No flash. The sound of the shots came some time after the lead arrived, so they must be at least a half mile off. The AK-47 will do the distance."

Murdock was right beside him a moment later. "No way to see anybody down there. Who the hell are they, and how did they get a location on the crash?"

"Who?" Lam repeated. "Got to be a cell of the Arabs who

live here and helped old Fouad get in and out of the Mexican airport. Who else? Somebody let out that Fouad's plane had crashed. Maybe one of the guys at the hangar. One of them must have understood English all the time."

The other four crowded up behind but kept on the reverse slope.

"So what is it," Mahanani asked, "a race for the crash?"

"Not from up here," Murdock said. "If they know where it is, they would beat us to it. But see that rocky area ahead? By the time they get there, they'll be so tired, they'll walk across it."

"Yeah, if they are heading upstream," Lam said. "What if they are waiting to see which direction we go? They could have seen the chopper circle something upstream and then come back and land."

Murdock studied the jungle below with his binoculars. He could see no movement, no armed men, nothing unusual.

"There," Lam said. "Almost straight down the slope and two fingers to the right. A whole flock of birds just flew out of those trees. Something down there disturbed them. Like a squad of men."

"So we wait them out," Murdock said. "They might kick up a few more birds as they move up the ravine."

Murdock checked his Motorola. It was on. "Flyboy One, this is Murdock. Come in."

"Yes, Murdock. Figured you were cutting your way through the damn vines out there. How far did you get?"

"We're at the top of the ridge. We can see you. Just got shot at, so we have unfriendlies somewhere below us in the crash gully. Some of them might come looking for you. You'll have no notice if they do. If your petrol is good, you better lift off for a new LZ. If you get out of radio range, fly over this area every two hours. We'll contact you with what we're going to do."

"Roger that. We're out of here. Talk later."

"Another bunch of wild birds flew out down there," Lam said.

"Cap, want us to put a couple of twenties into that last bird fly?" Prescott asked.

Murdock shook his head. "No. Then they would know we

were armed and they wouldn't go anywhere near that bald spot. Let's wait awhile longer."

A half hour later, Lam reported. "Cap, I've seen three more bird flyouts. Looks like their lead man must be about thirty yards from the bald spot. So will they cross it or go around in the cover?"

"Cover," Canzoneri said.

"Cross it," Bradford said. "They're civilians not in condition. By now they are dead tired. They'll take any gift they can find."

Prescott snorted. "Yeah, cross the bald spot. I've got a fiver if anyone wants to cover me."

"We have three twenties," Murdock said, "and the sniper rifle. If they cross it in a group, we all fire when they are bunched. Time to play our cards. Let's lock and load."

It took the men below ten minutes to get to the rock face. Then one figure burst out of the trees, ran across the first twenty-yard section, and paused. He looked ahead, then up at the ridge. He carried a rifle. At last he waved the men forward with the classic infantry arm motion.

Six men came out of the trees and started running across the rock.

"Now," Murdock said. The four weapons fired almost at the same time. They had been sighted in and the gunners awaited the command. Murdock watched through the scope on his twenty. The first round hit just below the first two men in the group. The blast riddled them with shrapnel and blew them ten feet to the side. Neither moved again.

The other two 20mm rounds exploded on the near side of the men; two more died and one crawled toward the jungle. With the sniper rifle Canzoneri stopped him ten yards short of his goal. Two men were missing.

"The scout ahead got away," Lam said.

"I saw the last man in the group turn and run back the way they came a second before we shot," Bradford said. "He must have figured it out."

"At least we lowered the odds," Murdock said. "Let's move on up this ridgeline to that bend and see if we can spot the wreckage."

Five minutes later they hadn't come to the bend, but the

ridge had flattened out into a mesa, which Murdock figured must be two hundred yards wide. Near the ridge edge the trees multiplied and grew much taller and denser. Lam had been out thirty yards in front of them, and he came back now to Murdock, sporting a strange expression.

"Not sure I believe what I'm seeing," he told Murdock softly.

"Why? What did you see?"

"From where I stopped it looked like five or six moss-covered buildings made of rough-hewn stone. One of the buildings is three stories tall and partly in ruins. The other smaller ones are mostly caved in and the jungle is claiming them as its own."

"Might be some old ruins of an Aztec city," Murdock said. "Or were they farther north? I don't remember. Let's take a look at it."

The six SEALs stared in amazement at the stone blocks that some ancient people had hoisted into place, some thirty feet high.

"Blocks must weigh a ton each," Lam said. "How did they get them all the way to the top?"

They saw some doors and openings that might have been primitive windows. "Don't go inside any of them," Murdock said. "They might come crashing down at any time."

Before he finished the sentence, Prescott let out a muffled scream and staggered against Mahanani, who almost fell down.

"I'm hit in the leg," Prescott shouted.

Mahanani lowered him to the forest mulch on the clearing around the buildings.

"It's an arrow," Mahanani said softly.

"Everybody go down on one knee and don't use your weapons," Bradford said. "Got to be some primitive tribe in here that hasn't been contacted by the Mexican authorities. That's my guess. By kneeling, we show respect and subservience."

"What else would they respond to?" Murdock asked.

"Prescott got hit with a bird arrow, small, light, just a sharpened point on the stick arrow," Mahanani said. "Not sophisticated at all. Maybe if we sit down and put our weapons on the ground they'll come out, and we can make signs with them."

The SEALs looked at Murdock. "Yes, sit down. No loud talk and no threatening motions. If they shot just one arrow, they must be good with their bows."

The SEALs sat down in a defensive circle from habit, so they could observe in all directions. Murdock checked his watch. He'd give the shooter five minutes, then his team had to move. He wondered where the survivors of the shoot-out down below were. They were an hour ahead of the SEALs to get to the wreck if they'd kept going. Murdock used the Motorola.

"Flyboy One, can you read me?"

"Just barely, I moved two miles downstream. If you go much farther, I'll lose your signal."

"We're held up here in an old ruins. Come up past the wreck every two hours on the hour. It's now ten minutes to the first hour."

"Roger. That's . . . I say . . . that's . . ."

"Losing him," Lam said.

They waited. SEALs are good at waiting without talking, without moving. Mahanani had pulled the arrow out of Prescott's leg. It had been imbedded only two inches. There was almost no blood. He cut a slice in the cammie pants and put a bandage on the wound, then taped the pants leg tight to his leg.

Just before the five minutes were up, a solitary figure, holding a bow and nocked arrow and wearing only a short breechclout, stepped out from behind the wall of the tall stone building. The brown man stood less than five feet tall, had long, dark-black hair, and was slender and muscular.

Murdock stood slowly, left his weapon on the ground, and held out his hands, palms up in what he hoped was a sign the small man would understand.

"We come in peace," Murdock said.

The small man scowled and Murdock could see tattoos on his chest and face. He chattered something and lifted his bow.

Murdock shook his head. "We will not hurt you," he said.

With that, the native let out a cry and twenty warriors his

size ran up beside him. All had their arrows nocked in the string, ready to be drawn and shot.

"Okay, somebody, get creative," Murdock whispered. "No way we're going to shoot down these aborigine men. We've got to think of something quick. These guys have lots of firepower and those dartlike arrows can cause great pain and death. Come on, men, some ideas."

29

Prescott stood slowly, took a deck of playing cards from his combat vest, and proceeded to do Las Vegas dealer tricks. He fanned the cards and collapsed them. He spread them out on top of a fallen log and reversed them in a flash. He threw a card in the air and watched it vanish. He moved to Murdock and showed his open hand, then withdrew a coin from Murdock's nose.

The small men's eyes lit up and they smiled.

"Magic," Prescott whispered as he walked slowly toward the aborigines. They watched him, curious. He came near them and reached out toward one. The man shrank back. He reached toward the first man who had shown himself and pulled a coin from the man's ear. He flipped it into the group. The small men cheered. He went from one to another of the men, who now stood their ground. Five times he pulled coins from the men's noses, ears, or mouths and gave each man the coin. Murdock couldn't see the coins plainly but they looked like Mexican pesos.

Prescott took a white handkerchief from his pocket and carefully stuffed it into his hand, then went to throw it into the air and it had vanished. The small men gasped in surprise. Prescott turned around slowly, his arms outstretched, his head bent back so he looked at the tops of the tall trees. Then he stopped and said a dozen nonsense words. He stepped back to the head man and slowly pulled the handkerchief from the man's ear. When it was all the way out, the small men dropped to their knees and put their heads on the ground. Only the head man of the tribe remained standing. He smiled and grinned and bowed.

Prescott sat down in front of the head man and motioned for him to sit as well. When he did, Prescott took out an

MRE package and tore it open. He displayed the many items of food and convenience on the mulch of the forest ground between them. He took out one of the energy bars and opened it; he broke it in half and took a bite of it. Then offered the other half to the head man.

For a moment the aborigine hesitated; then he watched Prescott chewing and taking another bite. The native nibbled on the bar a moment, his face frozen in worry and curiosity. Then he chewed and smiled. He ate the rest of the bar quickly and searched through the contents of the MRE for another. Prescott found one, tore off the wrapping, and gave it to him. He held it up, turned to his men, and shouted something. They all stood and hurried away.

The head man finished the second bar quickly and both he and Prescott stood. The head man waved his arms and motioned forward. Prescott smiled and nodded, and the SEALs stood and walked with caution past the small man and along what now became a trail near the side of the bluff that looked down into the valley where the crash had occurred.

The head man ran to the front of the group and made motions to Lam, who was leading. They were follow motions, and Lam moved in behind him.

"I think he wants to lead us down this trail," Lam said.

"Just so we stay near the valley on the left," Murdock said from the end of the group.

The small, dark man led them forward along what they now saw was a well-worn trail. Vines and brush had been systematically cut back, and they moved quickly.

A quarter of a mile farther up the incline of the mesa, the trail turned left, and below through the trees they could see the tendrils of smoke and the gleaming side of the airliner.

Lam stopped and pointed down, then pointed to himself and down the slope again.

The small man shook his head. He pointed ahead and held his hands a foot apart. Prescott had moved up and stood beside Lam. The aborigine looked at Prescott and smiled, and then he made the same motion with his hands.

"My guess is that if we go up a short way, the small native

has an easier way for us to get down through the jungle," Prescott said.

"Let's give it a try," Murdock said.

Lam nodded and waved forward. The small man grinned and went ahead at a slow trot. The SEALs followed. A half mile on the trail along the lip of the mesa ridge, they stopped. To the left they saw another path that had been cut through the brush and vines. The small man pointed down and motioned them. Lam reached into his combat pack and handed the native one of his MREs. The aborigine smiled and nodded and bowed, then dropped to his knees and put his head on the ground. He remained that way until the last SEAL had passed, and then he stood and ran on down a continuing trail, laughing and holding up the MRE.

Murdock moved up beside Prescott. "Where in hell did you come up with that magic idea?"

"These looked like simple people, without a lot of imagination or smarts. A little magic could work wonders with them, I figured, and it did. Just glad that I had those Mexican pesos in my pocket and that old handkerchief. If I'd had my props, I could have put on a real magic show for them."

"You did enough. Those MREs are valuable currency out here."

The trail dropped rapidly, and within fifteen minutes they had moved down over a mile toward the crash site. Twice Lam stopped and searched the area around the airliner with binoculars.

"Don't see a thing, Cap," he said on the radio. "Nothing moving down there. Can't be any survivors in a crash that bad. Don't see any birds flying up either, or any sign of those two escapees from our quick little firefight."

"Move on," Murdock said.

The trail ended at the creek, now larger due to the rain. They found where the aborigines evidently came to the stream for water or bathing or ceremonies. A small cleared place beside a large pool may have been used for tribal rituals.

Lam turned them downstream. "Not more than a hundred yards to the end of the burn swath," Lam said. "Probably are parts of the plane up here. Maybe the wings or the cockpit."

Twenty minutes of tough jungle battling later they came to the first part of the plane. It was still on the end fifteen feet of one wing.

"No fuel in this end," Murdock said. "So it didn't burn."

They walked through the burn strip now, since it was easier. Lam came past another chunk of the plane and kept going. He stopped fifty yards from what looked like the nose of the plane that had buried itself into the streambed. The rest of the group came up beside him.

"Cockpit must be ten feet into the ground," Bradford said. "Anybody in there when it crashed is sleeping with the fishes."

"The bomb couldn't have been up that far in the plane," Murdock said. "Let's go around this and get to that big section of the fuselage."

Before Lam could move out, a rifle blasted from ahead and a single bullet tore into Bradford's left shoulder. The six SEALs dropped into the brush and rolled behind trees. Two more shots came with the flat, booming sound that could only be an AK-47.

"I caught one in the shoulder," Bradford said.

Mahanani crawled over to him and went to work.

The shots came from the half of the fuselage ahead of them fifty yards. Murdock motioned for Lam and Prescott to circle to the left. He and Canzoneri went to the right. "Halfway," Murdock whispered.

Lam led out crawling through the brush and vines for ten yards to the left, then he stood beside a tree and looked at the crash. He shook his head and moved forward, down the gentle slope for thirty yards, slithering through the vines and brush by crawling, not walking. Easier that way, he knew, but slower. Prescott came behind him, following the scout's lead. This time when Lam stood in back of a tree, he saw they were directly opposite the large piece of the airliner, but forty yards away. He saw no shooters. He waited. Two minutes later a man in cammies dropped out of the broken-off rear section of the fuselage and worked slowly forward. He carried a rifle.

Lam moved his selector to 5.56 barrel and zeroed in on the man. Brush and trees got in the way of Lam's sightline.

Then the man stepped ahead and the brush thinned, and Lam triggered off three rounds. The gunfire in the softly silent jungle sounded like thunder, then it quieted again.

The man with the rifle turned, as if surprised anyone was near him; then he bent in half, dropped the rifle, and sprawled in the edge of the stream beside the airliner. For ten minutes nothing moved around the broken aircraft. Then a machine gun chattered off two twelve-round bursts. The sound came from the other side of the crash site, twenty feet up the slope. The bullets snarled and thudded and ripped through the trees and brush around where Lam and Prescott lay. None hit them.

"Hear that, Cap? We've got a chatter gun on your side of the crash."

"Heard it. We pulled back. We almost ran into a squad of twenty men. Some in uniforms, some in civvies. A ragtag bunch, but all have good-looking rifles and then that damn machine gun. Pull back to where we were, and we'll try to figure this thing out."

"Roger that," Lam said, and he and Prescott started their slow but invisible crawl back to their assembly point.

The six men lay in an arc aimed at the aircraft, watching for any movement toward them. "We pull back to the end of the trail," Murdock said. He checked his watch. Almost noon. He made a radio call, and the sputtering sound of the chopper came in.

"Read you, groundlings."

"Sky man, cut out for the city. Bring back the rest of the platoon. Stuff them all in your bird. Remind them to bring MREs and double ammo. Land where you did before. We'll have a guide to meet them. Do not fly over the crash site. We have some unfriendlies there."

"Understand. How many men?"

"Ten men. We don't need any more axes or machetes. Get them here as fast as you can."

"Roger and wilco."

Lam frowned. "Haven't heard that word for years. 'Wilco,' that means what, will obey your command?"

"Close enough," Murdock said. "Now let's get back and

set up a base camp at the pond. Bradford, how is the shoulder?"

"Not the best, Skipper. But I can still do the duty."

"Good. Canzoneri, you heard the transmission. You've got two hours to get up the hill and to the brush beside that burn LZ. Then bring the rest of the troops down here. We'll wait until it gets dark, then move in on a black raid and try to take them out. The twenties won't work as well in all this brush and trees, but we'll get their attention. Where in hell did Fouad get twenty-six to thirty men for an operation like this? And is the mastermind still alive or did he go down with the plane?"

"Oh, he's down and dead," Lam said. "He probably left instructions for the worst scenario. This is it, and somebody recruited a bunch of loyalists or mercenaries to come in and check out the bird and rescue the bomb if possible."

"A lot like us," Murdock said. "Only we haven't seen a chopper from the bad guys."

"We will," Lam said, "tomorrow."

Ten minutes later, Lam moved over to Murdock.

"Cap, I'm going out as an FO. I don't feel good not watching that site down there. We should know what they're doing."

"Right. Go. Be careful. Keep your radio on."

Twenty minutes later Lam was on the net.

"Hey, Cap, funny stuff going on down here. Not sure what. I hear what might be hammers. Some pounding. Maybe they're trying to get the bomb out of the crate. Would it be in a wooden crate?"

"Could be. If you see anyone outside, pick them off, then move like crazy. Wonder if we should send a couple of twenty-millimeter rounds into the trees over the crash. Might slow them down."

"I'd vote for that. Let me move a little so I can see the scene better. You have to move to get a clear shot?"

"Some. I'll let you know before we fire."

Murdock motioned to Fernandez, and they moved down the trail they had made to the burn swath. Still out two hundred yards to the body of the wreck, they stopped.

"One round each, airburst in the trees uphill on that blind

side of the aircraft," Murdock told Fernandez. "Lam, two rounds, you clear?"

"More than clear here."

They fired, and the resulting airbursts in the trees showered the top of the crashed airliner with hundreds of chunks of shrapnel. It could do great bodily harm to anyone in the open near the back of the length of fuselage.

"Well, the pounding stopped," Lam said. "Nobody is venturing out on this side of the plane. The body that was there has been taken away."

"Watch and wait. We have another two hours before we will have our whole platoon in hand. Then we figure out exactly what we're going to do as soon as it gets dark."

Lam kept watch on the crash site. The hammering had stopped and didn't start again. He reported spotting no one at the scene.

"What the fuck are they up to?" Lam asked on the radio.

"No good, count on that," Bradford said. He was moving his shoulder and arm to keep it functioning.

At sixteen-hundred, Canzoneri came back with the rest of the platoon. They all wanted to look at the crash site, and Murdock sent them up two at a time to the closest viewing spot.

"No noise and don't make the brush shake or you'll get a machine gun searching for you with hot lead," Murdock told them.

Just at dark they settled down for an MRE dinner. They were the new ones that heated up when you broke a seal. After that they huddled and Murdock laid it out.

"Tonight we take them out," Murdock said. "Here is how we're going to do it."

30

It had gone from daylight to dusk to dark in a matter of five minutes, casting a cloak of invisibility around the SEALs. They clustered around Murdock to find out how they would attack and subdue the mercenaries holding the crash site.

"This will be a silent operation for as long as possible," Murdock said. "We go with our best knife men first, Rafii and Lam. They will move in ahead of our main body. The mercenaries know someone is out here, but they don't know just who we are. They'll have security out, but we hope it isn't well enough trained to do much good. Lam and Rafii have as their first jobs to eliminate that security and call us forward. Depending on what we find, we'll move in with our silenced weapons and use them if we have to."

"How far out you figure their security is?" Lam asked.

"In this cover, I'd say not much over thirty to forty yards at the most. They must have some sort of camp in the jungle behind the plane. We have to find it and eliminate as many of them as we can and scare the rest of them off. Let's hope they don't have any RPGs in their weapon group."

"What about our twenties?" Jaybird asked.

"We use them only if we get surprised or they are too good for us to get inside their ranks. You all have knives. The silent approach here is best all the way around. We can't work in our usual formation. It could be one man at a time moving up in a file and then slanting off into something of an assault line. Just depends what we find, how thick the jungle is right up there, and where they have their camp."

"When do we go in?" Rafii asked.

"We wait an hour, then start downslope on the trail into the burn area. Right there somewhere, maybe four hundred yards from the fuselage, we'll make our base camp and wait on Lam and Rafii."

"How about a third knife man?" Prescott asked.

Murdock considered it only a moment. Prescott was good with his hands in the magic tricks. "Yes, go. Lam is lead man, go where he indicates. All silent as hell."

The men moved out in a perimeter defense without being told to. It was second nature. They lay in a circle with their feet nearly touching, all facing outward with weapons loaded and ready.

"Bradford, can you set up the box?"

"Yes, sir, no problem. Hell, do it with one hand if I had to. Give me about two minutes." Bradford pulled the SAT-COM off his back, turned on the switches, and aimed the fold-out antenna until he captured the sky-roving satellite. Then he handed the hand mike to Murdock. "All set on the channel Stroh told us to use down here."

"Murdock to Stroh. You have your ears on?"

"On and waiting. Where you been?"

"Busy." Murdock brought Stroh up to date on what they had found and the opposition. "My guess is that they are mercenaries with good equipment. We're moving in on them in about an hour. We'll see how well they function in the dark."

"How did somebody beat you to the prize?"

"Got me, Stroh. Could be one of our helpers at the hangar is more than just a maintenance man. Get rid of both of them. Don't let them hear anything you plan."

"Right. I can do that. We've contacted your SH-60. The pilot elected to stay there overnight. He'll do a flyover at eight A.M. and contact you on the Motorola. He knows not to fly directly over the crash site."

"We're covered. Our job now is to rout these pretenders and go in and make sure that the bomb is on the plane. It must be, or why else would thirty men go in here to protect and try to get it out? We'll talk tomorrow."

"Take care, and don't get shot in the butt with any of those pigmy arrows."

Murdock closed down the set, and Bradford put it on his back and strapped it down.

A half hour later, Lam checked Rafii and Prescott. Nothing on their gear jingled or rattled. "We'll use hand signals. Beyond about ten feet we won't be able to see each other. Use your penlight aimed away from the target for recognition of placement. Radio beeps will be two for come forward, one for wait where you are. Remember, we might lie in one position for ten minutes watching for any movement in the brush and jungle ahead."

He stopped talking and signaled for them to move ahead. They vanished into the night and down the improvised trail, on their way to the burn swath where the aviation fuel had charred a fifty-yard path a dozen feet wide burning everything in the way.

Fifty yards from the spot where they saw the faint moonlight gleaming off the white side of the airliner, Lam stopped them. They knelt, then went prone and watched the jungle ahead. Lam did as he had for years. He quartered the scene, then divided it in eighths, took one sector at a time, and studied every aspect of it he could see, memorizing the position of branches and trees. When he was satisfied nothing was dangerous in one sector, he moved to the next. It was in the third square of jungle that he saw something out of place. He put his thermal imager scope on it and checked again. Yes, a man's leg and boot stuck out from a foot-thick tree. Rafii had the other imager. He looked over his part of the vegetation and brush and vines directly in front of him. Twice he saw blips on the dark screen, white figures that scurried away and out of range. Some small animal, he decided and kept looking.

Lam slithered through the moist leaf mould on the jungle floor. He went over roots, around trees, and under more brush. It took him five minutes to work to within ten feet of the leg near the tree. The foliage thinned here. Another section of rock. He moved to the near side of the tree, worked around it in the darkness, and came up soundlessly behind the sentry. The caution was not needed. The man wore a uniform cammie shirt and blue jean pants. He had a rifle cradled in his arms and his head rested on the tree trunk. He snored softly.

Lam grabbed the man's head from behind, jerked it back-

wards, and sliced his fighting knife across the man's jugular
vein and his right carotid artery. The artery spurted hot blood
six feet into the air each time the sentry's heart beat. Then
it lessened more and more until it dribbled out. Lam let the
man's lifeless body down gently to the ground and picked
up his AK-47.

He touched his Motorola mike twice. It would transmit a
slight beep to all the rest of the sets. It was their signal for
the other two men to come forward. As he waited for them
to catch up with him, Lam studied through the trees ahead.
He figured he was still forty yards from the plane's cockpit.
There had to be more guards. Where were they? The scent
came faint at first, and then increased until he was certain.
Cigarette smoke and he was downwind. He tried to find the
angle it came from, but he couldn't. He used the imager and
checked the areas he could see. No white images of hot blood
showed on the tube. There had been no match flare. But the
smoker could have lit a new one from the old one.

Prescott slid in beside Lam, who turned, surprised. He
wasn't used to men slipping up on him unnoticed. He
grinned. The kid was going to be okay. He handed the thermal imager to Prescott and pointed in the areas he hadn't
covered. He made smoking signs with his fingers from his
mouth and Prescott nodded.

Rafii knelt on Lam's other side.

Lam studied the area just ahead of them. The land was
on a gentle slope downward. Here it fell off more sharply.
They were in a section beyond the burned swath. Evidently
the flaming wing had broken off and gone through the air a
hundred feet or more before it hit the ground and kept burning and skidding forward. The growth was sparser here,
probably from a rocky plate. A good spot for the enemy to
lurk behind, waiting for someone to try to cross the fairly
open space.

Prescott tapped Lam on the shoulder and gave him the
imager. To the left Murdock saw the white outline of a man
standing, probably beside a tree. Then the white ghost vanished. He must have stepped behind the tree. Lam showed
Rafii where the figure was and he held up the second imager.
The ghost showed on the far side of what Lam figured had

to be a tree. A long line crossed the white figure. The rifle
he carried would not show white. Lam pointed to the area,
and then to Rafii. The small man moved at once to the left
and without a sound worked his way past some brush and to
a sturdy tree with a two-foot-thick trunk. He paused and used
the scanner again.

Yes, the ghostly white showed, this time moving from the
dark spot forward six or eight feet and going prone, head up
and probably looking at the spot Rafii had just left. Rafii
touched the send button once on his Motorola, the danger
signal.

Rafii judged the distance. The ghost figure in his scope
was twenty feet away, facing away at a forty-five-degree angle. Too far for a good knife throw. Rafii edged forward, this
time on his belly, moving slowly and watching through the
scope. When the sentry's head turned toward him, Rafii
stopped and didn't even breathe. The head turned away and
Rafii slid forward.

It took him five minutes to work to within ten feet of the
man, who was still prone. Rafii had selected the knife he
would throw. It had a four-inch blade and a heavy handle,
one of his favorites. He could throw a knife and cut a match
in half that was taped to a wall twenty feet away. Now he
waited for the head to turn away from him. It did.

Rafii lifted up on his knees, cocked the blade behind his
head, and threw. The knife turned once in the air and the
razorlike blade drove deeply into the prone figure's back. It
sliced through half of the spinal column, paralyzing the man
from the neck down. He croaked out a cry, and the next
moment Rafii was on him, a second knife slicing cross the
man's throat, stopping the cry.

Rafii touched his radio button twice. He pulled out his
knife and cleaned it on the dead man's shirt, then rolled him
over. He was dressed in civvies and carried a submachine
gun Rafii did not recognize. He was a dark Mexican, of In-
dian ancestry. Lam came up and motioned to the side, where
there was more cover. The three SEALs slid behind trees and
watched ahead.

Lam touched his radio. "Murdock, move up now."

He put Prescott twenty yards back along the cleared trail

to meet the rest of the platoon. Lam and Rafii worked silently
forward. Lam had held up two fingers, then gave a thumbs-
down sign. Then he held up three fingers and pointed ahead.
There would be at least one more guard.

The two were ten feet apart, moving slowly, sometimes
crawling, sometimes walking. They went twenty yards and
stopped. Ahead Lam saw the red glow of a cigarette. He
motioned to Rafii, whom he could barely make out. Rafii had
seen it as well. The imager showed only a hand beyond a
tree or some other cover. They waited. A minute later a white
figure left the tree, moved over three steps, and stopped. The
legs spread and the man put one hand on his hip. He's piss-
ing, Lam thought. They were still ten yards from the man.
Rafii waved at Lam, stood, and, moving silently through the
cover, came to a tree ten feet from the man. He had finished
urinating and turned back toward the tree. Rafii threw the
same knife he had used before. It turned over once and the
blade drove through the man's shirt, sliced between two ribs,
and plunged three inches into the man's heart. He staggered
a step, then fell forward, ramming the blade up to the hilt in
his dead chest.

Both SEALs hurried up. Rafii took back his blade, wiped
it on the dead man's cammie shirt, and looked at Lam. The
scout whispered, "Go back and meet Prescott and the rest of
the platoon and bring them to this spot. Safe country. I'll
work ahead. Thought I heard someone talking a minute ago.
Go."

Rafii turned, jogged back, and worked through the brush
as quietly as a spirit. Lam looked forward. He could see the
side of the cockpit of the big plane. Most of it was buried
deeply into the soft ground just to the side of the small
stream. The water chattered softly, and gave Lam enough
cover to move forward. He kept the scope up but could find
no warm bodies.

He eased up another eight feet and touched the white
painted side of the nose of the plane. It had broken off
cleanly. The fuselage was behind it. Lam couldn't remember
how far. The camp for the mercenaries would be to the right,
away from the stream, slightly up the hill.

The sound of voices came again. Spanish. He couldn't

catch the words. He frowned, searched the area beside the cockpit, and then back toward where the fuselage should be. No white ghosts on the black screen.

Then he had a thought. Suppose that the mercenaries were sleeping inside the fuselage? It would have doors on both sides, they all probably broke off in the crash. There would be lots of room inside with just one nuclear bomb in there. He slipped back the way he had come, stepping across the three-foot-wide creek and waiting behind a tree.

Rafii led the group down the slope. Lam caught their movement while they were fifty yards away. When they came near him, he stepped out.

"Boo," he said softly. "You guys are all dead."

Murdock stifled a chuckle. "So, what did you find?"

"I think these guys are living inside the broken-off section of the fuselage. If so, they're fish in a barrel."

"Are you sure?"

"No, but I can't find any camp in back of that section of the plane. It's thirty feet long or more. The whole tail section has broken off; we saw that from the air."

"Would grenades thrown in there harm the bomb?" Rafii asked.

"Probably not," Murdock said as softly as the others were talking. He nodded. "How much farther do we have the way cleared?"

"All the way to the cockpit jammed into the ground. About thirty yards."

"Gardner, move the rest of the platoon up near the cockpit and take cover. Lam and I will do one more recon."

Murdock took the imager from Rafii and let Lam lead out. They moved cautiously, not making a sound. The jungle floor here was soft and moist, and each step was an adventure to find out if something underfoot would snap or some animal would scream in protest.

At the nose of the plane, they looked around. They could see the faint image of the ragged front of the fuselage where it had broken off. Behind it they saw nothing. Lam motioned up the hill. They moved at a right angle to the plane, working thirty yards into the jungle growth, worming under much of it, stepping over roots and branches and sliding around trees.

At that distance, Lam turned a right angle to the left and
worked until he figured they were in front of the middle of
the stricken aircraft. He pointed down the slope and they
edged that way through the trees and underbrush. Each step
they took was only after a quick sweep of the area ahead
with the thermal imagers. They spotted no guards. Another
rocky place allowed them to move faster, and soon they were
with thirty feet of the plane. They stopped. A low murmur
of voices came. Then a match flared somewhere inside the
dark outline of a door that had been torn off the big aircraft
in the crash.

Murdock and Lam looked at each other and nodded. Murdock's whisper came softly.

"We need four men on the far side of the plane at the
other door. They might try to get out the far door. Two men
to cover the broken-out front of the tomb and two at the tail
section. Bring the rest up here by a shorter route. The quicker
the better. We'll use three beeps on the radio when each unit
gets into place. After four of the signals, we'll be ready. Tell
the three off-side units to toss in grenades as soon as they
hear five beeps from me. Go now before the mercenaries and
their friends miss those three sentries they had out. When
everyone is in place, the party will begin."

31

Murdock waited twenty minutes, and then he crawled forward inch by inch until the thirty feet from the plane had been cut in half. He had one fragger in his hand and the other hand held the Bull Pup set on the 5.56 barrel. He watched the dark hole in the white-painted airliner fuselage. Now he could hear a soft mumble of voices. No one that he heard inside tried to quiet the men. He wondered how many there were. Twenty? Even thirty? They were probably mostly mercenaries, but they had fired at his men and they were working for a terrorist. That made them fair game, and many of them would die within the hour.

Five minutes after he was in his chosen position to throw two hand grenades into the airliner door, he heard the first three-beep signal on the radio earpiece. The in-ear signal could not be heard by anyone without the Motorola.

That would be the men at the broken-off front of the fuselage. It would take the other two units longer to get in position. Another five minutes crawled past before he heard the next series of three soft beeps in his earpiece. Then two minutes later the last set of three signals came through. All units in place. He dug out the second grenade and laid it beside his rifle. Then he pulled the safety pin on the hand bomb and held down the long thin metal handle that would arm the grenade once it flew off. He touched his radio and sent five beeps. The next second he lobbed the first grenade into the open door. Before the 4.2-second fuse train on the bomb set it off, he threw the second one through the door and ducked behind a fallen log.

Then the night roared with explosions. His bomb in the mid door went off first, followed by two near the front of the fuselage. Then he couldn't tell from where the blasts came. He did count nine grenades going off. Two men came screaming out the door in front of him and jumped to the ground. Murdock cut them down with a three-round burst for each one from the 5.56 barrel. He heard screams from inside. He watched but saw no flames; nothing had caught on fire from the explosions. Good.

"I've had two jumpers out the side door," Murdock said in the mike. "Hold your positions. Any more jumpers?"

As he said it, he heard gunfire from the front and from the far side of the dead airliner. Then all went quiet.

"Three in front who jumped their last time," Gardner said.

"We've had two try to get out the back section," Jaybird said. "They didn't make it. Count is seven down."

"Hold your positions. Where is the other thermal?"

"At the nose," Gardner said.

"See if you can get a man up to the opening without any danger and scope the inside. There have to be some live ones in there."

A minute later the radio came on. "Fernandez has the imager and is now working up to the opening. We haven't heard anything from inside. Not a cry or a groan or any screaming."

"Waiting us out," Murdock said.

Another burst of gunfire from the rear of the plane.

"One more jumper," Jaybird said. "It's four feet to the ground. He's down and out of the game."

"Skipper, I'm back down," Fernandez radioed. "I was shielded by some boxes but I caught two white images. I didn't take them out."

"You did good, Fernandez. We might need a live one. Let's give them another twenty minutes. Then I want you to get up near the same place you were and call into them in Spanish to turn on a flashlight and go to the mid door in the left-hand side and give themselves up. Tell them if they try to run they will be killed."

"Right, Cap. I could hear a few words but not well enough to understand them. They were Spanish. I'll go in twenty on your command."

Ten minutes later, Murdock had moved closer to the open door. He was less than six feet away, behind a tree that had survived the crash. His head jerked around when he heard a pounding on the plane just inside the door. The three poundings came again. He listened carefully. Bang bang bang. A pause. Bang-bang-bang. A pause. Then bang, bang, bang. Murdock snorted at the poor man's SOS.

Murdock's thermal imager lit up with a man standing in the open door.

"Okay. Give up. Okay, no shoot."

From near the front of the aircraft sharp commands came in Spanish. The man turned and looked forward, then laced his fingers on top of his head and sat down on the edge of the floor in the open door.

"Salto," Fernandez's voice bellowed from the front. The man jumped off the plane and landed on the brush four feet below. Murdock grabbed him and moved him up and away from the plane.

"Cap, how fast does a body cool off so it won't show on the imager?" Fernandez asked.

"No idea. They forgot that in our training."

"I've got some faint images, but nothing starkly white. My guess is that there are no more live ones inside the plane. I'm in the front of this section, so no more grenades in here, you guys."

"Roger that. I'm putting cuffs on this live one, and then I'm coming inside from here. So hold."

Murdock put a plastic riot cuff on the Mexican's wrists behind his back and then one around his ankles. The commander looked at the floor level of the big plane four feet off the ground. Just like the OC. He jumped, caught the opening with both arms, and levered himself onto the floor. He brought the imager out and scanned what he could see of the inside.

"I'm in, Fernandez. Check the front. I'll clear it back here. Use your flashlight after scoping."

"Aye, aye, Cap."

Murdock scanned the back twenty feet of the plane, but found no white ghosts on his small screen. Then he turned on his three-cell flashlight and scowled. Four feet behind him sat a large wooden crate six feet wide and probably twice that long.

The nuclear bomb.

He looked around it. He counted eight bodies in that section, and then turned toward the front.

"Cap, I have six bodies, none showing any signs of life on or off the scanner. I'd say we're clear up here."

"Clear in the rear. Okay, men, come on board. Fernandez, out the left-side door, up the hill you'll find our one live one. Have a talk with him. Find out everything you can. Tell him he gets to live if he tells you all he knows: who hired him, why, who any non-Mexican men are."

"Roger that, Skipper. I'm coming back your way."

Within three or four minutes the plane held fifteen SEALs. Their first job was to search all the dead, looking for any papers, orders, or instructions.

Gardner drew the winning hand. "Got something here, Skipper. Not sure what it is. Small notebook and several letters, all in Arabic I'd guess, and a money belt with plenty of cash—U.S., Canadian, Peso notes, and a lot of dinars. It's all in a fancy briefcase that used to have a lock on it. Should I have Rafii take a look?"

"That's a roger, J.G."

"Where are you, J.G.?" Rafii asked on the radio.

"Near the front, can't miss me."

Murdock examined the crate that held the bomb. The nuke was completely hidden under boards and what he figured were lead blankets. The crate had been lashed down with cargo straps and heavy ropes, more than a dozen of them, from tie-down points on the floor and both of the side walls. Murdock checked the floor. The big box had slid forward more than four feet during the crash, even with the overkill on the tie-downs.

"At least it stayed on the sled," Lam said. He had been checking out the cargo as well.

"Sled?" Murdock asked.

"It's on skids, the whole thing. We just hook up a small tractor to it and slide it up to the loading hatch."

"Which is where?" Murdock asked.

Lam shone his flashlight to the stream side of the craft. There the door was three times as wide as the one on the left. Half of it had been torn away, the other half swung outward at an odd angle where it hung on only half its hinges. Murdock judged the distance. It was almost twenty feet from the front of the crate to the hatch.

"So where is our tractor?" he asked.

Lam laughed. "Hell, Skipper, we've got sixteen little engines here who think they can. If you remember the little train story. Some air force guys I know said they sometimes had a problem with heavy items they parachuted out the end hatch of their planes. They carried a bucket of heavy grease with them and simply greased the front of the runners and then pushed and pulled like crazy. That was before they got rails and rollers and all that."

"Let's cut these tie-down straps and see what we have," Murdock said. "Bradford. Find a spot and set up the box. We need to talk to Stroh."

"Take me about five," Bradford said on the net. "I'll be outside the right-hand hatch."

They undid some of the straps, cut others, and at last had the large crate free.

"Now, if we move this forward twenty feet, are we going to roll over this half of the aircraft?" Murdock asked. He and Lam went out the hatch and checked the way the big body had come to a stop against the side of the slope and the creek bed.

"This half of the fuselage won't move an inch without a lot of C-5," Lam said. Murdock agreed.

"Skipper, I've got the mighty one on the set," Bradford said on the Motorola. Murdock found Bradford and took the handset.

"Oh, Mighty One," Murdock said.

"Enough. Did you find the package?"

"We've got it and one live prisoner to question. Problem is how to get it out of here. Can the SH-60 lift something this heavy?"

"How much does it weigh?"

"When is the Pope going to convert to Islam?"

"Been talking with the navy. We figure that the sixty can't do the job. Too damn heavy, especially if they used a lot of lead blankets. So we've brought in a special helper for you. They call it the Skycrane. We borrowed one from the my army command in Miami. They call it the S-64. Skorsky builds it. It's flying in here tonight. You know what time it is?"

"No idea. After dark and before daylight."

"Will that be a hot LZ?"

"Stroh, you pick up on the lingo fast. No, this should be a secure LZ. We think we contained all of the terrs in one place. Oh, when the crane comes in here at daylight, have him bring two five-gallon buckets of heavy industrial grease."

"Grease?"

"Grease. We've got to get the package up to the cargo door."

"Sounds reasonable. The SH-60 gave us the coordinates. This bird has all the equipment needed for a lift—the cables, the slings, the hooks, the works."

"Where are they taking it?"

"First back to Benito Juárez Airport. We're making sure the officials there don't know what it is. Then wherever it goes is not my concern, or yours."

"Right, it's out of our hands and we're done and heading back to San Diego, right?"

"Maybe, maybe not. We're working on something. First, who were the men helping what we understand was one Arab cohort of Fouad here in town? Oh, you haven't said anything about survivors. Did Fouad or any of the three crew members survive?"

"We don't think so. The nose of the plane is buried ten feet deep in a big pile of dirt. We haven't even looked at it yet. We don't know yet who the men were who helped Fouad's man. Rafii might have something for us on that. We found a notebook and a bunch of letters, all in Arabic. I'll touch you later."

"Yeah. You guys do good work. Later."

Murdock looked at his watch in the flashlight's beam. It was only 2240. He'd figured it was at least midnight.

"Skipper, you better get up here," J.G. Gardner said. "We're finding out some things."

"Inside, forward?"

"Right."

Fernandez had the prisoner in the front of the plane where the cargo bay had not been damaged much by the grenades. The prisoner sat on a box and stared at the side of the plane. Fernandez went first.

"Skipper, he says he's Jesus Orlando and he's only been with the group for six months. They call themselves the Toros Patriotico Nationales. They are dedicated to overthrowing the central government and setting up their own country here in central Mexico. Their leader was contacted two days ago to be ready for some action that would help the cause. This Arab man said he would contribute a million pesos to their war chest."

"How did they know about the crash?"

"Their man at the airport told them, and they were gone an hour later in four medium-sized helicopters that the Arab man hired. They got here but found no survivors, and were waiting for a big helicopter to come and lift out the package. He doesn't know what is in the crate."

"Is he wanted by the Mexican *Federales?*"

"He says he is. Something about a bank robbery last year to help finance their movement."

"We'll turn him over to them when we get back to the airport." Murdock looked at Gardner and Rafii. "What is in the book and the letters?"

Rafii frowned. "I'm not sure of all of it. Some is in code. But evidently these were the notebook and papers that Fouad carried. The letters are addressed to him. The notebook has a sketch of the bomb, and the three cities of choice for detonation: San Diego, Los Angeles, or San Francisco. Evidently it depended on how much trouble or lack of it they had getting over the border. They were scheduled to land at Tijuana Airport and go across at the Otay Mesa truck border crossing. They would use a truck with a fake center area where the bomb would be, and regular merchandise that goes across all the time would fill the rest of the truck. They had three border inspectors bribed. It shows their names and amounts of cash. Fifty thousand pesos each, that's five thousand U.S. dollars' worth."

"So Tijuana was the destination."

"There's more from the letters. They are to and from two

of the cells that could be al-Qaeda operated. One is in Tijuana, and the other one is in La Mesa, right there next door to San Diego."

"Does Stroh know about this?"

"We didn't tell him," Gardner said.

"He must have it from other sources. My guess is that we're not quite done yet. My money is on a cooperative effort with the Mexican *Federales* in Tijuana and then a co-op with the FBI in La Mesa."

Murdock nodded as if agreeing with himself. Then he got back to business. "Okay, not much more we can do here tonight. J.G., put out two guards on four-hour shifts. Set up the changes. Tell the rest of the men they can have an MRE and find a nice dry spot up the slope to sleep. We'll be busy enough when that flying crane gets here tomorrow. Sounds like overkill. That thing can lift half a regiment at one time."

Murdock scowled at the prisoner. "Give our little friend here part of an MRE and then tie him up for the rest of the night. The *Federales* are going to have fun with him."

32

Murdock woke up with a jolt. Then he relaxed. There were more than a dozen different birds calling and screeching and singing at each other. He knew at once where he was and what was at stake. He lifted up from the soft, dry forest mulch, moved the Bull Pup off his chest, and looked around. It was shortly past daylight. Some of the SEALs were up and moving.

Jaybird stood guard twenty yards away against a tall tree.

"Oh-six-thirty, Skipper. Figure that Skycrane will be here about oh-seven-hundred. Anything we need to do before he gets here?"

"Eat," Murdock said. "It might be a few hours before we have the chance again. Any more of the terrs show up?"

"Quiet as the inside of a mortuary, Cap. Tomblike, you could say."

They heard the big chopper coming when it was half a mile away. Jaybird threw out a red flare and Murdock checked his Motorola.

"Crash Site, this is Crane One. You still have the package?"

"Crane One, have it and ready. You sending down a couple of sling specialists on hoists to help us get this one ready?"

"Plan on lowering two men to assist. They come with the two buckets of grease. Good thinking."

Moments later the big, skinny-looking chopper came over. It was the stripped version with no cargo or troop pod, just the cockpit and the six rotors powered by twin turbines. The boom fuselage looked like a long stick with a rudder and a four-bladed propeller. It hovered two hundred yards downstream, where it could drop down to fifty feet and miss the tall trees. Two men came down on slings, which were promptly pulled up. The grounded men hiked up toward the crash, each with a bucket.

Murdock met them.

"Morning, Commander," one said. "I'm Sergeant Caldwell and this is Corporal Broderson. Where's the package?"

"Morning. I'm Murdock. Glad you could come to our party." He took them into the fuselage and showed them the prize. The terrorist's bodies had been dragged out of the plane and dumped out the uphill passenger side door.

The two lift specialists shook their heads at the problem. "We have to get it up to the door, then reach in the cables and rig them on this crate, all around it if possible."

"If not, will the sides of the crate hold the weight?" Jaybird asked.

"That's what we'll find out," Broderson said. "If they won't, we'll know it before we pull it out of the plane." He went to the open door and waved at the Skycrane pilot. The big bird came down to about a hundred feet and let down a pair of cables. Attached to them was a sling made of cables that looked welded together. Caldwell unhooked the sling from the drop cables and they were hoisted back into the Skycrane, which moved off to lessen the rotor wash below.

It took six SEALs on each section of the heavy cable sling to get it up to the plane's cargo hatch and hoisted inside. Caldwell stood staring at the crate.

"Don't tell me what's inside. I don't want to know. I just have to figure out where to put the slings. First, let's use that grease and some of your men and see if we can pull this creature up near the door."

Broderson spread the grease in front of both of the four-by-four timbers that served as the skids for the package.

"It's always easier to pull an object than it is to push it," Caldwell said. They attached some of the cables to the front of the big crate, and ten SEALs on both sides pulled. The crate moved slowly until more of the grease came under the skids, then it eased forward until it was directly opposite the outside door.

"Have to go through endways," Caldwell said. The men pushed and tugged and turned the crate sideways until it was aimed at the door. Then Caldwell and Broderson went to work with hammers. They broke out part of the crate at the bottom near the front and back on both sides and fed the heavy cables through and under the crate, then out holes on the far side. After a half hour of tugging, swearing, and sweating, the SEALs and the air force men got the slings in position and the large inch-thick lift rings chained together on the top of the crate.

Caldwell took out a handheld radio and talked to the pilot.

"Sir, have the package ready for a try. Slings are under the whole crate, so no problem of the crate breaking and spilling the goods. Drop down so we can attach the cables to the sling. We'll have to bring the cables inside the fuselage, then let you lift it as much as you can and ease it out the door without letting it roll down the hill."

"I have the picture, Sergeant Caldwell. Moving now. Cables down in about three."

The inch-thick hoist cables slithered down from the big crane in the sky, with heavy foot-long hooks that had safety clamps dangling from them. The air force men grabbed them as they eased down to the freight hatch on the big plane.

"Easy, Cap, easy, three feet more. Now we're hauling them inside and making the hook." Two SEALs helped on each of the big hooks, dragging them inside and lifting them to the top of the crate.

"Easy, Cap. Hold her steady." It was Caldwell on his radio. The hooks were both on the sling and the safety clamps in place over the open throat of the hooks.

Caldwell waved at the SEALs. "Out of here. Clear back at least thirty yards on each side. Count your men, Commander. I don't want to mash up a SEAL down here today."

The SEALs scattered. Caldwell and Broderson remained in the fuselage, one on each side of the big crate.

"Ready, Cap," Caldwell said on the radio to the pilot. "Move us easy at first until the slack is taken up. Aye, that's the way. Now a bit more. Right, the crate is sliding toward the door. Easy, easy! Slower. Yes. We're at the door. Now get directly over us so you can lift it straight up at the roof of the aircraft in here."

"Moving slightly forward," the pilot radioed. "Yes, now. Slowly."

"Good, Cap, she's off the floor, hold her a minute, yes, all looks right. Now ease away from the fuselage. Away. That's right. More, you can see the crate now halfway out of the craft, off the floor, not hitting the top of the freight hatch. More, another four feet. Yes!"

The big crate eased forward and upward again, fully supported now by the sling and the cables. Then the sky pilot pulled the heavy crate out of the confines of the BAC One-Eleven. It was free and clear. It swung slightly as the Sky-crane put on more power and lifted it straight into the air, then swung to the southeast and headed toward Mexico City's Benito Juárez Airport.

The SEALs cheered. Murdock grinned.

"Bradshaw," Murdock bellowed.

"Over here, sir. We're all set up and the great one is on the edge of his seat."

Murdock took the handset.

"Your baby is out of the nest and flying home. You should see him at your home base in about an hour. Not sure of the speed of this windmill but I'd give him an hour."

"Good. I'll breathe easier when the package is safely here. Then we worry about getting it back in town where she belongs. That's part of a song you may know, Dolly. We've had some more developments."

"About the cells in Tijuana and La Mesa?"

"How the hell you know that, Murdock?"

"Some letters we found here. Maybe we didn't tell you about them. We have names and addresses."

"I'll look at them later. Your SH-60 should be in his LZ. Give him a call and wake him up. Then haul out of there and take those two air force guys and the prisoner with you. It's now eight-fifteen. You should be here by ten o'clock. We'll have you on the Gulfstream II out of Benito at two o'clock, or fourteen hundred."

"Tijuana?"

"No. North Island in Coronado. We want to check your gear and get some briefings from Tijuana *Federales* before you hit TJ."

"We better be moving. I'm out of here."

"See you in about two hours."

Murdock handed Bradford the mike. "Gardner," he bellowed. "Tell that SH-60 jockey to get his rig warmed up, we're on the way with three extra passengers."

"Can do," Gardner said on the net.

Sergeant Caldwell saluted Murdock. "Sir, I hear we're hitchhiking back to Benito with you. Is that right?"

"It is, Sergeant, unless you want to walk."

"Rather fly, sir. How far to the new LZ?"

"About two miles. Think you're up to it?"

"We'll both give it a try, sir. Like you say, it's one hell of a lot better than walking all the way back."

Benito Juárez Airport
Mexico City, Mexico

By the time the SEALs returned to the airport, the Skycrane had long since departed. Stroh didn't tell them where it went and they didn't ask.

Stroh talked to them on board the Gulfstream.

"First, I'm going with you to San Diego."

There was a chorus of shouts and whistles.

"Thanks for the vote of confidence. Yes, we're going to work with the *Federales* in Tijuana. For those of you who don't know, that federal-sounding word is just that, the Mexican federal police. Sort of like our FBI but not at all like them. Sometimes they are loose cannons themselves. But this time we trust them and they heard about your trip into León and asked us to come and help them wrap up the TJ end of things. We still know more about it than they do, and we'll keep it that way.

"Yes, we have hot meals on board courtesy of Mexicana Airlines. It's their first-class flyer dinner. Not sure when we get into San Diego because we now stop in Tijuana first. We'll refill ammo for anyone who's almost out and get ready to take a bus ride into Tijuana. Our Mexican neighbors want this cleared up as soon as we can. Any questions?"

"What about La Mesa?" Gardner asked.

"Not sure on that. The FBI and the area task force are

working it. They might not need us. We'll watch and wait on that one. Mexico first."

The copilot waved at Stroh from the cockpit door. "Okay, we're next in line to take off," Stroh said. "So sit down, belt in, and dinner will be served as soon as we reach our cruising altitude."

"Thank you, miss," Jaybird cracked.

Stroh grinned. "Murdock, next time we go fishing, let's use cut bait. I think Jaybird's mouth would make some tasty morsels for the blue sharks."

There were cheers and catcalls and general approval of the comeback.

Lam held up both hands. "That's a score. I'm counting. The long-term results show that currently our totals are: Jaybird one thirty-four and Stroh one twelve. I think the old man is gaining on the upstart."

The cheering cut off as the sleek jet's throttles rammed forward and the seventeen passengers were pinned to the backs of their seats as the craft thundered down the Mexico City Airport runway and lifted into the sky.

33

The sleek jet took off from Benito Juárez Airport in Mexico City and climbed to its usual cruising altitude of twenty-five thousand feet. The pilot told them on the speakers that their flight time to Tijuana would be two hours and fifty-eight minutes.

Jaybird yelped. "Freeze-dried tomatoes on a hamburger bun. We're two hours ahead of San Diego time. We gain two hours going that direction so we get there fifty-eight minutes after we take off from here. On the clock that is. Damn. Always wanted to get somewhere before we left. Didn't quite make it this time."

"You're full of shit, Jaybird," Wade Claymore said.

"That's probably true," J.G. Gardner cracked. "But the fact is he's right. If you could fly fast enough this direction halfway around the world, you could get to that destination twelve hours before you left."

"Until you hit the international dateline out there in the Pacific and you gain a whole fucking day," Canzoneri said.

"Enough already," Luke Howard roared. "Where's the food?"

"Coming at you, girls," the crew chief said, coming out of the cockpit. He was a first-class petty officer and grabbed the closest SEAL, Fernandez, to help him pass out the food.

The clock showed slightly before noon when they landed at Tijuana Airport. It had been some time since Murdock had seen it and they had made some improvements. He didn't see much of the new part as their plane taxied to the transient hangars where a bus and two police cars met them. Each

SEAL wore his cammies and combat vest and carried his assigned weapon and double ammo. The civilian-clad *Federales* met them and talked with Murdock. Their spokesman was fluent in English.

"Welcome to Mexico. You guys travel fast." He held out his hand. "I'm Lieutenant Roberto Perez." Murdock shook his hand.

"Lieutenant Commander Blake Murdock. Hope we got here in time."

"You did, we waited for you to start. You came fast. I know this plane. She goes almost ten miles a minute."

"Good to be here," Murdock said. "How can we help you wrap up this end of the problem?"

The Mexican *Federale* looked to be in his thirties, Murdock thought. He was just over six feet tall and slender, with heavy muscles showing through his lightweight suit. He was clean shaven, with close-cropped dark hair. His darting black eyes took in everything as the SEALs came off the plane and lined up in squad formation, weapons slung and muzzles pointing down. The cop looked around the area, then at his two men, who nodded.

"First we get your men on the bus and out of sight."

"On the bus," J.G. Gardner barked. The men broke ranks and moved into the bus. As they did, the Mexican cop waved Murdock to one of the cars. Murdock pointed to the J.G. to go with the men.

In the car the cop relaxed. "The sight of those weapons could get told to the wrong people. We have an operation set up. You gave us the name and address of the cell leader here. He had been on a watch list for six months, but we never had enough evidence against him. Now we do. We've had his place under surveillance for six hours now and he seems to be inside and has not left. No one has come to his house. It's in a good neighborhood. We'll try to go in quietly and hope there is no gunfire. Tell your men they are backup. We have a force of twelve men waiting to take down the house."

"Why do you need us? You seem to have everything covered."

"You never know here in Mexico. They might have been

tipped off we're coming. Last month one of our top leaders in the Tijuana *Federales* force was arrested for aiding and abetting one of the larger drug cartels. So you just never know. We keep trying."

The cars led the group out of the airport and through ten miles of streets and highways and more streets until they came to a section of Tijuana that looked like any U.S. city, with paved streets, sidewalks, good three- and four-bedroom, two-story houses with neatly tended lawns.

"The target is two blocks from here," Perez said. "Half of my men will go down the alley and set up. The rest of us will come from the front. All are dressed casually as locals. All have automatic weapons. We'll want half your SEALs blocking the near end of the alley. The other half will move within fifty yards of the target and conceal themselves behind houses and trees. Then when all is ready, we will break down the door and go in."

"Sounds reasonable," Murdock said. He and Perez had just exited their black Buick when Murdock heard a sharp report.

"Rocket-propelled grenade," Murdock bellowed and he caught the Mexican cop and pulled him to the ground. He heard the report of a second grenade. Just then the first one hit four feet from the far side of the heavy Buick, smashing all the windows, showering the body metal with deadly shrapnel. Murdock had dove facing away from the car and dragged the cop with him. He felt the sting of the shrapnel when the round went off and felt some hit the soles of his boots. His left arm stung where a hot chunk of the RPG had cut a slash through his cammie shirt and gouged out a half inch of flesh.

He heard the second RPG round go off behind them. It hit the rear wheels of the bus the SEALs were still in and dumped it over on the side. The blast ruptured the fuel tank and flames roared through the back of the bus. Murdock ran that way. He saw his men kicking out windows. The door was flat on the ground under the tipped-over bus. He got to the rig and helped the men crawl out. Two had burns. A third had trouble getting out the window.

Murdock jumped up and lifted the man out. It was Prescott. His pants were burned off and both arms burned as well. They carried him away from the flaming bus and stretched him out on a lawn. Mahanani hovered over him.

"He needs an ambulance right now," the medic said.

Murdock looked for the J.G. He found the man away from the bus, lying on a lawn. He had bad burns on his arms and face.

"I'm okay, Skipper, just singed a little. You get a count?"

Murdock ran back to the men and began counting. The men sat and lay on the closest lawn. Murdock found Senior Chief Neal.

"Senior Chief, we're one man short. Who is missing?"

They went over the men again. Murdock found all of his squad. Neal came back shaking his head.

"It's Wade Claymore, the radioman. Can't find him anywhere."

"Did everyone get out of the bus?"

"Not sure."

Murdock called the men around him. "We can't find Claymore. Anyone know where he was sitting in the bus?"

"Toward the back," Jaybird said. "I remember Tate teased him about having to go to the back of the bus."

"Anybody seen him since you got out of the bus?" Neal asked.

Nobody answered. They all looked at the bus, which was thirty yards from them. The entire vehicle was one mass of flames. Then they heard the ammunition going off.

"What weapon did he have today?" Murdock asked.

Fernandez spoke up. "Usually he carried a Bull Pup, but we switched today. He wanted to use my MP-5."

They heard more rounds going off. Murdock said a swift little prayer that they weren't the ten twenty millimeter rounds exploding that would have been in the fire if Claymore had kept his Bull Pup.

"Okay, we've taken a casualty. Now spread out and look alive. Whoever shot those RPGs is still out there."

He ran back to the first Buick with the glass blown out. He found the Mexican *Federale,* Perez, sitting where Murdock had pushed him down. He had a graze on the side of his head that bled down his ear onto his suit. He held his left arm cradled against his chest.

"Broke my arm," Perez said. "Sliced it to hell. You saved my worthless life just now. Thanks. My second in command has taken over. He's Lieutenant Castro. He's sent our men to take down the house. If they knew we were coming, they all won't be there now. Can you put some men on this end of that alley right over there?"

He pointed half a block down and to the left.

"Done. We won't shoot. Your men must be down there somewhere at the back door. We'll block."

"How are your men?"

"We think we lost one in the fire. Some burns. Most okay. Did somebody call for an ambulance?"

"Castro did. He wasn't hurt. Should be one here in ten minutes. Sorry about your man. Maybe we'll find him yet."

"I'll get my men in position."

Murdock went back to his SEALs and told the burned men that an ambulance was coming. He left Mahanani with them and took the rest up to the alley mouth. It seemed strangely quiet. He called Lam over.

"Let's take a look. It's the fourth house down on the right. Supposed to be a fence next to the alley."

They worked down the alley in the bright sunshine, moving from what cover there was to the next. They saw no Mexican lawmen in back of the house. They heard nothing from the front.

"Give them five," Murdock said. The fence behind the place was concrete block, six feet high with a three-foot-wide gate in the center. Block walls showed on both sides of the house as well.

Four minutes passed and Lam signaled to Murdock they should go through the gate.

Before Murdock could signal back, gunfire exploded at the front of the house. He heard what could have been a door blasting open, then more gunfire. Two men ran out the back door. Lam ran to the gate in the fence, pushed his Bull Pup around the opening, and cut down one of the runners with a three-round burst. The other man stopped, dropped his weapon, and held up his hands. A third man ran out the door screaming. He had blood running down his face. He carried an RPG launcher without a round in the end. He looked at the man with his hands up and swore at him, then went for the gate. Murdock jolted him backwards with six rounds from his 5.56 Bull Pup.

The terrorist in the backyard stood there like a pole, his hands high over his head, his face a mask of anger and fear.

Shooting inside the house quieted. A man edged out the door and looked at the two bodies on the ground, then at the man with his hands up. The *Federale* shot him four times in the back, screaming at him. Then he ran back in the house. Murdock and Lam stood behind the fence and waited.

It was five minutes before one of the men Murdock had seen at the airport came out the door.

"SEALs, you there?" the man called in English.

"Right," Murdock said. "Is that house clear?"

"Clear and dead," the *Federale* answered. "Take your men back to the bus."

"Right," Murdock said. He and Lam jogged back to where they'd left most of the platoon and went with them back to where the bus still smoldered and smoked. Two police cars were parked nearby. An ambulance pulled away quickly, and another one rolled in and down to the target house.

Mahanani sat on the grass scowling.

"Wouldn't let me go with them," he said. "They didn't even speak English."

"They took Prescott, Fernandez, and Perez, the *Federale?*"

"Yeah. Hey, Cap, can you wrap this a little tighter? I'm no fucking good with my left hand."

Murdock saw the burn then. Half Mahanani's right sleeve had been charred and the arm under it wrapped with a roller bandage. Murdock straightened out the bandage and taped it in place.

"You could have been on that ambulance, too."

"Yeah, but I didn't let them see my burn. Just a scratch. Didn't even burn to the bone."

"Did Claymore ever show up?"

"No. Sorry, Cap. I think we lost him. He must have been right over the blast, or close to it. Then that damn gasoline went up and we had to scramble. I was only halfway back in the bus and it was scorching even there. Lucky we didn't lose half the platoon."

One of the Mexican *Federales* walked up. "Where can I find Murdock?"

"That's me. Did you get your men?"

"I'm Castro. We got most of them. They knew we were coming but couldn't all get out in time. The RPGs were meant to give them time. Good thing our men were in position. But two did escape. We're not sure if they were the leaders or not, but we suspect they were. We're interrogating one of the survivors now. Thanks for stopping those two trying to get away out the back."

"About the one who had given up . . ." Murdock started.

Castro's face turned dark and he scowled. "You have your way, we have ours. We already had a prisoner. We didn't need that one."

"Expendable?"

"Yes, good word." He paused and a smile nearly broke through his stern face. "I'll have two vans here in a half hour to take you back to the border. We thank you for your help."

"You're welcome."

The Mexican man saluted smartly, did a military about face, and walked toward the undamaged Buick.

J.G. Gardner came up, looking worried and angry. "If these Mexicans knew that the bad guys were on to us, why didn't they stop the rigs farther down the street? We can't find Claymore anywhere. He has to be in that burned up bus. How do we go about getting his body? We have to send him home. We aren't about to start leaving men on foreign soil."

"We'll have Senior Chief Neal take the men back to Coronado," Murdock said. "He can phone from the border for a pickup by a navy bus. You and I will stay here until we can find out what is left of Claymore and get a body bag and take him home."

Gardner nodded, his face relaxed a little, and his clenched fists opened and fell to his sides. "Yes, sir. I like that. I'm going back down there. Most of the fire is out. Still no firemen on scene. Where the hell are they?"

Five minutes later two large vans pulled up and the

SEALs loaded into them. Senior Chief Neal told Murdock he would get the men back to their base.

Murdock went down to the lawn near where the bus still lay on its side. He touched the metal top of the rig, but it was still too hot to crawl up so he could see through the broken-out windows. He sat down beside J.G. Gardner.

"First man you've lost. I know it's hard. That's the dark side of this little international game of cops and robbers that we play. That's why most men can't do this duty for long."

"But Claymore hasn't been with the platoon for long."

"That's what makes it all the more tragic." Murdock frowned as he saw two men half a block down step out from behind a concrete-block wall at the side of a house. He saw a glint of sunshine off metal.

"Terrs down there about forty yards," he barked. "Dive and roll away from me. Our job here isn't done after all."

Two shots came, drilling into the soft grass where the SEALs had been sitting. The two SEALs scrambled forward into the protection of the still-hot bus.

"I've got the front," Murdock said. "You take the back. Let's go down and meet those two killers and see what we can do with them."

The SEALs moved to the ends of the bus, motioned to each other, then both stormed around the bus, zigzagging to the next cover, a car at the curb twenty yards away on the other side of the street.

Murdock heard a shot and felt a bullet slam over his head as he kept running for cover.

34

Murdock felt a bullet clip his pants leg and tear on through; then he dove behind a gray sedan parked at the curb. When he peered around, he saw that the two gunmen had vanished. J.G. Gardner had slid behind the car just after Murdock did.

"Gone?" he asked.

"Down that alley they fired from. Cover me with a couple of shots while I get over to that block wall by the alley. Now."

Murdock surged around the end of the car and Gardner sent two three-round bursts of hot lead into the alley next to the block wall. Murdock made it safely the twenty yards to the alley mouth and looked around the block wall. He saw no one. He sent a three-round burst down the alley and waved at Gardner to join him.

On his next look down the alley, Murdock saw a man dive behind a large trash bin. The man hadn't come out. He kept watch. Another man farther down the alley jolted out from a gate in a wall, ran down to another block wall, and darted into an opening. Murdock didn't have time to aim and fire. He sent two more rounds into the trash container where one man hid.

Gardner nudged his elbow.

"We got one behind that trash bin down about forty feet. He can't get out and there's a ten-foot wall behind it," Murdock said, briefing Gardner. "You go down to that car parked in the alley about thirty feet down. I'll cover you. See if you can get an angle on the guy behind the bin."

Gardner nodded, surged around Murdock, and sprinted for the parked car. Murdock fired three spaced shots at the trash bin, and the man there didn't shoot back. Gardner slid in behind the car without taking any rounds. He stared through the windows of the car, then turned to Murdock and shook his head.

Murdock fired twice more on single shot—one under the trash container near the wheels, the second just past the front where the round slammed into the block wall. There was no reaction from the man behind the container.

Gardner held up a hand grenade, but Murdock shook his head. Too many civilians around. The hand grenade would cause too much noise and damage. He figured the gunman wouldn't give up. He must know what the *Federales* did with men who tried to surrender.

"Cover me," Murdock shouted. Gardner fired single shots behind the trash bin every three seconds. Murdock dashed from his position to the front of the trash container. He put his head out and jerked it back quickly. Two shots thundered from behind the bin.

Murdock pushed the Bull Pup's muzzle around the side of the container and triggered off three three-round bursts. He waited a moment, then heard a scream. He looked around and jerked back. No shot. He looked again. The terr sat against the back block wall of the indent for the trash bin. He held his stomach with both hands. Slowly his head fell forward, and then he tipped to the side and sprawled in the dirt and garbage of the trash area.

Murdock and Gardner looked down the alley. There was no sign of the other man.

"We got one of the two. Let's go back and see how that fire is doing."

When they got back to the bus, a fire truck had arrived and the men had the fire out and the metal cooled down with the cold water. The *Federale* officer who had talked to them before, Castro, came up and watched a moment. He came over to Murdock.

"You have a casualty in the bus?"

"We believe so. One of our men is missing."

"I'll have the firemen look for him." The federal man went to a fire lieutenant and talked. Then two firemen went down through a broken-out window. Murdock and Gardner waited.

It was almost five minutes later before a head appeared

in the broken-out window. The fireman talked to his officer, who talked to the federal cop. He went to Murdock.

"They have found a badly burned body inside. It must be your man. We'll get the bus tipped back on its rims and bring out his remains. Our nation appreciates the sacrifice your team has made here today. You'll receive an official commendation."

"Nothing public," Murdock said. "We're always undercover. We were never here. You understand."

It was a half hour before a tow truck arrived with a winch that hooked on and tipped the bus back on its axles. All the tires had burned off. An ambulance had been waiting, and now the paramedics went into the bus with a body bag and a stretcher. Murdock tried to get inside, but the firemen kept him out.

Another ten minutes passed before the medics brought out the heavy black body bag on a stretcher. They unzipped the end of the bag. Murdock and Gardner both looked at the face of the man inside. There was enough of it left for them to recognize and identify Wade Claymore.

The *Federale* put his radio away and motioned to Murdock. "You both can go with the ambulance to the border. I've radioed ahead and a U.S. ambulance will meet you at the border on this side and transfer the remains. We thank you for your assistance."

They stepped into the back of the ambulance and stared at the black body bag.

"I'll write the letter," Gardner said. "He was a good man and I hate to lose him."

At the border a South Bay Ambulance Company rig waited for them at the turnaround on the Mexican side. The two paramedics were surprised to see the body bag.

"Get us to Balboa Naval Hospital's emergency entrance," Murdock said. "No siren. As you can see there is no rush."

At the hospital it took Murdock ten minutes to get Claymore into the system and his body sent to the morgue. Then he contacted the Shore Patrol at the hospital and told them he needed transportation to Coronado.

"We can't do that, sir," a phone voice said.

"Put on your commanding officer," Murdock said.

Two minutes later a navy sedan pulled up at the emergency entrance and the two SEALs climbed in. The driver looked in surprise at the weapons and the cammies.

"Some maneuvers or an exercise, sirs?" the driver asked.

"No, sailor, it was the real thing. Now get us to NAVSPECWARGRUP-ONE just south of Coronado, on the strand."

"Yes, sir."

It was just seventeen-hundred when they walked across the quarter deck at their Coronado base. Master Chief Petty Officer Gordon MacKenzie met them.

"Confirmed about Claymore?"

"Confirmed, KIA," Gardner said. "He's at Balboa."

"The right place." MacKenzie nodded. "I hear you men did well. I'll be looking for your after-action report tomorrow. No rush." He hesitated.

"Was there something else, Master Chief?" Murdock asked. "Anything about La Mesa?"

"No, the FBI took care of that quite handily. Oh, your fishing partner, Mr. Stroh, did call. He said he was ordered back to D.C. for an early meeting tomorrow."

"Just as well," Murdock said. "The fish count is way down anyway."

"See you in the morning, Master Chief," Gardner said.

"Better make it about noon. Nothing pressing. Sleep in and, Murdock, you can get acquainted again with that woman."

Murdock brightened. "Now there is a great idea. Let me check in this hardware and I'm out of here."

35

Coronado, California

In their Coronado condo, Gunner's Mate First Class Miguel Fernandez had the longest hot shower he could remember. The platoon had arrived at the base about fourteen-hundred and the senior chief released them all on a three-day liberty. Miguel had hugged Maria for about ten minutes when he walked in the door, and she knew he was still worried about being a SEAL.

"You have a hot shower and I'll fix you afternoon waffles and bacon and sausages and some hot maple syrup," she said. She slapped him on the bottom. "Now scoot. We can talk when your stomach is full."

He got out of the shower and Maria was waiting for him in the skimpiest little nightie he had ever seen her wear. She pulled his towel off and guided him to the queen-sized bed.

It was almost an hour later that they sat on the edge of the bed, dressing before Linda came home from school.

"The skipper said you and I needed to talk about my being in the SEALs. We did a little before I left, but not much. I need to know exactly how you feel."

Maria kissed him softly on the lips, then leaned back and shrugged into her blouse.

"You are my man. You're the other half of me, and sometimes I think more than that. My life wouldn't be complete without you. I thought that way after the first few dates we had, and I still do. It is a joy being your wife and bearing our child. So, you're in a dangerous profession. What if you were a race car driver? A much higher percentage of those men get killed than do SEALs. You're in the navy. I knew that when I married you. I'm a navy wife and that involves a lot more than being able to go to the commissary to buy our food and supplies. It covers a lot of go-it-alone behavior, a lot of sucking it up and getting the jobs done. A lot of single parenting when you are out of the country. I know all that and revel in it because I know that I'm tough enough to do it.

"So I'll do a lot of things for you. I'll cover for you here with Linda, I'll do the PTA thing, and I'll be the good navy wife. I'll nurse you back to health after you get out of Balboa Naval Hospital. But I absolutely, and with no chance of changing my mind, will never go to your funeral. There I draw the line."

Miguel finished dressing and stared at Maria.

"You're telling me things you never have said in our eight years of marriage. Now you think I need to know all this so I can decide if I should stay in the SEALs?"

"Yes."

He sat down on the bed and hugged her until she gurgled. It was their little signal that the arms were too tight. He let her go and she pulled on her pants and shoes and they went to the living room.

"Right after Linda asked you what your job was, when you were playing with the dominoes before you left for your last mission, you seemed to tighten up. What didn't you tell her your job is in the Navy SEALs?"

"I told myself that, quite plainly, my job is killing people."

Maria looked up. "Well, sure, sometimes. You're not a cold-blooded hit man. You go after the terrorists and the bad guys . . . Somebody has to do it."

They sat on the couch and he held her hands. "Have I ever told you about a phrase we use when we're in a hot combat situation, called 'making sure'?"

"No, you've never said anything about that."

"Say we're on a quiet mission to penetrate ten miles inland in hostile territory. We must remain quiet and unseen. Whoa, two guards spot us and we get in a small firefight and knock them out. We think. But a man can get shot a number of times and stay alive. So Murdock or the J.G. will say, 'Okay, Fernandez, get up there to their position and make sure.' "

Maria frowned. "You mean, somebody has to go up to the enemy and make sure that they are dead?" Her eyes widened and her mouth came open in surprise.

"That's exactly what it means."

"What if one of the two, say, isn't dead?" she asked.

"Then whoever goes up uses a silenced round or a knife and makes sure that they are all dead. That person executes the wounded man or men."

They were both quiet for a time.

"But if the wounded man had crawled back and notified his officers, the whole regiment could attack you and kill all of the SEALs in the mission," Maria said. Her eyes went wide again and slowly she nodded. "So the wounded ones had to die so they wouldn't give an alarm. It had to be done. You had to make sure."

She stopped. "Oh, God! That's been your job sometimes during the past six years?"

He nodded slowly.

She grabbed him in a hug so tight that he gurgled, and she relaxed a little but held him.

"I never knew. I knew that you had killed some enemies with your rifle, but that making sure . . ." She stopped and shivered. Maria leaned back. "Miguel, how many times . . ." She faded out.

"I don't know. I don't even like to remember, let alone count the times and the wounded. I've never dwelt on it before. It kind of slithered off my back and I forgot it."

"Now, because your little girl asked you what you do for a living, it's all crashing down on you and threatening to bury you."

Neither one spoke for a few moments; they simply sat there holding each other.

"Six years I've been a SEAL. Most men don't last that long. Yeah, some leave because their knees give out or some other injury that makes then unfit for SEAL duty. I've known several guys who got their first gunshot wound and next thing we knew they had transferred back to the black shoe navy. One or two just freaked out after a mission and went back to regular duty. Only four of us are left who were in the platoon when Murdock took over. You know them from our barbecues: Lampedusa, Jaybird, Ching, and me. What a turn-over."

She pushed back, kissed his nose, and then stared at him with unblinking brown eyes. "So, sailor, where are we? You haven't even mentioned the great things that the SEALs do. Haven't you rescued some embassy people, and that senator who got stuck in China, and a ship you freed down in South America. You SEALs do a lot of good things that the public never hears about. Then the Koreans who invaded us and you tracked down a whole batch of them."

"That was a witness for the defense, I'd guess," Miguel said. "I don't know where I am. Maybe I should talk to our priest. I know, I know, I don't get to church often enough. Still, Murdock said I should have a chat with him. He is in a navy town, that might help. Father MacDouglas. I've got a three-day liberty. I'll call him tomorrow and set up some-thing."

Maria shook her head. "Not a chance, sailor." She handed him a phone. "Call him right now and see him this after-noon."

Father D. MacDouglas was in his office working on his hom-ily for Sunday when the call came. The tension and the tenor of the voice alerted him, and he agreed to see the young sailor in a half hour. They met in his office, where the priest had set out cheese and crackers and two glasses full of diet, caffeine-free Coke.

"So, you're one of our SEALs, Miguel. I hear a lot of good things about your work. I know most of it you can't talk about, but I hear things. Some excellent undercover jobs you boys do."

"That's what I need to talk to you about, Father."

"Your work. I know a Marine who used to tell me every week at confession that his job was killing people. If he ever had to go to war, he would be killing every enemy that he could see. He asked me if this would be a sin. I told him to ask me that on his first confession after he came back from his war."

"That's the trouble, Father. I've been at war, shooting-and-killing warfare for the past six years."

The priest nodded. "Yes, my son. When I told you that about the Marine, I realized that your missions were not search and rescue, or diplomatic. I've seen your demonstrations in the bay; I know you men are experts at killing the enemy. So I would assume that you have done that in the past. Is that what is bothering you, taking the life of another human being?"

"Yes, Father. I've been a SEAL for six years. I can't remember how many missions I've been on. Every one has been violent and deadly, and each time we prevailed."

"So you have killed?"

"Yes."

"Several men? A dozen?"

"Many more than that, Father. That's what we do to gain our objective. It's a small war. Our sixteen-man platoon against usually a much larger force, and we must win." Miguel stopped. "Father, whatever I say to you is privileged, right? You can't tell anyone?"

"That is the basis of the confessional."

"We just came back from a mission to recover a nuclear weapon from a terrorist. In the process, in the middle of a Mexican jungle, we killed twenty-nine men. We sacrificed those men so terrorists couldn't explode the bomb on San Diego or Los Angeles, where it would have killed a million human beings. We had a noble purpose, but we also snuffed out the lives of twenty-nine human beings. Were we justified?"

Father MacDouglas shivered. "They actually had a nuclear weapon that close to us? San Diego could have been vaporized off the map." The priest closed his eyes and said a silent prayer. Then he opened his eyes, dried wetness from their corners with a tissue, and nodded.

"You certainly were justified. No priest on earth would condemn you for what you did. Still there are the feelings of the individual men who were involved, including you. Do you think you did the right thing by killing those men and recovering the nuclear bomb?"

"Absolutely. Somebody had to do it. But if I hadn't been there, the job would have been done. I wasn't vital. I was just one of the incidental killers."

The priest peaked his fingers and stared at Fernandez. "So your moral dilemma is did you do the right thing for the sake of the masses of people you saved. You've answered that yourself. Now you have to deal with the aftermath, with the continuance. That's why you are here, isn't it? You need to decide if you want to remain in the SEALs, where you go to a killing war every couple of months, or if you want to go back to the black shoe navy, where war comes every ten to fifteen years."

Murdock nodded. "Father, how did you get so smart?"

"A God-given talent, Miguel. Then, it doesn't hurt that I was a navy chaplain on active duty for ten years. I was in the Gulf War."

"Yes, the eight-day war."

"No, that was Israel earlier. We worked at it for six weeks before we subdued Iraq." The priest stopped talking and watched Miguel. "My son, have you reached a decision about what you want to do with your life?"

Fernandez sipped at the Coke, then put down the glass and stood. "Father, that I have. I thank you for your counsel."

"I'm glad. It would be good to see you in church from time to time. And remember, confession is good for the soul."

Fernandez laughed, his tension gone. "I guess I deserved that zinger, Father. I'll really try to get to mass more often."

Fernandez hurried out of the church and into his car. He drove carefully back to his condo and ran up the steps. Maria saw him coming. She held Linda in her arms as he came in the door. Fernandez grabbed both of them in a bear hug.

"You can keep my black shoes in the closet, Maria. There's a lot more work I need to do with Third Platoon, Seal Team Seven."

SEAL TALK

MILITARY GLOSSARY

Aalvin: Small U.S. two-man submarine.

Admin: Short for administration.

Aegis: Advanced Naval air defense radar system.

AH-1W Super Cobra: Has M179 undernose turret with 20mm Gatling gun.

AK-47: 7.64-round Russian Kalashnikov automatic rifle. Most widely used assault rifle in the world.

AK-74: New, improved version of the Kalashnikov. Fires the 5.45mm round. Has 30-round magazine. Rate of fire: 600 rounds per minute. Many slight variations made for many different nations.

AN/PRC-117D: Radio, also called SATCOM. Works with Milstar satellite in 22,300-mile equatorial orbit for instant worldwide radio, voice, or video communications. Size: 15 inches high, 3 inches wide, 3 inches deep. Weighs 15 pounds. Microphone and voice output. Has encrypter, capable of burst transmissions of less than a second.

AN/PUS-7: Night-vision goggles. Weighs 1.5 pounds.

ANVIS-6: Night-vision goggles on air crewmen's helmets.

APC: Armored Personnel Carrier.

ASROC: Nuclear-tipped antisubmarine rocket torpedoes launched by Navy ships.

Assault Vest: Combat vest with full loadouts of ammo, gear.

ASW: Anti-Submarine Warfare.

Attack Board: Molded plastic with two handgrips with bubble compass on it. Also depth gauge and Cyalume chemical lights with twist knob to regulate amount of light. Used for underwater guidance on long swim.

Aurora: Air Force recon plane. Can circle at 90,000 feet.

Can't be seen or heard from ground. Used for thermal imaging.

AWACS: Airborne Warning And Control System. Radar units in high-flying aircraft to scan for planes at any altitude out 200 miles. Controls air-to-air engagements with enemy forces. Planes have a mass of communication and electronic equipment.

Balaclavas: Headgear worn by some SEALs.

Bent Spear: Less serious nuclear violation of safety.

BKA, Bundeskriminant: Germany's federal investigation unit.

Black Talon: Lethal hollow-point ammunition made by Winchester. Outlawed some places.

Blivet: A collapsible fuel container. SEALs sometimes use it.

BLU-43B: Antipersonnel mine used by SEALs.

BLU-96: A fuel-air explosive bomb. It disperses a fuel oil into the air, then explodes the cloud. Many times more powerful than conventional bombs because it doesn't carry its own chemical oxidizers.

BMP-1: Soviet armored fighting vehicle (AFV), low, boxy, crew of 3 and 8 combat troops. Has tracks and a 73mm cannon. Also an AT-3 Sagger antitank missile and coaxial machine gun.

Body Armor: Far too heavy for SEAL use in the water.

Bogey: Pilots' word for an unidentified aircraft.

Boghammar Boat: Long, narrow, low dagger boat; high-speed patrol craft. Swedish make. Iran had 40 of them in 1993.

Boomer: A nuclear-powered missile submarine.

Bought It: A man has been killed. Also "bought the farm."

Bow Cat: The bow catapult on a carrier to launch jets.

Broken Arrow: Any accident with nuclear weapons, or any incident of nuclear material lost, shot down, crashed, stolen, hijacked.

Browning 9mm High Power: A Belgian 9mm pistol, 13 rounds in magazine. First made 1935.

Buddy Line: 6 feet long, ties 2 SEALs together in the water for control and help if needed.

BUD/S: Coronado, California, nickname for SEAL training facility for six months' course.

Bull Pup: Still in testing; new soldier's rifle. SEALs have a dozen of them for regular use. Army gets them in 2005. Has a 5.56 kinetic round, 30-shot clip. Also 20mm high-explosive round and 5-shot magazine. Twenties can be fused for proximity airbursts with use of video camera, laser range finder, and laser targeting. Fuses by number of turns the round needs to reach laser spot. Max range: 1200 yards. Twenty round can also detonate on contact, and has delay fuse. Weapon weighs 14 pounds. SEALs love it. Can in effect "shoot around corners" with the airburst feature.

BUPERS: BUreau of PERSonnel.

C-2A Greyhound: 2-engine turboprop cargo plane that lands on carriers. Also called COD, Carrier Onboard Delivery. Two pilots and engineer. Rear fuselage loading ramp. Cruise speed 300 mph, range 1,000 miles. Will hold 39 combat troops. Lands on CVN carriers at sea.

C-4: Plastic explosive. A claylike explosive that can be molded and shaped. It will burn. Fairly stable.

C-6 Plastique: Plastic explosive. Developed from C-4 and C-5. Is often used in bombs with radio detonator or digital timer.

C-9 Nightingale: Douglas DC-9 fitted as a medical-evacuation transport plane.

C-130 Hercules: Air Force transporter for long haul. 4 engines.

C-141 Starlifter: Airlift transport for cargo, paratroops, evac for long distances. Top speed 566 mph. Range with payload 2,935 miles. Ceiling 41,600 feet.

Caltrops: Small four-pointed spikes used to flatten tires. Used in the Crusades to disable horses.

Camel Back: Used with drinking tube for 70 ounces of water attached to vest.

Cammies: Working camouflaged wear for SEALs. Two different patterns and colors. Jungle and desert.

Cannon Fodder: Old term for soldiers in line of fire destined to die in the grand scheme of warfare.

CAP: Continuous Air Patrol.

Capped: Killed, shot, or otherwise snuffed.

CAR-15: The Colt M-4A1. Sliding-stock carbine with grenade launcher under barrel. Knight sound-suppressor. Can have AN/PAQ-4 laser aiming light under the carrying handle. .223 round. 20- or 30-round magazine. Rate of fire: 700 to 1,000 rounds per minute.

Cascade Radiation: U-235 triggers secondary radiation in other dense materials.

Castle Keep: The main tower in any castle.

Cast Off: Leave a dock, port, land. Get lost. Navy: long, then short signal of horn, whistle, or light.

Caving Ladder: Roll-up ladder that can be let down to climb.

CH-46E: Sea Knight chopper. Twin rotors, transport. Can carry 25 combat troops. Has a crew of 3. Cruise speed 154 mph. Range 420 miles.

CH-53D Sea Stallion: Big Chopper. Not used much anymore.

Chaff: A small cloud of thin pieces of metal, such as tinsel, that can be picked up by enemy radar and that can attract a radar-guided missile away from the plane to hit the chaff.

Charlie-Mike: Code words for continue the mission.

Chief to Chief: Bad conduct by EM handled by chiefs so no record shows or is passed up the chain of command.

Chocolate Mountains: Land training center for SEALs near these mountains in the California desert.

Christians In Action: SEAL talk for not-always-friendly CIA.

CIA: Central Intelligence Agency.

CIC: Combat Information Center. The place on a ship where communications and control areas are situated to open and control combat fire.

CINC: Commander IN Chief.

CINCLANT: Navy Commander-IN-Chief, atLANTtic.

CINCPAC: Navy Commander-IN-Chief, PACific.

Class of 1978: Not a single man finished BUD/S training in this class. All-time record.

Claymore: An antipersonnel mine carried by SEALs on many of their missions.

Cluster Bombs: A canister bomb that explodes and spreads small bomblets over a great area. Used against parked aircraft, massed troops, and unarmored vehicles.

CNO: Chief of Naval Operations.

CO: Commanding Officer.

CO-2 Poisoning: During deep dives. Abort dive at once and surface.

COD: Carrier Onboard Delivery plane.

Cold Pack Rations: Food carried by SEALs to use if needed.

Combat Harness: American Body Armor nylon-mesh special-operations vest. 6 2-magazine pouches for drum-fed belts, other pouches for other weapons, waterproof pouch for Motorola.

CONUS: The Continental United States.

Corfams: Dress shoes for SEALs.

Covert Action Staff: A CIA group that handles all covert action by the SEALs.

CP: Command Post.

CQB house: Close Quarters Battle house. Training facility near Nyland in the desert training area. Also called the Kill House.

CQB: Close Quarters Battle. A fight that's up close, hand-to-hand, whites-of-his-eyes, blood all over you.

CRRC Bundle: Roll it off plane, sub, boat. The assault boat for 8 SEALs. Also the IBS, Inflatable Boat Small.

Cutting Charge: Lead-sheathed explosive. Triangular strip of high-velocity explosive sheathed in metal. Point of the triangle focuses a shaped-charge effect. Cuts a pencil-line-wide hole to slice a steel girder in half.

CVN: A U.S. aircraft carrier with nuclear power. Largest that we have in fleet.

CYA: Cover Your Ass, protect yourself from friendlies or officers above you and JAG people.

Damfino: Damned if I know. SEAL talk.

DDS: Dry Dock Shelter. A clamshell unit on subs to deliver SEALs and SDVs to a mission.

DEFCON: DEFense CONdition. How serious is the threat?

Delta Forces: Army special forces, much like SEALs.

Desert Cammies: Three-color, desert tan and pale green with streaks of pink. For use on land.

DIA: Defense Intelligence Agency.

Dilos Class Patrol Boat: Greek, 29 feet long, 75 tons displacement.

Dirty Shirt Mess: Officers can eat there in flying suits on board a carrier.

DNS: Doppler Navigation System.

Drager LAR V: Rebreather that SEALs use. No bubbles.

DREC: Digitally Reconnoiterable Electronic Component. Top-secret computer chip from NSA that lets it decipher any U.S. military electronic code.

E-2C Hawkeye: Navy, carrier-based, Airborne Early Warning craft for long-range early warning and threat-assessment and fighter-direction. Has a 24-foot saucer-like rotodome over the wing. Crew 5, max speed 326 knots, ceiling 30,800 feet, radius 175 nautical miles with 4 hours on station.

E-3A Skywarrior: Old electronic intelligence craft. Replaced by the newer ES-3A.

E-4B NEACP: Called Kneecap. National Emergency Airborne Command Post. A greatly modified Boeing 747 used as a communications base for the President of the United States and other high-ranking officials in an emergency and in wartime.

E & E: SEAL talk for escape and evasion.

EA-6B Prowler: Navy plane with electronic countermeasures. Crew of 4, max speed 566 knots, ceiling 41,200 feet, range with max load 955 nautical miles.

EAR: Enhanced Acoustic Rifle. Fires not bullets, but a high-impact blast of sound that puts the target down and unconscious for up to six hours. Leaves him with almost no aftereffects. Used as a non-lethal weapon. The sound blast will bounce around inside a building, vehicle, or ship and knock out anyone who is within range. Ten shots before the weapon must be electrically charged. Range: about 400 yards.

Easy: The only easy day was yesterday. SEAL talk.

Ejection seat: The seat is powered by a CAD, a shotgun-like shell that is activated when the pilot triggers the ejection. The shell is fired into a solid rocket, sets it off and propels the whole ejection seat and pilot into the air. No electronics are involved.

ELINT: ELectronic INTelligence. Often from satellite in orbit, picture-taker, or other electronic communications.

EMP: ElectroMagnetic Pulse: The result of an E-bomb detonation. One type E-bomb is the Flux Compression Generator or FCG. Can be built for $400 and is relatively simple to make. Emits a rampaging electromagnetic pulse that destroys anything electronic in a 100 mile diameter circle. Blows out and fries all computers, telephone systems, TV broadcasts, radio, streetlights, and sends the area back into the Stone Age with no communications whatsoever. Stops all cars with electronic ignitions, drops jet planes out of the air including airliners, fighters and bombers, and stalls ships with electronic guidance and steering systems. When such a bomb is detonated the explosion is small but sounds like a giant lightning strike.

EOD: Navy experts in nuclear material and radioactivity who do Explosive Ordnance Disposal.

Equatorial Satellite Pointing Guide: To aim antenna for radio to pick up satellite signals.

ES-3A: Electronic Intelligence (ELINT) intercept craft. The platform for the battle group Passive Horizon Extension System. Stays up for long patrol periods, has comprehensive set of sensors, lands and takes off from a carrier. Has 63 antennas.

ETA: Estimated Time of Arrival. The planned time that you will arrive at a given destination.

Executive Order 12333: By President Reagan authorizing Special Warfare units such as the SEALs.

Exfil: Exfiltrate, to get out of an area.

F/A-18 Hornet: Carrier-based interceptor that can change from air-to-air to air-to-ground attack mode while in flight.

Fitrep: Fitness Report.

Flashbang Grenade: Non-lethal grenade that gives off a series of piercing explosive sounds and a series of brilliant strobe-type lights to disable an enemy.

Flotation Bag: To hold equipment, ammo, gear on a wet operation.

FO: Forward Observer. A man or unit set in an advanced area near or past friendly lines to call in artillery or mortar fire. Also used simply as the eyes of the rear echelon planners.

Fort Fumble: SEALs' name for the Pentagon.

Forty-mm Rifle Grenade: The M576 multipurpose round, contains 20 large lead balls. SEALs use on Colt M-4A1.

Four-Striper: A Navy captain.

Fox Three: In air warfare, a code phrase showing that a Navy F-14 has launched a Phoenix air-to-air missile.

FUBAR: SEAL talk. Fucked Up Beyond All Repair.

Full Helmet Masks: For high-altitude jumps. Oxygen in mask.

G-3: German-made assault rifle.

GHQ: General Headquarters.

Gloves: SEALs wear sage-green, fire-resistant Nomex flight gloves.

GMT: Greenwich Mean Time. Where it's all measured from.

GPS: Global Positioning System. A program with satellites around Earth to pinpoint precisely aircraft, ships, vehicles, and ground troops. Position information is to plus or minus ten feet. Also can give speed of a plane or ship to one quarter of a mile per hour.

GPSL: A radio antenna with floating wire that pops to the surface. Antenna picks up positioning from the closest 4 global positioning satellites and gives an exact position within 10 feet.

Green Tape: Green sticky ordnance tape that has a hundred uses for a SEAL.

GSG-9: Flashbang grenade developed by Germans. A cardboard tube filled with 5 separate charges timed to burst in rapid succession. Blinding and giving concussion to enemy, leaving targets stunned, easy to kill or capture. Usually non-lethal.

GSG9: Grenzschutzgruppe Nine. Germany's best special warfare unit, counterterrorist group.

Gulfstream II (VCII): Large executive jet used by services for transport of small groups quickly. Crew of 3 and 18 passengers. Maximum cruise speed 581 mph. Maximum range 4,275 miles.

H & K 21A1: Machine gun with 7.62 NATO round. Replaces the older, more fragile M-60 E3. Fires 900 rounds per minute. Range 1,100 meters. All types of NATO rounds, ball, incendiary, tracer.

H & K G-11: Automatic rifle, new type. 4.7mm caseless ammunition. 50-round magazine. The bullet is in a sleeve of solid propellant with a special thin plastic coating around it. Fires 600 rounds per minute. Single-shot, three-round burst, or fully automatic.

H & K MP-5SD: 9mm submachine gun with integral silenced barrel, single-shot, three-shot, or fully automatic. Rate 800 rds/min.

H & K P9S: Heckler & Koch's 9mm Parabellum double-action semiauto pistol with 9-round magazine.

H & K PSG1: 7.62 NATO round. High-precision, bolt-action, sniping rifle. 5- to 20-round magazine. Roller lock delayed blowback breech system. Fully adjustable stock. 6×42 telescopic sights. Sound suppressor.

HAHO: High Altitude jump, High Opening. From 30,000 feet, open chute for glide up to 15 miles to ground. Up to 75 minutes in glide. To enter enemy territory or enemy position unheard.

Half-Track: Military vehicle with tracked rear drive and wheels in front, usually armed and armored.

HALO: High Altitude jump, Low Opening. From 30,000 feet. Free fall in 2 minutes to 2,000 feet and open chute. Little forward movement. Get to ground quickly, silently.

Hamburgers: Often called sliders on a Navy carrier.

Handie-Talkie: Small, handheld personal radio. Short range.

HE: High Explosives.

HELO: SEAL talk for helicopter.

Herky Bird: C-130 Hercules transport. Most-flown military transport in the world. For cargo or passengers, paratroops, aerial refueling, search and rescue, communications, and as a gunship. Has flown from a Navy carrier deck without use of catapult. Four turboprop engines, max speed 325 knots, range at max payload 2,356 miles.

Hezbollah: Lebanese Shiite Moslem militia. Party of God.

HMMWV: The Humvee, U.S. light utility truck, replaced the honored jeep. Multipurpose wheeled vehicle, 4 × 4, automatic transmission, power steering. Engine: Detroit Diesel 150-hp diesel V-8 air-cooled. Top speed 65 mph. Range 300 miles.

Hotels: SEAL talk for hostages.

HQ: Headquarters.

Humint: Human Intelligence. Acquired on the ground; a person as opposed to satellite or photo recon.

Hydra-Shock: Lethal hollow-point ammunition made by Federal Cartridge Company. Outlawed in some areas.

Hypothermia: Danger to SEALs. A drop in body temperature that can be fatal.

IBS: Inflatable Boat Small. 12 × 6 feet. Carries 8 men and 1,000 pounds of weapons and gear. Hard to sink. Quiet motor. Used for silent beach, bay, lake landings.

IP: Initial Point. This can be a gathering place for a unit or force prior to going to the PD on a mission.

IR Beacon: Infrared beacon. For silent nighttime signaling.

IR Goggles: "Sees" heat instead of light.

Islamic Jihad: Arab holy war.

Isothermal layer: A colder layer of ocean water that deflects sonar rays. Submarines can hide below it, but then are also blind to what's going on above them since their sonar will not penetrate the layer.

IV Pack: Intravenous fluid that you can drink if out of water.

JAG: Judge Advocate General. The Navy's legal investigating arm that is independent of any Navy command.

JNA: Yugoslav National Army.

JP-4: Normal military jet fuel.

JSOC: Joint Special Operations Command.

JSOCCOMCENT: Joint Special Operations Command Center in the Pentagon.

KA-BAR: SEALs' combat, fighting knife.

KATN: Kick Ass and Take Names. SEAL talk, get the mission in gear.

KH-11: Spy satellite, takes pictures of ground, IR photos, etc.

KIA: Killed In Action.

KISS: Keep It Simple, Stupid. SEAL talk for streamlined operations.

Klick: A kilometer of distance. Often used as a mile. From Vietnam era, but still widely used in military.

Krytrons: Complicated, intricate timers used in making nuclear explosive detonators.

KV-57: Encoder for messages, scrambles.

Laser Pistol: The SIW pinpoint of ruby light emitted on any pistol for aiming. Usually a silenced weapon.

Left Behind: In 30 years SEALs have seldom left behind a dead comrade, never a wounded one. Never been taken prisoner.

Let's Get the Hell out of Dodge: SEAL talk for leaving a place, bugging out, hauling ass.

Liaison: Close-connection, cooperating person from one unit or service to another. Military liaison.

Light Sticks: Chemical units that make light after twisting to release chemicals that phosphoresce.

Loot & Shoot: SEAL talk for getting into action on a mission.

LT: Short for lieutenant in SEAL talk.

LZ: Landing Zone.

M1-8: Russian Chopper.

M1A1 M-14: Match rifle upgraded for SEAL snipers.

M-3 Submachine Gun: WWII grease gun, .45-caliber. Cheap. Introduced in 1942.

M-16: Automatic U.S. rifle. 5.56 round. Magazine 20 or 30, rate of fire 700 to 950 rds/min. Can attach M203 40mm grenade launcher under barrel.

M-18 Claymore: Antipersonnel mine. A slab of C-4 with 200 small ball bearings. Set off electrically or by trip wire. Can be positioned and aimed. Sprays out a cloud of balls. Kill zone 50 meters.

M60 Machine Gun: Can use 100-round ammo box snapped onto the gun's receiver. Not used much now by SEALs.

M-60E3: Lightweight handheld machine gun. Not used now by the SEALs.

M61A1: The usual 20mm cannon used on many American fighter planes.

M61(j): Machine pistol. Yugoslav make.

M662: A red flare for signaling.

M-86: Pursuit Deterrent Munitions. Various types of mines, grenades, trip-wire explosives, and other devices in anti-personnel use.

M-203: A 40mm grenade launcher fitted under an M-16 or the M-4A1 Commando. Can fire a variety of grenade types up to 200 yards.

MagSafe: Lethal ammunition that fragments in human body and does not exit. Favored by some police units to cut down on second kill from regular ammunition exiting a body.

Make a Peek: A quick look, usually out of the water, to check your position or tactical situation.

Mark 23 Mod O: Special operations offensive handgun system. Double-action, 12-round magazine. Ambidextrous safety and mag-release catches. Knight screw-on suppressor. Snap-on laser for sighting. .45-caliber. Weighs 4 pounds loaded. 9.5 inches long; with silencer, 16.5 inches long.

Mark II Knife: Navy-issue combat knife.

Mark VIII SDV: Swimmer Delivery Vehicle. A bus, SEAL talk. 21 feet long, beam and draft 4 feet, 6 knots for 6 hours.

Master-at-Arms: Military police commander on board a ship.

MAVRIC Lance: A nuclear alert for stolen nukes or radioactive goods.

MC-130 Combat Talon: A specially equipped Hercules for covert missions in enemy or unfriendly territory.

McMillan M87R: Bolt-action sniper rifle. .50-caliber. 53 inches long. Bipod, fixed 5- or 10-round magazine. Bulbous muzzle brake on end of barrel. Deadly up to a mile. All types .50-caliber ammo.

MGS: Modified Grooming Standards. So SEALs don't all look like military, to enable them to do undercover work in mufti.

MH-53J: Chopper, updated CH053 from Nam days. 200 mph, called the Pave Low III.

MH-60K Black Hawk: Navy chopper. Forward infrared system for low-level night flight. Radar for terra follow/avoidance. Crew of 3, takes 12 troops. Top speed 225 mph. Ceiling 4,000 feet. Range radius 230 miles. Arms: two 12.7mm machine guns.

MI-15: British domestic intelligence agency.

MI-16: British foreign intelligence and espionage.

MIDEASTFOR: Middle East Force.

MiG: Russian-built fighter, many versions, used in many nations around the world.

Mike Boat: Liberty boat off a large ship.

Mike-Mike: Short for mm, millimeter, as 9 mike-mike.

Milstar: Communications satellite for pickup and bouncing from SATCOM and other radio transmitters. Used by SEALs.

Minigun: In choppers. Can fire 2,000 rounds per minute. Gatling gun-type.

Mitrajez M80: Machine gun from Yugoslavia.

MLR: The Main Line of Resistance. That imaginary line in a battle where two forces face each other. Sometimes there are only a few yards or a few miles between them. Usually heavily fortified and manned.

Mocha: Food energy bar SEALs carry in vest pockets.

Mossberg: Pump-action, pistol-grip, 5-round magazine. SEALs use it for close-in work.

Motorola Radio: Personal radio, short range, lip mike, earpiece, belt pack.

MRE: Meals Ready to Eat. Field rations used by most of U.S. Armed Forces and the SEALs as well. Long-lasting.

MSPF: Maritime Special Purpose Force.

Mugger: MUGR, Miniature Underwater Global locator device. Sends up antenna for pickup on positioning satellites. Works under water or above. Gives location within 10 feet.

Mujahideen: A soldier of Allah in Muslim nations.

NAVAIR: NAVy AIR command.

NAVSPECWARGRUP-ONE: Naval Special Warfare Group One based on Coronado, CA. SEALs are in this command.

NAVSPECWARGRUP-TWO: Naval Special Warfare Group Two based at Little Creek, VA.

NCIS: Naval Criminal Investigative Service. A civilian operation not reporting to any Navy authority to make it more responsible and responsive. Replaces the old NIS, Naval Investigation Service, that did report to the closest admiral.

NEST: Nuclear Energy Search Team. Non-military unit that reports at once to any spill, problem, or Broken Arrow to determine the extent of the radiation problem.

NEWBIE: A new man, officer, or commander of an established military unit.

NKSF: North Korean Special Forces.

NLA: Iranian National Liberation Army. About 4,500 men in South Iraq, helped by Iraq for possible use against Iran.

Nomex: The type of material used for flight suits and hoods.

NPIC: National Photographic Interpretation Center in D.C.

NRO: National Reconnaissance Office. To run and coordinate satellite development and operations for the intelligence community.

NSA: National Security Agency.

NSC: National Security Council. Meets in Situation Room, support facility in the Executive Office Building in D.C. Main security group in the nation.

NSVHURAWN: Iranian Marines.

NUCFLASH: An alert for any nuclear problem.

NVG One Eye: Litton single-eyepiece Night-Vision Goggles. Prevents NVG blindness in both eyes if a flare goes off.

NVGs: Night-Vision Goggles. One eye or two. Give good night vision in the dark with a greenish view.

OAS: Obstacle Avoidance Sonar. Used on many low-flying attack aircraft.

OD: Officer of the Day.

OIC: Officer In Charge.

Oil Tanker: One is: 885 feet long, 140 foot beam, 121,000 tons, 13 cargo tanks that hold 35.8 million gallons of fuel, oil, or gas. 24 in the crew. This is a regular-sized tanker. Not a supertanker.

OOD: Officer Of the Deck.

OP: Outpost. A spot near the front of friendly lines or even beyond them where a man or a unit watch the enemy's movements. Can be manned by an FO from artillery.

Orion P-3: Navy's long-range patrol and antisub aircraft. Some adapted to ELINT roles. Crew of 10. Max speed loaded 473 mph. Ceiling 28,300 feet. Arms: internal weapons bay and 10 external weapons stations for a mix of torpedoes, mines, rockets, and bombs.

Passive Sonar: Listening for engine noise of a ship or sub. It doesn't give away the hunter's presence as an active sonar would.

Pave Low III: A Navy chopper.

PBR: Patrol Boat River. U.S. has many shapes, sizes, and with various types of armament.

PC-170: Patrol Coastal-Class 170-foot SEAL delivery vehicle. Powered by four 3,350 hp diesel engines, beam of 25 feet and draft of 7.8 feet. Top speed 35 knots, range 2,000 nautical miles. Fixed swimmer platform on stern. Crew of 4 officers and 24 EM, carries 8 SEALs.

PD: Point of Departure. A given position on the ground from which a unit or patrol leaves for its mission.

Plank Owners: Original men in the start-up of a new military unit.

Polycarbonate material: Bullet-proof glass.

PRF: People's Revolutionary Front. Fictional group in *NUCFLASH,* a SEAL Team Seven book.

Prowl & Growl: SEAL talk for moving into a combat mission.

Quitting Bell: In BUD/S training. Ring it and you quit the SEAL unit. Helmets of men who quit the class are lined up below the bell in Coronado. (Recently they have stopped ringing the bell. Dropouts simply place their helmet below the bell and go.)

RAF: Red Army Faction. A once-powerful German terrorist group, not so active now.

Remington 200: Sniper rifle. Not used by SEALs now.

Remington 700: Sniper rifle with Starlight Scope. Can extend night vision to 400 meters.

RIB: Rigid Inflatable Boat. 3 sizes, one 10 meters, 40 knots.

Ring Knocker: An Annapolis graduate with the ring.

RIO: Radar Intercept Officer. The officer who sits in the backseat of an F-14 Tomcat off a carrier. The job: find enemy targets in the air and on the sea.

Roger That: A yes, an affirmative, a go answer to a command or statement.

RPG: Rocket Propelled Grenade. Quick and easy, shoulder-fired. Favorite weapon of terrorists, insurgents.

S & R: Search and Rescue. Usually a helicopter.

SAS: British Special Air Service. Commandos. Special warfare men. Best that Britain has. Works with SEALs.

SATCOM: Satellite-based communications system for instant contact with anyone anywhere in the world. SEALs rely on it.

SAW: Squad's Automatic Weapon. Usually a machine gun or automatic rifle.

SBS: Special Boat Squadron. On-site Navy unit that transports SEALs to many of their missions. Located across the street from the SEALs' Coronado, California, head-quarters.

SD3: Sound-suppression system on the H & K MP5 weapon.

SDV: Swimmer Delivery Vehicle. SEALs use a variety of them.

Seahawk SH-60: Navy chopper for ASW and SAR. Top speed 180 knots, ceiling 13,800 feet, range 503 miles, arms: 2 Mark 46 torpedoes.

SEAL Headgear: Boonie hat, wool balaclava, green scarf, watch cap, bandanna roll.

Second in Command: Also 2IC for short in SEAL talk.

SERE: Survival, Evasion, Resistance, and Escape training.

Shipped for Six: Enlisted for six more years in the Navy.

Shit City: Coronado SEALs' name for Norfolk.

Show Colors: In combat put U.S. flag or other identification on back for easy identification by friendly air or ground units.

Sierra Charlie: SEAL talk for everything on schedule.

Simunition: Canadian product for training that uses paint balls instead of lead for bullets.

Sixteen-Man Platoon: Basic SEAL combat force. Up from 14 men a few years ago.

Sked: SEAL talk for schedule.

Sonobuoy: Small underwater device that detects sounds and transmits them by radio to plane or ship.

Space Blanket: Green foil blanket to keep troops warm. Vacuum-packed and folded to a cigarette-sized package.

SPIE: Special Purpose Insertion and Extraction rig. Essentially a long rope dangled from a chopper with hardware on it that is attached to each SEAL's chest right on his lift harness. Set up to lift six or eight men out of harm's way quickly by a chopper.

Sprayers and Prayers: Not the SEAL way. These men spray bullets all over the place hoping for hits. SEALs do more aimed firing for sure kills.

SS-19: Russian ICBM missile.

STABO: Use harness and lines under chopper to get down to the ground.

STAR: Surface To Air Recovery operation.

Starflash Round: Shotgun round that shoots out sparkling fireballs that ricochet wildly around a room, confusing and terrifying the occupants. Non-lethal.

Stasi: Old-time East German secret police.

Stick: British terminology: 2 4-man SAS teams.

Stokes: A kind of navy stretcher. Open coffin shaped of wire mesh and white canvas for emergency patient transport.

STOL: Short TakeOff and Landing. Aircraft with high-lift wings and vectored-thrust engines to produce extremely short takeoffs and landings.

Sub Gun: Submachine gun, often the suppressed H & K MP5.

Suits: Civilians, usually government officials wearing suits.

Sweat: The more SEALs sweat in peacetime, the less they bleed in war.

Sykes-Fairbairn: A commando fighting knife.

Syrette: Small syringe for field administration often filled with morphine. Can be self-administered.

Tango: SEAL talk for a terrorist.

TDY: Temporary duty assigned outside of normal job designation.

Terr: Another term for terrorist. Shorthand SEAL talk.

Tetrahedral reflectors: Show up on multi-mode radar like tiny suns.

Thermal Imager: Device to detect warmth, as a human body, at night or through light cover.

Thermal Tape: ID for night-vision-goggle user to see. Used on friendlies.

TNAZ: Trinittroaze Tidine. Explosive to replace C-4. 15% stronger than C-4 and 20% lighter.

TO&E: Table showing organization and equipment of a military unit.

Top SEAL Tribute: "You sweet motherfucker, don't you never die!"

Trailing Array: A group of antennas for sonar pickup trailed out of a submarine.

Train: For contact in smoke, no light, fog, etc. Men directly behind each other. Right hand on weapon, left hand on shoulder of man ahead. Squeeze shoulder to signal.

Trident: SEALs' emblem. An eagle with talons clutching a Revolutionary War pistol, and Neptune's trident superimposed on the Navy's traditional anchor.

TRW: A camera's digital record that is sent by SATCOM.

TT33: Tokarev, a Russian pistol.

UAZ: A Soviet 1-ton truck.

UBA Mark XV: Underwater life support with computer to regulate the rebreather's gas mixture.

UGS: Unmanned Ground Sensors. Can be used to explode booby traps and claymore mines.

UNODIR: Unless otherwise directed. The unit will start the operation unless they are told not to.

VBSS: Orders to "visit, board, search, and seize."

Wadi: A gully or ravine, usually in a desert.

White Shirt: Man responsible for safety on carrier deck as he leads around civilians and personnel unfamiliar with the flight deck.

WIA: Wounded In Action.

WP: White Phosphorus. Can be in a grenade, 40MM round or in a 20MM round. Used as smoke and to start fires.

Zodiac: Also called an IBS, Inflatable Boat Small. 15 × 6 feet, weighs 265 pounds. The "rubber duck" can carry 8 fully equipped SEALs. Can do 18 knots with a range of 65 nautical miles.

Zulu: Means Greenwich Mean Time, GMT. Used in all formal military communications.